of Rachel Caine

Unknown

"A kick-ass heroine ... ready to sacrifice anything.... *Unknown* is high-octane from the first page, weaving a tantalizing mix of mystery, romance, and paranormal power. Fans of Rachel Caine will not be disappointed."
—Romance Reviews Today

"'Nail-biting' doesn't even begin to cover how intense these books are.... *Unknown* is a white-knuckle thrill ride from opening sentence to bittersweet end, and it's addictive as hell.... As per Ms. Caine's usual, the characters are made of awesome." —The Book Smugglers

"A light fantasy novel, with just a hint of smoldering romance; perfect for anyone who wants something new instead of the same old paranormal themes."
—Night Owl Reviews

"Full of passion, action, and memorable characters."
—Whatchamacallit Reviews

Undone

"Fast-paced ... plenty of excitement.... A cliff-hanger ending will keep fans eager for the next installment."
—*Publishers Weekly*

"This is a good read, full of nail-biting action, some really creepy kids, and a final chilling revelation." —*Locus*

"A lot of action and a fast-paced plot. The cliff-hanger ending will make you want to find out what happens next." —SFRevu

continued ...

Books by Rachel Caine

WEATHER WARDEN

Ill Wind
Heat Stroke
Chill Factor
Windfall
Firestorm
Thin Air
Gale Force
Cape Storm
Total Eclipse

OUTCAST SEASON

Undone
Unknown
Unseen

THE MORGANVILLE VAMPIRES

Glass Houses
The Dead Girls' Dance
Midnight Alley
Feast of Fools
Lord of Misrule
Carpe Corpus
Fade Out
Kiss of Death
Ghost Town

Rachel Caine

UNSEEN

OUTCAST SEASON, BOOK THREE

A ROC BOOK

ROC
Published by New American Library, a division of
Penguin Group (USA) Inc., 375 Hudson Street,
New York, New York 10014, USA
Penguin Group (Canada), 90 Eglinton Avenue East, Suite 700, Toronto,
Ontario M4P 2Y3, Canada (a division of Pearson Penguin Canada Inc.)
Penguin Books Ltd., 80 Strand, London WC2R 0RL, England
Penguin Ireland, 25 St. Stephen's Green, Dublin 2,
Ireland (a division of Penguin Books Ltd.)
Penguin Group (Australia), 250 Camberwell Road, Camberwell, Victoria 3124,
Australia (a division of Pearson Australia Group Pty. Ltd.)
Penguin Books India Pvt. Ltd., 11 Community Centre, Panchsheel Park,
New Delhi - 110 017, India
Penguin Group (NZ), 67 Apollo Drive, Rosedale, North Shore 0632,
New Zealand (a division of Pearson New Zealand Ltd.)
Penguin Books (South Africa) (Pty.) Ltd., 24 Sturdee Avenue,
Rosebank, Johannesburg 2196, South Africa
Penguin Books Ltd., Registered Offices:
80 Strand, London WC2R 0RL, England

First published by Roc, an imprint of New American Library,
a division of Penguin Group (USA) Inc.

First Printing, February 2011
10 9 8 7 6 5 4 3 2 1

ACKNOWLEDGMENTS

The Stone Coyotes (thanks, Barbara!)
Joe Bonamassa
Lexi Waller
As always . . . Cat, without whom . . . well, you know

WHAT HAS GONE BEFORE

MY NAME IS CASSIEL, and I was once a Djinn—a being as old as the Earth herself, rooted in her power. I cared little for the small, scurrying human creatures who busied themselves with their tiny lives.

Things have changed. Now I *am* a small, scurrying human creature. In form, at any rate. Thanks to a disagreement with Ashan, the leader of the True Djinn, I can sustain my life only through the charity of the Wardens—humans who control aspects of the powers that surround us, such as wind and fire. The Warden I'm partnered with, Luis Rocha, commands the powers of the living Earth.

I find myself caring too much about Luis, and his niece Isabel, and others who never would have mattered before. The leader of the Old Djinn tells me that I must destroy humanity to save the Djinn, and all other life on Earth. I do not believe that. I cannot.

I have become too . . . human.

Before, that would have seemed like a curse.

Now I believe it may be a blessing.

Chapter 1

FIRE IS A LIVING, malevolent thing. It eats, it breathes, it moves with fluid grace and eerie, destructive beauty.

I could still appreciate the astonishing power of it, even as my hair crisped at the ends and the heat seared across my fragile human skin. Flames poured like liquid down the walls of the office, rippling and twisting out onto the floor, devouring the furniture. Everything seemed trapped in its own frozen moment of destruction, as if the fire had become amber. I couldn't focus my stinging eyes for more than a few seconds; everything seemed too bright, too hot, and in the next instant smoke billowed black and choking around me.

I fell to my knees and crawled, breathing oven-hot toxic fumes until my searching hand fell on something soft. Skin—a woman's hand. It wasn't moving. I grabbed hold and pulled her back toward me; her black suit had caught fire, and I batted the blaze out as coughing fits threatened to rip my lungs from my body.

The woman I had found was unconscious but still breathing shallowly. Smoke had made her face a grimy mask.

"Cass! Get your ass out *now*!" A raw, ragged shout pierced the roar of the fire, and I looked around to see a sheet of fire racing across the floor toward me. A sudden chemical blast of white foam snuffed it out. It was a temporary measure, but it gave me precious seconds to find the strength to move.

Luis Rocha, still holding the sputtering, empty extinguisher, stumbled into view out of the thick smoke. My Warden partner looked as if he'd been through a fierce battle—clothes torn and burned, skin singed. He'd lost part of his shoulder-length black hair to the flames. "Cass, come on—we're losing it! Gotta go!"

I poured raw Earth power—thick, golden power that flowed like honey—over the woman I'd found, into her, and saw her breathing and heartbeat steady. I stood up and grabbed her around the waist. She was a small thing, and I was tall; even so, the weight of her draped over my shoulder caused me to stagger. The fire roared its defiance and ignited a chair only a few feet away; it burned fast, upholstery charring into black lace and revealing bones of springs and wood.

I stopped, momentarily overcome. Nothing looked good right now, and I couldn't find the exit. *You will die here*, something told me. It sounded like the cold, dispassionate voice of Ashan, the leader of the Old Djinn—my brother, in a very real way; my king, in every way that mattered. *Why do you do these things for them?*

For humans, he meant. I was not born into flesh; being here in the mortal world was my choice, just as I'd chosen to run into this burning building alongside Luis.

I had my reasons for doing both of those foolish, potentially fatal things.

At least the part of me that was stubbornly Djinn, immortally powerful, saw it as foolishness. There were times—and this was one—when the human part was tempted to agree with it.

A blessedly cool draft of air fanned my face, and I gulped it in as I staggered blindly into an area of the building not yet fully involved. A glass door had shattered at the end of the hall, and the strong breeze flowing past me was drawn by the sucking pressure of the fire behind me. We had, at best, only moments before it would lash out with explosive force in a fireball, scorching everything it touched along the way.

Ahead of me Luis was shouting something as he headed for the doorway. I couldn't answer. My lungs were choked with smoke and soot, and all I could do was cough, stagger, and brace myself against a black-smudged, too-warm wall. My eyes were watering and stinging, and I wanted to sit down against this wall, drowning in the cool, blowing air—but I knew that if I did, I'd be dead, and the woman I was trying to save along with me.

I felt a sudden wavering pause in the air flooding past me, and my skin prickled in instinctual alarm. It felt like the silence before a lightning strike, but I felt no weather-working in play. No, this was physics—physics of a different kind.

And then the fire exploded through the door behind me, crawling and leaping along the hallway's ceiling and walls in thick, fiery tendrils. Hungry, and grabbing for its food.

"Cassiel!" Luis shouted, and plunged back toward me. Too late, of course; he couldn't outrun that fire, any more than I could. I felt it with a kind of fatalistic calm: I was, indeed, going to die here, now, in this moment.

I was going to die a failure, trapped in human flesh, unable to prevent the disaster that was coming, or my own foolish end.

And it might have been so, except that a child walked calmly out of the hellish burning heart of that fire, through the doorway, and extended her hands toward me. She was a small, lovely girl with long, silky black hair and the caramel-colored skin of her uncle Luis. When I had first met Isabel, she'd been a laughing, happy child. Now she was far too grown-up for her very young age—almost six. Her eyes had a depth and sadness that spoke of trauma, and as she extended her chubby little hands toward me she closed them into fists, and the fire that was racing toward me . . . died.

It was as if there was some barrier over the doorway she had stepped through. The fire boiled and roared there, but couldn't pass to reach the cooler air beyond. Even the breeze had ceased.

There was not a mark on Isabel. Not a singed hair, nor a single smudge of ash. Her pale blue T-shirt had a cheerful rainbow on it, vibrant as ever, and even her white sneakers were clean.

She said, very soberly, "We should go now, Cassie." Isabel was the only person in the world I permitted to call me that. It was a reminder of happier days, and a happier Ibby. I continued to cough as she walked past me toward her uncle Luis. He shook his head and met my eyes briefly, and I read in his gaze how disturbed and worried he was by seeing her this way. There was nothing to be said, though. He took Ibby in his arms and carried her toward the broken glass door.

I followed, with my own unconscious burden.

Outside, the scene was a confusion of flashing lights, the harsh glow and roar of the fire, the squawk of radios and shouts of men. Fire trucks unrolled great white snakes of hoses, and men and women in heavy protective gear rushed toward the building. One took the woman from my shoulder and hurried her toward a waiting ambulance and team of paramedics.

I sank down to the grass, still coughing, and spat out black, vile-tasting mucus. I don't know how much time passed—a minute, maybe two—before a paramedic knelt next to me and held up an oxygen mask. I sucked gratefully on the cool, sweet breath of life, feeling my head clear and my lungs ease. He handed me a packet of premoistened towelettes and gave me a thumbs-up motion, with eyebrows raised. I nodded. He moved on.

I scrubbed the damp fabric over my grimy face, and realized that my hands were trembling. I could have used Earth power, drawn from Luis, to clean myself off and start to heal the damage done to my lungs, but I chose not to do so; Luis, at the moment, needed his strength, and I was not seriously injured. My vanity could be satisfied with mere human cleaning methods for now.

A well-dressed man with a badge hung on a cord around his neck took a knee beside me. He wasn't looking at me so much as at the burning building, and his expression was remote and focused. His credentials said his name was Guilder, and he was wearing a crisp black suit, white shirt, and businesslike blue tie.

"You're Cassiel," he said. "The Djinn." He didn't say it the way a Warden who'd grown up with the idea of supernatural genies locked in bottles would have; he pronounced the word carefully, awkwardly, like an entry in a foreign dictionary. "I'm Guilder. FBI."

I nodded. I had expected the agents to descend on us quickly; I was simply surprised that he wasn't one of many. I removed the mask (a little regretfully) and said, "You want to know how it happened." My voice hardly sounded like my own; my vocal cords were strained, and had the husky growl of a longtime smoker. "We warned you."

"I've been briefed already about your warnings," he said, still watching the blaze as the firefighters began to train their hoses on it. "You really think a child caused all this?"

"Not just any child," I said. "A child who can control fire and bend it to his will. We warned you not to keep any of them here. You're not equipped to handle them."

The children had been rescued—or abducted, depending on which side you might be on—from camps across the United States run by the Church of the New World, a fringe organization that had recently twisted itself in dangerous new directions: either one that abducted children with blossoming Warden powers over Earth, Fire, and Weather, or subverted the parents to believe that the Church was the only possible way to protect their young ones. Part of the Church's teaching was that the Warden organization, the official gathering of those gifted with these powers, intended harm to the children. I was the first to admit that the Wardens were not perfect, but I knew they meant the best, especially for the talented innocent.

The Church, on the other hand, taught that the Wardens were ruthless, cruel mutilators who would rip the talent away from the children, leaving them psychic cripples at best, or dead at worst. That could happen, of course, if a child manifested a talent that was dangerous to everyone else, and had to be stopped. It was rare, but possible. The Wardens didn't always err on the side of mercy.

The Church preached it as an everyday occurrence, as a plan. And many people had believed, and given the Church children to *train*—or the Church had, in some cases, abducted those it thought were the most valuable, the most vital, to its cause.

Such as Isabel.

Those children—the few we had managed to free from the Church compounds across the country—were dangerously gifted, trained too early, burdened with power that they were not equipped, either emotionally or physically, to handle.

I had warned the FBI not to keep the children here, in their offices. At the minimum, Wardens should have been kept on duty to ensure that the children didn't panic and use their abilities irresponsibly.

As one of them clearly had.

Guilder didn't argue the point. "We thought we knew the risks," he said. "We underestimated the situation."

In earlier months I would no doubt have informed him just how badly they'd miscalculated, but I had learned, at great cost, when to let a subject go, for politeness' sake. Tact was not something for which I had a natural gift. "How many casualties have you sustained?" I asked.

"Zero, since you got Agent Littleton out." There was a slight warming in his tone, and he glanced at me, finally. "Thanks for that."

I nodded and coughed a little more, but the pressure in my lungs had eased. I was beginning to feel a monumental wave of exhaustion building, and knew I'd have to rest soon, but in the meantime there was a pleasant feeling of warmth and relaxation. Even my burns stung only lightly.

Impossible, in my state, to miss the surge of feeling that had come from the FBI agent—a complicated mix of gratitude, worry, and . . . love. Not for me, of course, and it was rare that I could feel emotions from anyone save Luis, but it appeared that Agent Guilder had at least a latent Earth-based ability, something too mild to be called a true power.

The love was not for me. It was for the agent I had saved. Agent Littleton.

I met his gaze and said, "Is there not a regulation against agents becoming . . . close?" So many euphemisms, in human speech. But the imprecision helped, I'd found; I didn't know his relationship with the other agent, but I sensed its depth. And secrecy.

He hadn't expected that question at all, and I caught the surprise and discomfort in his expression, despite the reserve that he had surely learned as a law enforcement professional. He just as quickly smoothed it away. "No code against being happy a coworker survived," he said. "I'm pretty sure there isn't. I read the rule books."

That made me smile, as he no doubt intended. "I'm sure you're correct," I said. "The children are not harmed?"

He shook his head. "The rest of the kids are all okay. The only one unaccounted for is the boy who kicked off the fire, and he took off once he got the whole thing revved up to Mach Three; this was basically a big, fiery distraction to cover his escape. Your niece and another boy protected the other kids and as many of the agents as they could."

"She's not my niece," I said. It was an automatic response, but I almost immediately regretted saying it. I cleared my throat and tried again. "She is the niece of my partner, Luis Rocha. Her name is Isabel."

"Hmm. She calls you Aunt Cassie."

"I know." I looked away from him toward the fire. "She was recently orphaned. It's been—difficult for her."

"From what I've heard, it's been difficult for all of these kids," Guilder said, and finally rose to a standing position, still looking down at me. "We're going to need a statement about what happened inside. Not tonight, though. Tomorrow. We'll call you and Mr. Rocha in for that."

"You'll have offices again so soon?" I asked. He smiled. It was a deep, charming sort of smile, a professional weapon he wielded with surgical accuracy.

"That's why God made laptops," he said. "And cell phones. Not to mention credit cards."

He nodded and walked away toward the ambulance, where he bent over the agent I'd pulled from the fire. She looked very small on the gurney, and he was quite tall, bending over her. I was certain he did not intend to reveal what his body language so clearly communicated.

It was probably a good thing for him that Agent

Littleton was unconscious. If she returned his affection, it would be awkward for them both; if not, it would be heartbreaking.

My attention drifted from Agent Guilder to Luis Rocha, who was sitting on the curb beside Isabel, with his arm around the child. He looked tired and smoke-stained and singed around the edges, but the smile on his face was genuine and very lovely. The smile was for Ibby, but as he looked at me, the smile . . . stayed. If anything, it grew warmer.

I looked away, suddenly unsure what an appropriate social response might be. The feelings that ripped through me were too jagged and confusing to sort out now, and the exhaustion wave was cresting inside me, drowning me in a need to lay my head down and rest. He felt that, of course; it was almost impossible for me to hide that sort of exhaustion from Luis, as closely as we were connected. He hugged Ibby and stood up, with her hand in his. The light from the fire caught and flickered on his skin, especially his bared arms, where flame tattoos twisted in skillfully inked patterns.

I watched the tattoos flex and move as he walked closer. It was easier than looking into his face.

"You're tired," he said, and it wasn't a question. "I'm taking you home, Cass."

I nodded, because it sounded like a very acceptable idea. Isabel and I were almost on eye level, since I was sitting down, and when I glanced at her I saw she was watching me with wide, luminous eyes. I couldn't read a thing from her expression, and her emotions were closely concealed within as well.

Until she threw her arms around my neck and hugged me.

I embraced her in return and put her on my lap. "Hush," I whispered, even though she was making no sound at all. "Everyone's all right. Even us."

"I'm sorry," Ibby said. "I tried— He was so mad, Cassie. I couldn't make him stop. He thinks you want to hurt us. Hurt him. I just couldn't make him understand."

"Nor should you have to," I said. "It was brave of you to try, little one. And to get the others to safety."

She shrugged that off. "It's only fire," she said. "That's easy."

"For you. Not so for others." I nodded toward the firefighters and their hoses. "They risk their lives against fire daily, without a scrap of power to protect them. Don't underestimate how dangerous your element can be, Ibby. Even to you, if you lose control."

She nodded, but not in a way that meant she really understood. I wondered when she'd learned to be so diplomatic; it wasn't a child's usual response. I supposed that part of the training—no, the *abuse*—she'd undergone had taught her how to avoid conflict. It was sad, because Ibby had been such a forthright girl when I'd first met her.

I sighed. "Yes, I believe it's time to go home." I kissed Ibby's clean, sweet-smelling hair, all too aware that I reeked of smoke, singed cloth, and very human sweat.

Luis lifted Ibby off my lap and offered me his hand. I took it, and felt an immediate surge of fresh energy cascade into my body. "Stop," I said. "You need—"

"Don't tell me what I need, *chica*," Luis said. "I know, believe me, and it involves a beer, a shower, and a bed, in that order. But anyway, this will keep us both going a while longer."

Luis's truck was parked a few blocks down—a big, black, shiny thing, with painted-on flames down the sides. Still flawless, even after all the damage the two of us had heaped on it—or else it was a new replacement. I wasn't sure. Likely the latter, I decided, since the interior smelled and felt fresh. He hadn't told me, and I hadn't bothered to ask.

My motorcycle, a new Victory Vision in smoky silver, was parked just a little distance away. Luis, without a word to me, slid a ramp down from the tailgate of the truck and walked the bike up into the bed, carefully laying it down on a padded blanket. When he got into the cab with Ibby and me, he caught my stare and shrugged. "What?" he asked. "You'd just get up in the middle of the night and come back for it anyway. Better do it now so you don't wander around scaring people at four in the morning."

He was right about that. I loved my motorcycle with a devotion I reserved for only a few things, and I knew I wouldn't rest easy unless I'd made sure it was taken safely with me. Having successfully second-guessed me, Luis was almost grinning. I schooled my face to its customary mask of indifference, and wiped my hands again with a moist cloth from the package sitting on the dashboard. My pale skin still looked ashen with grime. I wasn't sure I'd ever get clean.

Luis started the truck, and the engine caught with a deep rumble. Air-conditioning blasted out of the vents and bathed me in a soothing chill, and I sighed in pleasure. Instead of putting the truck into gear, Luis reached for the cloth in my hand. "You missed a spot," he said, and gently wiped my face with the moist fabric. It felt . . . unexpectedly intimate. I blinked, and found myself smiling, just the smallest amount. He stared at me for a few long seconds, then handed the cloth back. "That's better."

"Yes," I said. "Better."

I was acutely aware of him—his warmth, his strength, his power—all the way home.

I lived in an apartment—a spare, empty place with only a few sticks of furniture and the occasional mistaken gifts people had given me to try to "warm it up." I didn't understand the need to stamp a personality on a set of rooms that was, essentially, temporary. It was shelter, and a place to rest. A storage unit with a bed and some hanging space for clothing.

For instance: I had no idea why I would need a ceramic statue of an angel (a gift from a well-meaning neighbor who'd been moving away), but Luis had said it was polite to accept. It was, in fact, the only thing I possessed that was of no practical use, which made it seem awkward and singularly strange. I thought often of throwing it away, but the more I stared at the thing's serene porcelain face, the more irritated I became with it. Becoming human, I'd discovered, seemed to come with a thousand invisible strings tugging at you, and each and every one of them conferred an obligation, and unexpected benefits.

Luis didn't take me back to my apartment after all, so I didn't have to gaze at the blank-eyed angel and wonder how long the grace period would be before I could safely dispose of it.

Instead, Luis took me home—to *his* home. This home had once belonged to his brother Manny Rocha, my first Warden partner, and in contrast to the awkward sterility of my apartment, it felt ... warm. Permanent, and saturated with the loving life of those who'd inhabited it. Manny's and Angela's deaths had stained it, but Luis was slowly repairing that psychic damage, and the house now felt ... welcoming. Even to me, even with the guilt that always struck me when faced with the reality of Manny's and Angela's absence from the world.

"Yo, Ib," Luis said as we entered the front door. "You want some dinner?"

"No, thank you," she said, primly polite. "I'm tired. I just want to sleep."

"Right there with you, kiddo." He kissed the top of her head. "You need me to tuck you in?"

"I don't need tucking in, Tío," she said. "I'm almost grown-up." His smile faded, and I saw the concern in his eyes as she walked away.

It wasn't, I understood now, the correct developmental behavior for a child of Isabel's age. And yet it didn't seem there was any way to undo what had been done to her, body and soul, during that time after she'd been taken from us. We still didn't know all that had happened; Ibby was reluctant to talk about it, and Luis wanted to respect her wishes.

But it worried us both, deeply, that she seemed to have aged so quickly.

She was almost to her bedroom door when she spun around and ran back to Luis, threw herself into his arms, and gave him a kiss on the cheek. "Good night, Tío," she said, and then wiggled free to run to me and receive a hug, though I could tell that she did it more from duty than enthusiasm. "Good night, Cassie."

"Sweet dreams," I said, which was something I had heard Ibby's mother, Angela, say to her once. I missed Angela. She would have known what to say, what to do ... but it appeared I had not done so badly, because Ibby smiled and kissed me on the cheek, too.

Then she ran down the hall, suddenly acting her age, and shut her bedroom door with a slam. Luis winced and shook his head. "Kids," he said. "They don't know how to shut a door without breaking the hinges, but I guess I shouldn't complain; at least she's not breaking my heart so much as she was. So. Food?"

"No."

"Ah. Beer, then?"

"Yes."

He disappeared into the kitchen and came back with two frosted bottles, tops already removed. He handed me one and clinked the glass. "Cheers," he said, and took a deep, thirsty gulp. His eyes closed in almost indecent pleasure. "Ah, damn, that's good. I've been thinking about that all night."

It was good, chasing away the ashy taste from my mouth and burning bright and cold down to my stomach. I sighed and sat down on the couch, only belatedly thinking of the state of my clothing and its effect on his furniture. But Luis motioned me to stay seated, and sank into place next to me. "I'll flip you for the shower," he said. I had a mental image of him tossing me head over heels, and couldn't imagine why that would be any kind of decision-making choice. He must have seen my confusion, because he laughed and clarified. "A coin. Two sides, heads and tails. Understand?"

"Yes," I said. I took another long, considering drink of my beer. "But there are two baths in this house."

"Yeah, there are," he said. "It was kind of a figure of speech, but anyway, the hot water heater's crap. One shower at a time or we both shower cold."

"Oh." I considered that. I had experienced cold indoor showers before; it was surprisingly less pleasant than being caught in the rain. Perhaps it was the fact that one deliberately chose it. "Then I will let you go first."

"Oh?" He was draining his bottle quickly, and cut a sideways glance toward me. "Thanks." He didn't sound especially grateful. I wondered what subtext I had missed in the conversation. Again. It was especially frustrating when I was tired and felt so grubby. I would have been glad to go first, and the fact that I had offered so selflessly seemed, to me, to be worth some gratitude on his part.

And yet, when his gaze lingered on me, I felt all that melt away. Luis and I had been ... close ... for some time, but never *close*, in the euphemistic way humans sometimes used the word. When he gave me that kind of considering look, it felt unexpectedly intimate, as if a door had opened between us. I wasn't under any illusions that it was a change in our relationship; one of us always slammed the door shut at some point. My background didn't lend itself toward absolute trust and honesty, and his—well, I suspected his didn't, either.

And still he watched me. I stared back, my eyebrows slowly climbing, and finally said, "What are you thinking?"

"Nothing," he said, and tilted his bottle up for the last of the beer.

"Really." I sipped mine. I was less than half finished, but the beer combined with the exhaustion from the effort made me feel light-headed, in a pleasantly drifting sort of way. "That's odd. It looked as if you had something on your mind."

"Don't you think I know when I'm thinking of something?"

"I would assume you would."

"And you think I would tell you all about it."

Ah. There was the interesting point. "Why wouldn't you?" I asked. "Unless you think I am thinking something entirely different."

"Cass . . ." He sighed. "Damn, girl, I never know which way to jump with you. When it's all action and danger, we're synced like a sound track; when it's just you and me, I never know what you're thinking, or what you're feeling, if you're feeling anything. I look at you and you just . . ."

"Just what?"

He shrugged, frowning. "You just reflect," he said. "Like steel."

That surprised me, and it hurt a little. "I am *not* steel," I said. "I am human. Blood and bone and muscle, heart and feeling and vulnerability. Don't I show that?"

"Not even a little. Not here." He sounded almost apologetic about it. "Probably not your fault, you know.

You've adapted so well to everything else, it's not surprising you can't shed that last little bit of Djinn."

I drank a quick, cold mouthful. "I was a Djinn for aeons. I've been a human for months. Maybe you're judging me a little harshly, Luis."

"Oh, yeah, I know. I see your point. It just doesn't make it any easier to get a vibe off of you, that's all."

"What *vibe* are you trying to feel?"

That made him look away at the empty beer bottle in his hands, which he turned slowly, finding something intensely interesting in the label. "Just want to make sure you're okay, that's all. And you get all closed up."

He was lying. I was expert enough in human feelings to feel *that*, at least. And suddenly I understood what it was he was seeking—what it was that I'd been holding back, hiding behind my Djinn mask. I had not lied. I was human, and vulnerable, but my instincts were never to disclose that soft, unprotected side to anyone. Not even to Luis, who most needed to see it.

And the thought of letting down that wall, of exposing my true feelings to him . . . that was terrifying, in the same way that it would be to stand on the fragile edge of a cliff with a killing drop below. If what the humans said was correct, I would float, not fall. But all my instincts went against it.

I reached over and touched my fingertips to his cheek. It felt rough against my skin, stubbled with a day's growth of beard, and the sensation roused all kinds of odd feelings inside me—instinctive feelings, nothing summoned by my conscious mind. Curiously powerful rushes of chemicals in my bloodstream that overrode, for the moment, all that caution and hesitation.

He looked over at me, startled. The contrast of my pale fingers resting against his dark bronze skin made my heart run faster. I held his gaze this time, and the wall I'd put up weakened, melted, and was gone. "Now can you see?" I asked him very quietly. "There's much between us, good and bad, but can you see past all that, to what I feel?"

He put the bottle down. I mirrored him, without stopping the slow caress of my fingers across his cheek, down the warm, damp column of his neck, the harsh rasp on his chin, the startlingly soft skin of his lips. They parted under my fingers, cool from the beer. "Hey, Cass?" he asked, and his voice had taken on shadows, weight, deeper registers. "Are you sure you know what the hell you're doing?"

"No," I said, with complete honesty. "I trust you to tell me when I do it wrong."

"Jesus," he whispered, with an odd expression of utter concentration. "Seriously. You know what you're not exactly talking about, here? Because I'm not sure you do."

I stared straight into his rich brown eyes and said, "I want to make love with you. Is that not what you want, as well?"

"Oh," he said, after a second's stunned silence. "I guess you do know what you weren't talking about. Sorry. Just didn't want to get that wrong, and *madre*, Cass, I still don't know if you—"

I stood, turned, and straddled his lap as he sat on the couch, kneeling on the cushions to either side. At that distance, there was no possibility of barriers or mistakes for either of us. And I kissed him.

There was something so astonishingly sweet to the taste of him, sweet and spicy together, heady and overwhelming and powerful in ways that I could only dimly grasp. Kissing him seemed to temporarily still a howling hunger inside me, but it only moved to a different place to set up new, strange aches. While our lips were sliding together, damp and striving, I couldn't feel the pressure of the world around us, the weight of all that responsibility and fate and desperation.

All I felt was light, and silence, and a trembling, silvery sliver of breathless anticipation.

I pulled back just far enough to breathe into his open mouth, "Is that clear enough?"

"*Claro*," he whispered back. He put a finger to my lips and said, "We can't do this here, *querida*. Ibby. Come with me."

I nodded, and followed him to the bathroom—not the one in the hall, which was close to Ibby's room, but the one in the master bedroom. He closed the door after me and turned the lock, as I stripped away my white leather jacket. It would need repairs later, a simple enough matter when I had energy to spare, but for now it simply looked grubby and battered. I began to unbutton the soft pink shirt beneath, but Luis reached out and stilled my fingers. "No," he said. "Wait. I know you already made it pretty clear, but—I just want to put it out there. You sure you want to do this? All the way?"

"I already said that I did."

"Cass—" He shook his head. "Okay. Then slow the hell down, will you? It ain't a race to the finish line."

He took his time at it, slowly slipping each button through its anchoring hole, and tracing warm fingers down over the revealed pale flesh. Three buttons down he uncovered the pale pink of the satin bra I wore, and I felt his heartbeat move just a bit faster. Mine was well ahead of his, heating my flesh to warm ivory, pounding in my temples and veins, pooling heat like sunlight into the lower part of my body. Preparing me, I realized.

He slipped the blouse from my shoulders, and I shivered, though the air in the bedroom was warm enough. The shivers intensified as he trailed his fingertips over my bare skin. He bent very close and put his lips to my ear. "Turn around," he murmured. I did, not moving any farther away from his body than the movement required. He unhooked the clasp of my bra and slipped the silky straps down my arms. The fragile thing fell to the floor, next to my shirt. Then he reached around my waist and unsnapped the leather pants, then unzipped them and slid them slowly down my bare legs. I found myself leaning back against him, mesmerized by the simple, catastrophic explosions of feeling in my body as he slipped his hand inside the thin underwear . . .

I gasped and bit my lip as an entirely new sensation fired through me, and found myself pressing against his fingers. A sound escaped me, completely beyond my control. I had no idea what was guiding me, but it must have been something coded deep into the human form. I'd always thought that Djinn who grew fond of wearing skin were somehow flawed, but now—now I understood. There were delights in a Djinn's natural form, of course, but nothing quite so . . . intense.

"Easy, girl. We've got a long way to go," Luis said, still in that low murmur that somehow only intensified the pleasure I was taking from his touch. "Let's get these off of you first."

He pulled his hand away, which made me almost cry out in protest, and slipped the underwear down my legs. I realized that I was naked, but I didn't feel exposed or vulnerable. Quite the opposite. I felt . . . powerful. Clothed in trust.

I turned to face Luis, breathing hard, and found that he was still dressed. I helped him pull his charred, ragged shirt over his head, and before it hit the carpet I had my hands on him. I'd seen him without his shirt before, but that had been like looking through an obscuring filter. Now, in this moment, I saw how beautiful he really was. The light and shadow of his muscles as they tensed and relaxed; the smooth, velvety skin, the deeper brown of his tightened nipples. The dark hair that drew a line straight down beneath his waistband, and tickled my fingers as I unfastened the riveted button. It yielded with a soft snap, and I unzipped his pants and hesitated, not sure what he wanted of me. Luis gave me no signals. He watched me with intense, opaque brown eyes. I could feel the emotions roiling inside of him, and when I looked at him in Oversight, overlaying the aetheric world native to the Djinn with that of the human reality, I saw him glowing in incandescent, intense colors—colors of passion, of need, of life itself. Breathtaking, and overwhelming.

I looked into his eyes as I carefully slid his pants down his legs and left him in his underwear—tight, defining a growing tribute to our attraction. Then I took a deep breath and pulled those down as well.

Then, with nothing between us, and before I could allow any sensible objections to overcome me, I stepped forward, pressed my body against his, and kissed him.

Power flowed out in a torrent from him at that first touch of our lips, thick as melted amber, drenched with the essence of all living things, the slow pulse beat of Mother Earth herself. I felt my skin scrubbed clean, and my hair blew back in an invisible wind. I felt . . . reborn. New. Perfect.

His lips warmed to fever heat against mine, damp and urgent and sweet to taste, and I shuddered against him as his hands traveled down my spine to the small of my back, then caressed the swell of my hips. His lips parted, and I felt the soft stroke of his tongue against mine. My blood felt on fire now, and my heart pounded hard. I didn't know how much of what I felt came from his use of Earth power, and I didn't care. It was intense and beautiful and utterly involving.

I couldn't believe I had avoided it for so long, being daily in his company. I'd yearned for it, and yet I hadn't even known why.

An odd sensation—the areas of the flame tattoos on his arms felt different. The flame tattoos seemed warmer, as if the dark borders banked in actual fire instead of only ink.

Luis broke off the kiss and buried his face in the hollow of my neck, breathing hard. His breath pistoned hot against my skin and fluttered my pale hair. "Slow down," he finally said. "You're going to get me off too soon. Relax. I told you, it's not a race."

"Then what is it?" I asked. "Because my body seems to want to rush to the finish."

He laughed. "Stop feeding back my energy and I'll show you. Shower first, though."

"We're clean." Thanks to that initial burst of power from him, which had scrubbed our skin and hair and left us deliciously fresh.

"That's not why we take the shower," he said. "You trust me?"

"Yes." I always had, at a very deep level. This was not different ... and yet, it was. This was a physical kind of trust that I found hard to imagine outside of this moment, and yet here and now it seemed perfectly inevitable, and perfectly right. "Of course I do."

He slipped his hand down to grip mine. "Then come on. Get wet with me, girl."

Somehow, that phrase had connotations I had never really considered ... ones shadowy and exciting, a sudden burst of spice on the tongue. It made my breath quicken, and my pulse beat faster.

I allowed Luis to pull me along to the bathroom. That door, too, he shut behind us, and locked with a quick snap of his wrist. He sensed me watching him, and raised his brows. "Only so Ibby—look, I don't want you to think I'm trying to push you into anything. Is that what you think? Because you can stop this anytime you want."

I smiled. "Do you believe you *could* force me to do this if I didn't want it?"

"Ah, good point. You'd hurt me so bad."

"At the very least," I said, and put my pale hands on his darker shoulders. "And I hope I am not driving *you* to do anything beyond what you wish."

He laughed. "*Chica*, you don't know guys very well." He took a second to sweep his gaze down my body, and then let out a slow breath. "Their loss, too. You are so beautiful." He moved his focus back to my focus. "You don't believe that, though, do you?"

I didn't, in truth; to me human beauty was a very different thing—a thing of weakness, of vanity, of misdirected goals. I was strong, tall, perfectly serviceable in form, but I had never felt any need to be beautiful.

Now, suddenly, I did. For him, I did.

"I believe you believe it," I said in a very low voice, and kissed him again. This time, I kept myself from reaching out to the core of his power, and this was merely flesh, warming and responding, perfect and natural. He backed me against the wall, and I gasped at the cold lick of tile on my skin, but the mild sting was quickly forgotten in the blur of the moment. Luis broke away to lean into the shower and turn on the controls, and as the water began to spray he pulled out towels from a cabinet and put them at the ready. In a moment steam was billowing inside the shower's glass cubicle, and I saw moisture beading on my skin.

We stepped under the hot spray together, sealed so close together the water had a difficult time finding entrance between our bodies. The sensations overlapped, melted, blurred into a blood-warm, pulsing tide. I couldn't distinguish between the heat of his hands, and the spray of the equally hot water. It was like being caressed everywhere, all at once, and as Luis's fingers slipped again between my legs I put my arms around his neck for support.

What he was doing to me sparked miniature explosions inside of me, tremors that signaled something much, much greater on the approach. I found myself arching against his body, head back, lip caught between my teeth. That seemed to please him as much as it did me, a mysterious alchemy of feelings that I had never truly imagined was possible among humans. He didn't speak. The water pounded down on us, hot as blood, and at last, at last, he lifted me by the waist, strong arms flexing and shedding water in bright silver streams, and braced my back against the warm, damp tile wall.

"Ready?" he asked me. I didn't know what he was asking, but I nodded. I knew in principle, of course, but knowing and feeling were proving to be completely different things. "I'll go slow."

I had expected pleasure, not a searing, startling flash of razor-edged pain, and cried out more in panic than delight, putting my hands flat against his chest in protest. Luis froze, shocked, and held himself very still as I regulated my breathing again. In the next instant the pain wasn't as great, but the surprise remained. I felt betrayed by my body, which had led me to suppose this would be nothing but sweet sensation.

Luis seemed just as astonished. After a few long seconds, he said, "Jesus, Cass, you didn't tell me you were a *virgin*. I didn't think . . ." He pulled in a deep breath, and I saw he was angry at himself. "Stupid. Of course you're a virgin. You came straight into human flesh—you haven't been with anybody—"

He was right. I hadn't been in this compromising, exceptionally intimate and vulnerable position with anyone else since my rebirth in human skin. I was, in many ways, more virginal than any human woman or girl, and yet I felt—not at all ignorant or unready.

Just betrayed by my own biology.

"It's all right," I said, and kept my voice low and steady, staring into Luis's warm, cinnamon-colored eyes. "I'm all right."

"No, I hurt you. I didn't mean—"

I wrapped my legs around his waist and slowly, inexorably pulled him closer. Farther into my body, until we were completely joined. Then I fitted my hands around his face and smiled. "Since taking human form, I've had a great deal of pain," I said. "That was a . . . momentary discomfort. It's done. Now help me forget it."

He made a groaning sound low in his throat and dropped his head forward, into the warm space between my shoulder and neck. I felt his legs trembling, and then, by slow, gentle increments, he began to move.

"Tell me if I—" He was, even now, struggling to be gentle with me. With *me*, a being so old and powerful that even fellow Djinn had always treated me with caution. It made me laugh, and it made me warm with sweetness toward him. I solved his hesitancy by showing him my own urgent need, a furious bonfire of lust and heat, passion and delight.

No one had ever described what it felt like, to be consumed in that fire together, in an all-consuming, mind-destroying blur of hands and mouths, thrusts and silky caresses.

There were no words, and no real equivalent in the Djinn world. It was a humbling realization, one that made me understand, finally, why so many of my kind found solace in human form.

The world broke apart into sounds, and lights, and colors, frantic racing hearts and sweating skin, and then a slow, featherlight spiraling descent from an aetheric height I hadn't known humans could scale. When Luis finally let me slip away, we stayed in the sheltering heat of the pounding water until it turned cool on our skin.

He shut it off, and we looked at each through the fog of steam still in the air.

Luis smiled. It was a beautiful, unguarded expression, and I saw in that moment that he truly had loved me for some time now—months, perhaps. I felt the same tide of emotion inside my own body, and felt a similar wild, uncontrolled smile bend my lips. I ached in odd places, felt strangely warm in others, and a lassitude had settled in that made me want to curl up on the damp tile floor and sleep. All that stopped me was the knowledge that there was a warm, waiting bed just a few steps away.

Luis dried us both with a burst of power, and I followed him to the wide, clean bed, draped in dark red silk, that was his place of rest. I'd never touched it before, but now I sank without hesitation onto the soft mattress, beneath the weight of the covers, and then burrowed through the cool sheets to meet him in the middle. We were both still warm, and a little damp, and our lips met in slow, dreamlike kisses as we twined together, again.

Luis eventually chuckled, a rumble deep in his chest, and I pulled back to regard him questioningly.

"I keep waiting for the other shoe to drop," he said. "You know?"

"I'm fairly certain our shoes—"

"No, I mean we get interrupted a lot by people trying to kill the hell out of us. Seems like every time we get anywhere near doing this, someone comes along and tries to ruin our good time." He looked around. "Nothing yet. I think that might be a good sign."

I kissed him again, savoring the sweet spice of his mouth. "Yes," I agreed. "I think it's a very good sign."

Nothing disturbed us for hours, and hours, except when we fell asleep at last curled together in delicious, delirious exhaustion.

Chapter 2

BEFORE DAWN, there was a knock at the front door.

Luis woke up fast, sliding out of my arms and out of the bed before I'd finished opening my eyes. He had a pair of blue jeans draped at the end of the bed, and pulled them on with hardly a pause, still zipping and buttoning as he moved to unlock the bedroom door and go down the hall.

I found a thick black robe hanging on the back of the closet door, and belted it as I followed him. He'd already reached the door and was reaching for the knob as the knock came again—an official kind of summons, fast and confident.

"Yeah?" he yelled through the wood, and motioned me off to the side. "Who is it?"

"Police, Mr. Rocha," said a male voice from the other side. "Open up, please."

"Let's see a badge first," Luis said, and cracked the door just enough. I glimpsed something that glittered brass in the porch light, and Luis nodded and stepped back. A uniformed officer came inside, noticed me in the next instant, and I found myself being summed up in a quick, head-to-toe glance that held no trace of emotion—just analysis.

There was a strong tingle of power from him, and a quick look on the aetheric assured me that he was, in fact, a Warden. One of the few who had assumed a mainstream occupation ... but I supposed that there were considerable advantages to having Earth powers, as a police officer. Strength, and speed, and the ability to bring down a fleeing suspect with knots of grass and the flailing limbs of trees, to begin with—and I hadn't considered how useful Earth powers might be for tracing a suspect, or evaluating clues left behind. Theoretically, an Earth Warden could be a walking laboratory, much like a Djinn, within those close confines of the limitations of his power.

If he was at all pleased to meet us, I couldn't see any trace of it in his manner, which was cool and businesslike. "Warden Rocha," he said, and held out his hand, palm out. The Warden's stylized sun symbol glittered there briefly, fired by a tiny burst of power—another form of a badge of authority, and one I didn't have, though I could have easily enough. He transferred his cold, guarded gaze to me. "Cassiel. I'm Lieutenant Cardenas."

I supposed that I didn't merit the title of Warden, even though I certainly did the work. Interesting. That offended me a little. "And which organization are you representing at the moment? The Albuquerque Police Department or the Wardens?"

"Warden Bearheart sent me," he said, which was answer enough. "She wants you two to bring the girl with you and come to meet her people for handover."

"Handover," Luis repeated, in a voice that wasn't anything like friendly. "What the hell do you mean, *handover*?"

Cardenas shrugged. "As in, you bring her, you hand her over, you drive away. That kind of handover. Didn't think there was anything unclear about that."

Luis made a move, and I grabbed his arm in a tight, sanity-inducing grip, hauling him to a stop. "No," I said. "We've had enough trouble with the police." I meant that *he* had, and he knew that; I saw the fury slowly bank itself down in him, and he took a deep breath and nodded to me to let go. I did, but I didn't back off far.

"Maybe you don't know," Luis said, his tone gone carefully flat, "that my niece is only five years old."

"Almost six," Cardenas said. "And I understand how you feel, but this ain't optional. She needs to go to Warden Bearheart. Nothing bad's going to happen to her."

"No."

"You know what you're saying?"

"No way is Ibby being *handed off*."

"I ain't arguing about it," Cardenas said. "Just delivering the message, that's all. You can do whatever you want about it. I've got plenty to do without being your own personal message service, so if you want to tell Bearheart no, you call her up yourself."

Luis's jaw was stubbornly set, but he wasn't being reasonable; his reaction was emotional, and I intervened on his behalf. "And where would Warden Bearheart like us to go?" I asked. When Luis shot me a furious look, I said, "It doesn't obligate us to anything to know the intended destination."

He had to nod, unwillingly, at that. "All right," he said. "And why do this now? Ibby's under control. She's doing just fine."

She was not, in fact, fine, and he knew that, but I understood his intense desire to protect the child from more trauma and harm. The Wardens didn't have a spotless reputation for caring for their own, and I knew that made him wary, and very reluctant. Still, I had heard no ill of Marion Bearheart, and nothing but good about her healing craft. If anyone could heal Ibby's wounds, it would be someone like her.

"There's a rendezvous point in Nevada," said the police officer. "I was told to give you the map." He reached into a breast pocket and took out a compactly folded

piece of paper. It was simply a computer printout of a
state map, with no directions or locations highlighted.
He held it out to Luis, who didn't make a move to take
it. I passed my hand over the map, using a small amount
of power even as Cardenas said, "That won't work; I already tried it. It's—" His voice died, because under my
touch, an invisible route sparked to life in glowing blue. I
quickly killed the glow before it could reveal much. The
Wardens were being secretive with the purpose of all
this, and highly security-conscious. This map had been
keyed specifically to Luis and me. I folded the paper.

"Thank you," I said very firmly. "Was there anything
else?"

"Guess not," Cardenas said, and turned to go. Luis
stopped him at the door.

"Wait. Did she say anything about why she wanted
Ibby? Does she think we're not safe here?"

"No clue. Like I said, I'm just the messenger. You
want answers, get Bearheart on the phone. If she'll take
your call, you're higher up than me."

Luis weighed the risks, and finally nodded. "Fine," he
said. "Thanks."

"No problem." Cardenas the Warden disappeared,
and Cardenas the policeman reasserted himself. "Sorry
about your loss, by the way. I worked that drive-by of
your brother and sister-in-law. Bad stuff. I heard the
gang's almost out of business these days. Local *jefe* had
himself some kind of meltdown, decided to go straight
and start doing charity work." There was knowledge in
that stare, and it worried me; Luis had taken steps on his
own, and I'd seen him do it. In altering the gang leader's mind, he had violated one of the principal ethical
codes of Earth Wardens. Of course, luckily for him, the
Wardens were pressed on all sides now with emerging
threats, so disciplining their own probably didn't rank
highly at the moment.

"Sounds like a good outcome for a scumbag like that," Luis said. "Better if he'd had his change of heart before he pulled a gun on my family."

"Yeah." Cardenas nodded. "Better if that had been the timing, for sure. How's the little girl doing?"

"Nightmares," I said. "But she seems to be adapting."

"Kids do that. Got two myself." He touched the shiny brim of his uniform cap. "If something like that happened to my family, I might want the same kind of change of heart for that guy, too. If I couldn't put a bullet in him, I mean."

He was, I realized, obliquely telling Luis that although he knew—or at least suspected—the illegal alterations Luis had performed on the gang leader, he wasn't going to report it. I hadn't realized how much of a danger that might have been until I felt the cold, close passage of it.

Luis had gone just a fraction of a shade more tense, and now he nodded and opened the door. Cardenas gave us both good-byes and walked down the path to the police cruiser waiting at the curb. We watched it drive away. I still had the piece of paper clutched in my hand.

"Let's see it," Luis said. I unfolded the map out on the nearest flat surface, and moved my palm over it to wake the glowing symbols again. Blue flowed down roads, over what appeared to be open spaces, ending in a deserted area marked by a simple sun symbol. On the map, there were borders, but no reference marks.

Luis whistled. "What do you think about that?"

I raised my eyebrows. "I don't think anything." Because I had no idea what he was talking about.

"Area 51?" When I didn't react, his eyes widened. "Come on, seriously? You never heard of Area 51? Dreamland?" When I shook my head, he sighed. "Got to get you a pop culture makeover one of these days. Boiling it down, this means the spooks all of a sudden like us enough to throw open the borders to one of their most secure facilities. Wardens have never been welcomed there before; maybe they're letting us in because they don't like all this weird Church business a whole lot more. They've had some bad experiences dealing with those kinds of cults."

His moment's fascination with the map faded, and he walked away, clearly thinking.

"What?" I asked him. I couldn't follow what logical—or illogical—leaps he was making, but I could sense the changes in his mood quickly enough, and it had darkened considerably.

"Area 51's a hell of a secure spot," he said. "But I really can't see the government letting the Wardens set up shop in there. If they're letting us in at all, they've got some kind of ulterior motive about it."

"Like what?" I asked. He turned and looked at me for a long second, then shook his head.

"Could be Ibby," he said. "Could be they want all these kids for themselves. Could be they want you, Cass."

"Me," I repeated, surprised. "Why?"

"Because the feds have never had an actual Djinn, they never could even come close to grabbing one. You, you're vulnerable, and you're the next best thing—you can spill all the weaknesses, and give them an idea of Djinn strength, too. I don't like it, and no way am I going to risk Ibby, either."

I had never thought of myself as vulnerable, and the idea surprised me far more than I'd expected. "I could fight them," I said.

"Yeah, sure you could. But this is something you don't understand about humanity, *querida*—you can kill one, or five, or ten, but they keep on coming. I guarantee you, in Area 51, if they want you, they've got you."

Unsettling. "Then what do you want to do?" I asked.

He locked the door behind Cardenas. "I want to find

out what the hell Marion thinks she's doing, because I'm not taking Ibby—or you—blindly out into the field of fire. Not ever again."

It took two hours to get a return call from Marion Bearheart. When it finally came, Ibby was eating cereal in the kitchen with us, and Luis gestured for me to finish pouring her orange juice and follow him into the other room. Ibby watched us go, too much awareness and calculation in her face, and I wondered just how much we could really keep from her. I leaned over to stroke her silky hair back from her face. "Just a moment," I promised her. "You'll drink your juice?"

That got a well-remembered, brilliant smile from her. "I know, juice is good for me," Ibby said, which wasn't the same thing.

"Promise me."

"I promise," she sighed, and reached for the glass to down a mighty mouthful, to prove her point. I kissed her forehead and followed Luis.

He was pacing, with the cordless phone held to his ear. I knew that particular style of restlessness in him; it meant he was deeply worried, and very angry on some level he was determined not to convey. His knuckles, however, were pale where he gripped the receiver. "Yeah," he was saying. "Yeah, I *know* the kid needs help, Marion; that's not what I—" He paused, clearly interrupted, and his dark eyes met mine briefly before the pacing carried him onward. "Ibby lost her mother and father; that's enough trauma for any kid her age. Then those nutcases triggered her powers too early. They filled her head full of lies about the Wardens; they told her I was dead—showed her I was dead. They showed her how Cassiel killed me. And now you want to put her in some kind of *camp*— No, shut up and let me finish. I don't care if you call it a ranch or a camp or a hospital or a school; it's nothing but more of the same. She's had enough terror and brainwashing for a lifetime, Marion. She needs a home, and I'm not sending her anywhere like that!"

Marion was patient—and kind—enough to allow him to finish his rant without interruption. Then she responded, something quiet and brief, and Luis hung up the phone. He stood there, head down, shoulder-length hair—now more than a bit ragged, from the fire we'd faced—hiding his expression, and then turned and walked away from me without saying a word.

I followed him into the kitchen. He poured coffee and sipped it, watching Isabel eat her cereal with narrowed eyes. She glanced up at him with a smile, and he smiled back. It looked almost natural.

"Ibby," he said, "how would you feel about going away to school?"

She didn't answer immediately. She looked up at him, no particular expression on her sweet-featured face—perfectly composed. There was an unsettling amount of calculation in the level stare she gave him, and then Ibby said, "I don't like schools anymore."

"I know, *mija*, but this is a good school, one that will help you." He sank down at the table next to her and took her small hand in his large one. "You don't say it, but you're scared, aren't you? And hurting. You still miss your *mami* and *papi*—I know you do."

That broke through the crystal shell of her artificial calm, and she looked away and said, in a small voice, "All the time."

"Yeah, me, too," Luis said, and kissed the top of her head with such gentleness it made my heart ache. "I hate it that they're gone and they can't be here to tell you how brave you've been, and how strong you are. But being strong isn't everything. It doesn't make you happy, does it?"

He'd struck a nerve, one that I didn't even understand. Why wouldn't strength make one happy? Would
weakness? No matter which direction I turned the question, it remained unanswerable for me. A quintessen-
tially human thing, I supposed.

Ibby's dark eyes had filled with tears. "No," she said,
in an even smaller, more fragile voice. "Being strong
makes me sad, too. I don't want to hurt people. Even the
bad people. I just want people to leave me alone."

That, too, I failed to grasp. Among Djinn, things were
much more straightforward. One had allies, friends,
adversaries, and enemies. Behavior of others dictated
responses, measure for measure. I couldn't imagine
having an ethical stand that would somehow keep me
from striking out at those who wanted to hurt me. There
could be no justice unless someone was willing to wield
the sword.

But I saw in Ibby something else . . . something that
I was almost certain was placed there by her mother,
Angela. I did not doubt that Angela would defend her
child to the death, but Angela was one who forgave others. She had tried to find the good in people even when
it was vanishingly small, or absent altogether.

She had passed that noble desire on to her daughter,
and now it was a slender, precious thread holding Isabel
away from the pit into which our enemies had tried to
plunge her. They'd sought to use her as a weapon, but
Ibby wasn't anyone's tool.

I sank down into the chair across from Ibby and Luis,
watching the two of them together. There was a sweetness to it that held a strength of its own.

I didn't know why, but I reached out to Isabel as well,
and took her left hand in both of mine.

"Your uncle and I will fight the bad people for you," I
said. "They'll never hurt you again. I promise you that."

Djinn didn't promise lightly; we were bound by oaths,

when we swore them in the old, formal ways. An oath sworn by a Djinn had once bound our entire race, and put us at the doubtful mercies of humanity. My promise was well meant, but it would require dangerous commitment to keep.

But I did not regret it, especially when I saw some of the deep fear in her start to lose its hold. She sniffled, and her eyes overflowed. I let go of her hand as Luis put his arms around her and gathered her up in his lap, rocking her as if she were a much younger child. "Hush, *mija*, nothing's going to happen. See, Cass and I are on the case. The bad people, they're gonna take one look at us and run."

She pulled back to give him a frowning look. "Why?"

"Why what, little duck?" He caught her nose gently between thumb and forefinger, and made a quacking sound.

Ibby suddenly reverted to her age, and giggled and put her arms around his neck. "Why would they run away?"

"Because," I said, "your uncle is very scary."

Luis snorted and said, "Yeah, coming from the Auntie War Goddess, that's funny. I'm just freaking terrifying."

"You can be, when you wish," I said. I was telling the literal truth. "I'd fear you, should we be on opposite sides."

He started to laugh, but then he got a curious look and said, "I think you actually mean that."

"I do," I said. "Were I your enemy, I might run away, too."

He held out his hand, which was curled into a fist. I glanced at it, then bumped it lightly with my own.

"You'd scare the crap out of me, Cass," he said. "If you ever went all avenging angel on me."

"Then you and I must try not to land on opposite sides," I said, straight-faced. Ibby giggled again, a sound like tiny silver bells that woke joy in my heart. "You know, I am younger than Isabel, in terms of my human life," I said. "I think I might go to this school to learn how to better use my own powers. That is the point of the training, isn't it?"

Luis seemed surprised, but he controlled it quickly and nodded. "Might be tough for you," he said. "I mean, you like to be head of the class, Cassiel. I can think of a lot of kids who'd be much better at this than you, you know."

I raised my eyebrows. "Such as?"

"Oh, I don't know." He winked at Ibby. "Maybe this one, here."

"I am formidable," I said. "Do you think you can learn more quickly than I can, Isabel?"

Ibby turned her head to look at me. "If I wanted," she said. "I'm a fast learner, faster than anybody. The Lady said so . . ."

Her face shut down, and I knew I'd made a mistake leading her down a memory path that would inevitably bring up images of Pearl, and her time shut up at the Ranch.

Time, events, that she still hadn't fully revealed to either of us.

She turned her head and buried her face in the soft material of Luis's shirt, like a younger, shyer child. "I don't want to go to any school," she said. It was almost a wail. "Tío, don't make me go!"

He kissed her hair again and hugged her tight. "No, sweetie, I won't," he said. He sounded miserable, and whether Ibby knew it or not, I could sense that he was lying. "I won't make you do anything you don't want to do."

My body felt a sudden bite of chill, even though I rarely felt shifts in temperature unless they were extreme and sudden. I cocked my head and studied him.

He mouthed, *Not now*, very clearly, and I inclined my head just a fraction.

For Ibby's sake, I would let his lie go unchallenged.

For now.

The day passed without much incident—or at least, much beyond the normal chaos of having a restless child-Warden roaming a household. Luis and I were required to be on call for the Wardens at all times, but remarkably, this was a day without an emergency, other than a few small aetheric maintenance requests to relieve seismic pressure in one area and build it in another to maintain the balance.

It seemed almost artificially calm, and it worried me.

Luis didn't discuss the order from Marion Bearheart until Ibby went to take a bath that evening—a thing that I supervised, albeit from the hallway, as Isabel's body image was starting to form and she was going through a period of shyness. As she splashed in the tub and soaped her hair, I looked down the hall toward the kitchen, where Luis retrieved a bottle of beer, opened it, and then turned to face me. I glanced at the bathroom. Ibby was singing something in Spanish, and making fanciful shapes in her shampoo-inflated hair.

"You lied to her," I said quietly, still watching her. She wasn't paying us any attention. "What did Marion tell you on the phone?"

Luis took a deep drink of beer before he said, "Marion said I could bring her, or they'd come and get her, but either way, it was going down. I was tempted to tell her to bring it, but I was afraid she'd take it literally. Marion's kind of like that. She's not giving us any choice."

"And will you fight them when they come for her?" I asked. "Because you know Ibby will resist. She's too afraid to surrender again."

"I know she will. And the truth is, I haven't decided yet." He sounded very troubled, and very serious. "I can't let her get dragged off again, not on my watch. Not gonna happen. But if Ibby and I put up a fight, people will die on their side, and maybe on ours. And innocent people for miles around, probably."

"Not only that," I said, equally softly. "If Ibby fights with lethal force, it only proves their point that she can't be left on her own among other children. It will destroy any chance she has for a free future. And she will kill, if she thinks you are in mortal danger. She saw you die before, even if it was a false vision. She won't allow it to happen again without acting."

He closed his eyes and pressed the cold bottle to his forehead. "Jesus, what a mess. I should have asked— what are *you* gonna do?"

"Like you, I have not decided," I said. "But I don't care for the idea that anyone should try to take her by force, even if they believe it's in her best interests. I don't like that all."

"Well, we've got that in common."

"Neither do I want to see her, or you, die," I continued, as if he hadn't spoken. "Or myself. I find I rather value myself."

He laughed. "No kidding."

"I am an important asset to the Wardens," I said, possibly too earnestly and too literally. "Should I not admit I am valuable? Is that wrong?"

"No, it's not wrong, Cass," he said, and put the beer down. He walked to me and put his hands on my upper arms. His right was cold, his left warm, but the temperature quickly equalized; I forgot the sensation as I looked into his eyes and saw the regard and strength there. "You maybe stretch the reasonable limits of self-confidence sometimes, but it's not wrong. You *are* valuable." His hands glided up my arms, and his voice softened and deepened. "God knows, I can't put a price on what I feel for you. You know that, right? You feel that?"

I put my hands flat on his chest, but not to push him away; I savored the feeling of his lungs moving, his heart pumping. Life, in all its odd, complex glory.

Luis, too, was irreplaceable. As was Isabel. As had been Manny and Angela.

And in that moment, I knew the decision had already been made for me—that I couldn't possibly allow Luis and Isabel to fight without me, whether the cause was good or bad. And yet I knew that fighting might bring terrible consequences.

There might come a time when we would all have to surrender.

Luis might have known it, too, but he wisely didn't pursue the subject. He kissed me instead, a sweet, warm lingering of lips and tongues, and I felt tension gathering inside, golden-hot, when I heard Isabel say, "Tía Cassie?"

Unthinkable as it might have been, I'd forgotten her completely. I broke free of Luis's embrace and turned, to find that she'd emptied the bathwater, wrapped herself in a towel, and was standing there on the tile floor, dripping. Her eyes were huge, and full of curiosity.

"Are you in love with my uncle Luis?" she asked.

I looked at Luis, who stared back, on the verge of laughing. He spread his hands helplessly. "Hey, she didn't ask *me*," he said. "Good luck."

In this, at least, I was determined to be truthful. I sank down to one knee in front of Isabel, which put us almost on eye level, and said, "Yes. I love your uncle very much. Is that all right?"

She cocked her head a little to one side, thinking; clearly, she hadn't expected such a direct response. From the choked sound Luis was making, neither had he. "I suppose," she said, a little severely. "But don't make him sad. I won't like it if you make him sad."

She continued to watch me with a serious expression, until I nodded with equal gravity. What Luis might not have picked up from her words was the underlying threat. She still doubted me, at some very deep level; my once-Djinn-sister Pearl had gone to great lengths to try to create me as the villain in Ibby's life, to paint me as a monster and a cruel murderer, to twist the child in the direction that Pearl wished her to go, for whatever obscure and dangerous reason. It would take time for Ibby to get over that completely, even if on a rational level she was trying to believe in me again.

I didn't yet know what Pearl was trying to achieve by abducting and altering these children, but I knew one thing: They were powerful, and dangerous when angered.

The subtext of what Ibby had said was quite clear: *If you hurt him, I'll hurt you back.* And she meant every unsaid word of it. She might not *want* to hurt bad people, but she would, for Luis, make a definite exception to her rule . . . even if the bad person was me.

I nodded, holding her gaze. There was no doubt between us what she meant, or what I had agreed. Ibby, satisfied, grabbed her pale pink nightgown, the one with bright cartoon characters woven in the fabric, and shut the door to change.

Luis had watched the entire exchange, and now, as I glanced toward him, I saw that he hadn't missed any of the subtexts, either. "*Dios,*" he breathed. "She really would take you on if she had to, wouldn't she?"

I nodded. "For you, she'd take on anyone. You're all she has, Luis."

"No," he said. "She has you, too. Even if she doesn't really know that yet."

I wanted to believe that, but I had choices to make—small ones now, and larger ones looming like storms in the distance. The wrong decision at any time would have catastrophic consequences, not just for me but for everyone I had come to love in the human world. I had, in a very real sense, been sent here by the Djinn to halt a disastrous, still-unknowable chain of events that Pearl had put in motion, by breaking a weak link in the chain itself.

The link of human life, from which Pearl was drawing her power.

Perhaps even the right decision this time would still mean that I would become the villain Ibby so feared, destroy my fragile relationship with her uncle, and set me adrift and alone.

Choices.

I hated them.

I felt a burst of power from the bathroom, and reacted without thinking to what could have been an attack upon Isabel; I banged the door open and charged in, and caused Ibby to yelp and back up fast against the wall. She was wearing the nightgown, and her hair was dry and crackling with energy. Too much energy. There wasn't a trace of water drops in the tub or on the floor, but there was a faint smell of singed fabric in the air.

I stopped, but not before Ibby had formed a ball of white-hot fire in the palm of her hand. She was staring at me with huge, terrified eyes, and I knew she was seeing something that Pearl had shown her—me, killing her uncle. It was a lie, but it was so hard for her to forget the images, and I had just triggered a flashback with my overreaction and violence.

I held up both hands to her, palms out. "Peace, Isabel," I said, in my most soothing voice. "I am sorry I frightened you. I was only worried for you. I thought something bad had happened."

She didn't quench the flame immediately; she kept watching me, wary and unhappy, until Luis appeared behind me in the doorway. "Ibby," he said. "Stop."

She closed her fist, and the flames died, leaving a brilliant aura I could still see when I blinked. "I didn't *do* anything," she blurted, and her pouting lips quivered, as if she might burst into wails at any moment. "She scared me! I didn't do anything wrong!"

"You used power," I said. "You promised you wouldn't, except in self-defense and with our guidance."

Now the pout was more pronounced, and her small features took on a stubborn, set look. "I was wet. I just wanted to get dry."

"Ibby, you can't do that," Luis said, and eased around me to put himself between the two of us. "You promised me, sweetheart. You promised you wouldn't use power just because it was easy."

"But I was *wet*. *You* dry yourself off. I've seen it."

"That's true, but we're older. There are a lot of things you can do when you're older that you shouldn't be doing now."

"Like what?"

"Like drinking beer. Or kissing. Or using power just because it's there. It's dangerous, Ibby. It can hurt you, and maybe hurt other people, too." For a man who had never expected to have these sorts of conversations with a child, he was doing well, I thought.

Ibby, however, still had her doubts. "But you *wanted* me to save those people in the fire. You said I should."

"And you were very brave," I said, when I saw the indecision on Luis's face. "But that was when we were with you, to help and make sure you didn't get hurt. You shouldn't do things on your own."

"You think I'm bad," Ibby said, and her face became a hostile mask. "Like the Lady said. The Wardens think we're all bad. They want to punish us and take away what makes us special. And now *you* want to do it, too, to me. You want to take it all away."

"No," Luis said. "We want to make you safe. That's all. You have to trust me, Ibby. You do, don't you?"

He sounded so sincere, so warm, that I couldn't imagine how anyone could have distrusted him even for an instant. Ibby wavered, and finally nodded. "I trust *you*." She still wasn't forgiving me, I noticed. "You're not going to make me go to that school place, are you?"

"No, I'm not going to make you go," he said. "We're not going to let them take you away, either. So don't be afraid, okay?"

"Okay." She fidgeted for a moment, then walked to Luis and hugged him. "Can I go watch a movie now?"

"One, and then bed," he said. "How about that movie with the fish? You like that one."

She brightened immediately, and nodded. She even turned a sweetly dimpled smile on me, and I smiled in turn, feeling a little of my unease abate. She moved away down the hall, excited by the prospect of fun, her fright forgotten.

But she'd not forgotten the rest of it. I knew that. She didn't trust me.

And the truth was she was right not to.

Chapter 3

EMOTIONS ASIDE, there was really no question of whether Ibby would go to the Wardens' retreat, or hospital, or school—whatever they wished to call it. At her tender age, with the kind of trauma and training (if one could call it that) that had been visited upon her, I did not believe that she could be counted on to learn right from wrong when it came to her powers, even with our guidance. In the worst case, Luis and I would be hard-pressed to contain her without damage, should it come to that, and keeping her in a situation in which others would be put at risk was a very bad idea. Isabel's gift was explosive ... literally. She had a second gift of Earth powers that would be much slower to develop, but I'd seen that element misused just as badly as fire, in the wrong hands. But fire—fire was disastrously easy for her, and it was one of the most visible, terrifying gifts. Humans—and I now counted myself among them—had a distinctively sharp fear of burning. I knew she would eventually learn to use that to get her way. What child her age wouldn't, in the end?

So no matter what Luis had said, or what he (or I) had promised, Isabel would have to be taken to a place of safety and seclusion until her powers could be curbed and properly directed. Betraying her like that would damage the fragile trust she had in me, particularly, but I couldn't help it.

Even Djinn understood that standing responsible for

children meant not always being liked. Luis couldn't
make that decision.

I could.

After Isabel was asleep, I poured Luis a glass of water (he had not been drinking enough) and, when he
reached for another beer, closed the refrigerator door
not quite on his hand.

"She has to go," I said. "You know she has to go, no
matter what she thinks. No matter how hard it will be.
You'd never forgive yourself if she injured herself, or
others, because we tried to protect her too much."

He took the water glass, turned it in his fingers, and
stared into it without acknowledging what I'd said. Finally, he drank it in one long, choking gulp and handed
the empty back. I refilled it for him.

"I promised her," he said. "You think I'm going to
break my word?"

"No. *I* am going to break *my* word. You'll bear no
guilt."

Luis looked up, frowning. "It's not about my conscience, Cass."

"I think it is, and I understand why. But you know
that Marion's arguments are sound. Ibby needs more
help than we can give her alone, and better training and
protection. If she's around children with similar experiences, it could be helpful to her."

"She doesn't want to go!"

"She's *six years old*. Of course she doesn't want to
go. But one of us must make the choice to do what's
necessary."

"And that's you," Luis said. "Always you." He handed
the water back again, and walked away, head down. "All
right. You're right—I know you are. What now?"

"We'll have to be careful in how we go about it," I
said. "You know that she will fight us, and it can turn
very dangerous. This house could easily be destroyed."

"Hell, we could destroy the whole neighborhood if this goes bad," he said, and sighed. "I've been thinking about it, too. I talked to Marion. She's not bending—we bring Ibby within the week, or she sends an extraction team, and things get real damn messy. But even if we agree to take Ibby ourselves, things could still get messy."

In solidarity with him, and in compensation for his lost beer, I drank the rest of the water. I had several sips before I said, "Can't you catch her sleeping, and deepen her rest to a coma so she doesn't wake?" It was an Earth Warden skill, but it was tricky, and required constant monitoring to ensure that a false coma didn't become a true one.

"I could," he said, and frowned unhappily. "No, I *should* be able to, but honestly, I think she's on guard against stuff like that now. Pearl's training was thorough. I'm afraid she'll wake up, either as I'm doing it or when we're traveling, and all hell will break loose. I can't keep somebody down who's fighting it without serious risk. She doesn't really trust you, and we can't afford to make her feel the same way about me. If she starts distrusting me, I don't see how we can be sure she won't be able to block us." He drank some of his water, not very eagerly. "You think you can get to her quickly enough to take her down without problems?"

I was even less likely to succeed, and I shook my head. "Yet it must be done."

"Yeah, I know." Luis was deeply troubled, not only by the risks of keeping her here, or moving her elsewhere, but by the emotional cost to the girl. "Cass, I can't help thinking that maybe this is what Pearl wanted. To have us rescue Ibby and bring her out here, into the human world, where she can do maximum damage. She could use Ibby to keep all of us pinned down and working twice as hard as we should. She could set these kids off like time bombs."

I had a difficult time deciding what Pearl's motivations might have been, at any point; she had always been hard to anticipate even when I had not been her enemy, though that was aeons ago, in a very different world. She could be cruel for cruelty's sake, or cruel to a purpose, and it was impossible for me to know which her abduction of Isabel had been. But she had a plan; I knew that.

And it ended with the destruction of the Djinn, which was an insane goal; it meant ultimately the death of the world itself. Pearl hated everything, and hated it enough to be willing to sweep it all away in her blind rage. Humans, Djinn, animals, plants, the rich life force of the planet itself. She might expire with the rest of it, but she would survive long enough to look on a barren, dying ball of rock, and the death of all that lived. Dying last was her definition of winning.

There was a simple enough way to stop her, if I had the courage to choose it; it would mean the destruction of Isabel, of Luis, of all humans with whom I shared this strange, fragile life—a kind of firebreak, cutting Pearl off from the source of her power. But one species sacrificed for the sake of the planet . . . one species out of so, so many. It had been done before.

In dooming me to mortal flesh for refusing his orders, though, Ashan had inadvertently convinced me that killing humanity was the last thing I wanted to do. I was determined to find another way, any way, to defeat my former sister.

But I still didn't see what that way could be.

"Cass?" Luis's hand closed over mine, drawing me back from the cold reaches of speculation to a warm, surprisingly sweet present. I felt an instant spark to him, an opening of my attention that surprised me, and I felt myself smile. "We're going to figure it out. Don't go there."

I raised my eyebrows. "Where?"

"To that closed-in, dark place where you always go. Sooner or later, if you go there, you won't come back to me, and I can't stand that. I really can't."

I knew what he meant, and laid my other hand over his in a silent promise.

I would always come back.

For him.

The solution presented itself to me in an odd way. Ibby herself suggested it the next day, when she grew bored with the things that used to interest her, before her abduction. First she wanted movies, then books, then stories told to her. Toys failed to entice. By noon, she had driven Luis mad with her demands, and I had watched, bemused, as he ran out of ways to try to deal with her patiently.

"That's enough," he said, when she shoved the latest game—some sort of puzzle—off the table onto the kitchen floor in a petulant tantrum. "Enough, Isabel. Stop acting like you're two."

"Stop pretending like you care," she shot back. She folded her chubby arms, tucked her chin down, and glared at him, and at me, as I watched from a safe distance. "It's boring. This is all *boring*. You're treating me like a little kid."

"Then what would you like to do?" I asked her.

"Go somewhere."

"Where?"

She sighed dramatically. "Anywhere!"

I exchanged a glance with Luis, but only a brief one. I couldn't tell what he was thinking, but I didn't really need to know. The glance was only to warn him not to interfere. "Would you like to ride on the back of my motorcycle?"

He frowned at me, and silently mouthed, *What are you doing?* I shook my head slightly in response, and he subsided.

Ibby, regardless of her trust (or lack of it) for me, brightened immediately at the prospect of doing something implicitly dangerous. "Yes!" She wriggled down from her chair and dashed away.

"What the hell, Cass?" Luis asked, as soon as she was out of earshot. "You're not going to take her—"

"No," I said, knowing what he was asking. "Not directly. I'm taking her to see an object lesson."

"Where?"

"You won't like it," I said. "It's best I don't tell you about it. Not yet."

"You want me to come with?"

"No," I said, as gently as I could. "This needs to be just the two of us. I'm sorry."

That was asking for a great deal of trust, and I saw it warring inside of him, but he finally bent his head stiffly and said, "Okay." He wanted to say more, but at last he let it go. "Girl talk. I get it."

Ibby came back. I couldn't see that she'd done anything at all to prepare for the trip. "You have to change clothes," I told her. She was wearing a pale pink flowered dress, one more suited to a party than a motorcycle ride.

"Why?"

"Because you'll be on a motorcycle. A dress is not suitable for a motorcycle."

"Why?" Ibby's dark eyes were wide, and the set of her mouth was dangerously stubborn.

"Because your dress can blow up."

"So?"

"It's not appropriate to—" I struggled for an explanation, and glared at Luis as he started to laugh. "Just put on pants, Ibby." Impossible as it seemed, I found myself being concerned about the child's appropriate attire.

How the Djinn would have laughed.

Isabel stomped off to change clothes, frowning, and

Luis chuckled and leaned over to kiss me lightly on the forehead. "Very good," he said. "Outstanding. You're getting the hang of this parent thing." I felt myself frowning, which made him laugh and kiss me again, this time on the mouth. That felt warm and wet and delicious, and I wished that I hadn't committed myself quite so quickly to taking Isabel out. Surely we could find something to occupy such a young child for an hour . . . or possibly two.

I found myself winding my fingers in his hair, deepening the kiss. The strands felt like warm silk against my skin, and I had a flash of sense-memory that told me how good it would feel brushing against my skin . . . elsewhere.

Luis pulled free with an appreciative gasp. "Later," he promised, and put his finger across my damp lips. "Wish I didn't have to say that."

"I wish you didn't, either," I said. If I'd still had my powers as a Djinn, I would have stopped time, created space, made a secret hideaway for the two of us. There we could have done as we both wished, for as long as we wished.

Djinn were indulgent, easily seduced creatures. I missed being a Djinn.

A racket of noise from down the hall made us step apart even farther, and Luis shook his head. "A gang of bikers on meth on a Saturday night couldn't make as much noise as she does just putting on a pair of pants," he said. He raised his voice. "Isabel, you'd better not be doing what I think you're doing!"

I looked at him, mystified. "What do you think she's doing?"

"No idea," he said. "Doesn't matter. That's something her mother taught me—kids always assume you know what they're doing, even if you don't."

The mysteries of humankind.

Isabel appeared a few moments later, neatly dressed in a pair of small blue jeans and a pink knit top. Her cheeks matched the color of her shirt, and I wondered exactly what it was she had been doing that she felt the need to blush. "Something broke," she said. "But it wasn't my fault."

Luis went off to see what it was, and I got down my leather jacket and Isabel's small, cheerfully stained cloth one, embroidered with smiley-face flowers. Ibby treasured that jacket, and I knew it would be a sad day when she outgrew it; her mother had sewed the flowers with delicate, loving precision, and as long as Ibby wore it, she would feel a connection to Angela.

I had, not long ago, bought a child's helmet. I had never felt so glad to have made that impulsive purchase. I was prepared to risk my own skull readily enough, but not Ibby's.

We waved to Luis from the driveway, and I boosted Ibby up on the seat behind me as I straddled the motorcycle and ignited the engine, which caught with a growl and a throb of power. Ibby wrapped her arms around me and squealed in delight. Her helmet, decorated with glittering Disney characters, glowed a shocking shade of hot pink in the sunlight.

Luis was holding two halves of a broken vase, which he juggled in order to wave back. He almost bobbled half of it when I reached out with our shared Earth power and tapped his eardrum, formed vibrations of sound. *Stay here*, I told him. *I have to convince her to do this of her own accord. Pack her things, and ours. Be ready.*

He nodded, face shutting down to blankness. That didn't stop me from feeling his uneasiness, and alarm. *Cass—what the hell are you doing?*

Trust me, I said in reply, and got a stiff, grudging nod. I had earned that trust, I knew, but this was Isabel, and

Luis would not forgive me if I did something that caused her to be hurt.

Then again, I would never forgive myself, either.

I eased the bike out onto the street, and gradually picked up speed, still keeping it well under the posted limits. Isabel wiggled with excitement behind me. "Are you holding on?" I asked her.

"Yes!" she shouted back, and tightened her grip on me to prove it.

"Are you sure you're holding on?"

"Yes!"

"All right, then."

We had come to an intersection, and I stopped for the light to change. When it went to green, I pushed the throttle hard over, and the Victory roared out a challenge and shot into the open road. Isabel couldn't fall off, because I had taken the precaution of using a fair amount of Earth powers to bind her hands tight together around me. Even should we crash—an extremely unlikely event—she would be thrown clear with me, and I would protect her from any injury.

I was taking her somewhere. This was not a joyride, although I could tell that for Isabel it certainly was, as she squealed in delight and turned her face into the wind. For me, it was cold-blooded manipulation. I thought again about the Djinn categories of how we saw others—friends, allies, adversaries, and enemies. I moved from friend to ally with Isabel, and I had been all the way to enemy. At the moment, I fell squarely between ally and adversary, I thought.

I wondered how she would feel about it afterward.

The road was indeed lovely, cool winter desert unspooling on both sides of us once we reached the freeway, a gleaming black line cutting through the ochre wilderness. Overhead, the sky was cloudless and merciless, the way it often seemed in this part of the world.

Vultures spun lazy circles in the distance, and I felt the slow pulse of this world around me—animals foraging, hunting, sleeping, mating; plants living their obscure and hidden lives of sun and shade, pollen and seeds. It was a world in which all things consumed, and were in turn consumed.

All things except the Djinn.

It was the best day I had ever spent with Isabel, a delirious whirl of riding the roads, eating at roadside diners, shopping at odd little dusty stores. We were both filthy from the road's dirt by the time we got to where I had planned to take her all along—Mabel's Exotic Pets, a nearly deserted place in a very empty area outside of Albuquerque, where the mountains were only a smudge on the horizon. It was a single building coated with thick, faded white stucco, with small barred windows and a creaking sign that rattled in the wind. COME SEE THE REPTILE GIRL! the sign blared in red, dripping letters.

I released the binding on Isabel and let her climb down; she looked very small and uncertain as she stood there in her handmade jacket and Disney Princess helmet. Even her sneakers sparkled with glitter. "Why are we going here?" she asked. "It looks scary."

"It is, a little," I said, and held out my hand. "There's someone I want you to meet." When she hesitated, I said, "And they have ice cream inside."

She brightened immediately and took my hand. In that moment, I felt a surge of something dark and sticky boiling up from my stomach—guilt, and the sick certainty that I was doing the right thing, no matter how unpleasant it would be for either of us.

Luis would be furious when he found out.

There were only a few other vehicles in the parking lot. One was a rusted van with a giant, crude painting of a woman with a cobra's head, and red letters that screamed SEE THE SNAKE WOMAN! ONLY AT MABEL'S EXOTIC PETS!

Ibby was looking more and more apprehensive. I'd left my helmet with the bike, but she had chosen to keep hers on, and her hand was clammy and sweaty as it gripped mine tightly.

I pushed open the door to the shop. It gave out a rusty sound not unlike a shriek, and Ibby flinched and pulled back. I looked down at her, and she looked up at me, and then she finally nodded and gave me a trembling smile.

That smile almost broke my resolve, but I looked away and walked inside Mabel's Exotic Pets, bringing the girl in with me.

Inside, the place was no chamber of horrors—it was surprisingly clean and cool, with dim lighting that somehow managed to seem soothing instead of sinister. Ringing the four walls were rows of tanks, lit with bluer-tinted fluorescent bulbs and the reddish glow of heat lamps. Within each tank was a tiny ecosystem, painstakingly preserved . . . a desert for the bearded dragons of Australia, who sat happily in their sand under the heat, watching us pass with curiously cocked heads. In the next tank a Chinese water dragon luxuriated in a jungle of leaves and raindrops, and Ibby stopped to examine the lizard's bright jewel-green color. At another tank she shrieked in horrified delight as a large blue gecko licked its own eye; it didn't seem in the least impressed with her, choosing to chase after a cricket in its tank.

I heard a dry rustle of beads, and a warm woman's voice said, "Can I help you folks?"

Ibby, engrossed in the discovery of a truly huge iguana stretched out, uncaged, across a branch at the back of the shop, didn't even register the question. The sign next to the iguana read, YES, YOU CAN PET ME AS LONG AS YOU'RE NICE. She tentatively reached out and ran her fingers over the iguana's giant, jowl-heavy head, and it lazily opened a golden eye and then closed it again. She patted it, and the iguana held up its head for more. I heard the silvery glitter of Ibby's laughter, and it hurt me—it felt in that moment as if I was on the verge of destroying all the innocence left in her.

I looked at the women who'd spoken to us. She had come out of the back of the shop—middle-aged, dried out by age and the sun, with gray streaks through her shoulder-length dark hair. There was a bearded dragon riding on her shoulder, looking at me with perky interest.

I held out my hand, and the dragon leapt without hesitation from her to me, where it sat in my palm and stared up at me. It was lighter than I had expected, and very warm. Its skin was soft and dry, and it cocked its head quizzically, as if asking a question I could not hear.

"Hello, little brother," I told him, and touched my finger lightly to his head. He settled down comfortably in my palm, and I handed him back to Mabel. She took him back with raised eyebrows.

"You're different," she said. "Djinn, right? I used to have a Djinn, back in the day. He was a big fella, scary as hell. Used to really have to watch my step around him. Part of why I got out of the business when I did."

"The business" being, of course, the Warden business. Mabel was a former Warden—Earth, of course—who had elected to have her powers blunted and leave the service. I had no doubt she still retained a strong influence over the living creatures in her shop; they were uniformly healthy and happy, from the snakes to the lizards to the arthropods like tarantulas and scorpions, who were surprisingly complacent.

"My name is Cassiel," I said. "I came to introduce young Isabel there to your friend."

Mabel's face, which had been open and friendly, shut down completely. I felt the entire mood of the shop shift, and the iguana moved on his perch under Isabel's hand, lifting himself up on strong, muscular legs. His large, mottled dewlap came down from concealment, making him look even larger, and he bobbed his head up and down in rapid, aggressive movements. Ibby took a step back in surprise, but the iguana was looking at me, not her.

"Costs five dollars each to see the Snake Girl," Mabel said. Her words were monotone, stripped of any kind of emotion. She held out her hand. I opened my wallet and placed a ten in her palm, and she met my eyes. Hers were black, bitter, and hard. "She ain't my friend," Mabel said. "And I only do this because she wants me to. If it was my choice—"

But it wasn't, clearly, because she shook her head and stalked over to the swaying beaded curtain in the doorway. She held it open, face averted.

"Ibby," I said, and held out my hand. "We have someone to meet."

"Can't I stay here?" she asked. Her voice sounded faint. "I like the iguana. He's nice."

"His name's Darwin," Mabel said. "He's very nice. Maybe the kid ought to stay here."

"She needs to see," I said.

Mabel looked up, startled, and I could see the calculations moving through her mind until she finally nodded. "All right," she said. "All right, then. Come on, little one, your friend's already paid for you. Darwin will wait for you, I promise."

Isabel frowned, looked back at the iguana with real misgivings, but he laid his head back down on the branch with every indication that he was agreeing with Mabel's statement.

I took Ibby's hand, and together we went to meet the Snake Girl.

The first indication of something unusual was that there were bars at the end of the hallway—a gate, one with a lock. Mabel walked ahead of us, keys jingling in her hand. She unlocked the gate and slid it aside with a scrape of metal. The air was warm, and smelled feral.

"Right," she said. "Rules. Snake Girl is on the other side of the glass. Don't touch the glass. Don't get her upset; it takes days to calm her down. Don't try to talk to her, either. You only look and you go. Okay?"

"Okay," I said. I didn't intend to follow any of those rules, but Mabel didn't need to be advised of that fact.

"Straight down on the left," Mabel said. She slid the gate in place behind us and locked it. "I'll wait here until you're done."

Despite the warm, musk-scented air, I felt a chill move through my body. I felt it in Isabel, too.

Was I doing the right thing?

It was too late to change my mind. *It's for the best*, I told myself.

And I hoped that I was right.

Isabel and I walked down the narrow brick hallway, which ended in an arched doorway that opened into a larger room. Half of the room was closed off by a giant glass barrier—heavy glass, at least four inches thick, with steel reinforcing wire inside. At the back of the room was another door, one with no handle on the inside. There was a slot at the bottom wide enough to admit trays for food.

Inside the room, sitting on a battered sofa that had once been antique gold in color, was a young woman of about twenty. She was stunningly beautiful—an exotic Aztec cast to her perfectly proportioned face, and skin like rich, glowing copper. Her eyes were black, and so was her hair, flowing in ebony waves down her back.

She looked annoyed. She was lying slumped on the sofa, clicking a remote control at a big flat-screen television across the room. She finally gave it up and tossed the remote to a nearby coffee table, which held stacks of well-thumbed magazines and soft drink cans. She seemed partial to Dr Pepper.

"What?" she snapped at us, finally giving us her attention. Her voice came through clearly, but off to the side from a speaker installed in the wall. "You never seen a Snake Girl before? *Vámanos*, losers. You've got your five bucks' worth."

The girl was perfectly human down to her waist, and wearing an old, faded T-shirt that featured the same cartoon character decorating Isabel's crash helmet. From the waist down, however, her body turned into the muscular coils of a serpent—massive, and patterned like a rattlesnake in tan, brown, and black. The scales glistened in the light, and as the coils began to move, undraping from the sofa, I saw the gleam of white bone at the end of her body.

She had a long rattle, and it began to set up a relentless buzzing, like a thousand hives of agitated bees.

Isabel, wide-eyed, had said nothing at all. Finally, she looked up at me and said, "What happened to her?"

Snake Girl laughed. It was a harsh, unpleasant sound like knives stabbing a chalkboard. "*Mira*, it talks. What you think happened to me, little bitch? I got cursed by an evil witch. What else? Only I *was* the evil witch." She stopped laughing and moved with frightening speed to the glass, her top half swaying above the massive, muscular snake's body as she stared down at us, but especially at Isabel. She finally looked directly at me. "You. You look Djinn."

I shrugged. "I was."

"Explains how you knew I was here," she said. "I don't take out ads in the Yellow Pages. Didn't think the Djinn paid that much attention to the Wardens' failures."

I didn't blink as I watched her; there was something very predatory and primally frightening about her. "The Djinn never forget a failure like you," I said.

That seemed to please her, in some bizarre, obscure way. She focused again on Ibby. "And you. You're just like I was when I was your age. Maybe a little skinnier. But I was shorter."

Ibby took a big step back, but I wouldn't let her run away. Not yet. She tried to pull free, but I exerted a little Earth power to freeze her feet where they stood. Snake Girl pressed both her very human hands to the glass, then squashed her face against it, too, turning the beautiful features into something alien and monstrous. Then she pulled back and laughed, clearly delighted by the discomfort she was causing.

Ibby was shaking with it.

"I was so *smart*," Snake Girl said. "I knew better than anybody. See, I was good, and I learned really fast. Eight years old and I was setting bones and curing diseases. Ten, and I was making crops grow out of dead ground. I was a fucking *miracle*, that's what I was. They all said so, all the *curanderas*." She smiled, but it was deeply unpleasant, and her body twisted sinuously to one side, then the other. It was mesmerizing and terrifying, and I could feel Isabel trembling. "I could do anything. To anybody. For anybody. You understand how that feels?"

Isabel didn't nod, but I did. I understood all too well how that felt.

"Well, I *thought* I could do anything, anyway," Snake Girl said. "But how do you know if you don't try? So I wanted to see if I could." She hesitated, studying me, then Isabel. "You sure you want me to go into it?"

"Yes," I said. Isabel said nothing.

"Your nickel," Snake Girl said with a shrug. "I started small, with animals, making them into other things. Some died. Some went all crazy. But I kept going, because why not, okay? I turned dogs and cats into bears and lions, only it didn't go so well most of the time. Big messes to clean up and hide. I figured I'd messed around with animals long enough, so I finally changed a couple of kids, made them grow six feet tall in a day." Her fierce, malicious smile faded. "They said they wanted to grow up. Well, I made them grown-up. Only they didn't do any better in the end than the dogs and cats, and there was an even bigger mess to clean up. And I got caught."

I knew the next part of the story, the part that involved the Djinn—it was something all Djinn knew—but Snake Girl seemed reluctant to continue, or else she enjoyed dragging out the suspense. The silence stretched until I said, "And then?"

"And then the *curanderas* got a Djinn to come and stop me. I almost won, you know. I turned myself into a giant rattlesnake and I bit him, but not before he turned it all against me. I killed him. I killed a Djinn. Can you believe that?" She laughed, and this time the huge white fangs in her mouth came down with terrifying ease, glinting and wet with venom. "But he got his revenge. He trapped me like this. Not human enough to live, not snake enough to die. A freak show. And while I'm a freak show, I'm damned sure going to make money from it!"

There was silence after she'd finished, except for the dry rustle of her coils.

And then, unexpectedly, Ibby spoke. "Aren't you sorry?" she asked. "For what you did?"

"Sorry?" Snake Girl tossed her hair back over her shoulders and gave the other girl a look of smoldering arrogance. "Why should I be *sorry*? I didn't ask for all this power in the first place. What, did you? You get yours at the Internet store, *idiota*?"

"I'd be sorry about it," Ibby said very softly. "If I did what you did. I'd feel sick. I'd hate myself."

Snake Girl's face distorted with something like fury, and her warning rattled sharply again through the speakers. The writhing coils of her body slammed against the glass with such force that a crack appeared in its surface. Just a small one, but it was significant.

I let Isabel go. She ran to the far corner of the room, still facing the Snake Girl, as if she couldn't stand to turn her back to what she was seeing. I couldn't, either, but I let none of that show on my face, and I did not retreat. I refused to retreat from the murderer of a Djinn.

"You can't hurt anyone now," I said, not so much for the Snake Girl's benefit as for Isabel's. "You're frozen—no power to shift yourself to either side. And so you will live, and die, between things. Between worlds." *Just as I will*, I thought, but at least my predicament was not so dramatic. "Didn't the Wardens try to help you?"

Snake Girl laughed. "Oh, yes. They tranquilized me, and they had their best Earth Wardens try to fix me. I guess that Djinn was just a little too good. Too bad, really. If they'd restored me, I'd have destroyed all of them."

"Why?" I asked only because I wondered if maybe, just maybe, this peculiar creature could give me a glimpse inside the mind of Pearl, my enemy. I didn't particularly care about Snake Girl, just as she didn't particularly care about the victims she had destroyed. It was a fitting, Djinn-style punishment, what had been done to her. Better she should suffer.

"Why not?" Snake Girl asked, and laughed again. She looked very pretty in that moment, and very insane. "Because they'd stop me from doing what I wanted, of course. They say I used too much power. I say I didn't use nearly enough. But the truth is, they could have killed me and they didn't. So I kind of owe them for that, I guess."

She stopped talking and stayed there, swaying back and forth, then whipped around suddenly as a steel door opened in the back of the room, and a rabbit hopped through, hesitant and worried. It sat up to survey the situation, not quite sure what to make of Snake Girl.

She moved in a blur of scales and fangs, all prettiness vanished into a deadly fury, and I caught a glimpse of the nightmare of her face distended, jaw unhinged to take in her prey, just before the rabbit discovered its last, fatal mistake.

I turned my back on it and went to Isabel. I didn't hold out my hand to her; I knew she wouldn't take it. Her gaze was wide, and fixed past me to the glass, and what was happening behind it.

I crouched down to put myself even with her, and said, "Ibby. Look at me."

She didn't at first, but finally, with a great effort, she transferred her attention to me. I expected anger, but I didn't see any. What I saw, very clearly, was fear.

"You wanted me to see," she whispered. "You wanted me to see what happens if I do the wrong things. If I become like her."

I nodded slowly. "One possibility of it," I said. "People are not Djinn; Djinn are born to power, bred for it, shaped for it. People are . . . fragile, even the best. And power is a heavy thing; it warps even the strongest. I know this is much for you to learn, but you have too much ability not to understand what you could risk."

We both looked at Snake Girl, who was swallowing the kicking feet of the unfortunate rabbit. She smiled at us with bloodied teeth.

I expected Isabel to flee, but she didn't. She walked around me, right up to the glass, and stared Snake Girl full in the face. Snake Girl, for her part, bent her body in a sinuous curve to put herself on a level with Ibby. "What?" she demanded. "You not get your five bucks' worth, bitch?"

Isabel gulped, but her voice was steady when she said, "I just wanted to know your name."

For the first time, I saw Snake Girl surprised. In that moment, she didn't look much older than Isabel. Then her face hardened, and she said, "Snake Girl. That's who I am now."

"Who were you then? Before?"

"Why you want to know?"

"I just do," Ibby said. "Please."

It might have been the first time Snake Girl had been asked for anything since sealing herself in this cage—or being sealed in, perhaps. She was silent a moment, except for the restless writhing of her coils and the dry scrape of scales, and then she said, "Esmeralda. My brother called me Es."

"I don't have a brother," Ibby said. "But my *mami* called me Ibby. Thank you, Es."

"For what?"

Ibby shrugged. "Just thanks." In an act of courage so vivid that I could not quite believe I was seeing it, Ibby put her small hand flat against the glass. "I hope you feel better someday, Es."

Snake Girl—Esmeralda—stared at her with odd, troubled eyes for a long moment, then slowly reached out and put her hand against Ibby's, with four inches of glass and steel wire between them.

"*Adios*, Ibby," she said. "Don't trust the Djinn. She's a cold one, like me."

"I don't trust anybody," Ibby said. "Not really."

Esmeralda nodded, and Ibby did as well, and then she walked back to me. I rose to my full height, and Isabel held out her hand to me. I took it.

"I'm ready," she said.

"To leave?"

"To go to the school." She looked at me very seriously. "Isn't that what you wanted?"

Chapter 4

DARWIN THE IGUANA was indeed waiting when we came out from the back of the room, which brightened Isabel's darkened spirits a great deal. Mabel watched us with a frown. After consultation with Isabel, we decided that an iguana was too large, but that a bearded dragon was an acceptable substitute.

Ibby wasn't interested in snakes as companions.

I called Luis, who answered on the first ring, sounding worried. "Could you bring the truck?" I asked. "We have things to carry."

"Everybody all right?"

"Everything's fine," I said. "I bought Isabel a pet."

There was an interestingly long silence, and finally he said, "Is it poisonous?"

"Not that I am aware of."

"That's . . . surprising, somehow, from you. All right. You can explain it all to me later."

I gave him the address, and Isabel and I spent the hour until he arrived quite happily encountering wildlife, in the gentle glow of Mabel's benign residual Earth powers. Esmeralda was, I thought, in the best possible place; Mabel was protective of all her charges, including a girl who might be tempted all too easily to dangerous aggression. If Mabel was uncomfortable with the exhibition aspect of Esmeralda's situation, it was clear that

Es reveled in it; she enjoyed seeing the discomfort and horror on people's faces.

Although I believed that perhaps Esmeralda had gotten a bit more for her five-dollar charge than she'd bargained for, with Isabel.

Mabel gave us all of the care instructions and a supply of food for the bearded dragon, whose name Isabel immediately decided was Spike. Spike was tame enough to ride home sitting on Isabel's lap in the sun, dozing happily with his head resting on her palm.

Luis, however, kept casting it, and me, nervous looks. "This wasn't just a shopping trip," he said. Ibby had also succumbed to the warmth of the sun, and was asleep with her head tipped against my arm. She showed no sign of hearing.

"I had to show her something," I said. "I had to convince her. It seemed the only way."

"Scared straight?"

I considered the phrase. "Perhaps," I said. "And perhaps I just introduced her to a future ally, in which case we will have much more to think about later on. But for now I think Ibby will go to the school without a fight."

"Good," he said. "I just got another call from Bearheart, and she's not kidding about the deadline. How you want to do this? I'm not too keen on putting her in an airplane, and Marion says it's too late to meet at the rendezvous at Area 51."

"Driving is better," I agreed. "Besides, I doubt they would allow Spike on the plane."

The school that Warden Bearheart had established was in Normandie, Wyoming. That was as close to effectively the middle of nowhere as it seemed possible to be in modern-day terms. The drive was long and tiring, not the least because I could not possibly take my attention off the world around us for long; our enemies were still shadows in the night, but they stalked us, and there would be only split seconds between life and death for all of us if our vigilance failed.

Despite all that, I found that there was little I loved more than being on the Victory, with the road disappearing beneath the wheels. Wind battered me, sun broiled me, we were visited by torrential rains that drove us to shelter for almost a full day, and yet something inside of me found this vagabond life fiercely beautiful. The snow came next, falling in steady white curtains and veiling everything in thick drifts.

I suspect Luis and Isabel, in the truck, found the long trip merely very tiring.

When we finally arrived in Wyoming, I thought it a beautiful place, stark and lovely as only the most deadly things can be. Thick with snow, it seemed especially ancient, and implied that humanity was a recent, not very welcome visitor. I liked its character. It suited me well.

Outside of Cheyenne, Luis received a phone call; I saw him drop back and flash his lights, which was the signal to pull over to the side of the road. That wasn't difficult, despite the banked snow; we saw very little in the way of traffic on this road. I braced the motorcycle on its kickstand and walked back toward Luis's truck, watching the shadows around us for any hint of hostile action. Nothing more menacing than a rabbit was nearby—not that I would underestimate the rabbit.

Luis rolled down the truck's window as I approached; he covered the speaker of the phone and said, "FBI." I nodded, because that spoke volumes in the three simple letters. The FBI had been working with the Wardens to try to take down several of Pearl's compounds across the country, but we'd heard little in the past few days about any success—or failure. Luis mostly listened, but from time to time he would look to me, or Ibby (who was again sleeping, with Spike's plastic case on her lap to get full benefit of the heater), and I was not feeling overly confident based on what I saw in his eyes. He finally said, "Yeah, sorry about that, but we're traveling. Nowhere near Albuquerque right now. Won't be back for at least a few more days." He paused to listen, and smiled grimly. "Well, you can try to trace us if you want, but you're tracking Earth Wardens. Whatever that GPS chip shows you, we ain't there, man. And I'm not telling you where we're going. I'll call you when we're headed back. Best I can do. Okay. I'll hit you back."

He shut down the call and tossed the phone on the dashboard of the truck.

"Let me guess," I said. "The FBI agents would like us to inform them of our every movement."

"Preferably they'd like us to not move at all. But, yeah, failing that, they want us on a leash. Very sad for them. Maybe we should send them a gift basket." He drummed his fingernails on the steering wheel, looking out at the road ahead. "Thing is, they wanted us back bad for something in particular."

"What?"

"Don't know, and I don't like it. They're pretty damn cagey about details on the phone. They want a face-to-face briefing—now, they say, but since that ain't gonna happen, as soon as we get back."

What he didn't say was this was bound to not be a good thing; the FBI turned to us only when problems became far too bad for their agents to handle alone. It meant the situation was already messy, and would probably only get worse the longer we delayed.

"We could split up," I said. "I could go to the FBI. You could go on to the school."

He shook his head even before I'd finished. "Not a chance. We stay together."

I smiled a little, and held my hair back from my face as the icy wind thrashed it around in a pink-tinted storm. "Jealous?" I asked.

"As hell. You bet. I'm not letting any filthy feds get their hands all over your . . . assets." He grinned outright. "And we don't break up the team. *Clara?*"

"*Clara*," I said. "We go on, then."

"All night if we have to, but according to the GPS, we don't have more than a couple more hours to go," Luis said. "You good for that?"

"Always." I turned to walk back to the motorcycle. Luis leaned out the window and gave me a sharp whistle. I looked over my shoulder.

"We should have dinner later," he called. "Something hot. And in my room, while she's asleep."

"Maybe," I said, although that wasn't what I felt rushing through my body at that moment. No, that was definitely a *yes*.

I put my helmet back on and kicked the engine to life and got us back on the road.

Warden Bearheart's patrols picked us up almost a hundred miles outside of the location of the school; I first became aware of them as a disturbance in the aetheric, and when I checked I saw a vivid glow on that plane of existence that could only be a first-class Warden at the height of his powers. Male, most certainly, and by the signature of those powers, he was gifted with Weather. There were two others with him, in the traditional Warden triad of Earth and Fire, though neither could match him for strength.

They challenged us outright, on the road, by slamming a wall of air and snow into our faces and forcing us to slow down, then stop. Luis could drive through the gale-force winds, but not easily; on a motorcycle, I was much more vulnerable. If I'd sensed it as a threat,

I would have fought, and fought hard, but we had both expected the Wardens to have perimeter security.

Just not quite so far out from their actual location. I approved of the security initiative.

I parked the bike and dismounted, walking over to Luis as he climbed down from the truck. Ibby was awake, and climbing curiously around the cab of the vehicle to look at the view. She rolled down the window and said, "Tío Luis, be careful!" I noticed she left me out of her warning.

Luis turned his head, shoulder-length hair streaming like a black flag in the freezing wind, and said, "Stay inside the truck, Ib. I mean it." He'd put on a thick parka, and now jerked the fur-lined hood up over his head.

She nodded and rolled up the window, small face gone very serious. She clutched Spike's plastic container to her chest in anxiety.

I looked ahead of us to see three Wardens emerging from thin air. One of them, probably the Earth Warden, had a respectable cloaking technique. They stood motionless in a group, seeming very competent indeed; the man in the middle was the young Weather Warden, and he seemed hardly old enough to shave. The other two were women, one only a little older than he was, the other a grandmotherly gray-haired elder who wielded Earth.

"Yo!" Luis shouted into the wind. "Can we turn down the fan a little? I'm getting frozen stiff here!"

The wind slacked and then faded to a cold, thin breeze. The fact the Warden didn't kill the breeze completely told me something about him—despite his power, he had relatively little training. Although he wasn't in her class, someone like the strongest of the Wardens—say, Joanne Baldwin—would have been able to pull gale-force winds from stillness and stop them on a breath; he still required some starting point, and made it easier by continuing the flow of air molecules, albeit in a minor way. It was a weakness, though not one many would recognize.

I didn't need to tell Luis about this. I knew he would see it as well, should we require it.

"Thanks," Luis said, smiling. He held up his hand, palm out, and the other Wardens did the same. On each, the stylized sun symbol of their organization glowed, visible only in Oversight. I didn't bother to identify myself. They wouldn't mistake me for anyone else. "Friends?"

"We hoped you'd be coming," the grandmotherly woman said, stepping forward. She had a sweet, crinkled face and a cloud of soft white hair, and she radiated a soothing presence that made it difficult to keep my customary wariness in place. I knew it was a manifestation of her power, but even so, it was a powerful, subtle force. "Nice to meet you. I'm Janice Worthing. This here's my friend Ben, and that's Shasa." Shasa was the younger woman, who was darker-skinned and sharper-featured. She radiated mistrust in equal proportion to Janice Worthing's peace. "Stop glaring, Shasa—they've been invited."

"Not by me," Shasa muttered. She seemed to save her special dislike for me. I returned the favor by fixing her with a steady stare, of the sort that made the most powerful of Djinn flinch.

She didn't. In fact, she intensified her glare.

Warden Worthing evidently decided not to push for better relations between us; she stepped forward, still smiling and communicating that soothing, warm reassurance, and shook hands with Luis. Coincidentally, that brought her closer to the truck, and Isabel, who was still staring through the window. "Well, hello, sweetheart," Janice said, and gave Ibby a smile that warmed even me. "You're a pretty one! You must be Isabel. I'm Janice."

Ibby put Spike's container down, opened the truck

door, and jumped down, staring up at Janice with blank concentration for a moment. She finally said, "You can't make me like you, you know. I'm stronger than that."

Janice blinked. "I never had any intention of making you do anything, Isabel."

"Oh. You don't know you're doing it?"

"Doing what?"

"You make people feel safe, even when it's not true." Isabel studied her curiously. "I guess that's a good thing, though. There were lots of times I wanted to feel safe when I really wasn't. It would have been nicer."

Janice bent down and gravely offered her hand. "I hope you always feel safe with me."

Ibby looked to her uncle for permission, then reached out and took the woman's hand with great formality. I saw a visible relaxation in her—something that surprised me because I had not really understood until that moment that deep down, Ibby had never let go of her fear, her worry, her wariness. I had not been able to give her that sense of safety, and it hurt me in an unexpected way.

It hurt even more when Janice opened her arms, and Isabel hugged her. The old Ibby, the one I had first met, was a hugging sort of child, willing to give her love unreservedly; this one, the one we had taken out of Pearl's hands, was much more guarded. The burning sensation inside me was, I realized, jealousy. I had wanted to bring that trust out in her, but I had wanted her to feel safe with *me*.

Janice's bright blue eyes met mine over the top of Ibby's dark head, and I saw understanding in them, and pity.

Irritated even more, I turned away to slap dirt from my leathers. I wanted no pity, no understanding. I didn't even understand what I did want. It made me irritable.

"Guess we're not going to have a problem after all,

Shasa," Luis said, and gave her his famously seductive grin. "Sorry. I know you were looking forward to a bare-knuckle throw-down. Must get pretty dull out here."

She smiled back, but there was nothing seductive about it. It was pure malice. "Next time," she said, and kissed her fingers at him. Ben turned and looked at her, eyebrows raised; she gave him a dark, burning look and stalked away. There was a black SUV parked just at the bend of the road that became visible as she walked toward it. Shasa, I realized, was the one with the talent for disguise, not Janice. Unusual in a Fire Warden.

Ben finally came forward, to me, and offered his hand. "Hey," he said. "Ben Samms. Pleased to meet you, ah—" He fumbled for my name.

"Cassiel," I supplied, and we shook. "Yes, I was a Djinn once, before you ask."

His face took on a faintly pink tinge, as if he was surprised I'd anticipated the question, and he glanced over at Luis, who was watching us with an expression of mild interest. "Warden Rocha." Ben nodded, and got a nod in turn. "Hey. Nice to meet you. I've heard a lot of good things."

"Thanks," Luis said. "Nice gale you blew up on us. Took some skill, man."

"Thanks. I've been working at it."

Janice and Isabel were no longer hugging, but Ibby held on to the older woman's hand, looking happier than I had seen her in some time. Another stab of jealousy, followed by guilt, found its mark inside me, and twisted. "We should get going," Janice said. "Isabel, you want to ride with us, or with your uncle?"

"With you," Ibby said. "Can I bring Spike with me? He needs to stay warm."

"Spike?" Janice said, raising her eyebrows at Luis.

"Lizard," he said, and held out his palms to indicate the short span equating to Spike's size. "He's okay."

"Oh, certainly. All right, you get Spike," Janice said. Ibby climbed up into the truck, got Spike's container and supplies, and ran to the black SUV. I saw the flash of pain go across Luis's face, but it was only a flash, and then he smiled.

"Right, let's get moving, then," he said. "Cass? Time to mount up."

I was grateful to get back on my motorcycle. Things seemed simple there, stripped to bare essentials. While I was moving, slipping like a shadow through the world, I didn't feel so vulnerable to a child's smile, or an old woman's pity.

Or Luis's pain, which, like mine, had an edge of jealousy and guilt to it.

We passed through increasing layers of Warden security, some of it Djinn-provided, to reach the school itself, which lay in a snowy, shadowed valley surrounded by dramatic forested hills. A small frozen stream wandered its way through, gleaming silver in the light, and came within fifty feet of the fence that surrounded the school.

It was the fence that made me think of a prison. Twenty feet high, built of strong metal links fringed with icicles and topped with razor wire, it hardly seemed reassuring, but I also understood the need; it was as much to protect the children from those who might wish to harm them as it was to keep them contained, though the children might not see it that way. I wondered how Ibby would interpret it, and was suddenly glad that she was riding under the calming influence of Janice Worthing. That might prevent any unpleasantness, at least for now.

The fence opened for our little convoy of vehicles—not a gate, but an accordion-like folding of the metal that I was certain was done by Janice, or another Earth Warden. As the last car (Luis's) passed through, the fence repaired itself seamlessly.

Luis opened a communication channel in my ear. *Mira*, he whispered, *I hope they don't go and lose all their Earth Wardens at one time. That would be awkward.*

Especially if one of them was you, I replied soberly. I hoped that Marion Bearheart had thought all this through; I did not know her well enough to feel confidence in her decisions. Not that I really had confidence in anyone when it came to my safety or the safety of those I loved. A human saying had always struck me as apt: *Trust, but verify*. It might seem paranoid to some, but it made excellent sense to me.

At least they kept the interior of the compound refreshingly free of snow. I supposed that would be light work for a Weather Warden, creating a microclimate just large enough to protect those within from the winter weather. It felt warmer, though not by any stretch warm.

I had only just dismounted my bike, feeling every cold mile of the road in my bones and aching flesh, when the front door of the school opened and a woman rolled down the ramp in a wheelchair, picking up speed and braking with a flair that landed her perfectly in front of us. Bearheart. I knew she had been injured during the Djinn rebellion, but I hadn't known how badly; it was plain, when I looked at her in Oversight, that she would never walk again. No matter the skill of the healer, there were some things that could not be fixed in the human body once shattered. In a way, she had that in common with Esmeralda, the Snake Girl.

Bearheart met my eyes with her dark, glittering ones, and said, "No need to pity me, Djinn," she said. "I'm satisfied I came out a winner. Plenty of my friends didn't—on both sides."

"I wasn't pitying you," I said. "I was wondering how much of a disadvantage you'd pose for us in a fight."

She laughed. "Don't make me roll over your foot. I'm

heavier than I look, and I can build up a lot of momentum."

She was also one of the most powerful Earth Wardens I had ever seen in person, and I had certainly seen many thousands. Physically, she was in her late-middle age, with thick black hair worn long, threaded through with liberal silver. Her skin was a warm copper, her features sharp, and I noticed a sudden resemblance to the Fire Warden girl on the road, Shasa. There was something of the same commanding nose on both.

I took a guess. "Your—niece is impressive."

That took her a bit by surprise, but she nodded. "Shasa is my brother's kid. Bad temper, but a damn good Warden. Funny, most people think she's mine."

"I am not most people," I said gravely.

"Indeed you're not. I'm not sure you're *people* at all, actually. You're something else."

There was a great deal too much comprehension in her expression to please me, and I nodded toward Janice Worthing, who had gotten out of the SUV with Isabel. "Do you trust that one with Isabel?"

"I've not had the pleasure of meeting Isabel just yet, but I'm sure there's not a child in the world I wouldn't trust with Janice Worthing. She's the best there is." Bearheart fell silent a moment, watching me. "Unless you know something I need to know. Something other than what's in the official record?"

I shook my head. There was, in fact, nothing to incite my suspicions about anything I'd seen so far in this place. The Wardens had done a competent job of intercepting us and escorting us in, and I suspected my general distrust was a reflection of my own feelings. Until Isabel had turned her adoration on someone else, I hadn't realized how important the regard of the child was to me.

Without her, I felt . . . less.

"I'll want to go over what you know," Bearheart said,

clearly not convinced with my silent affirmation. "My office, one hour. Bring Warden Rocha once he's convinced
we're not organizing a sweatshop and letting them run
with scissors." A smile flickered over her lips, but it was
thin and not very amused. "Not that I blame him. Wardens don't have the greatest track record when it comes
down to dealing with our own kids. And yes, I've been
part of that problem from time to time, to my regret. But
we no longer have the luxury of worrying about each
other's possible future bad behavior. We have far too
much actual bad behavior."

With that, she pressed a control on her wheelchair
and sped off to talk to Luis, meet Isabel, and generally
do her duty. It said a great deal about her, I thought, that
she turned her back on me so readily. Either she had
underestimated me badly, or she had taken my measure
exactly.

I wondered which it was.

When no one seemed to be watching me, I strolled
around the side of the school, allowing the impressions
to roll in. First, it appeared that the fence, though impos-
ing, did not much reflect the quality of accommodations
inside. The building itself was large, built of an outer
facing of wood but, I sensed, with a core of cement and
steel worthy of a military bunker. There were no bars
on the windows, and the side doors I passed seemed
unguarded. They also proved to be unlocked, I found,
because as I was passing the north side one opened and
a girl of about ten came running out, almost barreling
directly into me. She backpedaled to a swift, scrambling
halt, and ran into the boy who was chasing her. He was
about her age, but taller, and he wrapped his hands pro-
tectively around her shoulders and moved her behind
him as he demanded, "Who are you? What are you doing here?"

He was a Fire Warden; that much seemed obvious. I could both see and sense the energy forming around his fingers. He was ready to stand and fight. I honored that.

"My name is Cassiel," I said. "I am a guest. And you?"

My polite tone must have reassured him, because he hesitated, then shook the fire off his fingers and nodded to me. Like Ibby, he was adult beyond his years. "Mike," he said. "Mike Holloway. We heard about you already."

Everyone had, it seemed. I wondered exactly *what* they had heard.

The girl, irritated, shoved Mike's protective grip away and said, "I'm Gillian." She raised her chin, almost daring me to do ... what? Declare myself the villain, attack, froth at the mouth like a rabid vole?

I smiled. "Gillian," I said, and bowed slightly. "I am sorry I alarmed you."

"You don't scare me," Gillian shot back. "I don't scare that easy. Right, Mike?"

"Right," he said. I could tell he really wanted to put his arm around her, but had good enough sense to know that she wouldn't welcome it. "Gillian is badass. It's the hair. Redheads are always badass."

Gillian did, indeed, have fiery red hair, of a brilliance that put me in mind of bright new bronze. She had it pulled back in a small queue at the back of her neck, tied up with some complicated arrangement of rubber bands that looked as if they'd be impossible to untangle without yanking out entire hanks. Gillian was a Weather Warden, and I could tell that beneath the surface bravado she was terrified of me.

Whether she was terrified because I was simply a stranger or because she knew that I'd once been a Djinn, it was obvious to me, as it must have been to Mike. She could raise her chin and pretend, but there was no doubt that I held some kind of very real terror for her.

I liked her for nevertheless standing her ground and glaring defiance.

"You a new teacher?" Mike asked me.

"Perhaps," I said. "For a short time. I don't know yet. I'll be speaking with Warden Bearheart in a moment."

"Well . . ." He eyed me doubtfully. "We need teachers who aren't afraid of us. You know—of what we can do."

"I'm not afraid of you."

"Yeah, I can see that." Mike grinned suddenly. "But you haven't seen what we can do yet."

"*We* haven't seen what *she* can do, either," Gillián put in. She punched Mike in the shoulder, hard enough that he winced. "Come on, we've got work to do."

With that, they escaped back inside through the still-open door and banged it shut between us. I eyed it thoughtfully. There were no handles to enter, but obviously it was unlocked from the inside. A fire exit.

Interesting.

I completed my perambulation, and arrived back at the front to find Marion Bearheart and Luis standing in the shade of the porch, talking. She waved to me impatiently, and wheeled herself inside.

I paused next to Luis, who said, "Do I sound paranoid if I say I don't like all this?"

"Yes," I said. "But I don't like it, either."

"Excellent. Glad I'm not the only one." He gave me a quick, furtive kiss as I moved around him toward the door, for which I rewarded him with a wide-eyed look of surprise and then, considering, backed him up against the wall and kissed him long and thoroughly. Which I felt was highly appropriate, given that it had been a very long drive and I could see no conceivable way that we would have a night of unfettered passion within the confines of this school.

After going still with utter shock, he finally joined in with a will, his lips warm and soft and sweet around mine, his hands moving slowly up my back as we kissed. It soothed some wild need in me that I hadn't actually known was present until it howled for release. Luis finally sighed into my open mouth, ran his tongue around my lips (which made me flare even hotter inside), and drew back to whisper, "We're keeping the boss lady waiting."

"No," Marion said, from the doorway. She had glided up unheard in her chair and was watching us with eyes that I was fairly sure seemed amused, and perhaps a little envious. "You're reminding the boss lady of what it is we're supposed to be fighting for. I'm all in favor of kissing breaks. But *now* you're keeping me waiting, so move your asses."

She zipped off, and with a shake of his head and a muttered imprecation in Spanish that I didn't bother to try to understand, Luis followed.

The interior door slid shut behind me as I stepped in, and I saw our friendly Weather Warden Ben standing off to the side, in a booth that was likely bulletproof as well as fireproof; he touched a series of controls, putting in motion security measures that I was fairly sure would come as a nasty surprise to any intruders. Which, I was also sure, applied to us, since we were not recognized as being part of the group as yet.

"Don't worry," Marion called back over her shoulder as she disappeared through another doorway. "You'll get DNA-keyed when we're done talking. All the doors will open for you, unless I override it."

The fact that someone still held the final power of life and death did not reassure me, even if it was someone so theoretically benign as Marion. "Explain the security, please."

"No," she said, very calmly but just as firmly. "I don't discuss the security arrangements with anyone but those on duty. Only I know all of the safeguards, and I'd like to keep it that way."

"And if something happens to you?" Luis asked.

"My friend, if something happens to me, you've got much bigger issues than how many gunports there are in the walls." She cast a quick look back at us. "I'm not an idiot. I've made provisions for information to be available if you need it, but my goal is that you never do. Clear?"

"Clear," Luis said. "But I don't like it."

"Nobody said you had to. This is why I'd rather you'd handed the girl over at the rendezvous and stepped aside; everybody involved wants to overrule everyone else for the good of the kids. We have a chain of command here, and you're going to obey it or leave."

That was blunt, and it had the ring of absolute authority. I exchanged looks with Luis, shrugged, and followed Marion.

I spared a quick look for the entry hall, which was warmly furnished in wood paneling and comfortable chairs and sofas, but with a faintly new feel to it. This building hadn't been standing for long, or if it had, it had been repurposed and redecorated.

I noticed there were no windows in the entry hall, and a quick check on the aetheric told me that it was less a room than a fortress. Anyone entering this far could be sealed here, in a room thick with concrete and reinforced with steel, and safely dispatched from a distance.

However, the alarms didn't sound, and the steel fire doors didn't drop to seal us in. We passed through, into what was a meeting room of some kind, with a large oval-shaped table and several matching chairs. And windows, although reinforced with wire and aetheric security. All seemed quite new, again. Marion rolled herself up to a gap where a chair would have gone, and indicated two others for us to take across from her. There was a bowl of fruit, and Luis reached in and grabbed an apple, which he tossed to me, then picked out a banana for himself, which he peeled while Marion fixed us with a silent, assessing gaze. Luis didn't seem bothered by her regard in the slightest. He seemed more concerned with the brown spots on the fruit.

I followed his example, took a quick, crunchy bite of the apple, and chewed the sweet, tough fiber with gusto.

Marion snorted. "Yeah, you're cool, you two—I get it. Lucky for me, I've been cracking tougher nuts than you my whole career, children, so let's drop the drama. Thank you for bringing the girl. It's going to save everyone a lot of trauma, not least little Isabel."

"Ibby," I said. "She prefers to be called Ibby."

"I'll make sure everyone knows. We want her to feel safe here, and at home." There was a manila folder sitting on the table in front of her, and Marion opened it and glanced inside. There were photographs; one was of Isabel, gap-toothed and smiling eagerly. The other was a family photo of Manny, Angela, and Isabel. I recognized the picture, because Luis carried one in his wallet and there was another framed on the mantel inside his house.

It was the last photo they had taken together before Manny and Angela had been gunned down.

"When exactly did the girl show her first signs of talent?" Marion asked. Luis took a bite of banana and shook his head. "Did her mother or father ever indicate they thought she might be manifesting any—"

"Nothing," Luis said bluntly. "Ibby was a normal kid, normal and sweet and perfect, right up until the moment she got snatched out of her grandmother's house. What they did to her made her like this . . . It's not normal."

"I'm aware of that."

"Yeah? You *aware* that they took these kids in for weird tests every day? That the ones that failed got thrown out to live like little animals or die? That Ibby was one of the ones they decided to keep, and when they realized they couldn't make her believe we didn't love her they got inside her head and made her think I was dead and Cass had killed me? They *showed* it to her, Marion. Showed me burning to death, to a kid her age who'd already seen both her parents die." Luis tossed his half-eaten banana on the table and sat back, crossing his arms. "Jesus, what's normal about her now? She wanted to protect herself. She wanted revenge. So she not only let them jump-start her powers; she worked at it she wanted it. She was scared to death. And what you get out of that is one hell of a strong Warden, untrained, way too young to handle that power."

Marion let him finish without saying a word, then looked down at her folder before she said, "I'm sorry that she's endured so much. I wish I could say it would get easier for her, but the simple fact is that it won't. There are only three paths from this point: She controls her powers; we shut down her powers; or she becomes a rogue." What Marion kindly didn't say was that there was a fourth option: death. Luis and I were already acutely aware of it.

"She's not turning rogue," Luis said. "She's got control."

"Luis, be sensible. She's *six years old.* No one, anywhere, has control at that age, especially of the kinds of powers she's manifesting. It'd be one thing if she'd stopped using them immediately after leaving Pearl's control, but that's not what's happened, is it? She's used her powers steadily since leaving the Ranch."

"Under our supervision, yeah. What else were we supposed to do? Pretend like she didn't have them? She wanted to act like a Warden, like her dad would have wanted. I'm not going to tell the kid she can't help when she can save lives."

"And so you brought her in direct contact—into *conflict*—with children with whom she trained at the Ranch. Do you think that was a good idea?"

Luis didn't answer, partly because he was getting angry and partly because—I felt—he knew she was right. I stepped in "With respect, Warden, there are few who could effectively counter these children. Is that not why you've set up this school? To handle the most dangerous yet most promising of them?"

She smiled, but didn't raise her gaze to meet mine. "Do you think we have that simple an agenda?"

"Surely you are not using them for another purpose." That gave me a very unpleasant sensation in the pit of my stomach that would rapidly build to fury. "These children have been used enough."

This time she looked up, and her eyes were calm and direct. "I am not planning on indoctrinating them in any way," she said, "other than by teaching them to properly use and judge their own strength and powers. But eventually they will be used, Cassiel, or they will be destroyed—make no mistake. Perhaps you're not aware how dire the Wardens' situation has become. There are things stirring beyond Pearl, and we have lost many, many more Wardens and Djinn than we could afford. So eventually these kids will have to fight. It's my job to ensure that they fight well, and for the right side." When Luis started to speak, she cut him off. "Don't think I feel good about that, boy, because I don't. These are *children*. They're our own, and they should be loved and protected, and they've already been injured. But they may well be the only hope we have left, in the end."

Marion's words were bleak, and I sensed the conviction underlying them. "The Wardens who followed Joanne Baldwin and the leader of the New Djinn, David," I said. "What's happened?"

"I don't know," she said. "Nobody does, at the moment. They've been out of touch for a long time, and it doesn't look good. We have to consider the strong possibility that they may not come back, and that's an enormous blow. Possibly a killing one."

That was a sobering thought—that the best and brightest, not just of the Wardens but of the Djinn as well, could already have been lost, somewhere far out to sea. "How many are left?"

"Wardens? Besides those here, about fifty, scattered across the United States, Canada, and South America. Maybe another two hundred in Europe and across Asia. Not so many, comes down to it, and most of them are scared out of their minds, and were second-rank talents to begin with." She smiled slightly, but very grimly. "Present company excluded, of course. I had to fight some pretty heavy battles with Lewis to keep you two here." Lewis being the head of the Wardens' organization, and without question the most powerful Warden of them all.

"Yeah, in the middle of you describing how we're all going to die, I'm going to worry about not getting flattered," Luis said. "Seriously, that's all? What about Djinn?"

"The ones who follow Ashan won't communicate at all, so we have no idea of their strength, or if they'd lift a finger to help us anyway. David's followers are working with us, and they're all that's held things together this long—but there aren't many who can be truly relied upon. They're Djinn. You can't assume they'll be willing to do it forever, or even into the next moment." A glance at me. "No offense."

"I take none," I said. "Because you're correct. Djinn will have little patience for the problems of Wardens, in the end. You've done little enough the past few thousand years to earn our trust, or our respect. Were I still Djinn, I would ignore you just as Ashan has done."

That might have been too much honesty, considering the look that Luis gave me. I shrugged. It was the truth.

"What about Ibby?" Luis said. "I want to know what you're going to do to help her. And I'd better hear everything, not just the sunny-side-up version—"

He would have continued, but there was a sudden shift in the mood of the room, something subtle but unmistakable. Marion shifted her weight in her wheelchair, staring behind her at the doorway, which banged open without so much as a courtesy knock.

"You'd better come," Ben said. The young Warden looked out of breath, and his aura almost sizzled with alarm. "It's Isabel. It's started."

We passed through a series of doors that I was certain were as secure as might be found in any prison, but I scarcely noticed, and I knew they made no impression on Luis. Nothing did—not the number of rooms, nor the number of people we passed. The only thing he was focused on was Isabel.

I confess, I was not much different.

Marion's wheelchair was capable of great bursts of speed, and she quickly outdistanced us, shouting as she went, "Make a hole! Make a hole, people!" There must have been bodies in the way for her to make that outcry, but by the time we reached the blockage it was gone, withdrawn into the corners of the rooms. I had a blurred impression of children whispering, of older Wardens comforting them, and then Marion's electric engine was slowing, bringing her chair to a gliding halt. Luis and I caught up only seconds later, but Marion blocked our way into the room—perhaps deliberately.

The room we saw through the doorway was small but comfortable—a twin bed, a small dresser and mirror, a chest in the corner, a television set, games, toys. It was a child's room, but impersonal as yet, without a stamp of personality on it. Isabel's new home. Spike's tiny desert in its plastic container sat on one of the tables, and the lizard was watching all the furor in the room with perky, unemotional interest.

Ibby lay on the floor next to the bed, curled into a ball with her dark hair covering her face. Her whole body was shuddering, and she was sobbing wildly. Next to her sat Janice. The grandmotherly woman was trying to comfort Ibby, but each time she tried to touch her, Isabel flinched and screamed, and the terror in it ripped through me like hooks through flesh.

I didn't think. I grabbed the handlebars of Marion's wheelchair and hauled it out of my way, rushed in, and gathered Ibby into my arms, rocking her.

She screamed again, fighting me. I caught my breath, feeling that scream break something inside of me with a harsh, glassy snap—not a bone but something more vital, more ephemeral.

Had I been born human, it would have been a broken heart.

"Hush," I whispered, and held her tight, rocking her. "Hush, Ibby. I'm here. Nothing will hurt you now. Hush."

She collapsed against me like a wet doll, gasping for breath in damp hitches. "It hurts," she whispered, a bare breath of sound. "It hurts inside and I can't make it stop, Cassie. Please make it stop!"

I felt cold, and looked across at Janice, whose creased face was set in lines of grim sadness. I turned my attention to Ibby, using Oversight, mapping out the aetheric emanations of her body and spirit.

She was burning so brightly that it seemed to sear my inner eyes. I couldn't distinguish colors, only an out-of-control conflagration of power that held a bloody core of violent crimson.

Something was wrong, very wrong. I'd seen her in pain before, but not like this.

"Hush," I whispered again, and kissed her forehead. It burned, too, with an unnatural kind of fever. "Hush, my love, you're safe now. I won't let anything harm you."

She cried for what seemed like an eternity, but eventually I felt the heat begin to cool inside her, and her tormented little body stilled in my arms, falling into a dazed sleep. It wasn't healthy, not in any way. I looked up, and saw that Luis was crouched next to me, staring at Ibby with a ghostly pallor on his face. Marion, beyond him, looked grim, as did Janice. I saw Janice shake her head in response to a silent question from the wheelchair-bound Warden.

Janice reached for Ibby. I hesitated. "Let me have her," she said quietly. "She'll be all right for a while now. She'll sleep. I can do her some good."

I sensed nothing from the woman but a sad pity, and I finally allowed her to take Ibby from my arms. The absence of her warm weight hurt in ways I couldn't define, and I had to fight the urge to cry out.

Luis put his hand on my shoulder, feeling what I felt, and looked at Marion. "What the hell happened to her?"

She exchanged another look with Janice as the older woman put Ibby in bed and drew the covers up around her chin. "We'd better talk," Marion said. "This way."

She led us back through the rooms and hallways, moving slowly this time, stopping to flash reassuring smiles at anxious children and Wardens. "Everything's fine," she said, again and again.

I knew she was lying, but there was no point in challenging her here, in front of those she was protecting.

She dropped the reassurance as soon as the doors were shut and we were locked into the conference room once again. Luis didn't hesitate. "What the hell just *happened*?" he demanded again, and, instead of sitting as she indicated, loomed over her to force her to look straight up. "What did you do to her?"

She did, without a trace of discomfort. "You may have noticed," she said, "that these days, most people are taller than I am. Please sit. I know you're upset, but that won't help the situation."

He was angry, but he wasn't insensitive (although I was tempted to be); he pulled out a chair from the table and sat down across from her, straddling it backward and crossing his arms over the top. I followed his lead, sitting a little farther away, just in case I needed for any reason to serve as backup.

Not that it would come to a fight, I hoped.

"Now," Luis said. "What did you do to Ibby?"

Marion sighed. "Nothing, I'm afraid. Your niece, like all the children in this facility, has had the channels that carry power forced open—nerves that weren't developed and mature enough to carry the kind of signals that Warden powers generate. It's very rare for a young potential Warden to manifest anything before the age of puberty, because that level of development is all-important. These children—" She paused and shook her head. "I don't like putting it this way, but it was a kind of clinical, cold rape, and it has consequences. What we will do here is try to repair the damage that's been done, because the nerves themselves are still immature and raw, and the power they're channeling is far too great. We have to contain it while the damage is healing. In your niece's case, we'll put in limiters to control her power flows. She won't be of any immediate use to anyone, not until she's healed enough to handle things on her own."

Luis was silent—shaken, I could feel that. He'd just been told, very bluntly, what he already knew, but in a way that brought it home to him in visceral terms. He didn't know what to say, except, "That doesn't answer my question. What just happened to her *now*?"

"What you just saw is the first signs that her body's defenses are fighting against what's been done to her. Once that cycle of feedback begins, it's very dangerous, both to Ibby and to everyone around her, because in a very real sense, she is fighting herself." Marion hesitated, then said, "It will get worse, I'm afraid. Much worse."

Luis swallowed. "How much worse?"

Marion regarded us both steadily and sadly. "These children are like road flares," she said. "They burn very hot, and very fast, and with very little control. Once their bodies begin acting against them, they burn themselves out quickly. I'm sorry, but the more your niece used her power, the more she damaged her ability to regulate it. . . . Think of it as developing a potentially fatal allergy. At the rate she's going, even if she avoids the obvious mistakes, she'll still be dead before she reaches puberty. Her body simply can't sustain the level of power being channeled through it, and with the body's instinct to fight the damage, it'll be further and irrevocably destroyed. It will cannibalize itself to keep going, but at a certain point, it won't be able to survive."

I felt—hollow. Numbed inside, but distantly aware that I had been injured, possibly dangerously so. Ibby was dying. Slowly, to be sure, but Pearl, *my own sister*, had twisted her, warped her, and was even now remotely killing the child in slow, cruel stages.

"No," I said. "No, that can't be true."

"You saw what happened just now," Marion said, not unkindly. "The fact is, this kind of thing will happen more and more frequently—waves of agony racing through her body, unbearable feedback from a system that isn't capable of channeling it efficiently, shredding her nervous system. The fits will come more frequently the more often she is allowed, or asked, to use her powers, until she simply stays in that state." Marion looked weary now, and a little sick. "That's why I asked you to bring her here. It's the only hope she has. Unfortunately, it does appear that we might have left it too late to allow for any kind of true recovery."

Luis took my hand. The warm feeling of his flesh on mine steadied me a little, until I looked at his face and saw the same pallid dread there. "Can you save her?" he asked Marion.

She didn't blink. "I don't know," she said. "It's going to take some time before I can even accurately assess the damage already done. I'm only giving you my preliminary impression. If Ibby fights me, it'll be worse, and she'll fail much faster. If she works with me, then I think I can prolong her life. I wish I could offer you more hope, but I have to tell you the truth. That's why it's important that she stay here, Luis. Without intervention, we stand a very good chance of losing her within the year. Not only that, but there's a risk she will take many, many other innocents with her." She paused, and then delivered the worst of it. "Even in the best-case scenario, it's unlikely she'll live to see adulthood. I'm sorry."

I felt the surge of fury and horror from Luis, and he shoved his chair back and rose to stride away, staring out one of the windows with blind intensity. He was on the trembling verge of violence, or of tears; it could go either way. Neither would be useful, not here.

I didn't even need to look at Luis to know we were in agreement. I said softly, on behalf of both of us, "What can you do for her?"

"There are treatments," she said. "Janice and I will administer them, as we do with all the children here who are displaying that kind of reaction. It'll take time, and I can't promise you it will be painless for her, but we can buy her time. That's the best I can offer. Time." She let that fall into silence, then said, "I could use your help. Trained Earth Wardens are precious here."

Luis and I answered at the same time.

"Yes, absolutely," he said.

And I said, just as decisively, "No."

We looked at each other. There was shock and disbelief in his face and, I was certain, in mine as well. "We can't just abandon her, Cass! What the hell?"

"We can't save her by staying here," I said. "It may be too late to save her at all. But what we can do, what we *must* do, is stop Pearl before any other children are mutilated and destroyed. Staying here may help your guilt, but it's not productive."

That turned Luis's eyes ice-cold. "Not *productive*? Look, I know you're not human, but just pretend for a second—"

"Wait," Marion said, and leaned across the table as if she intended to physically interpose herself between us. "Maybe Cassiel is right. Maybe there are two greater goods here. I'm selfish; I think keeping you here is the better option. But I can't deny that she's got a point. Neither can you, Warden Rocha, if you look at it objectively."

He was in no mood to examine anything objectively, and I had to admit that I wasn't, either. I was raw and furious over what I'd seen happen to Isabel, and so was he. Our instincts simply ran differently.

He wanted to protect. I wanted to attack.

"Do you even have a plan?" Luis demanded. I stared back at him without replying. "You don't, do you? You're going to run off and what? Run around screaming for Pearl to fight fair? Get a grip, Cass. She doesn't have to fight you. She's fucking *winning*."

"She'll fight me," I said. "If she hates me even a fraction as much as I hate her, she won't be able to pass up the chance to make me suffer."

"She's already making you suffer," Luis shot back. "Unless you just don't feel it. Is that it?"

I caught my breath, feeling his barb dig deep. "No. I feel it. But I can't just let it pass. You know that."

"You can't go without a fucking *plan*, Cassiel. It's stupid. And it's suicide."

Marion cleared her throat when neither of us spoke further. "All right," she said. "Let's take some time. Cassiel, stay with us for a few days while we decide together what the best course may be. Agreed?"

I was tempted to slam my way out of the room, get on my motorcycle, and ride away to find some way, *any* way, to avenge Isabel, but something stopped me.

The proud, angry yet vulnerable look on Luis's face.

"All right," I said. "Until there is a plan. But I can't stay here forever."

"I'm not asking you to," Marion said.

But Luis was, though he wisely was not asking it out loud.

Chapter 5

I HAD NEVER EXPECTED to work with children. Isabel, yes, but I had always considered her a special case in many ways—the first child I had ever met, after taking human form, and a very special, sweet, affectionate child at that. I had grown desperately fond of her, and I was aware that that was unusual for me. I am not fond of many things, really, and fewer people.

But almost immediately, I was put face-to-face with a great many individuals, and I was asked to care about them, deeply. As an Earth Warden, or at least a crippled Djinn sharing the powers of an Earth Warden, such connection was natural to me, and yet still sat oddly with my nature. Luis was compassionate. I was not . . . but the more children we met at the school, the more his compassion grew, and influenced me as well, overtaking my natural reserve.

I had already met Mike and Gillian, who proved to be the two oldest in the compound; Mike and Gillian, I soon learned, had been among Pearl's earliest captures and experiments, and while Mike seemed to have fared the best—or at least sustained the least long-term damage—he was having considerable difficulty with sudden crippling flares of pain and panic. Gillian was much worse, with episodes of paranoia that brought out uncontrollable manifestations of her powers—a potentially fatal problem for anyone around her. Mike, being a natural opposite to Gillian's Weather powers, was a good check and balance for her, and she for him, but Gillian was frighteningly fragile, and for all Mike's stoic strength, he was still only a boy—one forced to be a man far too early.

The others were worse. Elijah was a small African-American boy with a heartbreakingly beautiful smile, prone to sudden attacks of epileptic fits during which his artificially strong Earth power affected others around him. That connection triggered similar seizures at best, crushing injuries to the internal organs of others at worst. He had a constant Warden companion to monitor his status and try to head off the attacks, but they were becoming more and more frequent.

Little Sanjay couldn't speak, and his inarticulate rage triggered actual fiery explosions when his frustration grew too intense.

And they were not the most dire cases, by far. Janice, who was giving us an introductory tour, still radiated the warmth and soothing comfort that I now understood was so vital; even Sanjay, as angry and injured as he was, seemed calmer in her presence. But Janice couldn't be everywhere. There were, I realized, only four Earth Wardens present in the school, and only two were on duty at any one time, with rotating schedules. I could understand now why Marion had wanted us to stay. It was not merely for the benefit of Isabel—it was for the benefit of all her other charges as well, who had so little chance of long-term survival. She was hoping I would change my mind.

After the tours and introductions, we were served a quick, simple meal, and as I ate, I considered the future of these children. If Marion was successful in managing their conditions, then it was possible they could become useful Wardens and live approximately normal lives, for as long as their damaged bodies could sustain them. But that was not a cure, and I began to realize that there was never going to be a cure. Marion Bearheart was the best, most expert Earth Warden alive, and if she could not guarantee their health, then it could not be done.

Isabel had been dealt a mortal wound. It was simply killing her very, very slowly. That thought filled me with a sick, deadly rage that made me wild with the need to escape these walls, ride into the night, and exact revenge in the bloodiest way possible.

But Luis was right. I needed a plan, a real and solid one. Djinn were subtle, and we were known for our ability to outguess and outthink humans . . . but I was going to have to outguess and outthink the ghost of a Djinn who had more experience of strategy. I had never bothered with strategy. I had been too powerful to need it.

In the end, it was Gillian, red-haired Gillian, who gave me the plan, although I doubt she meant to do so. We were sitting together, with Mike as her constant shadow, sharing hot cocoa in one of the comfortable, quiet common areas of the school. And Gillian was talking about Pearl, surprisingly; few of the children ever mentioned her, except in euphemisms (such as calling her "the Lady").

None of them answered my questions about what she was like, except Gillian.

"She was like you," she told me. Mike grabbed her hand, probably to warn her to shut up, but she shook him off. "Pretty, I mean. And really cold."

"She doesn't mean you're cold," Mike said. "Just—"

"Not like us," Gillian finished. "And yeah, I meant *cold*. Don't tell me what I meant."

"You shouldn't be talking about this."

"Why?" Gillian tossed her red hair over her shoulders in a gesture that practically dared Pearl to appear and strike her down. "I *hate* her. The *Lady*. She tried to make me love her, but I never did. I hated her then, and I really hate her now."

"Gillian," I said, "this is important. How often did you see her?"

"See her?" She paused for thought, then shook her head. "Almost never. But she was always there, you know? You could feel her all the time."

"But she did show herself."

"Only a couple of times. She didn't look—right. Like wax or something, not a real person. It was weird and creepy." Gillian considered for a few more seconds before she added, "When she was there, when she was like that, it *did* feel different, though."

"Different in what way?"

"Like—less. Like she wasn't watching us, except when she looked right at us. Does that make sense?"

It did, and I felt an unreasonable jolt of excitement. If Pearl's omniscience limited itself as she took physical form, even as rough a form as Gillian described, then there were ways to fool her. Ways to hurt her.

"When did she take form?" I asked. Gillian, for the first time, looked at Mike, who shook his head mutely. "Please. This is important. I need to know."

"I'm going to tell," Gillian said to Mike.

"You know what she said. She said she'd know."

"Well, I don't care if she does." Gillian looked right at me and said, "It was after they woke up our powers. When there was one they thought was special, she'd come to see. Sometimes she showed things to us. Sometimes."

"What kind of things?"

"It's hard to explain. She showed us the future, I guess. And the past. And she showed us how our parents were gone and she was all we had." A muscle jumped in Gillian's tensed jaw. "But she wasn't. We had each other."

She was holding Mike's hand again, and her knuckles had gone pale. "We always had each other."

I nodded and stopped the conversation; I could sense that even Gillian, brave and angry as she was, would go no further with it. Mike pulled her away, leaving me alone to consider what she'd said.

As the fire burned down to ashes and the night settled in deep and cold, I murmured, "She comes to the camps. She comes in the flesh."

If I could get in, if I could get close, I could destroy her while she was in skin, or at least damage her badly. Gillian had given me the clue. She'd said that Pearl's omniscient presence had ceased when she was inside flesh. That meant Pearl couldn't maintain both things; she could be energy or she could be flesh.

Flesh was vulnerable. I knew that better than anyone.

I waited until the next day to speak to Luis, at the end of a silent meal. Our guides had left us, no doubt wanting us to process all the information we'd been given so far, although I had no illusions that there weren't ears listening, both mechanical and actual. "I'm going to say something you may not like."

He grunted and took a sip of Diet Coke. "Yeah, that's not really new, you know. You do that a lot."

I let the silence stretch for a moment, long enough that his smile faded, and I felt him tense in readiness for what I was about to say. "I'm not staying here."

He stopped, watching my face. I couldn't tell, in that moment, what he was thinking, but I knew what he was feeling: the same slow, rolling anger he'd been carrying since he'd first realized how damaged Isabel had become. The anger we shared, and the need for action. The difference between us was how we defined actions to be taken. "Why?"

"Because my fight is out *there*. Can I be of value here? Yes. But I could be of value anywhere, in any hospital, any war zone, any disaster. My *duty* is to find Pearl and stop her. I can't do that from here."

"You think I don't want to run off and get my revenge on? Damn straight," he said. "But I can't leave Ibby to face this alone. And neither can you. I know you better than that."

I swallowed. "You're wrong. I can."

It was black and brutal to say, but I needed to leave no doubt, and I was dreading the violence of his response . . . but not for the first time, Luis surprised me.

He looked back down at his plate, picked up a potato chip, and ate it with careful deliberation. Then he said, "You know these kids need our protection," he said. "And our help. *Isabel* needs our help."

"These children are Pearl's *failures*. Her castoffs. Her rejects, Luis. She won't threaten them; it's to her advantage to have them seeded out here in the world, causing mayhem and absorbing the best efforts of our Wardens. She throws the wounded and dying in our path to slow us down. Don't you see that?"

"No. I see kids who need help, and who the fuck do you think you are, calling them failures?" Now I'd made him angry—or, more accurately, given him a target for his rage. Me. "It takes more courage for them just to get up every day and face the world than you're ever going to know your whole life. You calling *Ibby* a failure? A reject?"

I had, of course. "That isn't a personal judgment . . ."

"The hell it isn't!" He shoved his plate aside, got up, and paced, glaring at me with sullen fury. "You cold *bitch*. You can really sit there and say this to me. I always knew you were some kind of alien inside, but damn. I thought you cared."

"I do. I love Ibby," I said. "And I love you. But I know my duty, and it isn't here. It isn't doing this. This is nothing but bandages on a mortal wound."

Luis Rocha let out a harsh bark of laughter. "*Love.* Yeah, I figured you'd be bringing that up sooner or later. You always hurt the ones you love, right? Well, fuck you. That's not love; that's selfishness. We don't need you. Just get your shit and go, if you're going to cut and run. Ibby's better off without you dragging it out. So am I."

I'd been prepared for this to hurt, but not this much. Not as if my intestines were being dragged out and burned. Oddly enough, it wasn't only the hurt, though—it was anger, too. I was right, and Luis knew it. He just couldn't bear to hear it.

And that made me see him as weak. As *human.* It made it perversely easier to say, "If you don't want me here, there's no reason for me to stay, is there?"

"None," he said. His eyes had turned obsidian-hard, and there was no trace of the man I'd kissed just yesterday. The man who had held me and shown me the sweetness of human life in ways I'd never imagined. The one who'd made me lose myself in him.

That man had been an illusion, a ghost, and now he was gone.

I kept my voice steady with an effort. "Then I'll leave tomorrow," I said. "I can't delay any longer."

"Yeah, I know, you've got a destiny and shit," he said dismissively. "Too important for all us little people to stand in your way. Especially us failures and rejects."

Hearing the words from his lips, I felt their sting, but they were still true. The longer I stayed here, mired in the hopeless struggle of these children, the more damage Pearl could do. I needed to engage her, and quickly, before she could carry out whatever obscure plan she was pursuing. It involved the children of Wardens, and

Djinn, and although the Wardens were now on guard against her, the Djinn were overconfident. Always overconfident.

The fact that all that was true didn't make the cruelty of my decision any less biting, and I couldn't think what to say to make it any easier. Luis would accept nothing short of complete compliance with his wish to stay close to Ibby; I couldn't give it, though I deeply desired to make them both happy. We were in a war, and there was triage to be done, no matter how much it hurt.

"How are you planning to stay alive?" he asked me bluntly. "You need me, Cass, unless you all of a sudden got some plug-in to the Djinn I don't know about." That was startling; we rarely talked about my . . . disability in not being able to reach the aetheric realms the same way the Djinn could, to draw their life energy directly.

It was a handicap I didn't like to remember—and one that gave him unspoken power over me.

I stared steadily at him. "I plan to stay alive the same way I have so far," I said. "Do you really mean that you will cut me off from your power? That you'll send me away to die?"

His mouth opened and closed. I knew he wanted to strike at me, but even now he couldn't do that. Not that. He knew what a risk I was taking, and how much power he really held over me. But he also knew that he couldn't stop me, not with threats. Not even with action.

Cutting me off from his power would damage me, weaken me, force me to find other sources . . . but it wouldn't change my mind.

"No," he said. "I wouldn't do that. I know what's at stake here. But you're wrong, Cassiel. You're wrong to go off after her like this."

"And you're wrong to hide," I said. "Because this fight has to go to her. She's already brought it to us, and she'll keep hurting us until we're unable to fight at all. I *have* to do it. Please understand."

He did. He just couldn't admit it, and it made him unreasonably furious.

"Then you should go right now," he said. "I can explain to Ibby why you dropped her off like a puppy at the pound, but not if you stay a couple of extra days and then abandon her. I can't explain that at all."

"I know you think I'm cruel, but this is—"

"No," he said, and there was quiet venom in the word that stopped me cold. "No, don't you try to tell me all the reasons why you're right. I know you're right, I damn well *know* you're right, but I can't forgive you for it. Don't ask me to do that, because if you loved her, *you wouldn't leave us*." The rage was still there, but his voice broke at the last, and I sensed that the anger was a thin crust now over a bottomless well of grief. Like Ibby, he'd never truly come to terms with the loss of Manny and Angela; like Ibby, he still blamed me, deep down. He didn't want to, but he did.

And yet, he wanted me to stay here. With him. He wanted it so badly that it put tears shimmering in his eyes. He hid them by turning his back on me.

I was breaking his heart, and mine, and there was nothing I could do that would heal that wound. It was better to let it bleed out the poison . . . if that was possible.

I wasn't sure that it wouldn't kill us both.

I got up and left the room, found Marion, and said, "I'm leaving tomorrow. What do you need of me tonight?"

She frowned, then looked from me to Luis, still seated in the conference room, head down. "Oh," she said, and there was a world of sad comprehension in her voice. "Oh. He's not going with you."

"No."

"I'm so sorry. That must be difficult."

So was I, deeply and achingly, but there could be no going back now. "It doesn't matter," I said. "I want to help while I can." And I wanted to keep busy, and away from the aching black hole of pain that formed inside me when I was in Luis's presence.

"All right, there's plenty to do around here," she said. "Come with me."

Marion Bearheart was brilliant, and untiring in ways that defied my understanding; she should have been exhausted, but even in Oversight I couldn't see any trace of it throughout the next few hours. I certainly tired quickly, because the delicacy of what Marion was doing in her sessions with these children was extremely difficult, and a profligate use of Earth powers; all that I was doing was amplifying and concentrating the power that she wielded, much as a nurse assists a surgeon wielding the finest laser scalpel, and of course I helped keep the children calmed and under deep sedation. I made it only halfway through the first session with Sanjay before I realized that I would need to draw power from Luis . . . or from someone else. Preferably from someone else. I wasn't sure that his power wouldn't turn toxic between the two of us, as angry as he was with me now. He'd promised not to cut me off, but that didn't mean our relationship was the same as it had been—not in any way.

I didn't need to ask for help, after all. Marion looked up from what she was doing, met my eyes, and held out her hand without hesitation. I gripped her fingers, and a glorious flood of power spilled over me, warm and insubstantial as sunlight, sinking into every hungry cell of my body and filling the reservoirs completely in only a few seconds. Marion was a natural, almost frictionless conduit for the power of the Mother, and that was an amazing thing to experience. It was close to Djinn strength, and I acknowledged that with a hesitant dip of my head in honor of the fact. Marion smiled and went back to work. I put both hands on Sanjay's warm, sweating head, not so much to restrain him as to give him the comfort of simple human contact, and felt a tension inside of him ease. Children craved touch, even more than older humans did.

The fact that people were so hesitant to get near Sanjay was a sad additional burden of his condition. They were right to fear him, but that didn't mean it made his loneliness any easier to bear.

Two hours later, Marion sighed, lifted her hands from the boy's still form, and shook her head. "I can't do more for now," she said. "It should ease the frequency and severity of his attacks, but I can't prevent them; over time, with enough interventions, we should be able to reduce them to almost nothing, but the bigger issue is controlling his power and keeping him from accessing it. It's not going to be easy. I've put some blocks in place, but until the nerve pathways heal a little I don't dare block it completely. He's going to be a danger for some time to come. The worst thing he can do is to try to use his power consciously; that would undo everything we've accomplished."

She stretched out her arms and rolled her shoulders to release tension, and Ben, who was still on duty, came into the room to take the boy back to his quarters. He could have simply rolled the bed along with its sleeping burden, but instead he picked the boy up and carried him in his arms. I was glad; the boy needed contact, needed it badly. Even sleeping, he would feel that someone loved him enough to risk that simple human touch.

"Right. That's enough, I think. I don't want you working on Isabel," Marion said, as she checked the schedule on the wall. "She's in here next. Are you still planning to leave us after sunrise?"

"Yes."

"Better sleep fast, then. You've only got about two hours, and you need it whether you know it or not."

"I could help with—"

"No, you couldn't," Marion said, and rolled her chair around to face me. "Soldiers learn to sleep when they can; who knows when you'll get your next downtime. The thing is, you're going out there alone, and we both know what a risk that is for you. You're a great asset to the Wardens out there, but you're vulnerable. I wish Luis was going with you. Do you want me to talk to him?"

I shook my head. "He won't leave Ibby, no matter what you say. Even if you did manage to convince him, it would poison the two of us for him to leave now." If I haven't irreparably poisoned us already.

"I see," Marion said. "You're probably right. I like Rocha, but he's got issues to work through."

"Don't we all?"

She smiled and didn't answer.

"Should I say good-bye to him?" I asked it as a straightforward question, because in all honesty I was at sea with this, with all the tidal sweep of emotion in this moment. I hadn't seen Luis since we'd fought and caused each other such pain, but I hadn't ceased thinking of him, and aching within for the anguish we'd caused each other. "Would that be . . . kind?"

"Not to you," Marion said. "But it might be the right thing to do, yes."

"And Isabel?"

"She's asleep," Marion said. "I wouldn't wake her up, but you can look in on her."

And if she woke, what then? What excuse would I give to avoid seeing the betrayal and disappointment on the child's face? Would I lie to her to save myself the discomfort?

The hard fact was that when I left, she, like Luis,

would see me as a traitor—as the villain she had secretly believed I was. And that was my personal burden, because I could not stay here. I could not allow my personal feelings to get in the way of my duty.

Did that make me cold? Perhaps, from a human perspective, I couldn't think of it in such terms anymore, not if I hoped to prevent the ghastly atrocities I saw here at this school.

"Cassiel?" Marion raised her eyebrows.

"I think I'll rest first," I said.

I left, but tired as I was, I was unwilling to take the opportunity to sleep. I found myself wandering the school, watching the children sleeping, or at play, or studying. They looked normal, much of the time, the way Isabel did when watching her movies or playing her games. It was the flashes of ungovernable temper that were dangerous—or unstoppable fear. Those were the things that Pearl had woken in these children—or perhaps they were normal enough, except when paired with the fearfully strong gifts she'd woken as well. I saw Mike, as always serving as Gillian's protective shadow; I watched Elijah with his beautiful, brilliant smile charming his tutors, until the clouds once again crept over him and anxiety made him difficult to manage. I was standing in the corner, observing but not taking part, when Shasa entered the room, spotted me, and drifted in my direction. I thought she might be inclined to needle me, but she only leaned against the wall beside me, crossed her arms, and finally said, "You're probably wondering where their parents are."

I hadn't been, surprisingly, but now that it occurred to me I did wonder. Luis was so protective of Isabel—was that not the normal human condition, to be concerned for one's own?

I lifted a single shoulder in response. Shasa jerked her chin at Elijah. "Orphans," she said. "All orphans. Every one of them. Parents killed in the Djinn rebellion, or in accidents, or in storms, fires, earthquakes . . . the usual fate of Wardens, sure. But every one of the children Pearl really focused on was an orphan, including your Ibby. Ever wonder why?"

I considered it now. "Because it's easier to twist a child who has no roots," I said. "No one to care. No one to watch. No one to fight for her."

"Oh, believe me, we care," Shasa said. "We watch. We fight. And if I ever see that bitch, I'll make her understand that we're a community, we Wardens. We stick together." She sent me a sidelong look. "Maybe you can tell her next time you see her. From me."

"Yes," I said. "Perhaps I will explain it to her in great detail."

"Is it true she's one of you? One of the Djinn?"

"Not anymore," I said. "But then, neither am I, if you wish to be technical."

"So you say." Shasa seemed unimpressed. "My aunt seems to like you. She doesn't trust you, though. Seems that nobody trusts you, really. Including your own Warden."

"How do they feel about you?" I asked.

She laughed. "About the same. I don't go out of my way to be liked. Never seen much point in it."

We had that in common, it seemed. After a moment, Shasa pushed off from the wall and walked to Elijah, who was wavering between smiles and tears, and when he saw her his face simply lit up with joy.

There was much to be said for the judgment of a child, I thought. And for not much caring about the opinions of others.

"Shasa," I said as she lifted Elijah in her arms. "I'll be leaving soon."

"Yeah, I heard. I'm planning a party, with cake and balloons. You're not invited, though."

"Look out for them," I said. "All of them."

She looked up, holding a laughing Elijah on her hip, and frowned. "You got something to tell me? Something I should know?"

"Nothing definite, or I'd stay. But—it's too good a target, this place. These children."

"Yeah," Shasa said. "I know. We all know. But keeping them separately wasn't helping. At least together they can help each other. We haven't got a lot of choices."

I definitely understood that, but I still couldn't silence the tremor of doubt deep within that had started upon first glimpsing this place. They'd located it far from a ley line, which was a part of the network of aetheric forces that allowed Pearl to establish footholds and compounds for her own misguided followers. There were no obvious signs that Pearl's people were even aware of this location, and yet . . .

And yet.

I couldn't wait for the fight to come here, not with so many fragile lives at risk. I had to act first, and as aggressively as possible.

That meant abandoning Ibby, and Luis, and destroying all that I'd worked so hard to build with them.

And it hurt.

My God, it hurt.

I went to say my good-byes to Luis. His door was closed, and I knocked. I heard a rustle of sheets inside, but nothing else.

I knocked louder, and then I turned the knob.

Locked.

I snorted. That was only a token gesture—he knew perfectly well that a lock couldn't keep me out if I wished to come in. I snapped it and repaired it as soon as the door swung in, and shut it behind me. The room was dark, but after a second there was a click, and the bedside lamp flickered on to illuminate Luis, propped up on pillows, staring at me.

I felt nothing from him. He'd closed himself off. Only the quiet whisper of the connection between us was left, but nothing came through it to indicate to me what he was feeling.

"Come for the big scene?" he asked. "Sorry. I'm all out of drama. I thought you were leaving already."

"I am," I said.

"So go."

"I will. I came to see you first."

"Yeah, well, I don't want to talk about it. Locked door doesn't mean anything to you?"

"It means you're angry."

"Damn straight I'm angry. *Christo*, woman, how you think I ought to feel, like twirling on a mountaintop and singing? How you think Ibby's going to feel when I tell her you dumped us?"

"I think she'll feel very hurt," I said. "Especially if you lie to her about my motives."

He sat up, and the sheet slid down his bare chest. The light seemed to be devoured in the dark shadows of his flame tattoos that ran up both arms. His voice came low and almost savagely rough. "You'd better not mean that, *chica*. You'd better not say I'm a liar, because you're the one leaving, not me."

"If you tell her that I'm *dumping* the two of you, you're lying," I said. "You're lying to yourself, and to her, and that's unforgivable. I'm not turning my back on you out of some petty disagreement. I'm *fighting* for you."

"I never asked you to do that!"

"You didn't have to," I said. "I fight for you because it's my duty. And I fight because I love you, Luis, and because I love Ibby and I can't bear to see either of you harmed again. And I always will love you, no matter how you feel. Because that's the curse of being a Djinn;

we don't fall out of love the way humans do. That's why we so seldom try to love at all. I thought you knew that." I felt out of breath, saying it, and a little sick. There were some weaknesses Djinn don't want to admit, and this was the worst. Our constancy.

I wanted to stop this. I wanted him to reach out to me, love me, forgive me. I *needed* that from him, because I could never, ever go back to simply thinking of him as a friend, an ally, a disposable human being. He was real, and he had my heart.

Perhaps he could turn his back on what we'd built. As a Djinn, I didn't have that option. The pain would echo forever in the empty places that were left.

I turned to leave. I suppose I was hoping that he'd stop me, say something, *do* something, and that there would be a shining, soul-easing moment of reconciliation between us.

And he said, very quietly, "Cassiel."

I looked at him, and saw that a struggle was going on inside of him, one I didn't fully understand. "Cass," he said, "you're doing what you've got to do. I know that. I don't like it, and I don't agree with it, but I know. But there are things I have to do, too. Things you aren't going to like, either."

I felt my forehead wrinkle into a frown. "What do you mean?"

"Since we talked I—I took some precautions. For Ibby's sake."

"I don't understand. What precautions?"

He shook his head. "You wouldn't agree. Best I not tell you. But just remember—I didn't do it for myself. Just remember that."

He wasn't going to admit anything to me, I realized, not directly. I studied him, still frowning, and then nodded. "Be careful," I said. "Watch out for yourself, and her. And all of them."

He nodded, without a single word of comfort, of understanding, of acknowledgment. It was only as I walked away, feeling the burning weight of my own pain, that I realized I hadn't, in fact, told him good-bye at all.

But I believed that he had nevertheless understood what I meant.

Chapter 6

WELL BEFORE DAWN, I kicked my motorcycle to growling life in the fenced compound. Marion had gotten up to see me off, but there was still no sign of Luis. I felt ... unfinished. And deeply guilty, although I knew it was no fault of mine that duty drove me to this. I was acting to preserve him, and Ibby. I could do nothing else.

All I really wanted was his understanding, but it seemed he couldn't give it to me. I hoped that eventually he would at least be able to grant me forgiveness.

I looked back over my shoulder to where Marion's wheelchair sat on the porch; she was, as always, alert and seemed not to be tired, although I knew that the pace must be wearing her down. "Guess I can't talk you out of it," she said. "Even though you know you could do a lot of good here."

"I can do a lot of good anywhere. You know I'm right about this," I replied, over the engine's noise. "Tell Luis ..." I didn't know what to tell him. I didn't know what he would accept from me.

Marion evidently did know, because she nodded. "I will," she said. "He loves you, you know. That's what makes this worse for him. He's a proud man, and he wants to be with you."

"And I want the same things," I murmured, but I wasn't sure she could hear me. "Marion, be careful."

"Always. I've survived this long. I'll survive a few more years, I promise you." She held up her hand, palm out, in farewell. When I faced forward again, I saw a neat hole had been made in the fence for my motorcycle, an archway not unlike the entrance to an old church. Well, this was a holy place, in a sense. A place of refuge.

I hoped it remained that way until I was able to return.

The opening sealed behind me with a white-hot snap of power, and by the time I looked back, there was a veil over the entire school. No lights showed, nothing except blank, featureless woods covered in thick mounds of snow. Unless I took the trouble to mark its location on the aetheric, I'd never find it again. That eased some of my anxiety, but not all. Not nearly all.

Once I was on the road, which was mostly still navigable, though a challenge to even my driving skills, I triggered the cell phone embedded in my helmet, and called my FBI contact in Albuquerque, Ben Turner. "I'm heading back," I told him.

"Jesus Christ, Cassiel, do you know what time it is?"

"Before dawn."

"It's three fucking o'clock in the morning. I don't get up at this hour. I don't even make love with my wife at this hour. What is so important?"

"I'm heading toward you," I repeated patiently. "I should be there tomorrow morning. Where do you want me to go?"

That triggered an ominous silence, followed by, "You want to know where you should go *tomorrow*? At three in the morning?"

"I like to be prepared," I said. I also enjoyed making Agent Turner's life a living hell; he had done me a bad turn or two, fairly recently, and I still owed him all the petty annoyances I could imagine.

But I also meant what I'd said. I did like to be prepared.

"Luis got a phone call a few days ago," I said. "Someone in the FBI would very much like it if we came back to be debriefed. Do you know why? Was it you?"

"No," he said. "And at this hour, I mostly don't care, either."

"Find out," I said. "I need to know what's happening."

He swore at me and hung up the phone. I smiled a little, in the secret shadows of the morning, and thought that the score might have righted itself just a tiny bit—but he had much, much more unpleasantness due to him. Lucky for him, Djinn are very inventive.

My smile faded as I tried to imagine what had proven dire enough for the FBI to demand our presence in the first place.

I had expected to be distracted by leaving Isabel and Luis behind. What I had not expected was how much it would continue to fester inside me, like an unhealed wound. I told myself that I didn't need them; my reliance on Luis had been, in the beginning, purely practical, but I could drain power from any Warden, willing or not. I had no need to be tied down with the complications of an emotional relationship, with Luis or with a child. I had not been put here to indulge my own impulses. Ashan's curse, which had reduced me to human flesh, was never meant to make me truly human, only to teach me the risks and humiliations of failing to meet my Djinn obligations.

And yet, it hurt to leave that odd, precious relationship behind me. It hurt so much that two hours into my drive, as the sun rose in a glory of gold and red above the trees, I couldn't bear it any longer. The world had not changed. I had.

I pulled to the side of the narrow, still-shadowed road, yanked off my helmet, and threw myself into a run. I needed to feel my muscles working, my body screaming, but even then, it wasn't enough. I stopped, breathless, and sank to my knees.

The scream welled up in primal fury out of the very core of me, and I howled my anguish out to the world. It tore the tranquil quiet to shreds, echoing from stone and sky, and *still* it wasn't enough.

I sat on the ground with my forehead pressed to my knees, shoulders shaking, as my grief poured out of me in agonizing waves. I wanted Luis's arms around me. I wanted the warmth of Isabel's smile. I wanted to feel part of them, instead of so . . . cold. So alone.

But I *was* alone. I had always been alone, in a very real way; alone even among the Djinn, my brothers and sisters.

And now I was alone here, in this world, with nothing to bind me to it but necessity.

So cold, necessity.

Eventually, even that faded, but the anguish wasn't any less; I was simply too tired, too numb to give it voice. I had to keep moving, I knew that, but it still took a real effort of will to roll up to my feet, dust myself off, and walk back to where I'd left the motorcycle leaning by the roadside. On the seat was the helmet, and black fury twisted inside me as I contemplated putting it back on. I was no *human* to need that frail protection. I dropped the helmet and kicked it, hard; it skidded away into the trees.

I mounted the Victory and was about to bring it to life when a voice said, "I never thought you had the capacity to cry, Cassiel. Much less the impulse." It came from behind me, and I twisted around to see a Djinn sitting— reclining, actually—on the branch of a tree above me. He was a beautiful creature, and human only in form;

his skin was storm-gray, and his hair seemed to flow like liquid gold down his bare shoulders. All of him was bare, in fact, and as perfect as a Greek sculpture—every muscular line of him drawn with a master's eye.

His eyes glowed a vivid, warm violet, casting their own light in the shadows

His name was Rashid, and he had been useful to me before. I would not go so far as to classify him as an ally, because I could predict the actions of an ally with reasonable certainty; Rashid was fascinated with me, but it was a magpie's fascination with a shiny object. He might aid me, and he might peck at me simply for the amusement value. Still, he had definitely helped me before, which was why I didn't reach out and snap the branch he was sitting on with a bad-tempered burst of Earth powers for surprising me. He'd seen me cry. That was reason enough to dislike him, for all his naked glory.

And it was . . . quite glorious.

"Has clothing gone so far out of style?" I asked him. "I've not been paying attention to fashion."

He smirked. "I heard you'd begun to . . . appreciate the male figure," he said. "I hoped you might appreciate mine."

"I don't," I said. "Anything else?"

He rolled sideways, falling from the branch, twisting, and landing lithely on bare, perfectly formed feet. He still wasn't bothering to cover himself, and I had to admit, the manhood on display as he walked toward me was . . . impressive. Though only in a technical sense, of course.

"Well," he said, "I thought you might like to know that Pearl's taken a new group of children. Her followers struck in Denver, and they're moving their captives in a van toward a nexus of power."

All my theoretical appreciation of his form evaporated as I fixed my attention completely on his face.

There was no human sense of outrage there, only a distant and odd amusement. "Where?"

"Where are they now? Or where are they going?"

"Going," I said, and started the engine.

"Oh, you won't get there in time," he said. "They're driving fast, and they'll arrive at their destination in less than six hours. It would take you, oh, twenty to reach them, even if you pushed your machine and yourself to the limit. Once they're in the nexus, Pearl can transport them anywhere she wishes. You'll never find them again."

I bit back a growl of frustration. "Then why tell me?"

He grinned, and his teeth seemed sharper than before. "I thought you might be grateful for my help."

"And how do you propose to be of help, you useless naked fool?"

"Temper, Cassiel," he chided me, and kept his grin. "I can slow them down, of course. I could even try to free the children. For a price."

Bargaining was a way of life among the Djinn, but that didn't make it any more welcome at this moment. I needed a friend, not a mercenary. But I'd left my friends behind, and Rashid was what I had left.

"Don't look at me that way," he said, and leaned on the handlebars of my bike, propping his chin on his palm. "Don't you want to save those children? Isn't that the heroic Cassiel I've been hearing so much about?"

"Price," I growled.

"Simple," he said. "I want you to perform a service for me. It won't stretch your abilities in the least, and best of all, it fits your personality very nicely. In fact, I should think you'll find my request a definite pleasure."

I gritted my teeth. "I won't couple with you, like some animal in the forest. Don't disgrace us both by making the suggestion."

He managed to appear both shocked and delighted.

"Would I ask that? Well, I might now; so kind of you to put it on the menu of options available. But no, I promise you, my request has nothing whatsoever to do with reproduction, human or otherwise. Quite the opposite, in fact."

That cast a shadow over the conversation, a deliberate one. I frowned as I stared at him, reading nothing in his expression or his inhuman violet eyes. "Meaning?"

"Meaning that I'd like you to kill a man for me," Rashid said, and dropped all his playacting. In this, at least, he was deadly serious. "I trust that's not beyond your abilities. In fact, I think you positively enjoy it."

He was not completely wrong in that, but I'd not give him the satisfaction of saying so. "Whom do you wish me to kill?" I asked.

"No one you know. It has nothing to do with you."

"And why can't you kill him yourself?"

"Because I made another bargain elsewhere, and now I find myself . . . restrained," Rashid said. "But it doesn't mean I can't ask someone to do it on my behalf. It's a moment's work for you, Cassiel, and if you do it, I will save your innocent children from the clutches of the evil Djinn. What say you? I think the advantages are all to you."

As bargains went, it wasn't bad, but there were unknowns in it, things that made me feel uneasy. I can't claim that my conscience would prevent it; my conscience was not human, though there were moments when I liked to pretend. I had contemplated murder in the past, and still did think about it on a regular basis. The reason I didn't act on it—or at least, not usually—was that it so often came with complications.

So might this, as simple as it seemed.

"How far away is this unfortunate person?" I asked.

"Luckily for you, only about an hour's ride, if you don't spare the horsepower. He has a tent struck out in the woods. You don't even have to look into his eyes as you end him; a simple accident would suffice for my needs. Maybe something in a nice rockfall, or a tree flattening him. I'd prefer something that painful and lingering, but your pleasure."

"His name."

Rashid flipped his hand dismissively. "You hardly need that."

"I may not need it, but I want it."

His eyebrows rose, then drew together. "I have said, you don't know him."

"Is he a Warden?" Silence. I matched him frown for frown. "You want a *Warden* destroyed. At such a dangerous time, when the humans need all the help they can get?"

Rashid lost all his playfulness, and his beauty, as he glared at me. Anger sharpened the angles of his face, and the bones seemed to take on edges beneath the skin. "This one needs to be killed," he said, quite softly. "This one killed a Djinn."

There were ways to kill a Djinn, but not many, and few were within the reach of a human, even a Warden. Where it had happened, the end for the Djinn had been slow, agonizing, and appalling. "How?"

"Does it matter? A Djinn no longer exists, one who lived thousands of human lifetimes and was worth more than a river of human blood and a mountain of human bones. A Djinn who was *my child*." That last was a hiss, like steam escaping from a vent deep in the earth's core. "This Warden had him in a bottle, once. Then when he let him go, he ordered him to fight an Ifrit, to the death. For profit. My son died for *money*. Tell me I should show mercy, Cassiel. Tell me."

I couldn't. I watched Rashid's face for a long, silent moment, imagining what it would be like to know one's child had been devoured alive, eaten by a creature that existed by ending other Djinn. Rashid would have felt it, I thought. Connected by power and heritage, he would have felt every second of his progeny's ending.

"Why now?" I asked him. "Why here? You must have had months to gain your revenge."

Rashid's face changed again, melting back into its pleasing lines. "Oh, I tried," he said. "He had another bottle and another Djinn he could torture and destroy as he wished. He bargained for her release, under the condition that I should never harm him. I made this deal." That grin came again, but this time it had darkness in it, and cruel amusement seemed to fuel his glowing eyes to even greater brightness. "I made that bargain to save an innocent life. You should understand that, Cassiel. But I never said I wouldn't find *others* to harm him."

That was the Djinn's way; bargains were sacred, but there was no deal a human could make that a Djinn couldn't find a way around, or through, or under. We'd had too long to learn our skills, and by nature we were twisting and devious. It was part of our charm.

"How do I know you're telling me the truth?" I asked him. Rashid might be lying to me, for any number of reasons of his own; there were no codes between us that prevented lying to achieve a goal. If I failed to ask the relevant questions, then that was my problem, not his. And Rashid could spin a tale, a good one.

I felt that this one might actually be true, however.

"I'll swear," he said immediately. "Thrice. On anything you think necessary."

That was an open oath, and very powerful to us. I considered for a second, then nodded. "Swear upon the Mother," I said. No Djinn would swear on the Mother and not mean it. "Swear that every word you have said to me during this conversation has been true in every aspect."

He considered, too; I was asking for something exacting, and if he'd lied in even the smallest detail, he wouldn't swear. The consequences were too great.

Instead, he nodded, and said, "I swear on the Mother, and the blood of the Mother, that every word I have spoken to you during this conversation today has been true," he said. "I have not lied. Is that sufficient?"

"Swear it three times," I said. There was nothing more binding than that. And, to my surprise, he did so without blinking.

I said, "If I fulfill your request to me, you'll overtake those who've abducted the children in Denver, stop them, and return the children to their families, or at least to the place from which they were taken?"

"I so swear," he said. "If that Warden dies, I'll save your children. I'm the only one who can, Cassiel. But I won't act until he's dead."

That seemed fair enough. "Done," I said.

"Done," Rashid repeated. "The deal is struck."

He leaned back, and gathered shadows around him. When they settled, they'd formed a black suit, cloth that slithered like silk, draping him in perfectly tailored lines. On his feet shoes formed, in the latest style, polished and perfect. He even added a tie that looked spun of moonbeams and dreams and diamonds. It suited him very well.

"Next time," he said, "we'll bargain for something more intimate." His grin was half a leer this time. "I'll wait here until it's done."

"Where is he?"

For answer, he created a map in midair in front of me, glowing golden lines with a bloodred star marking the location of my quarry. He was right; it was about an hour's ride, and I didn't look back as I gunned the engine, leaned forward, and sped off on my mission.

I hadn't intended to be an assassin, but sometimes

one must do the unpleasant to prevent the unthinkable. Having more children twisted, destroyed, and dying was unthinkable.

This was merely unpleasant pest control.

The white dot indicating my location moved steadily over the map, as miles disappeared beneath my tires; despite the piled snow, the sky was clear. The Vision glided like a shark between the shadows as the sun climbed into the sky, and when the trees parted the silver gleamed knife-bright. My hair rippled in the icy wind, and I felt the air hissing over my exposed skin. I extended my Earth sense into the trees, feeling the slow, constant strength there, the bright sparks of life moving on their own journeys large and small. For the first time in a long time I felt like a Djinn again—free.

And that carried its own guilt, and sadness.

After almost an hour, my white mark was rapidly encroaching on the red dot, and I slowed to begin examining the road and forest more carefully. There, off to the east, I located the large ripple on the aetheric that indicated a human Warden's presence. A Weather Warden, from the feel of it. A man, of middle age. His aetheric signature was muddy to me, constrained as I was in flesh; had I been truly Djinn, I could have read his past, known the truth of what Rashid had told me written in the whispers that followed him through time. Some acts left ghosts. The one Rashid had described to me would have left screaming, bloody trails.

It troubled me that I couldn't read those signs, not now, not as human as I was.

I pulled the bike over and killed the engine; in the silence, the sounds of the world around me took on weight and depth. Birdsong, sweet and constant. The wet thump of melting snow falling from branches. The whispering rustle of trees, constantly in motion as they struggled for power, for position, for light and life. The smaller noises of rodents and mammals making their little lives.

And from a distance, the entirely inappropriate music of the Beach Boys came echoing through the trees.

I left the bike and walked on, dodging trees, maneuvering through thick brush that choked the areas between. Leaf litter coated the ground where the snow had melted, thick and spongy and filling the air with a thick, piney scent of decomposition. I sensed a snake making its sluggish, cool way through the leaves toward the sun, and changed course to avoid it.

Then, quite suddenly, I was in a clearing that was bathed in golden morning sunlight, and there was a dark green canvas tent angling among the surrounding trees. The grass in the clearing was artificially thick and green, and the man had scraped a round bare circle for a fire pit and lined it with stones. There was nothing in the pit now but ash and embers, burned down overnight.

The tent flap was unzipped and open, and a man sat cross-legged on a striped blanket in front, in the sun. He was dressed in a thick flannel shirt of red and blue checks, a sleeveless down vest, and a pair of much-worn and seldom-washed blue jeans, with battered hiking boots. His salt-and-pepper hair had scarce acquaintance with a barber, and he wore a three-day growth of beard, some of which glinted silver in the sun.

He was drinking a cup of something that steamed hot wisps into the cool air, and as I emerged from the trees he stopped in mid-gulp, staring at me.

He was, for a human, reasonably attractive, though worn by time—lines around his eyes, and at the corners of his mouth. He spent much time in the open, I thought, because his skin was leathery and well tanned. I could smell him from where I stood, a rich mixture of sweat, leather, and unwashed clothing.

He put down the coffee—I could smell it, too, now—and said, "Hello, there. You lost?" He turned down the machine next to him, which had finished playing the Beach Boys and moved on to another musical group I couldn't identify. He couldn't have missed my exotic look—the pale, pink-tinted ragged hair, the white cast of my skin, the vivid, not-quite-human green of my eyes. His face went hard and a little pale, and he put his hands down on his knees, affecting an unconcerned sort of body language. "So to what do I owe a visit from the Djinn?"

I didn't have to speak with him; my commission from Rashid didn't require me to know him at all, this man who'd committed such crimes against my brothers and sisters. But I inclined my head and said, "My name is Cassiel."

"Nice to meet you," he said, which was a patent lie. "Rick Harley. Weather. If you're looking for a Djinn, I'm not working with any right at the moment."

"I'm not looking for Djinn. I'm looking for you," I said, without any particular emphasis or menace. His eyes were blue, faded a bit from their sapphire sparkle of youth. He drank too much alcohol, and it showed in the tremor of his hands and the state of his body. "Did you participate in any gambling involving the Djinn?"

He looked ghostly now, and grim. There were pale patches around his mouth and eyes, and a muscle jumped unsteadily in his jaw as he said, "Don't know what you're talking about. If that's all—"

"I am speaking about the death of a Djinn," I said. "And you know what I'm talking about, very well. It disturbs your sleep. It makes you drink too much, and cut yourself off from your family and friends to hide out here in the wilderness. You are guilty, and it eats at you."

He said nothing to that. He stared at me as if I were the angel of death, come on this fine, sunny morning to reap his soul ... as I was. He seemed unusually composed, and resigned.

"Rick," I said, "I've been sent to kill you. This isn't my choice, although it's justice; your death serves a greater purpose, and will save innocent lives. Your death is the price I have to pay to ensure the safety of those innocents."

"Why are you telling me this?" he asked, and there was a grim, wry twist to his mouth at the end. "Do you think it makes me feel any fucking better? You think I'll be happy to put my neck on the chopping block because all of a sudden I'm dying for a good cause?"

"You might be," I said. "Your death isn't in vain. Your death is honorable, the way a Warden's should be. Your death redeems your life, and the mistakes you've made."

"Fuck you," he said, and stood up in an unsteady scramble. He was already drunk, I realized, even so early in the morning. His ears were flushed bright red, but his eyes were steady and focused, and frightened. "I knew one of you would come for me. I knew it would happen someday. Well, fuck you. I know I can't win, but I'm not giving up. Maybe you can kill me, maybe you can't, but I'm damn sure going to give you one hell of a ..."

He didn't have a chance to finish. His head exploded in a cloud of red mist, and it took me a shocked second to realize that someone had shot him, from a distance. Someone had put a high-caliber bullet through his head, blowing it apart like a ripe melon. Warm spray spattered my face and dotted my white leathers, and a second later I heard the rolling crack of the rifle shot.

I didn't think, only reacted, throwing myself down and to the side, rolling even as Rick Harley's body toppled dead to the ground. Another shot snapped into the dirt where I had been, and a third followed but missed by inches. I made it to the cover of the tent's bulk and paused, breathing hard as the facts began to hurtle through my brain at light speed.

One, I had been sent here by Rashid to kill a man.

Two, I wasn't the only one.

Three, and most important, I had never been expected to carry through on my task.

This was a trap, set not for Harley but for me.

Rashid was no longer my ally. He was my adversary, and he'd sold me out to my enemies.

That was confirmed as a very human voice called from the trees, near where the rifle shot had originated, "Come out, Cassiel. We'll let you live if you surrender peacefully."

Chapter 7

THERE WAS, in fact, no possibility of surrendering, because I knew that these had to be Pearl's human acolytes—and they were under orders to kill me if at all possible. Otherwise, they'd not have fired the shots they already had—or, in the next breath, fired through the tent, opening bright spots of sunlight that blazed into the shadows beside me. The last of these missed my head by no more than an inch.

I closed my eyes, blocking it all out, and went on the aetheric to assess the situation. There were four of them—one, probably the shooter, holding his position in the trees beyond the tent. A second was creeping slowly through the foliage around to my left, and a third was climbing a tree to try to get an angle down on me from above.

The fourth, and most worrisome, had abandoned stealth and was running fast, heading for my exposed right. Once I was flanked, I was dead—that much was clear. They were certainly all armed. I could control guns, but there were many moving factors in this that didn't play to my strengths.

I considered my options, which weren't plentiful, and then did the only thing I could.

I softened the ground beneath my boots into loose, frictionless fine sand, and sank quickly to my knees, then to my hips. I held my breath as the sand advanced to my breasts, and closed my eyes and held my nose as my body plunged completely into the earth.

I was no Weather Warden, to create breathable oxygen, but the earth and things within it responded to me; I kept my vision in Oversight, assessing the positions of my enemies, and swam silently through the ground and loose rocks, cutting through like a shark beneath the waves. I sensed the two others getting quickly into position, and felt the waves of alarm and confusion when I wasn't where they expected me to be. They would waste time assuming I'd somehow managed to make it to the trees.

The one who'd gone up into the tree had made a deadly mistake. I poured power through the tough, springy bark, waking thirst and hunger, and the branches began to twist, seeking sun. If he felt it, he must have attributed it to nothing more than the wind, until he paused and a tiny tendril of a new branch whipped around his ankle. Then another. Then another, pinning his knees. By the time he realized he was being restrained it was already too late, and bark was growing up and over his body with relentless speed.

It closed over his face and cut off his screams of alarm, and in another moment his final thrashings were over.

I achieved the safe shadows beneath his tree and emerged from the earth just enough to allow myself to take a quick breath. The air tasted sweet, and I had to fight the urge to gulp it in uncontrollable spasms that might be heard. I stayed very still. My enemies were down to three, but each of them had a good vantage point, and would be hard to take down if I came out of cover.

But there was no real need, I realized, as I assessed their aetheric signatures more closely. There were no Wardens among them; these were merely human hunters—which would have been enough, if I hadn't been warned and taken immediate action.

But once I was able to ready myself, they had no real chance at all. I proceeded to kill two of them, simply by reaching out and stilling their hearts. They had no concept of how to fight such an attack, and dropped without a sound. In a way, it was a pity, because I do enjoy a fair fight. But I love winning much, much more.

I saved the last one, who had no idea he'd gone from a position of strength to even odds in less than a minute. I sank back into the ground and swam again, avoiding the area where Rick's blood was seeping into the soil. I came up where one of the other hunters had fallen, with his rifle still clutched unfired in his hand.

I rose out of the earth and grabbed the rifle in the same motion, sank to one knee, and sighted.

Rick's killer saw the movement and started to turn, but I was quick, and although I wasn't an expert with a rifle, I didn't really need to be; his chest was a large enough target, and I hit him high on the right side, between heart and shoulder. Probably through a lung, possibly near or through a major artery. The rifle rocked in my hands, driving back against my shoulder, and I rode with it and kept it at ready position as my opponent staggered and tried again to raise his own weapon. He failed, and it slipped out to fall to the grass.

Another second, and his knees went out from under him to dump him to a kneeling position. He fumbled for the rifle, but even if he'd been able to grab it, he couldn't have fired it with the wound I'd put in his chest. I stood and walked over, weapon still held in a position from which it would be easy to fire. I stood over him.

Like Rick Harley, he was of middle age, but that was where the resemblance ended. He was a smooth-skinned man, with skin that spoke of clean, indoor living, a fattening diet, and the gentle ministrations of facial cleansers and massage therapists. He looked well-off, in other words. His rifle was clean and expensive; his clothing was designer-made, and the boots he wore seemed almost new. He radiated a kind of bland superiority that made me want to put another bullet into him, in a more painful spot.

"Name," I said, and put the barrel of the rifle against his throat. "Please."

He swallowed, and I felt the vibration through the metal and wood. "Errol Williams," he said. "You're one of them. The demons."

"You could say that," I said, and smiled over the warm barrel of the weapon's long, blued steel. "You could say I'm worse. Why are you here?"

"I don't have to tell you anything," he said. "You can't touch my soul."

"No? Are you very sure of that?" I cocked my head quizzically. Errol proved to be sensible. He stopped talking. "You were sent by the Church," I said. "The Church of the New World. Who told you where we'd be?"

He said a name that meant nothing to me, but I hadn't expected to have an easy solution. Ultimately, however the information had gotten to him, it was Rashid who had performed the simple, vital task of putting me in the same valley with them, at the right time.

And they'd known that I was leaving the school. Somehow, impossibly, they'd *known*.

That meant they also knew about the school, and Luis, and Ibby.

It meant they had someone inside, or on perimeter guard. Certainly, it had to be someone who was known to the Wardens, and trusted by them.

I didn't kill my would-be assassin. I left him there, naked and alone, without weapons or any protection from the elements. I left him tied by his wrists to a tree, with a rope I'd found in his backpack. He'd had a neatly packed restraint-and-murder kit in it—coiled rope, wide tape, plastic strips of handcuffs, knives, and guns. Meant for me, I assumed.

Foolish.

I hefted the pack on my shoulder, considering him— naked, he had lost any sense of menace or competence he'd had clothed—and said, "You understand that I could have killed you, as I did your friends?"

He nodded, watching me very closely. He couldn't speak. I'd used some of the tape across his mouth. He would work it loose, but for the present, I would not have to listen to his lies and protestations.

"Soon," I said, "you may well wish that I had."

I slung the rifle across my body and walked away, passing the clearing with Harley's bullet-ripped tent, past his gradually cooling corpse, and stopped to completely douse the embers of his fire before moving on.

I paused at the edge of the clearing to put out a call to the area's predatory wildlife. Most of them were smaller things—foxes, a few lynxes—but deep in the trees lived some bears, and a pack of wolves.

They might come to investigate an easy meal. They might not. It was still a better chance than he'd given Harley. Or me.

I reached my motorcycle and considered the rifle. It was a fine weapon, but I suspected that traveling with it slung across my body wouldn't win me any thanks from the highway patrols. With a certain regret, I stripped it of bullets and tossed it into the underbrush. A quick burst of power encouraged the bushes to grow up and around it. It wouldn't be found for some time, if ever.

I kept the bullets, which might come in handy. I sealed them in an inner pocket of the backpack, which I settled comfortably on my shoulders before I reached into my leather jacket and took out my cell phone.

Luis was on speed dial. I called, but it rang five times and then his recorded voice—still warm and friendly in this virtual contact, at least—invited me to leave a message. "Watch your back," I said. "Someone either inside or close to the school has a Djinn, and may be working for Pearl. I was trapped coming out." I considered reassuring him that I was all right, but that seemed obvious, considering that I was summing up events for him. "Find the traitor. It's the only way to protect the children. Look for someone with a bottle—" My phone exploded in a scream of static as the electronics inside it fried.

"That won't do you any good," said a voice from behind me. I dropped the useless corpse of the phone and rolled off the bike, then up to my feet facing the Djinn. Rashid was still as I'd last seen him—elegant and exotic, clothed in opaque, shifting shadows. But he no longer smiled. "Your warnings will do no good."

"You lied," I said. "On the *Mother*, you lied."

"No, I didn't. Every word I said to you was true. The Warden was guilty. And I wanted him dead."

"But you sent me into a trap. You knew Pearl's men would be there."

"That was the plan, to draw them out," he said. "And I trusted that you would escape without assistance."

"Trusted?"

"*Hoped* perhaps is a better word. Yes, I hoped you would escape. As you have." He studied me for a few silent seconds. "You've killed those who came against you. Without much regret."

"I never feel much regret," I said. "That's the legacy of being a Djinn. I wouldn't feel much regret in destroying you, either, under these circumstances."

"I'm not your enemy. I was put in a position that made it impossible for me to refuse to send you to that place, or to help you once you were there. You understand?"

I did. Djinn were, after their own fashion, consistent

and predictable; under a strict obligation, we would do exactly what we'd been told to do. He would have helped me if he'd been able to find a way to do so.

"I didn't fulfill my part of the bargain," I said. "I didn't kill Harley."

"He's still dead." Rashid shrugged. "I consider that you achieved the objective as it was worded. And I'm prepared to fulfill my obligation to you. You still want the children saved, I assume."

"I do," I said. "But I'll want something more, to right the balance between us." He bowed a little in silent agreement. "I want the name of the person within the school compound who passed word of when I would be leaving. This couldn't have been done without advance warning. Your part, certainly; you can go anywhere you wish. But Pearl's men had to be put in my path, and that takes timing."

"Clever Cassiel," Rashid said, and sighed. "I can't tell you that."

"Can't," I repeated. "Not won't?"

He didn't affirm or deny, simply looked at me with those fiercely glowing eyes, as expressionless as an owl. A bad feeling grew within me.

"Does this person," I said, "possess a bottle within which you're bound?"

No response, which was in itself a response. Someone in the Warden compound had a bottle, and had found a way to bind a True Djinn into it. I hadn't thought that was possible anymore, not since the death of Jonathan and the breaking of the vows that had made us vulnerable in the dim mists of time, but it seemed things had changed, again. The Djinn were vulnerable—which, curiously, might serve us in the struggle against Pearl. It might be harder to destroy Djinn who had masters to protect them; a Djinn inside a bottle was almost indestructible, unless his master ordered him to extreme measures. As compensation for slavery, it was weak tea, but I couldn't deny that it had saved Djinn lives from time to time.

"Were you bound by your own consent?" I asked. It was an important question; some Djinn allowed themselves to be so bound, for their own reasons. I could not understand it, but I did respect the legality of it.

Rashid bared his teeth. "No," he said. "Not by my own *consent*." Tricked, then. Ambushed and overcome. There was a fire in the violet eyes now, eerie and full of impotent anger. "I can't help you, Cassiel."

"I know." Djinn who were bound were impossibly constrained, if their masters knew how to properly set the boundaries—as this one did, apparently. "When you go back to the school, warn Luis if you can. I've left him a message, but I trust no one else there. Just tell him there's a traitor. Can you do that?"

"I can." He shrugged. "It still won't do you any good."

"Just do it. Thank you."

"You're not going back to them? Even knowing this?"

I shook my head. "The reasons I left are even more important now. Luis will find the traitor. I have to go on."

"And if he can't?" Rashid asked. "If I'm ordered to kill those children, I won't have a choice. I don't wish to do that."

"I know," I said. "But I know Luis. He won't hesitate to protect Isabel, at any cost. If you can find any way to delay, to exploit any weakness in your master, take it. If you give Luis an opening, he will free you. I know he will."

Rashid bowed his head. "As you say." He didn't seem convinced.

"Are you going to keep our agreement? Are you going to save the children who were abducted?"

He flashed me a sudden, blinding smile. "I will," he said. "Be safe, Cassiel. Watch for others. Your friends may not be your friends."

As he'd been the closest thing I still had to a living friend among the Djinn, I didn't think the warning was necessary, but I nodded in turn. The shadows swirled around him, arabesque patterns of black against his skin like living tattoos, and then he was swallowed up.

Gone.

I had no doubt he would fulfill his promise to me. That meant children saved.

All in all, a morning on which I'd won.

It still felt like a hollow sort of victory, since Rashid, despite all his evidence of freedom, was held captive, and a potentially deadly weapon against those I loved.

But I couldn't turn back. I *couldn't*.

I drove through the day, and well into the night beyond the snow line, until I was too tired to continue. I slept curled on a bed of leaves and pine needles, warded against the cold by layers of more forest litter. It was not a comfortable rest, but it did the job. I woke with the earliest songbirds, did my toilet duties (a thing that had ceased, finally, to horrify me), and washed my face and hands in a cold stream that left me tingling and shivering. I drank as much as I could hold, then got back on the motorcycle for another long day's ride.

At noon I spotted a roadblock on the freeway ahead, and slowed to assess the situation. It seemed simple enough—an overturned semi truck, with its contents spilled over half the lanes of traffic. Unfortunately, its cargo had been living—cattle, probably destined for an unpleasant end in the slaughterhouse. Some had seen an earlier demise than planned due to the violence of the crash; others wandered aimlessly, confused and frightened. Some were wounded, and limped or lay crying out in pain.

Simple enough for me to edge around the mess and keep going, but there was something in it that stopped me. Wounded men roused little in the way of pity from me, unless they were innocent bystanders in a conflict; humans had a violent, bloody past, and a violent, bloody present to match it. Cows, on the other hand, seemed destined from birth to a hard life and a bad end through no fault of their own.

I liked cows.

I parked the bike and walked past two or three stopped trucks to reach the wreck. Some people were trying to help round up the strays. I wasn't as concerned about them as I was the ones lying wounded in the road, struggling to breathe. I knelt next to one massive female with a broken right leg, and straightened and set it. That took a little more power than it would have on another animal; with so much stress on the bone, any flaw would cause the mended area to snap again, possibly in a worse configuration. The cow, sensing that the pain was gone, tried to get up, but I held her down until I was sure the repair would hold. Then she struggled up to her hooves, blinked at me with warm, simple eyes, and put her nose against my chest in a gesture that might have been affection. I patted her head with awkward good humor. "I didn't save you," I told her. "I only stopped the pain." For a cow, there were no roads that didn't end on someone's dinner table; this one had been a dairy cow once, but her days of prime milk production were over, and a farmer had no doubt rid himself of the burden of buying her hay.

Her trusting mind held memories of a child feeding her treats, of the sun's blaze on her skin, of the soft, sweet taste of grass and clean water, with the sharpness of dandelions cutting through. Of pain from calving, of pleasure from the rain falling down over her, of caring for her offspring and seeing them taken away either by time, or elements, or humans.

She'd had a good life, by cow standards.

I patted her head again. "Run," I whispered to her. "Run now."

She looked at me, as startled as it was possible for a cow to be, because I put an image in her mind of danger—of wolves circling for the hunt. She edged backward nervously, then wheeled with surprising grace and trotted away, moving faster and faster until she was headed for the truck driver, who waved his arms to scare her back into the makeshift corral.

She kept running. He threw himself out of the way, and she achieved the grassy edge of the road and plunged into the trees beyond.

I went on to the next injured cow.

Run.

It was the only freedom they could know. And maybe it substituted, a little, for the damage that I'd done in the world . . . and gave a little release to my own feelings of being trapped by my own existence.

Run.

I wished, for a moment, that I could follow my own advice. I wanted to run. The question I hadn't settled yet in my own mind was whether I would be running toward Pearl . . . or back to Luis. I knew what the logical thing, the *necessary* thing, was, but that image of Rashid kept haunting me.

There was a Djinn at the school, under the control of another with unknown motives. And Rashid was right . . . Anything could happen. A creature of Rashid's might wouldn't be easily countered, or controlled, even by Marion. If she wasn't aware of the problem . . .

No. It wasn't my problem. I'd delivered the information to Luis's cell phone, and Rashid had promised to tell him as well. I'd already done as much as I could do.

I was ready to leave the accident scene and continue when I heard a shriek of horror and anguish cut through—not animal grief or injury, but human. A woman's cry.

She staggered out of one of the wrecked cars, holding a bloodied child in her arms.

Isabel.

I realized in the next instant that it wasn't my Ibby—it couldn't have been—but the impact of the horror was visceral. By the time reality sank in, I was already moving, running for the woman. She sank to her knees, still holding the limp form of the girl in her arms. Ibby's age, or very close; like Ibby, the child had dark, sleek hair, and what skin that wasn't covered in blood was a similar coppery brown. She was wearing a blue Princess shirt, with butterflies and rainbows. It looked like something Ibby would have liked.

"Give her to me!" I demanded. The woman—young and very shocked—wasn't responding. She had a broken leg and, I thought, a concussion. "Let me have her!"

The child didn't have time for any hesitation; she was bleeding out very quickly from a slash across her femoral artery—the only injury she'd sustained, but a deadly one that had already gone on much too long. I grabbed her and laid her down on the pavement, focusing all my will and strength on her thin, failing body.

Someone grabbed me and pulled me away—the arriving police, meaning well but not understanding what they were doing. I cried out, summoned up Earth power, and threw them off their feet with a roll of the pavement as I lunged back toward the girl. Paramedics were setting down cases and equipment around the motionless child, but they would be useless; it was too late for what they would try, far too late.

She had seconds left, at best. I was her only real hope.

Something struck me in the back, bit sharply, and then my entire body spasmed as electric current slashed through me. My muscles lost all control, and I slammed facedown to the hot, blood-streaked pavement. I heard the metallic ticking of the Taser control, and as soon as it ended, there was a knee squarely in the center of my back, holding me down while my muscles continued to writhe in silent agony.

But worse than that, far worse, was seeing the paramedics kneel down, check the small girl's pulse, exchange a look that clearly said their efforts wouldn't be enough. Oh, they went through the motions, but I could feel it from where I lay pinned by the police—she was dying.

I could still save her . . .

And then, with a last flutter of breath, she was gone.

I didn't offer any more resistance. With the girl's death, the police lost any real interest in me, especially when the mother woke from her stupor to tell them I'd been trying to help. A simple nudge of influence that I'd learned from Luis was enough to have them release me, though I didn't immediately leave. Instead, I watched the paramedics load the body of the girl into their ambulance, and tried to understand what I was feeling. Inexplicable loss, yes. But more than that . . . fear, very real fear.

I could lose Ibby, so easily. Rashid's words came back to me with sudden, gut-wrenching force. *If I'm ordered to kill those children, I won't have a choice.*

It became crystal clear to me: I couldn't go on, not knowing what I knew now. There was someone hiding inside the school, with Isabel and Luis. I could fight all the battles I wished out here, but back there was the one that I *had* to win.

I'd just seen the unmistakable outcome of what would happen if I didn't. An omen of things to come.

I got back on my motorcycle, and opened the throttle as I raced back the way I'd come, and hoped—no, *prayed*—that I wouldn't be too late.

I was still two hundred miles out when the attack came, in the form of a thickly falling rain. It wasn't a normal storm, I could sense that, but I was no Weather Warden, and the purpose of the storm failed to come to me until it was too late ... until the tide of mud rushed down the steep hill on my left in a thick, choking rush. I didn't have enough warning, and though it was certainly of the earth, and under my control, the water in it was the active force, and the vast amount of power in it hit me with the force of a speeding train, knocking me and the Victory off the road and sweeping us along in a grinding roar of rocks, earth, and malice.

I kicked away from the bike and tried to move with the tide, but the churning, thick mud made me clumsy and slowed my efforts. I couldn't keep my head above the muck and, after a few uselessly spent moments of flailing, allowed myself to sink as I reached out for power ...

... And found myself almost exhausted. I expended what power I could to try to slow the avalanche of mud, but it wasn't enough. I fought my way toward the surface, slicing myself on tumbling rocks, and came up in a tangle of black roots that held me under the surface like a thick, fibrous cage. I was able to grab a quick, muddy gasp of rain and air before the tumbling flow pushed me down again.

Panic and lack of oxygen quickly robbed my limbs of strength, and I lost track of where I was or how much time had passed. I knew only that I had to get free, quickly, or I would never draw a clear breath again.

My flailing hand fell on something sharp, and I felt the sting of the cut even over the muffling grip of desperation. My fingers closed around it—a torn, razor-edged piece of metal about as long as my forearm. I gripped it hard and used it to slice at the roots that had wrapped around my head and neck, hacking wildly until I felt it give way and tumble away in the tide.

Then I touched rock beneath me, and with the last, fading glimmers of power, I launched myself up, out of the mud. I made it to the rolling top of the flow and saw a chance—just one—as it took me toward a thick overhanging branch.

I stabbed the metal into the tree branch and, screaming with primal effort, pulled my legs out of the muddy avalanche. I wrapped them around the wood and slowly, painfully crawled up on the thick, sheltering tree. I was freezing and shivering, and so caked with mud that I could hardly move with the weight of it. It seemed to take forever, but I gradually stopped shaking as the wet, sucking tide beneath me slowed to a stagnant pool of muck. Things surfaced from its depths: shredded plants, broken and unidentifiable; sad, muddy lumps of dead animals caught in the trap. I caught a glimpse of something metallic, and dropped down into the chest-high mud to wade toward it.

The Victory was buried beneath what seemed like a ton of slowly congealing mud, but the wheels were intact, and I managed to get it upright. I rolled/dragged it to a shallower area and finally got it up onto dry land again. The rain continued in a torrential downpour, but this time to my benefit, as it sluiced the thick, heavy coating of black earth from my body and the bike.

I didn't know if the Vision could possibly still be functional after that ordeal, and at first it seemed that it wasn't; attempts at starting her met with nothing but impotent sputters. I was beginning to think that I ought to abandon it, sad though the thought made me, but I gave it one last halfhearted try, and the engine coughed, struggled, and then roared in triumph.

I mounted the bike and leaned forward, resting my cheek on the handlebars. "Thank you," I whispered. "Thank you."

The Victory gave a rough purr beneath me . . . not perfect, but running with the same determination I felt myself.

I walked it downhill, until I found a trail, and then rode.

I didn't dare come at the school in the same direction as before; I would rather let my enemies think that they'd destroyed me. It was only luck and stubbornness that had saved me, in truth, but I couldn't risk another encounter. I didn't have the power.

Rushing into danger without it, though, was a fool's errand. I needed to draw power; the question was, from what. Or from whom.

The obvious and easy answer was Luis, but the relationship between us was, at present, neither obvious nor easy, and I wasn't sure he would respond . . . but he hadn't broken the link between us, which still pulsed and whispered deep within me. As I searched the aetheric for a better, less obvious route to where I was going, I also—very carefully—sent a wordless signal down the connection, like a tap on a wire.

I received a single, wordless pulse back from him. The relief I felt was immense, almost choking, and I had to steady myself for a moment before I tried to think what to do next. I was too weak to force open the connection wider on my end, and too weak to communicate with him in even that indirect whisper we'd used so often before. All I could do was signal, like someone walled up in wreckage, and hope that he'd act on his own.

My eardrum gave a peculiar flutter, and then Luis's voice said, *What happened to you?*

I couldn't really answer him. Instead, I tapped the connection again.

You're hurt, he guessed.

I gave him another single tap. *One for yes, two for no, okay?*

Yes.

What do you need—dammit, you can't tell me, can you? Are you out of power?

It was an excellent guess. *Yes*, I signaled back.

Hold on, he said, which was not the response I expected. *Are you close to the school?*

Yes.

Then come in. I'll let Marion know you're coming.

No! I added the emphasis by tapping harder, two times, then another two, just to be sure. *No!*

All right, I get it. Got your message about the traitor. You want me to come to you?

No.

Then what the hell do you want, chica?

I tapped the connection, steadily, five times, drawing attention to its presence. After a few seconds, he said, *You need power, yeah, I got that. Come in to the school first.*

NO! My signal this time was two strikes, as hard as I could make it. I gave out an audible growl of frustration.

Fine, he said. *I'll come to you. Got your position on the aetheric. Be there in half an hour.*

No matter how many times I tapped the connection, or how hard, he refused to speak further. I gritted my teeth in frustration, and rode the bike up the narrow, winding trail. I was approaching the school from the south, but off the expected road; I knew I'd be running into the school's first line of boundary defenses soon. Luis was taking his life into his hands coming out, but he still had a better chance of surviving that than I did coming in.

I needed to meet him halfway.

I was still well shy of the defenses—or so it seemed—when Luis appeared, on foot, at the top of the ridge above me. He didn't say anything at first; neither did I, as I idled the bike, then cut the engine and settled it on the kickstand. The descent from the ridge was steeper than I would have attempted, but Luis took the direct approach; he broke loose a thick slab of rock with a kick, stepped on it, and rode it like a surfboard down the rugged, snow-dotted hill, skidding to a halt in front of me.

Earth Wardens. So showy.

"Well," he said. "You came back."

"I had to," I said. "There's a traitor with a Djinn at his command inside the school. No one there is safe, and nobody can be trusted." He nodded, not looking away from my face. "You're not surprised."

"No," he said. "I'm not." He looked up the slope, and I realized that we weren't alone.

Rashid was standing there, looking spotless and sober in his black suit. He folded his hands and stared down at me with an expressionless intensity that made me feel very, very vulnerable. If I couldn't fight a mere Weather Warden's attack, how much chance did I have against a Djinn?

"You came back," Luis repeated. "I didn't think you would, Cass. I really, really didn't." And then he said, almost in a whisper, "I'm so sorry. I did tell you that you weren't going to like what I was doing."

Rashid jumped off the ridge and landed flat-footed beside Luis. No mistaking it; Luis hardly glanced his direction. No surprise at all.

The realization came to me slowly, but it brought with it a massive shift of perspective. Luis wasn't surprised by Rashid's presence ... because he knew that the Djinn was there.

He knew *why* the Djinn was there.

And there was only one person who could know that.

I stared at Luis, and after a moment he reached in his pocket and took out a small, thick bottle sealed with a simple rubber stopper. He held it up for me to see, then put it back.

"You," I said. "You have Rashid."

"Yes."

"Before I left you?"

"Yes," Luis said. His voice was soft, but definite. "After you told me you were taking off, he showed up, carrying a message from the other Wardens. It was a God-given opportunity, Cass. I couldn't take the risk that Ibby would be left without a last line of defense. That's what he's for."

"You enslaved Rashid." I felt sick, lost, and deeply betrayed. "Knowing what you know, you still did it, by force."

Luis had the grace to look away. "I wasn't sure it would work," he said. "But I had to have something in reserve. I couldn't depend on you; I knew that. You *told* me that, straight out."

I had. I just hadn't expected him to take me so literally.

"You're not turning against the Wardens, or the school," I said. "Then why—?"

"It was a strategy with Marion. We knew you'd leave us; we needed to flush out the threats along the way. I wanted to warn you. I tried to warn you." Luis seemed uncomfortable now, and reluctant to spell it out; Rashid, on the other hand, smiled and picked up the thread.

"What your faithful lover is trying to say is that Marion ordered Warden Harley to his position in the first place. When you left, Luis arranged for me to send you there as well—expecting that with Harley a sitting target, any opposition would be drawn to him." He shrugged. "I admit, the bargain to destroy Warden Harley was all my doing. But you didn't have to kill him yourself. No harm done."

"Shut up," Luis said, and uncorked the container.

Rashid gave him a sudden, startlingly violent look that dripped of hatred. "A moment," he said, voice still smooth despite the depth of that emotion. "She needs to know this."

"What?" I asked.

"You can't believe him," Luis said.

"*You* can't believe him," I corrected him. "He has no reason to lie to me. Rashid?"

"The children from Chicago," the Djinn said. "I know where they were being taken."

"It doesn't matter—she could have moved them anywhere . . ."

He smiled, but it wasn't at all friendly. "I was *thorough*. Their final destination was in New Jersey."

I could believe him or not, and clearly Luis wasn't prepared to trust his word, but something in Rashid's gaze prompted me to believe. I inclined my head slowly. "Thank you."

"Don't thank me," he said. "Destroy the bitch. That's why you're here, not for this mortal nonsense."

That broke Luis's temper with an almost visible snap. "Back inside the bottle, Rashid. Now."

Rashid stretched himself out into a thin black mist and flowed into the glass. Luis slammed the cork home and dropped it into his pocket. "I said it before—you can't believe him. He was supposed to warn you before sending you in there," he said. "I told him to do it, but I didn't make it an order. I didn't think I had to. I thought he was your friend."

"He was an ally," I corrected. "And it wasn't a strike

at me; it was a strike at you. I was incidental. Also, I thought *you* were my friend. But you used me."

"Had to. We needed to make sure we got all of Pearl's scouts."

"You sent me out *blind*. Knowing the odds."

"Yeah, that's how it worked out," he said softly. "What, did you think you were the only hard-ass on the team, Cass? The only one who could make the hard choices? I chose to do what I had to. I had to protect this school and the kids inside. I trusted you to do what *you* had to do to protect yourself. I didn't think it would send you running back here."

I bared my teeth. "I came running back here to *save you.*"

"I know that now," he said, and stepped forward. "And I'm sorry. I'm sorry I didn't trust you more than that, but I really thought Rashid would warn you. I really did."

I took in a deep breath. "Give me the bottle."

"I can't do that. We need him. He's the last defense for the kids."

"Only if you don't lose control of him, and he's already fooled you once, Luis. Managing a captive Djinn is something that even the elder Wardens did carefully. You can't expect someone like Rashid to just let you order him. Free him. He'll help you of his own will."

Luis shook his head. "I can't count on it. There are too many lives at stake, and this is too important. There's no traitor at the school, Cass. I have control of the Djinn. Let's leave it at that, okay?"

I gave him a long, dark look and turned away to mount my bike. I felt filthy, inside and out. Betrayed in a way that I'd never expected.

"Wait." Luis leaned on the handlebars of the Victory, stopping me as I kicked the engine to life. "You need power before you go. Let me do that, at least."

I hated it. I hated *him* for it. But I hated myself, worst of all, for accepting. Luis took my hand in his, and the familiar hot surge of energy swept through me, healing and sure. I would have sworn that the man wielding that power could never have betrayed me, or deceived me ... but he had.

And it sickened and frightened me, that I could so misjudge him in this.

As soon as it was practical, I pulled free of him and turned the bike on the narrow trail to head back the way I'd come.

"Are you okay?" Luis asked me. The warmth in his voice made me feel a little more betrayed, a little more angry. "Cassiel—"

"Think on this," I said. "If you're not the traitor, who created the mudslide that almost killed me on the way here?"

He had no answer for that.

"Watch yourself," I said. "And watch Rashid. He'll betray you if he can." I stopped short of saying what I felt: *And you would deserve it.*

Because even though I agreed with that, I loved him, dear God, I loved him, and that was utterly damning.

I put the Victory in gear and roared away.

Chapter 8

MANY HOURS LATER, I stopped for gasoline and a meal at a diner that proved to be delicious enough, though I avoided any kind of beef, in honor of my recent new friends from the cattle truck. It was, by that time, nearly six in the morning, and I dialed my friend in the FBI with great pleasure. "Hello, Agent Turner," I said, with a good deal more cheer than was perhaps called for. "I hope I didn't wake you."

"Matter of fact, you didn't. Sorry about that, Cassiel."

"I would never wish to cause you inconvenience."

"I thought the Djinn didn't lie."

"Who ever told you that?"

"Huh, good point. Where are you?"

"A diner outside of Albuquerque—the Adobe Bowl. You know where it is?"

"I'm not that far away. Stay put. I'll come to you."

"I'll be here." I hung up without any kind of conventional end to the conversation; in my experience, that left the other party feeling off balance and frustrated. I liked to have Turner frustrated; he tended to give more away than he intended.

I ordered pie and coffee, and nursed both while the sunrise turned the land to intense bands of color—purple for the mountains, dark green for the foothills, ochre and gold for the flatlands. There was a television running silently in the corner of the diner, tuned to a news channel. One of the stories was about an abduction of children that began in Denver and ended in Chicago, which had been foiled by a fast-thinking citizen. All the children had been recovered safely, and the kidnappers either dead in the ensuing gun battle with police or fled. A manhunt was under way.

I doubted they would ever find the bodies of those who'd "fled." Rashid had not been in a very good mood, and after posing as the "fast-thinking citizen," he would want his pound of flesh.

The children were safe. That made me feel a distant, cold satisfaction, if not happiness; but even the satisfaction was wiped out by the next story, which involved the grisly discovery of a shooting victim in the woods, two men dead of apparent natural causes and one who'd been torn apart by wild animals.

Luis had gotten what he'd wanted from me. Full value.

They hadn't found the one who'd been sealed alive inside the tree, but he was as dead as the others, no question about it.

"Gruesome stuff," said Turner as he slid into the booth across from me, a porcelain cup of coffee already in his hand. He was a thin, bland sort of man, and as usual he was dressed in what I considered the FBI uniform—a dark suit, a plain tie, a white shirt. Turner was, however, also a Warden—not very powerful but well trained, at least. I doubted his FBI bosses had knowledge of that particular aspect of his life. "What kind of pie was that?"

"Good," I said. He sighed, motioned to a waitress, and pointed at my pie.

"Another one of those, unless it's cherry. I don't like cherry."

"Coconut," the woman said. "That okay?"

"Brilliant." He sipped coffee and returned his attention to me. He'd showered recently; the ends of his hair were still dark and damp against his neck, and his face seemed freshly shaved. By contrast, his shirt seemed wrinkled and stale, and his suit hadn't seen recent cleaning, either. "Nice trip?" He glanced over his shoulder at the TV. "You pass that place along the way, the one with the dead guys?"

"I think I would remember something like that."

Turner had enough experience with me to recognize a non-answer when he heard one, and for a moment I thought he might continue to pursue it, but he decided not to, as his slice of pie was deposited in front of him. "I'm sure they needed killing," he said. "That would be the usual excuse, even if you're not from Texas."

"I thought you investigated things like that."

"Murder isn't a federal crime," he said, "luckily for you. Abductions are, which is why I was tracking this Denver thing until miraculously everything just went wrong for the kidnappers. Kids got out of it fine, which was another miracle considering the bullets that started flying around. Incidentally, although this isn't going out to the media, all of the adults in the plot were either recent converts to the Church of the New World or hired guns paid as muscle. And the kids were all Warden kids. You got any insights?"

"None that would be useful to you," I said. "But you didn't call me because of those kidnappings."

"Not originally," he agreed, and considered his next words over a bite of pie. "You said the FBI wanted you to come in for a case. Truth is, there is no case. They want you to consult on some hypothetical scenarios."

"Consult," I repeated, frowning. "I don't think I understand your meaning."

"I did some digging around to get this, so please, tip generously. I mean that some eggheads up in Quantico have developed a what-if idea about what could happen if our relationship with the Wardens goes sour, and they'd like you to render an expert opinion about how likely the FBI and other governmental agencies are to be able to contain the situation."

It was frankly laughable to think that, should humans somehow go to war with Wardens—much less with Djinn—there would be any scenario at all under which they would live, much less win, but I gazed back at him with what I hoped was a politely interested expression. "I should be glad to render my opinion," I said. "But I don't have time for such things at present."

"I'm afraid their response to that is that you're going to make the time," he said. "That's why I wanted to meet you out here instead of at my offices. They're going to, ah, require your immediate assistance. You understand what I'm saying?"

I thought so, and ate the last bites of pie instead of offering an immediate reply. "You think they will take me into custody and force me to do it."

"I think they'd try. Look, I don't agree with eighty percent of what the Wardens are up to these days, but I could say the same about the FBI, and that's why I think I'm getting less than half the story at any one time. Wardens don't trust me; my colleagues at the day job trust me even less. Officially what they're telling me is that you're under no obligation to help them, but I'm placing my bets that if you say no, you get strongly reminded that you're now a citizen of the United States of America, and there'll be some statute they invoke to make damn sure you don't go anywhere until they're ready to let you off the hook." He paused, licking coconut cream from his fork. "I know you well enough to know that detaining you when you want to be somewhere else is a really awful idea. So in the interests of you not melting down a wing of a government building and putting yourself on the Most Wanted list, along with every Warden who ever met you, let's get you heading somewhere else. Fast."

It explained much, including why the government had initially wanted Luis to bring Ibby, and me, to an area they controlled ... Area 51. They wanted me, and they weren't inclined to change their minds.

I signaled the waitress for another cup of coffee and, after due consideration, for another piece of pie. Watching him eat was making my taste buds crave another. "And you? They'll know you spoke to me."

"Yeah, they'll know," he said. "Fact is, though, they don't know what we talked about, and technically I don't know enough to have warned you off anyway. My story is that I tried to persuade you to come in, but you didn't want anything to do with it. You told me you were heading for Mexico."

I raised my eyebrows. "And where *am* I going?"

"Anywhere but Mexico. Look, I don't care. I don't want to know." Turner was concentrating very carefully on his pie, and no longer meeting my eyes at all. "I've seen the stakes. You need to get where you're going and put an end to this. I don't care if you do it by our rules or not. I've seen what Pearl has done to these kids. So have you." He suddenly looked around, frowning. "Where's your shadow?"

"Who?"

"You know who I mean. Big, tall guy, badass tattoos ... ?"

"Luis has other commitments," I said coolly. "He's not involved at present."

"Huh." Turner chewed his pie thoughtfully. "I'd have placed a bet that I'd never seen the two of you apart."

"You'd lose," I said.

"I wouldn't be the only one."

My pie and extra cup of coffee were delivered, and I slid the waitress a larger bill than necessary to pay for us both. "Margaret," I said. She looked up, startled, and I focused on her tired, faded green eyes. "Margaret, we were never here. You don't remember serving us at all." The money was for my FBI friend's benefit. The pulse of power—illegal to use in this way, for a Warden—was the real weapon I was wielding. In her mind, our faces blurred and became indistinct. "Keep the change."

She smiled vaguely and wandered on. I ate my pie quickly, savoring every bite, and drained the coffee in one long gulp. "The sun's up," I said. "You should go before you're late to work."

He looked at his watch. "I've still got plenty of—"

"Ben." Now I had his eyes, too. "No, you don't. You need to go, now. I'm sure you have paperwork to complete. Just forget you saw me today."

I had him now, too, caught in the hold of my gaze, and my borrowed powers. The pupils of his eyes widened, and I sensed that he was thinking now about getting to work, and wondering vaguely why he'd come all the way out here to eat pie, of all things, for breakfast.

Before he could focus again, I slipped out of the booth and walked quickly away, out into the hot spill of the morning sun. In ten seconds, I was on the bike and riding away.

I'd lost another ally. More critically, perhaps, I had gained an adversary of definite ability . . . the entire system of human law enforcement, which could be easily brought to bear upon me because of its vast size and scope. I was no Djinn, to slip quietly away. I was flesh and blood—powerful, but fragile. I could be hurt, imprisoned, or killed.

So be it. I would risk all that, and more, in order to ensure that Pearl was stopped from hurting another child as she'd hurt Isabel.

That was my only mission now.

*   *   *

My first stop was at an Albuquerque map store that sold detailed laminated illustrations of every area of the United States. I bought sets detailing roads, another with painstaking topographical detail, and colored markers. Then I stored it all in a plastic tube that I slung across my back, and rode my motorcycle to the interstate. It didn't much matter which direction I chose, so long as it was out of Albuquerque and heading toward a major city, so I picked the widest, straightest roads possible, and opened up the throttle. The buffeting of the wind numbed my skin and froze my hair into unruly spikes, and hours passed before I spotted a quiet, out-of-the-way motel that seemed clean. It had only two other vehicles in the parking lot—one, a battered pickup, almost certainly belonged to a staff member. The other was a dusty dark red sedan with out-of-state license tags and children's toys in the back window.

I paid for a room. It was all I wanted—simple, well maintained, without any of the luxuries so many travelers seemed to expect. I bought a bottle of water from a machine, sat down at the old, narrow table with my maps, and put down everything I knew.

Then I rose up into the aetheric and zeroed in on the closest of Pearl's compounds. That one, the Colorado facility, was long gone, dead and closed down, with nothing left to even mark it in the physical world. It wasn't so easy to erase the stains in the aetheric, though. A darkness still hovered there, and I directed my insubstantial body to step inside that quivering cloud.

It felt like heat, and rot, and hate, and even the ghost of it made me feel drained and exhausted—but I had what I needed, as quick as the encounter had been. I had the taste of Pearl's madness.

Now all I had to do was verify the information Rashid had given me . . . information that could be a lie, a trap, a useless waste of time, or—and this I believed—a golden opportunity to finish Pearl once and for all.

Tracking on the aetheric is simple for Djinn since it's their primary home, the environment in which they feel most alive, most comfortable. For humans, it is a closed door. For Wardens, there is access, but it is limited, and even the most gifted find it extraordinarily difficult to read the subtleties of that world; human senses, enhanced though they might be, are not meant to take in what is natural for Djinn.

But I had an advantage—I was a blind woman remembering sight. I could interpret what I could see in ways that most of the Wardens never could.

Distance was no barrier on the aetheric; my self-projection could travel easily enough without regard to the laws that governed the natural world. My next stop was California, where Pearl had established her second known camp. Like Colorado, this place had been closed and abandoned, but the traces were stronger. I didn't dare venture too close. The shimmering blackness above it warned me that it would burn. I recalled the fate of my friend Gallan all too well—he'd been the first Djinn to come in too close to Pearl's orbit, and he'd been destroyed. Utterly destroyed—unwound from the world, erased from existence. There were ways to kill Djinn, but in my opinion that was the worst.

The California facility still had a faint black shadow stretching out into the aetheric, fading to a thread-thin line. I followed it, careful to stay out of accidental touching range. Around me, lights flared and rolled in confusing shapes, coming and going in a brilliant neon flood. I was in an area rich with human history, from the ancient tribes who had first inhabited it to the flood of immigrants searching for land and gold to the modern-day prospectors panning for fame and fortune in an inhospitable land. Djinn were more difficult to spot than

Wardens—Wardens flared with brilliant sparks, but
Djinn were subtler, more inclined to fade into their natural environment.

I avoided them all as I raced after the fading trail of
Pearl's influence on the world. *Where are you, sister?*

The thread ended, fraying into gray smoke.

Gone.

I cast about, feeling more tired than I should. There
was no sign of Pearl, nor of any other Warden or Djinn. I
was standing in an utterly featureless area, one that held
the soothing, nacreous colors of a shell.

Ah. I was over the ocean. The huge amount of the
Earth's surface covered by water had its own aetheric
energy, but few features; humans traversed it, but made
little lasting impact. Had I been Djinn, I could have seen
the magnificent depth and variety of the life around me,
but Wardens were not so perceptive.

I had lost Pearl at sea.

I marked the spot and opened my eyes into the mortal world while holding the aetheric steady as well, overlaying the two, and found the spot on the map where
Pearl's trace had disappeared. I colored it with a thick
black dot, then drew a line from the rancid California
compound to where she'd last left a mark.

Off the coast of Florida.

Journeying on the aetheric was tiring, and I was
quickly burning through the power that I'd received before leaving the school. I should have taken power from
Turner, my FBI friend and enemy, but delay might have
cost me more than I would have gained. He wasn't especially powerful, on his own.

No, all in all, I really had very little choice. I was cut
off from the powerful Warden friends I might normally
call upon—Lewis Orwell and Joanne Baldwin, so nearly
equal in power and influence, had taken the majority of
significant Wardens with them out to sea, seeking to stop

a rogue Warden—or, possibly, something worse—from ripping a hole between universes and allowing destruction to pour forth. They'd been gone some time now, and the news had been ominously silent. We would know if they failed, of course. Success might well be heralded by a bland wave of sameness—and only the Wardens themselves could rejoice at that.

But whether success or failure awaited them, one thing was certain: My most powerful allies couldn't help me now. My options were small, and dwindling all the time.

I could still draw power from Luis without speaking to him; it would be a simple matter, since the connection between us still existed. My entire being resisted that necessity, but I am nothing if not practical.

I knew he wouldn't stop me, but I was reluctant to act like a parasite, preying on him for nothing more than existence. Even given what he'd done to breach the trust between us. I tentatively tugged on the connection between us, and got no response. I tugged harder, trying to open the flow of the low-level trickle that always existed between us, but he had blocked me.

I had no choice but to pick up the phone and call him. It was a difficult thing, to press the keys and initiate the contact. . . . I didn't want to talk with him, truly I didn't, and yet some part of me yearned to hear his voice. I wondered if he felt the same anger, anguish, need, and desire, all rolled into a dangerously spiked ball. I couldn't tell, truly. He was guarded now, more guarded than ever before.

Luis answered on the third ring, but said nothing. For a moment, it was a war of silence and static, and then I said, "I am close to finding a way to Pearl, but I'm running out of power. Will you help me?"

He was quiet for a long few seconds, and then he said, "Sure."

"Why didn't you simply let me draw what I needed?"

The pause this time was longer, and his voice was weary as he said, "Maybe I just wanted to hear your voice. Make sure you were okay."

That hit me hard, and I took the phone away from my ear for a few seconds, struggling to sort out my own torrent of feelings. I finally took a deep breath and said, "I am fine."

"Fine. Really."

"Yes." I wasn't, not now, not listening to his breathing, his voice, knowing how far separated we were by both distance and emotion. "Luis—"

"Yeah?"

I couldn't bring myself to forgive him, or even to acknowledge that I understood the decisions he'd made. I admired his ruthless dedication, but the scars were still too bloody. "How is Isabel?"

"Better," he said. He sounded relieved that it was a less controversial topic. "She's settling in, and the seizures are coming under control; Marion thinks we're making good progress. She helps out with Elijah; he likes her better than any of the others."

"But she's suffered more seizures."

"Yeah, one more," he said. "Not as bad as the first one."

"Have you given any thought to what I said? About the possibility of someone acting against you inside the school?" I hadn't discussed it with him, but that mudslide had not been any sort of natural occurrence, not at that time of year. It had been brought down on me by a Weather Warden, one subtle enough to do it without tipping his hand early.

"I've looked around, but there's nobody I can put my finger on. Maybe it was just random, Cassiel."

His use of my full name felt like a barb, even though his voice remained calm and neutral. I had grown used to his nickname for me, *Cass*. I hated it on anyone else's lips, but from him it seemed . . . honorable. And warm.

"I don't think it was," I said. "So please, watch yourself. And protect Isabel."

"I'd be able to do that better if you'd stayed."

"I couldn't. You know that."

His voice was sharp enough to draw blood. "You made your choice, Cass. We'll both get by without you. Sorry, but that's how it is. That's how you wanted it." He was silent for a moment, in which I fought the impulse to protest that I hadn't chosen this, not *this*, not this separation and anger and loss. I'd chosen him, and Ibby, to love, and that had been an enormous risk for me; it was duty that pulled me in a different direction, and I responded to it only because of my burning desire to keep them safe. *He* was the one who'd made the irrevocable decision to betray my trust, and I was certain that part of that was spite.

"Just tell me that she's all right," I said, and closed my eyes. I felt suddenly very weary, and very alone. "Tell me that you're all right, too."

His voice, when it came again, was lower, softer. "I didn't think you'd care whether I was or not."

"I don't know," I confessed. "But I told you: Djinn don't fall out of love that easily. And I do care about you, even if I wish I didn't."

"Ouch." He sighed. "Cassiel, please. Yeah, I should have told you about the guys waiting outside to pick up your trail. I was going to when you stopped by my room, but . . . You ever have one of those moments where you wish you'd done something, wish it with everything you've got? That was mine. I should have warned you. I didn't want you hurt."

It was an apology, but not the one I was seeking. "And Rashid?" I asked. "Have you freed him?"

"Cass—"

"Then there's nothing more to discuss. I can't trust you if you keep a slave against his will."

Luis cleared his throat uncomfortably and changed the subject. "Where are you?"

"Far away," I said. His voice sounded thin and distant now, fading as the connection fluctuated. "But never far from you if you need me. I hope you believe that."

"I do. Cass? I'm sorry for what I said before you left. Not that it wasn't true, but it didn't need to be that harsh. I didn't want that. I didn't want to hurt you."

"I know," I said. "And I'm sorry that my decisions have led us to this, but I couldn't see another way. Something must be sacrificed for the greater good."

"And that something's us," he said, recovering some of the cool distance to his tone. "Even if it puts Ibby at risk."

"I'm trying to save Ibby. And all the others. But I can't do it from there—you know that." Now we were entering the downward spiral of arguing the finer points again, and I knew where that would end—in pain. "Please take care of her."

"I will," he said. If there was the slightest emphasis on the "I" part of that statement, I supposed he could be forgiven for it. "If you need power, take it. I'm out."

And he was, ending the call without any further courtesies. He was learning bad habits, but probably from me.

I had learned so much from him, including how bitter a personal betrayal could be. It seemed only fair.

I closed my eyes, calmed my thoughts, and reached for the connection between us. It was a slender thing, but still strong, built of trust and experience; our recent discord had frayed that rope badly but not broken it. Over time, it would repair . . . if we survived.

There was an oddness to doing this now, a kind of strange, tentative worry that rose in me as I began to draw power out of him. This felt less intimate and more like a clinical transaction. That should have been a good thing; it held far fewer complications, for both of us.

But as the power sank into me, heavy and golden as liquid sunlight, I found myself thinking about his face, his mouth, his body, his skin . . . all the things that were now forbidden to me, by my own choice.

And it hurt, again.

I don't know what Luis felt, or thought, but as soon as I could, I cut the flow of energy between us. The contact had left me feeling restless and wild at a very deep, almost cellular level. I craved . . . something. And I didn't dare define what it might be.

I glanced at the maps again, and at the network of black dots I was slowly forming. I'd marked all the places where the FBI had identified either locations or suspected groups of Pearl's growing list of followers. I could visit each on the aetheric if I managed my power carefully enough. That would have been the smart, methodical way to approach it, but I believed Rashid. Right or wrong, I believed him. And if Pearl had planned to have those children brought to her in New Jersey, then it was possible that was where her training efforts were under way—and where she would be visible, flesh, and vulnerable.

I went straight to the camp location in New Jersey. As before, there was a thin, toxic shimmer to the aetheric mists over the location, but this was stronger than before—and it seemed to have a sense of me, as well. I stopped well short of the vague, twisting shapes that shrouded the area, but it seemed that I couldn't stop drifting toward them. Troubling—and then I realized that I had stopped, after all.

The mists were reaching out for me.

I quickly propelled my aetheric body backward, but a whisper of dark shimmer brushed me as I did, and a black, cold pain shot through me. It shouldn't have happened; nothing should have been able to affect me on the aetheric level, not in this form. But I felt it like a freezing electrical shock, and tumbled away from it, out of control, driven by a panic even I couldn't fully understand.

There was something there. Something alive. Something hungry.

It wasn't Pearl, but it was an aspect of her. An avatar, waiting for the unwary Djinn or Warden. The chill I'd felt had been her leech battening on me to drain away all of my aetheric energy . . . all that I'd borrowed from Luis, and all that powered the cells of my human body as well. This was new, and deadly indeed, if it could attack Wardens, and not only the Djinn.

Pearl was growing stronger, and I'd allowed that to happen. It was as Ashan had told me in the beginning: She was drawing power from humans, and from Wardens, and if she wasn't stopped, she'd soon have enough to destroy all of the Djinn as well—a ravening black hole consuming all that it touched.

I experimented a bit with the trembling black fog, seeing what triggered it to move closer and what it would ignore. That was a dangerous game, and it brought me into contact with the mist more than once. By the time I'd done my investigation, and gathered enough information, I was once again running dangerously thin on reserves—but it was worth it.

I knew enough to get a warning through.

My next call was to Luis, again, to give him the information, location, and findings; he would tell Marion, who would coordinate the Wardens and warn the Djinn, such as remained on speaking terms with us. Luis brought up the issue of power, for which I was thankful; I hadn't wanted to ask a second time. This time, the flowing energy was stronger, and the images and desires it woke in me more pronounced.

Not something I could share with Luis, but I was relieved when he said, a little hesitantly, "Do you want me to stay on the phone? I'm on some downtime. I could go up with you to take a look, see what you're up against."

The idea of seeing him, even in aetheric form, was irresistible, and the tone of his voice seemed to indicate that he wanted at least some kind of reconciliation. I forced myself to hesitate before saying yes, hoping I didn't sound as desperate as I felt; if he sensed it, he had the kindness not to say anything. Our good-byes were nonexistent again, but I left the phone on and the channel open, and rose into the aetheric. The cell phone would be a great help, since humans could not easily speak on the aetheric, and even Djinn sometimes found that their conversations took on confusing, unintended overtones in the realm of energy and intentions.

Finding each other was easy. The connection between us could be used as a guideline, and I flew toward him at dizzying speeds through the aetheric—native, to the Djinn, but confusing and wildly unreal to human senses. I felt the vibrations between us grow in intensity until I saw him hurtling toward me with equal urgency. I slowed, and so did he, until we were hovering just apart. His form glowed a soft gold now, with flickers of copper in the form of flames on his arms. Most Wardens chose other forms on the aetheric, but not Luis; he was himself, in all important aspects. I still wondered how he saw me here, in this place. It wasn't a thing I could witness for myself.

Speaking was all but impossible between us, but the feelings that cascaded back and forth were not. His hand reached for mine, and as he touched me I saw that my fingers glowed moon-silver on the right, dull copper on the left, because half of my left arm had been replaced and reworked with Djinn power in metal on the physical plane. It made little difference to me; sensations still came through, even touch, though perhaps a bit muted. I actually forgot about it much of the time.

On the aetheric, though, the contrast was striking.

Intoxicating as being in his presence again was, I knew we couldn't linger here; Luis's time was limited, and he needed rest. There was an underlying flicker of gray around him that spoke of exhaustion.

But he'd come to me, despite everything. And I knew, because I could feel it, that his instinctive pleasure in my presence was as intense as mine in his.

I held his hand as we shot up in a parabolic arc through the mists and lights, dodging dimly seen figures of other Wardens on their own affairs and Djinn who registered in ghostly flickers. We came crashing down toward the flat representation of the world at the black spot on my map, near Trenton, New Jersey.

More of that black shimmering curtain, but this one rose higher and twisted with more power than before. It seemed to move like a silently blazing fire, reaching up to brush the roof of the aetheric world and stretching down into the physical world below—a burning black tree of power.

Of all the things that I had seen so far of Pearl's influence, that was the most alarming. The power involved was staggering.

More than that—it felt *aware*.

She's here. She might not have taken physical form yet, but it was a certainty that her energy was stored here, readying itself.

Something in me reacted to her presence with a kind of longing, and panic, and I dragged Luis to a halt, hovering well beyond any approach to the column of force. Shafts of multicolored light crackled within it, lightning without a storm's logic, and on the real world I dimly heard Luis's voice on the phone say, "We can't handle this alone, Cass. This is way above our pay grade."

He wasn't wrong, but the fact was that there were no others to call on. Marion couldn't leave the children; most of the other powerful Wardens had been called out to the emergency at sea. Pearl had timed her move to active strikes just perfectly; Ashan wouldn't commit the Old Djinn to fighting her, and David couldn't. He'd already tasked them to the Wardens and to combat existing threats.

We were very much on our own, and very vulnerable indeed.

"Go," I said aloud, in the real world. "Break loose. I can't risk you."

"You can't do this alone. If she's that powerful, she'll destroy you in ten seconds and you know it."

"And your help will only add another ten seconds to our lives! I'd rather do this alone. Ibby needs you more than I do."

"You think I'm just going to back off and leave you? That's you who leaves, Cass. Not me."

On the aetheric, his glowing form turned toward me, and both our hands joined. We turned in slow, dreamlike circles, eddied by the currents of power. Beyond us, the fire of Pearl's black hatred danced, and the smoke it gave off in the aetheric was the ash of a thousand burning Djinn.

"I'm not going. Ibby needs us both," Luis said, down in the real world. "You can't fight her. Not alone, Cass. Not now. Please don't do this."

"It's the best chance we have to stop her," I said. "I'm sorry."

I hung up the phone.

In that instant, the bonfire ceased to shimmer its toxic colors upward, toward the roof of the Djinn world; instead, the tendrils suddenly whipped outward, flowing with wicked speed toward the two of us. We'd been at a safe boundary distance, I'd thought, but no longer.

Now it was coming for us.

Coming very, very fast.

I tried to push Luis away, toward safety, but he hung on with a tenacity I hadn't expected. Instead of pulling apart, he dragged me closer, closer ... and instead of a physical embrace, our aetheric bodies slid together.

They merged, sinking into each other, forming one heart, one spirit, one mind.

The resulting explosion of power was soundless, and bright as a star, and as Pearl's poisonous tendrils of shadow whipped around us, I realized that she couldn't touch us. Not as long as that brilliant light burned between us, within us.

I clung to Luis on the aetheric, and the power amplifying between us roared on, louder and louder, setting up resonances and waves that rippled in all directions. It disrupted the attack coming against us, and then broke in a soundless shatter against Pearl's central column of force.

But Pearl's column wavered under the attack, and came near to dispersing completely.

The blaze—Pearl herself?—pulled itself rapidly into a hard black shaft of swirling shadows, then into a ball, which contracted to a tiny pinpoint of darkness ...

And sped away through the aetheric, leaving behind the ghostly shimmer of power that I'd seen at other locations.

That was how Pearl moved from one of her camps to another. We'd just forced her to stage a hasty retreat.

On the physical plane, my cell phone rang, and I fumbled it open, still splitting my attention between the two realms of existence. "*Madre*," Luis's voice said shakily. "Can you feel this? What the hell is this?"

"I don't know," I said. We were still merged on the
aetheric, and it felt . . . incredible. I wanted to weep with
the beauty of it, and scream, and run away from its in-
timacy. There was nothing in my experience like it, not
even among the Djinn. This was . . . wrong, and yet it felt
so addictively right. "Let go."

"I can't," Luis whispered, from a great distance away.
"I can't let you go. I can never let you go. Don't you
feel that? God, Cass, no matter what happens, no matter
how we feel . . . this is right."

The truth of it echoed between us in breathtaking
clarity. That was the painful part, as well as the beauty;
we were not meant to feel this kind of connection, not
at this level. It was reserved for Djinn, and too powerful
for humans to channel.

I tried again to pull away, but I couldn't. I wanted . . .
I wanted to stay connected to him, in just this incredibly
powerful, intimate way, forever.

The light between us flickered, and I realized with
a jolt that he was the one fueling all this power, and it
was draining him dry. He would allow it, in this state.
He wouldn't feel self-preservation, or fear. Not when we
were too closely joined to differentiate ourselves.

I had to end it. Quickly.

It took the effort of my life, but I ripped us apart—and
the pain was unbelievable, cell- and soul-destroying. On
the physical plane, I heard Luis scream through the cell
phone, and heard my own agonized cry. On the aetheric,
we bled black waves of anguish as our conjoined bodies came apart, and wisps of our aetheric essence broke
loose to swirl in bright, then fading colors around us. The
wisps quickly cooled to ash gray, and fell away.

On the phone, Luis went ominously silent, and in
the aetheric his form went still, drifting aimlessly in the
visible and invisible currents of force. The colors of his
body, normally so bright, were fading to pastel.

He was injured.

He might be dying.

I was hurt, but not so badly; I could see places on my aetheric body where I continued to bleed off energy in brightly colored streams. I concentrated on stopping the flows, and slowly, painfully, the bleeding became trickles.

I let go of my hold on the aetheric, and the gravitational pull of my physical body snapped me back through a dizzyingly long distance, a rush of starlight and waves of color, a fall from heaven. . . .

I came upright in the chair in the motel with a gasp. I was still holding the cell phone, but there was only static and distant noise on the line. "Luis?" I said. "Luis, answer me if you can hear me!"

Nothing. I heard more noise now, other voices, and then a rustle as someone else picked up the cell phone. "Cassiel?" Marion's voice. She sounded guarded.

"Is he all right?"

"Don't know yet; he's out cold. No obvious physical damage, but I've had a good look at Luis Rocha these past few days, and if he's hurting, it's a real problem. What happened?"

I didn't want to tell her. There was something frightening and intimate about what we'd done; it felt forbidden, though as far as I knew there were no customs or laws against it.

But then, there never were until someone invented the newest perversion.

"We joined on the aetheric," I finally said, choosing my words carefully. "Not touched. Joined. Became one. I had to pull us apart; it was killing him." When she didn't immediately reply, I asked, "Do you know of this? Have you seen it done?"

"Not by humans," she said. "A very few times by a human and a Djinn, but it takes a strong bond to even attempt it. Maybe the Djinn have something like it among themselves . . . ?"

"No," I said. "I don't think there's anything like that in Djinn experience. Did I kill him, Marion? Did I—"

"No, he's not dead," she said. "Hurt, yes, but not dead. No worries, we'll take care of him here." She cleared her throat. "Perhaps you shouldn't—"

"Yes," I agreed. "Perhaps we shouldn't. Ever."

I hung up, staring thoughtfully at the blank wall in front of me. Djinn couldn't—or didn't, in any case— merge in the way that Luis and I had on the aetheric; that seemed to be reserved exclusively for Wardens and Djinn . . . but technically speaking, I wasn't even a Djinn, only the remnants of one.

Odd, that I was the first to discover this intimate, cruelly beautiful connection that could occur between two people on the aetheric—unless it couldn't occur to anyone but me. Perhaps that was one of the strange out-lying pieces of my once-Djinn self; perhaps Ashan had deliberately left that capability to me, to help me protect myself here on the aetheric from Pearl.

I wouldn't rule it out. Ashan played very long, very obscure games, and he had manipulated me from the beginning. If this was some kind of weapon left to me to discover, then it was a dangerously seductive one.

It appeared that I could protect myself from the worst that Pearl could do, on the aetheric. All I needed to do was kill the Warden who stood with me.

I rested my aching forehead on my palms, and quietly, deeply hated Ashan all over again, the smug and unfeel-ing bastard brother of my soul.

I left the next morning, as soon as I could be sure of re-covery from my adventures on the aetheric . . . because I had a new destination. It was far, far across the country, but the first new lead that I had on Pearl and her plans.

First, I had to get to Trenton, New Jersey, but I needed to do it without triggering the interest of the FBI, which had to be actively on the lookout for me now. I was an easy target to spot—after all, I was tall, thin, albino in coloring, with green eyes and a hand and forearm made of copper. Not exactly average, especially in my white motorcycle leathers and on the sleek Victory I was riding.

I needed a human makeover.

My first task that morning was standing in front of the mirror and concentrating very, very hard on altering my appearance, one feature at a time. The hair was the most obvious, and easiest . . . I slowly darkened it from pink-streaked white to a smooth cap of black. My skin was much harder to alter, and I decided not to try; I had seen others with similar coloring who achieved it through application of makeup, and although they attracted attention, I would be a stereotype, difficult to identify as an individual.

Hair completed, I went to a cheap, dingy thrift shop, where I found a tight, long-sleeved black shirt, a battered black jacket, and black nylon cargo pants covered with massive silver zippers and nonsensical pockets. When the clothes were paired with equally battered black boots, I looked . . . different. I studied myself in the mirror critically.

"Needs something," the clerk said. He was an old man, with rheumy eyes and a humped back from age and bone loss. What little hair he still had was a dirty gray. It stuck out like the mane of a lion and hadn't been washed in some time. "I got it. Hold on."

He shuffled off at a speed that was, for him, fast, and returned a few moments later with two things: a black collar studded with silver spikes, and a necklace. I dropped the chain of the necklace over my head, and a snarling silver skull with wings leered back at me.

I liked it.

The collar fitted around my neck with just enough room to feel comfortable, and I had to admit that the two additions made the ensemble memorable, and at the same time, utterly not matching the description of the woman the FBI would be seeking.

One problem remained. The Victory.

"If I pay you a fee, will you keep my motorcycle here for me, but not sell it?" I asked. "And my other clothes?"

He squinted at me suspiciously. "How much of a fee?"

"A thousand dollars to hold these for me here. You can place a price tag on them, but just be sure no one buys them." I gave him an unsettling smile, one I had learned from the best. "I would be *very* upset if I come back and they're not available."

"A thousand," he repeated, as if he'd never heard the word before. I watched the light slowly dawn in his eyes—the sunrise of greed, with dollar signs for rays. "Yes, sure, can do, missy. What name do I—"

"Jane Smith," I said.

"That'd have to be cash, missy."

I opened my backpack and took out an envelope. "That is fifteen hundred," I said. "For the clothing I just bought, and for your services. Please understand that even if you take this money and run, I will find you. I'm very good at exacting justice when someone tries to cheat me."

His Adam's apple bobbed in his scrawny neck like a golf ball trapped in a hose, and then he nodded. "Wouldn't think of it," he lied. "I'll guard your stuff like it was my own. Better, even."

"An excellent idea." When he tried to take the envelope, I held on to it. "This also buys your silence."

"Never heard of nothing," he agreed, and snatched the money away. "I'll put that bike in the back, put a ten-thousand-dollar price tag on it. That'll keep it here.

Nobody with ten grand to their name ever stepped foot in here, anyway."

It sounded like a perfectly reasonable plan. As long as the Victory was gathering dust and dreaming of the open road, I'd be far less recognizable.

I bought, at the last minute, a pair of black leather gloves with the fingers cut out. That disguised most of the oddity of my left hand. A few large silver rings drew attention away from the coppery skin even more. As I was admiring the effect, and thinking that these would be a great benefit if I had to punch anyone, I heard a harsh blatting noise from the parking lot. The clerk went pale and scurried into the back.

I headed for the door. A hulking man at least six and a half feet tall shoved in before I could reach it, and all six and a half feet of him—at least the parts visible—were covered in violent tattoos, mostly in reds and blues. A winged dragon graced his shaved head, its snarling maw open just over his nose like a helmet. His black leather jacket was heavily decorated with patches and paints, rips and scuffs, and I was fairly certain he was a murderer. Some people just give off that aetheric stench.

He barely gave me a glance as he stalked forward, bellowing, "You got any new blue jeans in, old man?" The jeans he was wearing were, in fact, splattered with a dark substance that could have equally been motor oil or blood. I decided I didn't need to know the technicalities, and walked out into the parking lot.

A large black and chrome Harley-Davidson motorcycle was parked at an angle in front of the shop, the leather tassels on its handlebars flickering in the breeze.

I smiled.

Really, sometimes it's just too easy.

The Harley was built for intimidation, not comfort, and it jolted me with every bump of the road—but the freedom it gave me was a wonderful thing. I called Marion before I left, but there'd been no real change in Luis's condition; he was still unconscious, though she'd been able to repair the physical damage, which had all been internal. She didn't think he was in any lasting danger.

I did. Ironic that I'd warned him to watch out for the traitor at the school, and then done him an injury myself, but that didn't mean the traitor wouldn't take the golden opportunity to put Luis out of the way when he was down.

After much debate, I told Marion. To my surprise, she already knew. "Luis told me," she said. "Not sure I believe it, but I agree, the timing of your mudslide was more than just coincidental. I'm watching, Cassiel. Trust me."

I did, or I'd never have spoken to her about it.

"I got a call from the FBI," she continued, without changing her tone at all. "They say you were supposed to show up for a meeting in Albuquerque. They're mildly peeved that you ditched them."

"Mildly?"

"Well, that's the story they gave me. I expect they're beating the bushes looking for you. I assume you're protecting yourself, including randomizing this phone."

"I am."

"Good girl. Go to it, then. I'll call you if anything changes with Luis."

"And Ibby?" I dreaded her answer, but it came readily enough, and cheerfully.

"The girl's doing well. Scared about her uncle right now, but otherwise settling in. She's a sweet little thing. Her seizures have stopped, at least for now."

I felt a stir of hope. "Does this mean she can recover?"

Marion's silence was a depressing omen of the words to come. "No," she finally said. "That's not what I meant. Ibby's damage goes deep, all the way to her core. I mean

I can stabilize her and extend her life, but I can't heal her. If she uses her power, I may not even be able to promise that much."

I knew that, but for a moment, I had felt an entirely unreasonable surge of hope. And it hurt, badly, to have it taken away. I had known there would be no miracles, and yet . . .

And yet.

"I have to go," I said.

"You don't have to," Marion said. "You could turn around. Come back. Ibby and Luis—"

"I have to go," I repeated. It made me feel cold inside, but I couldn't let her talk me out of this. Not now. Not when I'd seen how close Pearl was to the power she needed.

I had many miles to go, and I didn't intend to spend them talking.

It took three days, sleeping in short bursts at campsites, to reach the area where I'd sensed Pearl's presence. Not surprisingly, it was a fenced, guarded compound in the woods, and it was surrounded by federal agents and observers. No press, which was interesting; the FBI had succeeded in maintaining the press blackout so far, and it was an impressive accomplishment, considering the deaths and other criminal acts that had already been associated with the Church of the New World.

But now I had a dilemma. There seemed to be no real way to easily bypass the federal observers and enter the camp, and even if I did, they'd know I was an intruder. I needed a quieter, more thorough reconnaissance, one that required me to blend in to my surroundings—or as much as my costuming would allow. I could try a cloak, but that was one thing I was curiously deficient in as a skill; Luis was much, much better at it, and I could never keep it up for long. Certainly not long enough to make it into the compound, against the Argus-eyed guards Pearl would have set, animal and human.

There would be no way in without the cooperation of the FBI.

So I rode the Harley up to the front door of the communications trailer parked half a mile up a country road, raising a column of dust and frightening sheep with the motorcycle's unforgiving noise. I parked, walked up to the trailer's door, and knocked. The sign claimed that it was a telecommunications work van, but the man who cautiously opened the door didn't seem to me to be authentically blue-collar. He seemed ill at ease in his gray jumpsuit, and I doubted his name was really Earl.

"My name is Cassiel," I said. "I believe that the FBI is looking for me. I want to bargain."

Whatever they had expected, it wasn't this. The man stared at me for a few seconds. I stripped off the glove on my left hand and wiggled my coppery fingers in his face, made a fist, and then opened it again. "I assume your instructions said to look for someone with a metal arm," I said. "It's a great deal more certain than most distinguishing marks."

He looked over his shoulder at someone else in the trailer, then said, "Uh, excuse me for a minute, ma'am," and shut the door. I waited patiently, putting my glove back on and crossing my arms. The day was nice in New Jersey, though humid. Sheep ambled the hills, having forgotten the scare of my passage. I wondered if the cows I'd set free on the road from their slaughterhouse trip had ever found freedom—sweet grass and long life. Probably not. Life was rarely so simple, even for cows.

After a lengthy, but restful, few minutes, the door opened again, and Earl leaned out. "Ma'am? Please step inside." He said it politely enough, but it wasn't exactly a request, either. His tone implied the *please* was really just a formality.

Since it had been my choice, I allowed him his little
illusion of power and obliged.

Inside I found no fewer than four agents, all dressed
in gray jumpsuits with creatively rustic names embroidered on the front, under a corporate logo so vague as to
have been entirely mysterious. Three of them had weapons in their hands—FBI-issued handguns, extremely
effective at such close range, should I allow them the
luxury of firing.

"Please sit down," Earl said, and indicated an office
chair that, from the warmth of the cushions, had been
recently vacated by someone's rear. The FBI van was
stripped to the essentials, but at least the chairs were
reasonably comfortable, and there was coffee brewing
in the corner. "Special Agent in Charge Rostow is on the
way to talk to you. Until he gets here, please sit quietly."

I didn't know Special Agent Rostow, but I had no
doubt that he would be just as effective and efficient as
all of the other FBI representatives I had met. I had no
real desire to chat, and instead I studied the van workers
each in turn. I found nothing especially interesting, but
one of them, a woman, found my regard uncomfortable
and finally snapped, "What?"

"She's not doing anything, Andy," said the man sitting
beside her. They both had banks of monitors to watch,
and he'd never taken his eyes off of his responsibility.
"Stay focused. She's not our problem."

I wondered what their problem was, and so I focused
on the monitors as well. It was the compound, of course,
shown from a painstakingly thorough set of angles, and
both distant and close views. Beyond the gates, people
moved with every evidence of calm purpose. Some of
them were tilling a field, by hand, with hoes. A group of
women in pastel clothing was hanging up laundry on a
line strung between two trees, while another group had
taken on the task of scrubbing and wringing out clothes

in a series of large tubs. Still another group was preparing for a meal, and I watched them as they casually chatted and chopped vegetables for a pot.

Men, women, and, yes, children. All seemed totally at ease within their little world.

I envied them that, a little.

A few moments later, the door of the van opened without any knocking preliminaries, and three more men crowded in. The one in front was shorter than most federal agents, and wider; he was definitely a senior man, probably close to fifty, and although he looked soft, I was certain he was not. The benign smile and low hum of contentment emanating from him were treacherous; he seemed to have a touch of Earth power about him—something like what Janice Worthing radiated, but of course at a much lower level. It must have served him well in gaining trust and eliciting confessions.

"You must be Special Agent Rostow," I said. I dismissed the other two with him, and he didn't bother to introduce them, either. "I'm Cassiel."

He smiled reassuringly and gestured for a chair. One of the individuals watching the monitors got up and rolled his over; you had to be quick to catch the expression of annoyance that came across his face before the smile of compliance. Rostow seemed to just expect obedience, and get it. That said a great deal about his style of leadership, I thought.

He settled himself in the rolling chair and moved it to sit across from me, elbows resting comfortably on his thighs, hands dangling. Casual and relaxed. "Cassiel," he repeated. "I'm pleased to meet you. There are lots of stories going around about you. Is any of it true?"

"All of it," I said. "Especially the parts that say I'm dangerous."

"I think I'll take my chances," he said. His smile invited me to share the naughty conspiracy, but I didn't smile back. "So. Half the agency is turning over rocks looking for you, and you just show up here. To what do we owe this honor?"

"Necessity," I said. "I need to get inside the compound."

"Inside," he repeated, and leaned back in the chair. The back gave a small squeak of protest. "For what purpose?"

"If you're thinking you can keep me here and talking until you get a response from your superiors, I can tell you what it will be—detain me and send me on to Quantico," I said. "You don't want to know my purpose, because you won't care; in any case, you're not inclined to trust me at all, and you'd never help me get inside. Correct?"

He blinked a little, and some of the benign trust-me aura faded. I liked him better this way: suspicious. "I suppose so," he said. "I have no reason to help you, and plenty of reasons to do what my bosses tell me. For one thing, I'd like to retire in a few years on my hard-earned pension. So tell me what I ought to be doing for you and why. Make it convincing."

We were drawing glances from the monitor techs, and Rostow must have noticed; without moving his gaze away from me, he snapped his fingers rapidly and pointed to the monitors. "Eyes forward, people. Always forward."

There was a murmur of assent. He cocked an eyebrow at me, waiting.

"You're aware that the Church of the New World is involved in child abductions," I said. "And murder."

"Some of them," he said. "But it's a subgroup. Most of their activities are perfectly legal, which is why we're observing, not taking action. No evidence that this compound is anything but a bunch of people getting together to reject modern life. I'm not going Waco on a bunch of would-be Amish. Not unless I see evidence that something is really going on inside that needs stopping."

"There's something evil here," I said. "Or was, until recently. I need inside to find out what they're planning, because I assure you, they *are* planning something. Pearl wouldn't have been here if they weren't."

"Pearl," he repeated. "Who the hell is Pearl?"

"No one you can find in your monitors," I said. "You may think of her as—a spiritual leader. She influences others, the way Earth Wardens can; she found a ready audience in the Church of the New World, who already distrusted the modern world, and the Wardens, once they learned of their existence. Pearl has used her influence to make them increasingly afraid of you, and us, making them withdraw even more radically."

He didn't indicate whether he agreed with me. "And the children?"

"They believe they're saving them," I said. "Rehabilitating them. They think the Wardens will maim or kill them. Make no mistake, Pearl's followers believe they are *saving* the world, not bent on destroying it. That's the danger of fanatics. They're blind to everything but their own preconceptions."

"You're not telling me much I didn't find out from interviews with detainees," he said. "And?"

"And if Pearl was inside the compound—and I assure you that she was, recently—she may be back, especially if she has unfinished business there. It's our best chance to get to her, if we work together."

His gaze didn't waver. "Miss, we're the FBI. We don't cooperate with civilians in investigations, unless we're the ones doing the investigation and they're the ones doing the cooperating."

"I know." I smiled, with bared teeth. "But I believe that you might make an exception for me."

"Or I might slap some cuffs on you and hand you

over to Quantico, just like they're going to ask me to do."

"Not if you want to live," I said softly. I saw the agents around me stiffen, and a few reached quite calmly for weapons. Rostow didn't bother. "Please understand, threats are not my preferred method, but I can't lose this chance; she was here, and I believe she will return."

"I'd advise you not to make empty threats, ma'am."

"I can kill every one of you in this room by stopping your hearts, and there is nothing any of you can do about it. That is far from an empty threat. Do you understand?"

"Sure," Rostow said. He moved quickly, standing in one fluid motion, drawing his handgun at the same time, flicking the safety off, and firing three times in rapid succession.

Straight at my head.

Chapter 9

CLICK, CLICK, CLICK.

I was no Fire Warden, but I didn't need to be one to disrupt the bullets in his gun; in the past few moments, I'd chemically changed the powder in all of their bullets into a similar but inert compound that wouldn't fire, no matter how many times he pulled the trigger.

Rostow's eyes widened, but he took the shock in stride, and his people were well trained. It was close quarters, and they swarmed me . . . or tried to. But it was a metal van, and I was an Earth Warden. Metal flowed up over their feet, trapping them in place, tripping them up and binding them to the floor of the van wherever they hit.

I didn't kill anyone.

I didn't have to.

I'd left Rostow unbound, to make the point. His chair rolled a few inches, and stopped as it bumped into the leg of one of his two assistants, who was pinned to the wall of the van with a thick band of metal.

"I didn't have to be so nice," I said. "Do we have an understanding now about why you don't want to make me angry?"

He was beaten, and he knew it. Rostow looked down at the gun in his hand, flicked the safety back on, and holstered it with a quick, fluid motion. "What do you want?" His voice was clipped and businesslike now. He was done trying to persuade or reassure me. "If you've hurt any of them . . ."

"Bruises," I said. "And you tried to put three bullets through my skull, Agent Rostow, so I would suggest you have no grounds to expect too much in the way of restraint from me. What I want is for you to tell me how the people in that compound come and go."

"They don't," he snapped.

"They must. They can't be totally self-sufficient. Not yet."

He hesitated, then said, "They bring in supplies and new recruits once a month. One of them leaves to pick up the supplies and recruits in a minivan."

"Where do the recruits come from?"

"The Church has people out there proselytizing. We catch them sometimes, but not often. They've formed a kind of underground railroad that ferries converts from one place to another. The rally points change every time; we don't know where the next one will be."

"But you do know where they go for supplies?"

"They vary that, too. We haven't figured out how they place the order; probably through someone on the outside, because we're monitoring phones, cell frequencies, Internet, et cetera. We follow them when they leave, but we can't get ahead of them. What bugs we've managed to slip in have been intercepted and destroyed before they get inside."

That was not as much information as I'd hoped, but what had I expected—that Pearl would leave this facility as sloppily run as the one in California? No, she learned from mistakes, most definitely.

"Have you managed to get anyone inside the compound undercover?" I asked.

Without a flicker, he said, "Not yet." I couldn't tell whether he was lying; it was entirely possible he meant what he'd said. Still. it never hurts to cultivate a reputation for supernatural keenness, and so I gave him a slow, wicked smile, and said, "Liar. You do have someone inside. Who?"

He frowned, just a slight groove between his eyebrows. "Where are you getting that? I just told you we don't."

"I'm an Earth Warden. We know a lie when we hear one. Please, don't insult me by continuing to bluff."

For a long moment, I thought that *my* bluff had been called, but then he shook his head and said, "We did, until two days ago."

"What happened two days ago?"

"Our agent walked out of the gates, came to find me, and told me that she'd seen the error of her ways and she was quitting the bureau. Then she turned and walked back inside." He turned to the monitors, looking at each in turn, and then pointed at one of them— the field, and the people out in the sun using the hoes. "There. That's her."

"You're sure she wasn't just trying to get in deeper with them, or preserve her cover?"

Rostow's mouth set in a flat, grim line. "I know Stephanie," he said. "Known her a long time. I can tell you that wasn't an act, and it damn sure wasn't Stephanie. What went into that compound was a great agent; what came out to quit was a true believer. She got turned. I know it in here." He tapped his gut with one hand. I believed him. There was no reason for him to lie about it, and there was real pain in his expression. "I hate losing people, but I'd rather lose them honestly than have them brainwashed into a cult."

"You realize that she will have already told them everything she could about you, your operation here, and anything else that could be helpful to them."

His eyes turned blank and hard. "No shit. Surprisingly enough, I *did* think of it. So what other stunning revelations do you have to share with me, *Warden*?"

"If you help me get inside, I can get information back to you freely."

That made him frown. "Freely. As in, anytime you want."

"Exactly."

"How?"

I smiled, just a little, and fluttered his eardrum in a whisper. *I just can*, I said, and he jerked in surprise and clapped a hand over his left ear. "What the hell?"

"Warden abilities," I said. "You won't be able to communicate back to me, but I can talk to you across a considerable distance, as long as I can find you on the aetheric."

"I'm going to pretend that last part made sense," he said, "because I like the first part a lot. Trouble is, you're just a tad recognizable—maybe not as a Djinn, but you sure don't look like a likely recruit, either."

"I can manage."

"Do you have any idea of your own arrogance, lady?"

"Yes," I said. "Do you have any idea of yours?" One of the FBI agents pinned to the van let out a choked sound that was almost a laugh. I didn't blink. "I will let your people go if you promise good behavior. If not, you may wish to invest in some kind of welding equipment."

Rostow considered all that, and it was obvious that he really, really wanted to tell me to go to hell, but he finally nodded reluctantly. "All right," he said. "Last thing I want to do is piss off the Wardens right now. Let them go. I promise we'll play nice."

That did not seem to me to be an exact enough definition of cooperation—not for a Djinn—but he seemed sincere enough. I extended my hand, and after a hesitation he accepted the gesture and shook firmly.

As he did so, I released his people from their bonds.

Some, overbalanced, sprawled on the van floor; others grabbed for their weapons. "Enough of that!" Rostow snapped, still shaking my hand. "Stand down. Not sure your guns will fire any better than mine, and we don't need more excitement in close quarters right now."

The agents quieted down, positioning themselves carefully. I noticed they did so with an eye to firing cleanly at me, should that be necessary. I didn't mind. I would restore their ability to fire their weapons, but not until I left the van.

"Now," I said, looking Rostow in the eye, "tell me how you plan to get me into the compound."

"I can't."

"You can. You've already selected another agent, and you're planning to infiltrate within the next few days."

I had to give him credit—he really didn't allow me to shock him this time. "I don't know where you're getting this stuff, but it isn't—"

"It must be," I said, "because otherwise your superiors would be demanding action of some kind, and it's been quiet and tranquil here in what I can only think is your command center. No demanding phone calls. No tension. So you have a plan, which you are in the process of executing."

A couple of agents murmured in the background, while Rostow stared bleakly at me without speaking. I waited, then said, "All I ask for is a chance. Put me in the same way you're introducing your own agent. I can serve as backup, which could be the difference between success and failure, or life and death. I'm offering you help. Take it."

"Like I said"—he shrugged—"you're don't exactly blend in."

I closed my eyes and concentrated on my physical body. It took a great deal of power—more than I could easily spare—but I slowly, carefully altered the black of

my hair to a short, mousy brown, and my skin to something unremarkable for the area. My face I shifted to
one I'd glimpsed in Albuquerque months ago—not
pretty, not ugly, not memorable at all, except that I'd
noted it for future reference. I shortened my stature and
shifted the inert textures of my clothes to something
bland, blocky, nothing of any identifiable style at all.
After a moment's thought, I roughened the condition,
added dirt and spots of grime, and the smells of old food,
smoke, and unwashed sweat.

I looked like any of the thousands of struggling,
subsistence-level poor to be found in any city.

I opened my eyes, looked directly at Rostow, and
said, "Do I blend in now?"

I sensed it wasn't often that a man like him experienced amazement, but that was as close as he came—
widened eyes, slightly open mouth that quickly snapped
shut as he realized others were looking on. He needn't
have worried, though. His people all looked far more
thoroughly impressed, and unnerved.

"I guess that'd do," he said. "Can you—ah, do that
whenever you want?"

I smiled faintly. He had no real idea of what it had
just cost me. I had drained myself dangerously low, but
the important thing had been to make a definitive impression. I felt the cost was justified. "No," I said, and
didn't elaborate. "Will you trust me?"

"No," Rostow said. "But you've got a good point
about my agent needing on-site backup. So I may not
trust you, but you'd be damn useful right about now."

"You'll send me in."

"I'll recommend it," he said. "I've got bosses, lady."

I actually thought he was lying. Not about the bosses,
perhaps—I was sure he did, in fact, have those—but
about the need to run the question by them for approval. It was much more likely that he just wanted time

to think. I could understand that, and respect it, so I nodded my acceptance.

Everyone seemed to relax, including Rostow. "Right," he said, and pointed to one of his agents. "Langston. Get the lady some coffee or something."

"Water," I said. "And a place of privacy, if you have one."

Water, they could provide me; privacy, it turned out, was a bit more problematic. I finally walked away from the mobile truck, out into the surrounding trees, and sat down with my back to a tall, strong oak with roots that reached deep, both into the ground and into the past. There, I was able to sink into a light, comfortable trance and make connection with Luis through the aetheric.

He was asleep. Dreaming. I could see that in the muted blues and purples of his aetheric colors, and the way his body floated, weightless. The shapes of his dreams were faint whirls of color, slashes of blood red, white, night black. Luis's dreams were not restful.

Oddly, they were dreams full of fire—almost a physical thing, burning him from the inside out. I could see it in eerie flickers around him. It reminded me of the flickers I'd glimpsed, from time to time, on his tattoos. He was no Fire Warden, and yet there was fire in him all the same.

Ibby had both Fire and Earth powers. I'd always assumed that was a recent addition to the family's genetic heritage with her, but perhaps, in some small way, Luis had shared it as well.

In the aetheric, I put my hand on him, and breathed peace and light into him through the connection between us. The dreams hung on stubbornly, then subsided into warmer, kinder colors. I opened the connection wider and began to pull power from him.

The dreams darkened, and I felt both his aetheric and

his physical body thrashing, trying to resist the draw. I slowed it, frustrated and shaking with need, but he could give only so much without distress, and I didn't want to cause him pain. He'd once described the sensation of sending power to me as bleeding; it was no wonder that the feeling disconcerted him in his already troubled sleep.

Slowly, his power trickled through the connection, filling my empty reservoirs. I hadn't realized how weak I had been until some strength returned to me. Dangerous, that—all too easy to overestimate what I could do and then fail at a critical moment. I was alone now, and despite his willingness to help, Luis could not always be counted on to put my mission first, or to be strong when I needed his strength. He needed power to heal and protect the children at the school as much as I needed it to pursue my own agenda.

I took as much as I dared, and then stayed with him, drifting slowly through the aetheric. There was something unguarded about him this way, something pure and poignant. It was hard to turn away, leave him to his dreams and nightmares, but I had nightmares of my own to face.

Alone.

I made my way back to the FBI trailer and found Rostow deep in conversation with a man of average height, with roughly cut sandy hair and thick eyebrows, with skin that had seen too much sun and taken on a leathery, prematurely aged look. He had icy gray eyes, startling in that tanned face, and his hands were rough and scarred. He looked like a laborer, and dressed like one as well, in battered denim and canvas. His shoes had split under hard use and been patched with dull silver tape. There was dirt ingrained under his fingernails, and when he said, "This her?" I noticed that his teeth were uneven and discolored.

Rostow nodded. "Cassiel," he said. "But we'd better get you a name that isn't quite so memorable." He tapped one of his computer operators on the shoulder. "Jen, get her a good set of creds, something with a minor record—theft, vandalism, something like that. Something easy to remember."

Agent Jen nodded, bent to work at her keyboard, and then left the trailer. She returned a few moments later with an envelope, which came with a receipt I was asked to sign. I did so, and found in the envelope an Arizona identification card and bus pass in the name of Laura Rose Larkin. There was also a detailed sheet giving the past of Laura Larkin—parents' names, addresses, and dates of birth, schools attended, residence history, close associates, and crimes. It seemed very credible. Rostow nodded toward the paper in my hand and said, "Memorize it. You've got the night, but you need to be completely up to speed before we drop you and Merle here tomorrow. Oh, and this is Merle, by the way. You're in good hands. He's our best."

Merle didn't smile. He didn't seem to be much prone to it. I couldn't detect much in the way of emotion from him at all; I supposed that if he was, as he seemed, a professional undercover agent, then he'd long ago learned how damaging emotions could be. "Better know that stuff backward and forward," he said. "Word is, these guys test pretty thoroughly. You make mistakes, they'll dump you quick."

"I won't make mistakes."

"Well," Merle said, looking at Rostow, "she's confident. Give her that."

"If she screws up, don't go down with the ship," his boss replied. "Cut her loose. You don't know her; you just wound up standing in the same space. You, same thing. You don't know him. You've got zero history."

"Then we shouldn't be building one now," Merle said,

and nodded to me. "See ya." He left, slamming the door behind him, and I raised my eyebrows at Rostow.

"Learn your stuff," he said. "Don't expect Merle to cover your ass. You're there to back him up, not vice versa. Understood? Good. Now go get some sleep. Jen will show you to the racks. We'll get you up in a few hours and start moving you around. You're going to get off a bus in Trenton. We'll give you directions from there. You won't see Merle again until you're both met by the recruiters. Got it?"

There was nothing not to get, but I acknowledged with a slight nod. Agent Jen got up from her computer and walked me from the trailer down a path through the woods, which opened into a clearing where a small camouflage tent was pitched. A latrine tent was situated near the tree line.

"Rules," she said, as she opened the flap of the main structure. "Don't talk to anybody. Don't touch anything that isn't on your bunk. And if you snore, prepare to be smothered in your sleep. We don't get much downtime. What we get, we value."

I liked Agent Jen. She was forthright. She handed me a plate of fruit and sliced meats and bread, gave me a bottle of water, needlessly pointed out the latrine, and showed me to a narrow, neatly made bunk with a thin pillow and light blanket. I ate, then spent two hours reading over and over the material that I'd been given. When I was certain that it was as natural to me as any other thing in my unnatural life, I stretched out, wrapped myself in the thin blanket, and was asleep—unsnoring—by the time the next agent came to claim his bunk.

The next morning was a grim march. I was woken early, when the sky was still black, and hustled into a rusted pickup truck driven by a silent Hispanic man wearing a battered straw hat, who drove me two hours in the darkness to a deserted bus station. "Next bus," he said, which was two more words than he'd exchanged with me thus far. He handed me some crushed folded bills, soft from use, and a handful of loose change. "Get off in Trenton. Look for a blond kid in a hoodie passed out on a bench and with a skateboard and a backpack. Wake him up. He'll tell you where to go next."

That was the extent of our friendship. He drove off almost before the truck door had slammed, leaving me feeling unexpectedly alone and exposed under the glare of a spotlight in front of the closed bus station. I waited, pacing to ward off the cold, until a lone bus arrived in a huff of air brakes. I climbed on board and paid the driver, then huddled—like the others—in a plush but battered seat. No one noticed me; as I looked around, I saw a bus full of people wrapped in their own personal struggles and tragedies, with no interest in mine.

It was perfect.

Dawn broke as we arrived in Trenton, and I found the sleeping skateboarder, who looked hardly old enough to be in the FBI. He glared at me through glazed eyes, and then muttered an address. I repeated it, and he rolled over and went back to sleep, apparently. The bus station had a map on the wall, and I used it to locate the address, which was more than a mile away. I walked, hands in my pockets, head down, as the city began to come alive around me. I looked needy, poor, and a little desperate, and I soon realized that these were things that served to isolate me as surely as if I had been walking the street alone.

I found the address, which was a dreary-looking coffee shop. I didn't have instructions on what to do, so I ordered the smallest, cheapest drink I could with my remaining crumpled cash and sat in a corner, sipping slowly, practicing a dull, weary stare.

I was still practicing it when a woman came in dressed

in an expensive business suit and ordered coffee. Once she had it, I expected her to hurry on, as most everyone had done, but she picked up her briefcase and walked over to me with sharp, confident steps. She sat, opened her briefcase, took out an envelope, and looked at me as she sipped her coffee. Bright brown eyes, and an even, regular face. "What's your name?" she asked.

"Laura," I said. "Larkin. Hi."

"You come far, Laura?"

I nodded. "From Arizona," I said.

"Really?" She blew on the surface of her coffee lightly. "Whereabouts?"

"Tucson," I said.

"Where'd you hear about us?"

This was gray area, and I shrugged. "Around."

"Around where?"

"California," I said. That was a safe bet, I thought; it was reasonably close to Arizona, and not unlikely that if I'd been struggling to find food and shelter, I'd have made my way there at some point. "Near San Diego, I think."

She watched me for a few seconds, and I realized that this woman, whoever she was, had a shrewd sense about her—almost a Warden sense, perhaps. "You living rough?" she asked. "On the streets?"

"I get by."

"That's not what I asked."

"I lost my last apartment," I said. "My job went away. Not my fault."

She sipped her coffee, and finally said, "There's something about you, Laura. Something—special."

I didn't want, at this moment, to be special, not at all. I tried to think what I might have said or done that would create such an impression, but couldn't. Instead of letting that agitation show, however, I forced myself to seem encouraged. People always wanted to feel special, apart from their fellows. It was something ingrained in human DNA, and my reaction seemed to please the woman, who smiled slightly in response. "Yes," she said. "Very special. What skills do you have?"

"Um . . . I cook," I said. Laura Rose Larkin had been prepared with a specific set of things; I hoped no one would immediately ask me for proof. "And I'm good with the stuff nobody likes to do, washing, cleaning, that kind of thing."

"Not afraid of work?"

"No, just haven't had a lot of luck," I said. "Like a lot of people."

"Oh, I doubt you're like a lot of other people," she said. "Our job is to find the things that make you different, Laura. To bring out your gifts. Everyone has a gift. Pearl's taught us that."

Pearl's teachings were convenient for her, to say the least; she preyed on the human desire to become something more, something special, and slowly but surely warped that desire out of true, into her own tool.

But I nodded. "I want to learn," I said.

"And you've got nowhere else to go." I looked away, turning my empty cup in my hands. The woman reached out and patted me on the shoulder. "Nothing to be ashamed of," she said. "We get all kinds of people— people like me, who just aren't happy with the life that's supposed to be so great. We also get people who are lost and alone, even people who bring special skills because they believe in the cause. We're all unique, and we're all equal."

She said that, but I could sense from her that she didn't believe it, and never would; she believed that she was more important, and that sense of entitlement allowed her to speak to me as if I was a lost child that needed saving. *No*, I reminded myself. *Laura Rose needs saving.*

The part of me that was still stubbornly Cassiel didn't like it.

"So," she was saying, as she drained the last of her own coffee. "Here's what you do. You write down your name and social security number on the outside of the envelope, and take what's inside. We'll be back in touch."

She handed me a pen. I laboriously wrote *Laura Rose Larkin* and the number that I'd been given by the FBI, making sure that my handwriting was as bad as I could make it while still legible. She nodded, then took the pen back, and I shook out the contents of the envelope.

A cell phone, small and cheap. A small, bound number of bills. A blank business card with a number written on it in pen—not a phone number but a five-digit number.

"The cell won't make outgoing calls," the woman said. "It only receives calls. When you get a call, give them that number on the back of the card."

I looked up as she snapped shut the latches on her briefcase. "What do I do now?"

"Whatever you want," she said. "We'll find you."

She dumped her cup and walked out into the bright morning sunlight. I watched her from the window as she hailed a taxi and was gone in only a minute.

The phone, I was reasonably certain, functioned as a tracking device. I considered shorting it out, but that seemed unwise, given the circumstances. Instead, I put the money and phone in my pocket, along with the business card, and set out to walk the streets until I was called.

It took two days, during which I slept at cheap motels and ate even cheaper food; even with the frugality, my money didn't last long, and my stomach was growling in frustration as I considered the dollar left to support me through the night. I was carefully weighing the options between fat, sugar, or both when a new sound filtered up from my pocket.

The cell phone.

I pulled it out, pushed TALK, and heard a businesslike voice say, "Identification number, please."

I recited it from memory. There was a short pause, and then the voice said, "Go directly to the Trenton bus station where you came in and wait. Someone will be along."

It was dark, and chilly. I could have thickened the material of my coat, but it occurred to me that they would have been photographing and observing me these past few days. Anything out of the ordinary would be noticed.

I would, as Rostow had said, be dropped.

At the bus station, motionless people slept sprawled in chairs and on benches, or wandered aimlessly. There was a minivan parked outside, and a man beckoned to me as he slid back the door. Inside were four others. One was Merle, but he looked at me blankly, and I forced myself to give him the same basic regard as I dropped into a seat in front of him. The driver shut the door, climbed behind the wheel, and drove us on into the dark. Nobody spoke.

"Phone." I hadn't noticed, but someone was sitting in the passenger seat in the front, and was now turned toward me and holding out her hand. It was the woman I'd last seen in the coffee shop. Funny, I should have seen her; again, I felt the telltale tingle of some kind of power. She'd veiled herself—I was almost sure of it. I found my cell phone and handed it over, along with the business card. She tossed the phone into a bag with others. "Put on your seat belt, Laura."

I nodded and fastened it as the van sped on into the unknown.

*   *   *

To my surprise, we were not taken to the encampment that the FBI had been observing. We were taken instead to an old building on the outskirts of the city, which seemed to be unsettlingly isolated—I worried not so much for myself as for the others, excluding Merle, who seemed as expressionless as before. Our companions seemed to be honestly frightened for their safety.

I was not sure they were wrong.

"Inside," said the driver, and shoved open the front door. Light spilled out in a blinding fan, and we were hustled through quickly, not given time for our eyes to adjust. Merle, who was in the lead, suddenly froze and held up his hands in a position of surrender. I saw why, a second later; there were two men in the room, each in a separate corner, pointing guns at us.

Large guns.

"Sit," said the driver, and pushed the last woman into the room before slamming the door behind himself and locking it. Merle settled into one of the four dented chairs, and I sank down next to him, followed by our other two recruits

"One of you is a spy," the driver said, and walked in front of us. He was a big man, and it was hard to focus on his face. I realized that once again I'd lost track of the woman in the business suit. She was here, somewhere; I could feel her presence. With a little effort I could have broken through her veil, but I let it stand.

Nobody had responded to the big man's declaration, so he said it again. "One of you is a spy, sent by the government. I'll give you one chance: Say who you are, and we'll let you go."

I felt a perverse sense of relief. With *two* of us infiltrating, his supposedly insider knowledge seemed a throw of the dice at best. I almost glared at him, and remembered my timid exterior at the last second. Instead, I glared down at my own frail, shaking hands lying impotently in my lap.

"Ain't me," said the man on my left, a rawboned young man with smooth, dark skin and big, wickedly amused eyes. "Don't suppose they'd have me, anyway."

He seemed strangely cheerful about it. Maybe he found having a gun pointed at him exciting, which I found curious; I could count on surviving such an encounter. He couldn't. When the man kept focusing on him, the younger man lost his smile. "Dawg, you think you're scary? I been shot by grannies scarier than you."

"Show me," the man said. The young man stared at him for a second, then grinned in a flash of perfect teeth, stood up, and skinned his shirt up to hang around his neck.

"This one I got in a drive-by when I was ten," he said, pointing to a scarred dimple low on his right side. "Got this one two years ago." The other scar was both more recent and more impressive; it was in his chest, and it looked dire. He also had tattoos, a lot of them, subtle and dark against the tone of his skin. It reminded me irresistibly of Luis and his flame tattoos.

"All right. It isn't you," the man said. "Put your shirt back on."

The young man laughed and yanked it down as he sat. I risked a quick glance up to find that the gunman was staring at me. I looked down again and folded my trembling hands together. From my peripheral vision, I saw him shake his head. "Not you, either."

Merle sat back, arms folded. Unlike me, he was staring straight at the man, as stone-faced and immovable as ever. He didn't say anything. The gunman assessed him for a long moment, and then jerked his head suddenly to stare at the last one in our little group, a woman. "You," he said. "Talk."

She was an older woman, gray in her hair, heavy and

tired. I didn't need to be a Djinn to read the hardness of her life, the pain, the struggle. When she spoke, she had an accent—Eastern European, I thought. "I don't like police," she said. "I just want to have peace."

The young man, the one who was so scarred, looked sharply at her, and I could see in him in that moment that he wanted the same thing. Peace. A place to be safe.

It made me angry that Pearl was betraying them.

The gunman prolonged his drama a few seconds longer, then made a show of clicking the safety on his gun and holstering it on his belt. "All right," he said. "Wait here."

He walked away, into the shadows at the end of the room. I stared after him, and willed the shadows to fade, just for an instant—long enough to see the woman I'd met in the coffee shop in the veil. She'd been reading us, of course, monitoring our heart rates, our aetheric pulses. Earth Wardens were difficult to fool when they were focused on determining the truth.

He came back another moment later and said, "Get up." We did, with varying degrees of reluctance. "Go change your clothes. Strip down and leave everything, and I mean everything. Watches, jewelry, underwear, socks. You leave it all behind."

It was a wise precaution, and it wouldn't matter to me. I supposed Merle was prepared for it as well. I followed the gray-haired woman into the room indicated, and found that there were two stacks of clothing. I expected the fabric to be uncomfortable, but it felt surprisingly good against my skin. I left behind the items I'd been wearing—almost as colorless as what I had been given—and walked back to join the others. Merle and the young man were already in their chairs, dressed identically to me and, in another moment, the older woman.

Our driver then had us each stand up, and searched

us, by hand. At the end of each search, he looked over his shoulder into the shadows, where the Earth Warden—or whatever she was—would be scanning us on the aetheric for any hint of concealed items. Merle was clean, as was I. The young man had tried to keep a thin, flexible knife, which was found in the search. The older woman had kept pictures, old and faded, of young children. She wept at giving them up, but give them up she did.

We drove a long, weary way.

When the van finally parked, I knew we were there. I felt the tingle of power hissing around us, exhilarating and menacing at once. None of the others seemed to notice it, and I was careful not to react outwardly. I was in the heart of the enemy, and if Pearl wanted to destroy me, it would be hideously easy for her, hardly as much effort as slapping a bug. My only defense was anonymity.

But it was difficult not to feel a fierce surge of adrenaline. I was *here*. I was going inside, and I would have a chance, just a chance, to end this.

I missed Luis. I missed knowing that he was with me, connected to me, caring for me. It hurt to feel so alone, but it would all be worth it if this worked.

The van door slid open on a brilliant clear sky, and warmer air rushed inside, smelling of freshly turned earth and trees. Instead of the armed driver, there were two young people smiling at us from the other side—dressed in identical outfits to what we now wore, but accessorized with bits of color: a red and white kerchief over the girl's smooth brown hair, and a bright orange braided belt on the boy. They both looked well, happy, and eerily content. "Welcome," the girl said, and held out her hand to help the older woman out of the van. "You're very welcome here. I know the trip was a little scary, but you're safe now. You're with friends."

She hugged the older woman, who seemed surprised,

then hugged her back quickly and awkwardly, as if she'd forgotten the skill. I'd never really known it, but when the hug came for me, I was ready. No hug for Merle, who shook hands with the boy as he got out. The last one out was our younger companion on the journey, who was offered a handshake, too, *and* a hug. He seemed to enjoy the hug more. So did the girl.

The boy greeter produced a clipboard, consulted it, and said, "Merle?" Merle raised his hand. "You're going to be in the second lodge. Kale?" That was our younger companion. "First lodge. Laura Rose?" I slowly raised my hand, not very high. "Third lodge. Oriana, you're in third lodge, too. Everything's in there for you—clothes, toiletries, a little gift to welcome you to the family."

The girl took up the patter, smiling brightly. "A few rules before we let you go," she said. "I know, rules, we come here to get away from them—but these are simple, I promise. We share work and resources, but don't take anyone else's personal things without permission. There's no alcohol, drugs, or smoking allowed, because we believe in good health. We work hard, but we do have fun, too. Oh, and stay away from the fences. If you see any of the Outsiders, don't talk to them. Just come and get one of us wearing colors; we'll take care of it for you. Clear?"

The young man who'd come in with us, Kale, looked at her and said, very directly, "We got to go to church, too?"

"You don't have to," she said. "But we'd like it, of course. The Church is the core of our community. We're not all true believers, though, and we don't reject people just because they don't worship as we do. We believe our truth will become clear."

He looked doubtful, but also a little relieved. "And what about work?"

"We expect you to pull your weight, Kale. Nobody

gets a free ride here; we're not the Outside. But you do the work you can do, and want to do. We all pull together here, and we have a duty to one another and to our community."

"We get paid?"

This time she laughed. "No, we don't get paid. But we all get what we need. We've proved that you don't need money to have a society; you just need community."

She had the light and sparkle of a true believer, and even Kale—who I felt was probably as cynical as Merle, in his way—seemed charmed into agreement, at least for now.

"Oh, I forgot to tell you my name," the girl said. "It's Georgie. And this is Marcus."

And that, it seemed, concluded our introduction. Georgie and Marcus walked away to talk to another group. The four of us, momentarily bonded by our shared experience, looked at one another, and then Merle, with a nod, set off for his lodge—a long, barracks-style building clearly marked with a number. Kale shrugged and followed, and Oriana and I headed for the third building.

The compound was both what I'd observed from the outside and a great deal different. The smell, for one thing—it had a rich, healthy sort of smell, of growing things, flowers, grasses, trees, the dark spice of fertilizer. I hadn't expected the explosions of color—flower beds planted neatly along the paths, bordered with carefully arranged stones. The grass was kept clean and evenly trimmed.

It looked . . . peaceful.

The people didn't look the same as those I'd seen at the other encampments, either; they seemed to be happy, healthy, moving with purpose, and—when speaking or working with another—kind as well.

And there were children.

I felt sick at the sight of them, here, in this place, but

they were everywhere—dressed in bright colors, though in similar patterns to what the adults wore. I remember the feral children I'd seen in Colorado, but there was no evidence of that abuse here; these boys and girls ran and played happily. A guardian (or teacher) followed groups of them, but it didn't appear to be a sinister sort of caretaking.

It took me a few moments to spot the underlying pattern, but when I did, the dread grew stronger. The groups of children were not, as I'd first assumed, random. No, they were all composed of the same *number* of children—eight—and within each group there were four sets, two wearing blue, two wearing orange, two wearing green, and two wearing a golden yellow. They weren't organized by age, either; I saw older children and younger wearing the same color. Nor were they organized in any way by the gender of the child. In some groups, boys and girls were evenly distributed, but in others there was a predominance of one or the other.

I went back to the colors—blue, orange, green, gold.

Blue for water—Weather Wardens. Orange must be Fire, and green reserved for Earth.

But that left gold. And I didn't know what it meant.

We reached the lodge marked with our number, and entered. Inside, it was exactly what I'd expected—a long, low building, filled with two-level cots. Each cot was neatly made, and contained exactly the same things—sheets, a pillow, a blanket, and a small black pouch hanging from the end like a saddlebag. There were warm woven rugs on the bare floor, and gooseneck lamps at each bed. The windows were plentiful, and sunlight poured in to make the room feel almost comfortable. It smelled pleasantly of herbs and soap.

A middle-aged woman came forward, wiping her hands on a red-checked towel, and smiled as she offered me her hand. Her grip was firm and a little moist. "Hello, you must be Laura Rose. And Oriana?" She repeated the handshake. "Wonderful to have you join us. Please, come with me. I'll show you your bunks."

Our beds were near the middle of the room, and each of us had been given a top berth. It occurred to me that placing us so, in the middle and up high, made it very difficult for us to do anything unobserved, or to easily slip out. Their warm welcome to the contrary, they didn't yet trust us.

Under other circumstances, I would have approved of their caution.

On each bed was the same black saddlebag that I saw slung at the foot of each of the others in the room, but ours were sitting squarely in the center of the bed, and each had a small bouquet of flowers leaning against it.

"My name's Willa," our greeter said. "I'm the manager of the lodge, so if there's anything you need, anything you see that needs to be fixed or causes you concern, please come to me. Just ask anybody for Willa; they'll know me. Oh, and your kit there has soap, toothbrushes, toothpaste, deodorant, lotion, washcloths, towels. There are robes and slippers in the lockers at the back, so find some you like and put your name on the door. Any personal items you don't have that you need, let me know—that includes medications, okay? We have a library in the center of the camp if you need reading material."

Oriana looked nervous, but she said, "My doctor says I should take vitamins."

"Of course. What kind? I can pull them from the stores."

While Oriana stammered out her requests, I opened my saddlebag and examined the contents. One thing that Willa hadn't mentioned was that they had included feminine hygiene in their welcome kit, and—surprisingly—a pack of condoms. I took it out, examining it, and held it up to show Willa. She laughed.

"We're not prudes," she said. "And we're not crazy. Our rules are against people getting hurt, that's all. If you meet someone special here, you should be able to enjoy that."

Curious.

I dropped the condoms back into the saddlebag, closed it, and draped it at the end of the bed, fiddling until it matched the others in the room. Then, when Oriana turned away, I said, "So what do we do now?"

Willa was making a note on a clipboard, but she glanced up to say, "What do you want to do?"

"Sleep," I said, and yawned to prove it.

"Then you should go ahead. You can always start your orientation tomorrow, if you'd like. I'll wake you up for dinner."

Willa did not seem the harsh taskmistress I'd expected. Oriana tentatively said that she, also, would like to rest, and Willa readily agreed to that as well. I took off my shirt and pants and shoes, and climbed up on the bunk. It was comfortable enough—better than I'd expected. The blankets were thick and warm, and the pillow soft, and to my surprise, I was almost immediately sleepy. It had, in fact, been a hard few days, and here, despite that low-level tingle of power, I felt . . . peaceful. There was none of the ever-present noise that I'd come to associate with the modern human world; here, there was silence, except for Willa's footsteps and the creak of metal as Oriana climbed up to her own rest. I heard the wind against the roof, and the sighing of trees. The distant murmur of voices, and laughter.

Before I slipped off into the darkness, I reached out and located Agent Rostow. It was more difficult connecting with an ungifted human at this distance, but I'd taken care to memorize his aetheric signature. I didn't waste a lot on the report. *Arrived*, I vibrated the tiny bones in his ear to say. *No trouble.* I couldn't think of anything more to say. If he had questions—and I was sure he would—I wouldn't be able to hear them in any case.

After that I fell asleep without any hesitation.

I woke to the sound of murmurs and a gentle hand shaking my shoulder. "Time to wake up," a voice said. Willa, coming to wake me as she'd promised. "Dinner."

"Thank you," I said, and sat up. The air was cool now, and I shivered as I put on my shirt and pants and slipped on the canvas shoes. Willa had draped a sweater over the end of the bed, of nubby gray material, and I put it on to cut the chill. I smelled spices, meats, fresh breads, and it made my stomach rumble in frustration. Willa had moved on to rousing Oriana, and as I hopped down from the bunk, she said, "Go on out. The food hall is next door; just follow your nose."

I stepped outside. While I'd been sleeping, the day had slipped into twilight, and the sky was a translucent dark blue, with the black shapes of trees outlined against it. More surprising, though, were the streams of people moving past the lodge—gray-dressed men and women of all ages, all races, laughing and talking as they headed for their dinner break. I had expected a certain paranoia, a pervasive atmosphere of oppression, but it wasn't so, not at all. Somehow, these people seemed . . . happy.

I stood there for a moment, an outsider to the general feeling of community, and my gaze fixed on a man walking with a small group. Like all of them, they were animatedly talking, but there was something about him that caught my attention. A nice, mobile face, a little too firm in the jaw, and piercing gray eyes as he glanced my way. He had shaggy brown hair, and he was tall, with strength in the broad shoulders. I couldn't guess his age immediately—anything between thirty and fifty, though I guessed closer to forty, based on the slender strands of gray in his hair.

He slowed, and indicated me to his friends, then broke off to walk toward me. I was standing on a step that led up to the lodge, but even so, we were almost at eye level. "Welcome," he said. He had a deep, warm voice, and his smile had a sweetness I didn't expect. He held out a hand to me. "I'm Will. Very pleased to meet you . . ."

I was surprised by the warmth of his grip, and it took a moment before I could order my thoughts enough to say, "Laura Rose."

"Laura," he repeated, and somehow, he gave my name a beauty that I didn't think it should have possessed. "On your way to dinner, Laura?"

"I suppose."

"Great, join us." He beckoned to his friends, who came over, smiling. "Becca, Aiyana, Karl, Desmond— this is Laura." A blur of faces—all dramatically different but somehow similar in their friendly welcome—wished me well. "We'll show you the ropes. I know how strange the first day can be."

I felt a bizarre gratitude for the warmth with which they surrounded me; I hadn't realized how tense I had been until the muscles knotted inside me began to relax. Laura, I felt, would have been quiet and shy, so I said little as we walked to the food hall, but I listened to the others. They talked brightly about the day's work, about trivial things, but the affection between them seemed almost to shimmer like flakes of gold in the air.

I was included, although I didn't contribute; they glanced at me, shared smiles, touched me gently on the shoulders to guide me when I hesitated. I had never been a younger child in a family, but I imagined that was what it must have felt like.

When Will glanced my way, I felt a telltale illicit shiver, and wondered at my own odd behavior. Yes, I was lonely; yes, I missed Luis. But was it so easy for me to respond to another man's looks, his light and casual touches? If it was, what worrying thing did it say about my character?

"The food's good," Will said, steering me with one hand on my shoulder blade toward the line of people forming near a buffet. "We all take our turns in the kitchen, but thankfully, most people are better at it than I am. I can chop a mean carrot, but seasoning's best left up to the experts."

The food was, indeed, fresh and colorful, and it smelled delicious, from the vegetables and crisp breads to the thin slices of meats. I took a modest-sized plate and followed Will to a long wooden table, with the others. As I sat down, I asked, "Do you raise your own animals, too?"

"Some," Becca said, and nodded down at the slices of pork on her plate. "We've got some pigs, some sheep, chickens and some cows, but the chickens are for eggs, and the cows are mostly for milk. Horses, too, but not for eating, obviously."

"Rabbits," Desmond put in, mumbling around a mouthful of green vegetables I didn't recognize. "Love them rabbits."

"I hate to see them on the dinner list." Aiyana sighed. "They're so beautiful."

"Aiyana's vegetarian," Will said, and passed her some bread. She had only greens and potatoes on her plate, I realized, and blushed a little as Will pointed it out. "She'd starve rather than kill a chicken."

"That's only because she doesn't have to clean up af-

ter them," Karl said. He had a distinct European accent,
though I wasn't sure if it came of German origin, or another neighboring country. "Right, Aiyana?"

She blushed further, and looked down at her plate. "I
like the fields," she said. "It's peaceful."

I cleared my throat and said, "Do we get a choice of
what to do?"

"Not at first," Will said. "You'll rotate around, find
what you're good at doing. I work with the animals, and
sometimes in the fields; I also do the doctoring, when it's
needed. Becca teaches the kids, but she does real good
with cows, so she gets up early for the milking before
class."

Cows. I shook my head, wondering what I'd expected
from this—certainly not this homespun rustic conversation about milking cows and cleaning up after chickens.
Pearl's followers were fanatics, and they were dangerous.

Yet they didn't feel dangerous at all.

I accepted a glass of cloudy yellow liquid someone
said was lemonade, and turned the topic to something
else. "I don't see the children in here. Do they have their
own place to eat?"

"Oh, they eat earlier," Becca said. "Great kids, very
gifted, you know. We make sure they get to bed early;
they get tired out from their days, poor things."

I glanced around at the others, who were all eating.
"Are any of them yours?" I asked. Will almost choked
on his lemonade before he burst out with a laugh. Desmond pounded him on the back as he coughed.

"Definitely not," Karl said, and grinned before he bit
off a big chunk of his bread. "None of us, anyway. There
are a few at the other tables whose kids qualified for the
program."

I—or Laura—blinked in wide-eyed confusion. "Are
most of them orphans?"

My new friends looked at one another, and for the

first time, I saw a slight hesitation ripple through them. Eventually, Aiyana said, "Most of them are. And the rest weren't in good situations, you understand. They really were in danger. We're saving their lives."

Desmond followed that by saying, in a darkly determined way, "We're not going to let anybody hurt them. Not again."

That fit with what I'd understood—that Pearl had indoctrinated her followers to believe that the Warden children were abused, and in horrible danger of being killed by the very organization that should have been protecting them. It wasn't true, but it was a powerful message, and there was just enough truth in it to give the lie a believable flavor.

The others murmured support for that sentiment. Will was looking right at me as he did so, and I nodded, making sure that my gaze held his. "I don't like seeing kids hurt," I said. "Especially the young ones. Somebody needs to protect them."

That was all true; what they would not realize, I hoped, was that I would be protecting these young ones from *them*. At least, I planned to try.

Will seemed to suspect none of that. I felt no change in his warm regard of me. He finally scooped up a bite of pork and ate without further comment.

I spotted Oriana a few moments later, sitting with another group and talking animatedly, as if she'd woken from her earlier dull, almost drugged state. She seemed as happy as the others now.

It was difficult for me not to feel that way as well, as the evening slipped over us, and my newfound companions lulled me into a peaceful sense of belonging.

By the time we began to break up, it was full dark, and Will retrieved an oil lamp to walk me back to my lodge. It seemed peaceful and very beautiful here; I could hear no machines, not even the distant hum of traffic that seemed such a sound track to modern life. This setting reminded me of ancient times, as did the houses, the clothing, even Will's open, unguarded smile.

"There you are," he said, and raised the lamp to illuminate the steps to the lodge. He kept holding it up, and the golden light shimmered on his face and in his eyes. "I'm glad you joined us here, Laura. I think you're going to like it."

"I already do," I said. That wasn't a lie, either. I did like it, more than I had life outside of these artificially peaceful fences. Out there, it seemed trust was a dead language, and danger lurked around every corner. Here, I felt safe. And at peace. It was absurd, and yet it was true.

Will took my hand and, to my very great surprise, pressed a quick, warm kiss to my knuckles. It sent a marked wave of sensation through my body, from toes to the top of my head—a flash of heat I'd only ever felt at intensely personal moments, with Luis. It left me feeling shaken, and deeply vulnerable.

Luis. I closed my eyes for a second and felt the low, steady whisper of the connection I still retained with him. Images flashed through my mind—Luis, on his knees beside his murdered brother. Luis, holding me still as he healed me. Luis, with that incomparable light of passion in his eyes as he bent to kiss me.

This isn't real, I told myself. *Will isn't real. Luis is. What I have with him can't be duplicated.*

But Luis wasn't here, and there was something deeply, sweetly seductive about Will in a way that I had never encountered before. I felt a surge of panic. Djinn couldn't be so changeable, so easily swayed . . .

. . . But I was no longer a Djinn.

When I opened my eyes, Will was still holding my hand, watching me with those wide, lovely eyes. He started to say something, then evidently thought better of it, and turned away. I watched him go, bathed in golden light, until he disappeared into another lodge.

Then I went into my own new home, found my bunk among all its identical fellows, stripped off my gray clothes, and worried for only a few moments before I fell as deeply, peacefully asleep as I ever had since being reborn into the human world.

It seemed ironic that I should find the most peace I'd known in the most dangerous place I'd ever entered.

The next day came early, when dawn was still the same drab color as the clothes hanging at the end of my bunk. I woke to the creaking of metal springs, low-voiced conversations, the whisper of clothing, and the sound of water running in the bath at the end of the lodge. I stayed still for a long few moments, luxuriating in the sense of warm relaxation, and then regretfully rose, gathered clothing, and went on to the baths. These were communal showers, with no privacy to speak of, but the women seemed not to be much bothered by their displays of nudity. I had no ethical objections to it in any case, and enjoyed the hot water immensely, as well as the feeling of once again being clean. The soap was rougher than I'd expected—hand-milled, according to one of the other very wet women standing next to me under the spray. I passed the bar on to the next woman when I was done. It all seemed very . . . civil.

Dressed and reasonably groomed, I made my way to the food hall, where coffee and tea were available, as well as eggs, bacon, and toast. I didn't see Will or Becca, but Desmond, Karl, and Aiyana waved me over. We shared a pleasant few moments before they left on their morning duties, and I was finishing my toast when Will entered, filled a cup with coffee, and came to sit beside me.

"Did you sleep well?" he asked. It seemed a politely

empty question, and I replied with the appropriate civility. "Any idea what you want to do today?"

"Not at all," I said. "I thought I'd be assigned to something, I guess." It was a little dangerous, but I hazarded it anyway: "Perhaps something to do with the children?"

Will didn't pause in sipping his coffee, and he didn't look directly at me, but I still felt that same odd hesitation tremble between us. "Maybe later," he said. "They need some help on laundry duty today. Suzette's out sick and Topher got roped into felling trees. You don't mind doing laundry, do you?"

I did, in fact, but Laura Rose would not. "That'd be fine," I said. "Where do I go?"

"I'll show you."

Our meal finished, Will walked me outside. He kept his hands clasped behind his back, and exchanged smiles and pleasantries with people we passed. I didn't see weapons in evidence anywhere. The children streamed past us, heading toward what looked like a white-painted school. I saw no evidence of Pearl's presence anywhere, other than the general whispering sense of power in this place.

"Aren't there guards?" I asked. "I mean, it was pretty scary getting in. I thought someone would be—"

"Yeah, the vetting process is extreme, I keep telling them it's not necessary," Will said. "We always know when people try to get in who aren't genuine about it. We're not violent people. We don't want to hurt anyone; we just want to live a little differently from the way others do. I don't like it that they threaten people and try to scare them away. We don't have guards here. It's not a prison, Laura. It's our home."

"Are you in charge?" I asked it directly, and it startled a laugh from him—rich, full, and unguarded.

"Do I seem like a guy who'd be in charge?" he asked, and then sobered. "No, I'm not in charge. We don't have that kind of relationship here. There's no dictator; no government, exactly. We have an industry proctor who deals with work schedules, but that's mostly paperwork. Our food proctor works out farm and husbandry details and does the menus. We have a services proctor for everything else."

"How do you pick the proctors?"

"We all used to take turns," he said. "But certain people have a talent for administration, so right now Violet's our industry proctor, because she's great at scheduling and making sure everyone gets varied work and rest. We're still looking for someone to want the food and services proctor roles full-time; until then, we all take a week at it. Trust me, it works out. We're not perfect, and we do have conflicts from time to time, but surprisingly few, really. We don't need jails. We don't need courts, or lawyers, or drug rehab." Will hesitated, then shook his head to get long hair away from his eyes. "On the outside, I was a mess. I had a meth habit. I never fit in. Here, it's all different, Laura. You can just be yourself here."

That was ironic, considering what *being myself* meant, but at a certain level I actually craved the certainty I heard in his voice. He'd found his paradise. In a sense, I felt that under other circumstances it might have been mine as well.

But not for the children.

Pearl was the unseen cancer at the heart of this seemingly healthy community, and I hated her for it with a sudden, breathtaking intensity. Will would be broken in this, and so many others who didn't deserve to have their dreams shattered.

It would be as much my fault as hers, or they would see it that way; they would see me as a betrayer of the worst kind.

Even now I could feel the early echoes of the pain I would cause.

"Laura?" Will was looking at me in concern. I forced a smile.

"I don't know who I am," I said, again quite honestly. "How can I really be myself?"

"You'll find your way," he said. "We all find our own ways."

Chapter 10

THERE WAS A SURPRISING meditative quality to doing laundry; no mechanized washers and dryers, but there was water heated in the center boiler, and tubs, and I was part of a team of four who filled the tubs, dunked and scrubbed the clothing, rinsed, wrung, and hung it up to dry in the crisp sunlight. The smell of the detergent—homemade—was strong and a little astringent, but the warm water felt soothing on my skin, and so did the sun. I was surprised when the midday meal break came; we'd done almost the entire camp's laundry in a single morning. Rhona, one of the four working with me, explained that we would leave the drying until twilight, then take in the clothes for folding and redistribution. It seemed a steady, simple system. A few of the clothes had names inked in them, because they were especially sized or tailored for their owners, but most were interchangeable shirts and trousers and skirts. Bandannas of various colors signaled seniority within the groups, though there were only a few in for washing.

Lunch was spent sitting in the shade with a small picnic delivered from the food hall. Again, I felt that sense of ease, of peace, of a quiet and predictable life.

No one struggled here. No one felt isolated, afraid, unloved, unwanted.

Not even me.

It took three days of laundry service before I was moved to another duty . . . animals this time, cleaning up after the chickens, pigs, and horses. The sheep were grazed out on a hill, with two shepherds to guard them; the cows seemed placid and well fed as they grazed downhill.

There were two horses, both big rawboned beasts who assisted in plowing and cart pulling; neither was young, but they were healthy and well treated, and greeted me with the same placid friendliness as all the other animals. I liked the horses the best, I thought. Karl was right about the chickens, though the pigs charmed me with their bright, inquisitive ways.

I saw Becca occasionally, but Will was constantly in the periphery as well—not shadowing me, but working his days in the same spaces. It felt comfortable with him, when we had duties in common and chatted together.

It wasn't until the third day of animal duty that I realized I had failed to reach out to Luis, or to Agent Rostow. I felt a sense of dread, in fact, in contacting the FBI at all. It brought an unpleasant, gritty sense of reality to the illusion I was truly beginning to enjoy.

I kept it brief and to the point. *Nothing to report yet. Children are not their own in most cases. No evidence yet of weapons or abductions.*

It occurred to me, as I used that minor amount of power to deliver the report, that I had not felt the need to draw power from Luis for several long days, because I hadn't expended much, except the slight outflow to maintain my current appearance. When I closed my eyes and focused on him, I felt the ghost of his presence, so far away. After hesitating for what seemed an eternity, I tugged just slightly on that anchor between us, and after a moment, felt a slight popping of my eardrums before I heard Luis's voice echo in my head, *Where are you? Everything okay?* The reproduction of his voice was flawless, so good I could hear the concern in it.

Fine, I whispered back. It felt intimate, this contact, but left me wanting more. Aching for it, in fact. *And you? Ibby?*

We're all right.

Any sign of trouble there?

Not so far. It's quiet. If there is a traitor here, I can't spot him. Cass, what the hell did you get yourself into?

This has to be done, I said. *To safeguard Ibby. And you. And all of them. She's here. She's going to be vulnerable. I can do this, Luis. It's our best chance.*

Luis hesitated, then said, *Probably useless to tell you to be careful, right?*

I feel safe here, I said, before I could stop it. This time Luis's hesitation was much longer.

Hang on, chica. *You need to check yourself. You shouldn't feel safe. You should be scared out of your mind, because you're* not *safe. Don't forget it, okay? This ain't like you. You're not the joiner type.*

I joined the Wardens, I said. *I joined you.*

Wardens ain't there, Cass. I'm not there.

Will was, but I didn't want to bring Will up at all, not even obliquely. *I'll be careful*, I said. *No one here seems dangerous.*

It's always that way, Luis said grimly, *before somebody shoots you in the back. I know we didn't part ways too well, Cass, but—but I love you. I care, all right? I care what happens to you. Please. Don't let your guard down.*

I won't, I promised, but even as I said it, I knew I was lying to him. I already had let my guard down, and I didn't know how to raise it again. I didn't *want* to raise it again.

I felt too safe here. Too much a part of things.

I fell asleep soon after, to the soft breathing and snoring of the women around me.

And Luis was right . . . I should have taken more care.

*   *   *

I had slept deeply, and dreamlessly, for several nights, but that had turned out to be only a prelude to the nightmare—the silence before the start of the play.

I came out of the restful darkness to realize that I was standing on a rocky shelf on a mountain, with the frozen-cold wind rippling fragile cloth draperies around me, in the shades of storm clouds. My skin was ice-white, and my long hair whipped like a silk banner in the fierce gusts.

Across from me, on another mountain, stood a beautiful, exotic creature—human, yet somehow no longer holding to that shape, or to any shape. It flowed and flickered, drifted and snapped back to form. In the brief glimpses of a human figure, I saw a tall, slender woman with shining black hair, dressed in night-blue layers of padded silk. Her skin was flawlessly golden, and in her right hand she held a golden spear, with a black silk flag fastened to it. Black on black, a dimly seen darkness in a circular pattern almost hidden in the middle of the fabric.

It seemed that darkness was alive within the hissing, snapping fabric, and with every wave of the flag, it grew larger, and larger, until it broke free of the spear and flattened itself on the wind like a giant black bat, gliding in defiance of the prevailing currents.

"Sister," she said to me, beneath the darkness cast by that growing, oddly sinister silken cover. The circular inky spot in the middle seemed to be turning now, a slow and relentless rotation. "I've been waiting for you to come to me. Where are you?"

"Can't you find me?" I asked her. Pearl lost her human form, distorting into static, into a snarling beast, into a twisted, spiked tree, before regaining her beauty. "How do you know I haven't come to you already?"

She smiled. The banner flapping above her grew and grew, and the wind grew with it, ripping at my frail clothing, pulling my hair with the hands of cruel, invisible children. "O sister, I know you too well. Your arrogance can't be disguised. You shine like a fire in the night. But fire can be smothered."

The banner suddenly snapped on the wind and arrowed toward me, wrapping me in folds of choking blackness, waves of *nothing*. I felt it pulling at me, like the sucking mouth of a leech, and power poured out of me like blood from a new wound. The banner had felt colder than the wind that had brought it. I could no longer see Pearl, but I could feel her, hear her, and the smothering power of her presence was ripping at the roots that held me to the world . . .

But power rose up through those roots, rich and sweet and hot, burning red holes in the darkness, shredding it into rags. It was an overwhelming force, something I neither called nor commanded, but it saved my life.

The silky darkness that remained fell away from me and sought escape in the open cold air. I fell on the rocks, my face in my hands, my hair wild as a madwoman's. The wind had torn away my clothes. My skin was bleached and abraded, and rich red blood flooded from the cuts to puddle on the stone beneath my bruised knees.

Pearl raised her spear, and the banner flooded in a silk river across the open space between us to wrap itself around the golden shaft, shrink, and become a mere flag again. Pearl stabilized in human form, as perfect and beautiful as when I had known her in our youth, so long ago.

"You haven't lost your touch, sister," she said. "But you will. The Mother isn't as we knew her in the ancient days, awake and alive. And like her, we are not the same. Corruption can't be unseen or unfelt; it can't be healed, only endured."

"Pearl," I said, and raised my head to meet her eyes. "I'll destroy you. I don't wish to, but I will. Stop this before we have to raise our true forms."

"Dream on, my sister," Pearl said. "What I do must be done, to make way for what is to come. Only out of destruction can creation be born. Life in this place was an experiment, an accident of chemicals and light. It's time to cease the struggle, and let darkness have its time. Who knows what new forms can come from that? Because it's beautiful, my emptiness, the emptiness where you sent me so long ago. And it hungers, as life hungers. And it will feed, very soon."

Under my knees, the shelf of rock suddenly broke loose, and my body tumbled out into the endless gulf, falling, spinning, falling . . .

. . . until I crashed into my flesh, breathing hard, sweating and shaking.

All was darkness.

I no longer felt it was peace.

I waited for the death blow; surely, I thought, Pearl must have detected my presence so close to her seat of power. The next morning I spent tense and alert, waiting for any hint of an attack. My distracted behavior displeased the horses I was grooming, and I soon was the recipient of shoves and whinnies to remind me of my duties. The horses, at least, seemed to have no worries at all. I was midway through the last grooming when a group of eight children, wearing those four colors I had noted before, came for a barn visit, supervised by a woman in a red bandanna. I instantly sensed the tingle of power in her presence; Weather, I thought. The air seemed to taste of ozone around me. Of a surety, she was not Earth; the horses crowded closer around me, as if for protection. She gave me a close look, dismissed me as unimportant, and began tell the children about horses—a speech they blithely ignored, to pet the huge beasts and offer them apples.

This woman was far different from the warm comrades working the farm outside. I sensed from her that she held them, and me, in mild contempt. She was a wolf, hiding among the placid sheep, and she despised us even while she needed us.

This was the enemy I had been waiting for.

"Hello," I said, and directed it generally at her and the children. The boys and girls echoed it back. The Weather Warden did not. She gave me another long, level look. I gave it back to her, and held out my hand. "My name is Laura. I'm new."

"Clearly," she said, and cocked a single eyebrow. She must have decided that being overtly rude would risk questions from the children, and so she shook hands with me. "Mariah," she said. "I'm sorry, but we're all quite busy. Kids, we need to be moving on. We've got lessons this morning."

That brought out a general groan from the children. One of the older ones, a girl, was hidden from Mariah by the bulk of the horse between them, and I saw the fear that passed over her expression before she hid her face in the horse's thick mane for a moment. I wondered why she seemed afraid, and the others didn't. Possibly because this girl had seen something, or knew something more than she should have.

I edged up next to her, on the pretext of currying the horse. "What's your name?" I asked her softly. She was a pretty thing, delicate and dark, with wide black eyes and a pointed elfin face.

"Zedala," she whispered back. "Please, miss, can you find my parents? I want to go home."

I glanced at her and saw tears in her eyes. Mariah was, for the moment, involved in gathering up the playful younger children, and I took the chance to hug the girl for comfort before saying, "Be brave, Zedala. All will be well."

She looked hopelessly at me, and said, "You don't

understand." I ached to tell her more, to promise her that she'd soon be free, but the risks were too high. Even this lovely child could be a trap, set to make me betray myself.

I forced myself to smile and pat her shoulder. "We're all friends here," I said. "We'll take care of you. You don't have to be afraid."

"Zedala!" the other woman called, and I saw the shiver that went through the girl. She quickly wiped the tears from her eyes. "Zedala, hurry up!"

"Yes, miss!" She gave me one more troubled, pleading look, and hurried off. I brushed the horse with absent strokes as I watched Mariah hustle away her eight small charges.

Zedala knew there was danger; that much was obvious. The others didn't.

I needed to understand what she'd seen.

At lunch, I sat with Will and we split a small block of yellow cheese, some sliced ham, and fresh bread. It was delicious, and sitting so comfortably in the sun it seemed impossible to believe there was evil being done here, in the heart of this peaceful place. But the fear in Zedala had been real, and immediate, and I didn't have the luxury of ignoring the pain of a child.

"Some of the children came to the barn this morning," I told Will as I ate a slice of apple. We had no apple trees on the farm; I wondered if they traded for the fruit. "Why do they wear those uniforms?"

"We all wear uniforms," he said, and reached for an apple slice as well.

"I know, but the colors . . ."

"It's just to identify what their powers are," he said.

"Powers?"

"They're special," Will said, very softly. He kept his eyes focused on distant trees, but I thought there was a slight glitter there, a hardness that seemed very alien to what I knew of him. "They have gifts, not like normal kids. We have to protect them and train them for the end."

"The end?"

"The end of civilization," he said. "It's coming, Laura. It's why we're here. We have to learn how to live without all those things so-called civilization has given us, all the toys and machines and pollution. These children are going to help us survive it, and in turn, we're going to save them and protect them from those who want to hurt them."

"Oh," I said. It was what I'd expected to hear, but not from Will—not from someone I'd grown to like. "It seemed like they were a little frightened."

He shrugged a little. "They have to learn," he said. "Not all lessons are easy. It's good for them to be a little frightened."

I swallowed a piece of bread that seemed suddenly foul, and reached for the lemonade glass to wash the bad taste from my mouth. "I don't like to scare kids," I said. "Even if it's for a good cause."

"They have to be trained. Just leave it alone, Laura. Let the teachers handle them."

"All right," I said, and ate another apple slice. It didn't taste as sweet as it had.

Will ate in silence as well, until the plates were empty and the glasses drained, and then he stood up and stretched. I watched him, aware of how the sun filtered through the clothes and outlined the strong lines of his body. Aware of the gentle intensity of the stare he turned toward me, as he offered me his hand.

I took it, and he pulled me up—against his body. I didn't move away. There was an odd inevitability to this, a feeling of recognition, as if I'd dreamed this, or lived it in another life. I looked up into his face, into those lovely eyes, and felt myself falling into a great, gaping void from which there would be no return. It should have been frightening, but instead, it felt . . . reassuring. Like coming home.

Will let go and stepped away. I stood there for a moment, watching him, and then turned and picked up our plates and glasses. "I'll take them back," I said.

He didn't speak, not even to thank me. I felt his gaze on me, heavy and hot, all the way back to the food hall.

When I came back out, Will was nowhere in sight. I missed him, and hated myself for it; I had no business longing for any man here, including Will, whatever odd attraction had developed between us. I was here for a reason, and that reason had just crystallized for me in a single haunting image—the desperate tears in Zedala's eyes.

I went back to the barn and picked up the hay rake. As I did so, a pair of arms came out of the shadows behind me, grabbed me from behind, and attempted to yank me backward into the dark.

I suppose that Laura Rose might have screamed, but in that moment I was not Laura Rose. I was Cassiel, and Cassiel didn't cry for help.

Cassiel made *others* cry for help.

I drove my elbow backward with as much force as I could, and felt it connect solidly with flesh, muscle, bone. I heard an explosive exhalation of breath against my hair and neck. Before he—I was sure it was a he, from the feel of his musculature against me—could recover, I spun and slammed the heel of my hand in a strike for his nose, to break it or, in the best case, drive bone into his brain.

He caught my hand barely in time, and I belatedly realized that I knew him.

Merle. I had almost forgotten about my fellow implanted agent, since he'd been put into another work cycle altogether . . . but here he was, hiding in the dark.

"What do you want?" I hissed. Around us, the horses stamped nervously, catching the rush of adrenaline from our bodies. Merle looked worried. Haunted.

No, he looked *hunted*.

"I think they suspect," he said. "Get a message to Rostow. Tell him I need extraction."

"What did you learn?"

"Not a goddamn thing except how to run a plow," he said. "I can't find a way in, and they don't like questions. I think I asked one too many."

"Did they threaten you?"

"They don't threaten anybody," he said. "But one day, you just wake up in the cornfield, I'm guessing. Contact Rostow. Get us an exit."

"I'm not going," I said. Merle let go of my arm, and I stepped back. "I can't leave. Go if you wish, but I'll stay."

"You stay and you'll end up one of them," he said. "Or worse. Something's wrong here. I've been in cults before, but this one's a whole new rainbow of wrong. It's like it changes you inside out—not like brainwashing. I can resist brainwashing. This is something else."

What it was, I realized, was the low-level tingle of power in the camp. Pearl's influence, breathing around us, infiltrating our every thought, breath, heartbeat. Merle could feel it, even if he had no idea what it could be, and it had frightened him. It was eroding his sense of self, corrupting him from within . . . and it was doing the same to me, only for me it had created this false link with Will.

"I can't go," I said, as gently as I could. "But you should. As soon as possible." Merle, in struggling to keep his sense of identity and purpose, was making himself a target. They would know he wasn't one of them soon, if they didn't know that already. As good an undercover agent as Merle might have been in other circumstances, here in this place he was in grave danger.

"I'll let you know when it's ready," I told him. "Go back to work. Be careful."

He nodded, wiped his forehead with the sleeve of his gray shirt, and took a deep breath. Even so, he didn't look himself, I thought.

"Stay cool," I said. "You'll be out soon."

He nodded again and walked out into the sun, head down. Even his body language seemed wrong, when compared to the alert, confident strides of the others in the camp. I could see it. So could others.

Merle was in very real trouble.

I went back to raking the straw as I sank into a light meditative state and reached out for Rostow to deliver my message—a minor enough effort, and a nearly imperceptible use of power, but it still felt more difficult now, as if the walls around the camp were psychic as well as physical blocks. Perhaps it was only that something inside me longed for this life now—the simplicity, the clean and straight lines of it. The honesty and trust.

But the trust itself was a lie, and underneath was a black lake of toxic betrayal. I knew that, I did, but even so, it was difficult to separate *knowing* from *feeling*.

I reached out for Rostow, but before I could deliver Merle's plea, I heard shouts from outside. No one shouted here, not in that particular tone.

I looked out to see that it was the girl, Zedala. She was running across the field, stumbling on the carefully plowed rows. She looked terrified.

Mariah, her teacher, had stopped at the edge of the field, and stood watching her with a stiff, unforgiving expression. Next to her was another teacher in a green scarf, who extended her hand toward Zedala.

The next step the girl took tripped her, and she plunged flat onto the ground.

No.

Into the ground.

I dropped the rake and ran out of the barn. Around
the edges of the field, the workers had all stopped what
they were doing, but no one was moving to interfere.

Not even Merle, who was standing near the fertilizer
cart, clenching his fists.

Zedala didn't come up from beneath the ground.

I took in a deep breath and ran forward, shoving the
two teachers out of my way. I got only a few steps into
the field before it opened before me—not my doing—
and I plunged down into a thick, heavy darkness of fer-
tile tilled dirt, worms, and the sharp chips of rocks.

I could reach her, I realized. They didn't expect me
to be able to maneuver through the dirt, to use my
own Earth powers to guide me to Zedala. But if I did,
it would betray me utterly, not only to them but to
Pearl.

The frustration made me scream silently into the
darkness of my temporary grave.

I couldn't save her. I could only hope that their goal
was to punish, not to kill.

After what seemed an eternity, I felt the ground underneath me pushing upward, expelling me into the air
once again. I rolled over on my back, gasping and choking, wiping the black earth from my face with trembling
hands.

Zedala was lying crumpled and weeping twenty feet
away. She was filthy and terrified, but she was alive.

I coughed up dirt and blinked up at the bright yellow
sun, which was blotted out by one of the teachers. Not
Mariah. This one was, I was sure, an Earth Warden, and
a potentially quite powerful one.

He was also very, very young—no older than Zedala,
but with a shimmering cloud of power surrounding him
that was unmistakable to the eyes of anyone with a gift.
Possibly, I thought, the most powerful Earth Warden I'd
ever met, besides Lewis Orwell.

He had dark, empty eyes that held no pity, no reluctance, no doubt. The eyes of a fanatic.

"Go get her," he said to Mariah, who ducked her head in acknowledgment and hurried over the rows to grab Zedala and pull her to her feet. "Take her to the box."

"No!" Zedala screamed, but only once. The boy-Warden stared at her, and the next time her mouth opened, nothing came out. The panic and terror on her face spoke loudly enough, though. It was a horrible sight, but when I looked around, I saw that the gray-clothed workers had all turned away, intent on their own duties.

All but Merle, who was still watching, with his fists tightly clenched.

And, standing in the shadow of the corner of the barn . . . Will, whose clear gray eyes were fixed not on Zedala, but on *me*.

The two teachers dragged the girl away. I was left alone to stagger upright, slapping dirt from my clothes. Will strode forward, grabbed my wrist, and pulled me out of the field. Once I was on hard-packed ground, he took my shoulders and shook me, hard enough to make a rain of dirt fall from my body.

"Are you insane?" he demanded. "Don't you understand that whatever happens, we do *not* interfere with the training of those children?"

"Training!" I spat, and struck his hands away from me. "I didn't see *training*. I thought they were going to kill her!"

"Their methods may seem harsh, but—"

"It's cruel, Will! And I'm not sure they wouldn't have let her die, if we hadn't been watching! I couldn't—"

"*Listen to me!* You have to, Laura. You have to learn that they know best!"

"Or?" I lifted my chin and stared into his eyes. His pupils slowly widened in response, as if he was swallowing my image whole.

"Or you won't have a place here," he said very gently, and touched my cheek. "And I'd regret that. I'd regret that very much."

So would I, I realized. Even now. Even with the panic and pain in Zedala's face, the icy indifference in the boy-Warden's cruelty. I didn't want to leave this place.

I didn't want to leave *him*.

I took a step away, until my knees were steady enough to hold me, and walked back to the barn, head down.

Then I picked up the rake, and went back to work. As I combed through the straw, I reached out for Rostow, to deliver Merle's message.

I couldn't make contact.

There was only emptiness on the other side of the fence, where Rostow and the FBI agents should have been. Nothing. An eerie silence that made me pause in my work and rise up into the aetheric, just enough to see.

Beyond the forest's cover, the FBI trailer was still in place. So were the cars, the SUVs, the tent where the agents slept.

But there was no sign of them at all.

They had all just . . . vanished.

Every single one.

Merle and I were very much vulnerable, and on our own.

Chapter 11

THE REST OF THE DAY passed without incident, and I trudged back with the others to the lodge, where I showered, dressed in fresh clothing, and ate with Will's usual group of friends. They didn't mention the unfortunate Zedala, or my dip into the earth in a failed rescue attempt. No one did.

Merle sat alone at one end of another long table, head down. It was as if he'd already been ostracized from the group. I wanted to warn him that there was no rescue, no exit plan, but I didn't know if I dared now. If Pearl and her followers were powerful enough to abduct, destroy, or otherwise relocate the entire FBI presence, it would be dangerous to display any power that might draw their attention; I knew my aborted attempt to save the girl had already roused some suspicion. There was too much focus on Merle already.

I sipped my water and stared down at my plate as the others talked and laughed, and finally, very carefully, reached out and vibrated the delicate bones of his ear to say, *FBI presence is gone. We're on our own. Watch out.*

He looked up, startled, and checked himself before he stared in my direction. Instead, he stared at an entirely innocent Oriana, who was listening to someone else tell a long-winded story about a crow and a field of corn.

And I noted that a man near him was watching, and tracing any potential interactions Merle might have with others.

Merle's quick thinking had just preserved my cover—but had endangered Oriana, who was entirely innocent. And she didn't even know it.

My peaceful idyll here had, in a matter of hours, turned into a dangerous pit of vipers. The difference between me and Merle, or me and Zedala, was that I didn't intend to leave this place—not until I'd accomplished what I came to do.

I needed to lure Pearl here in the flesh, and find a way to destroy her—or cripple her. The Djinn side of me said that it was worth the cost of Merle's life, or the child's. Or of Will's, Oriana's, and the lives of all the other members of this cult who'd come here seeking escape from their own nests of problems. Collateral damage was inevitable now in this struggle. Surely it was better to sacrifice a few than to be forced to the extreme of slaughtering millions, or destroying the entire broad and lovely spectrum of the human race.

Surely.

Yet looking around the room, seeing the peace these people felt, the gentle love and regard they held for one another . . . I felt that this would be less a sacrifice than black, cruel murder.

Not that I wasn't capable of that, too.

I had only myself to answer to now. Not Luis. Not Isabel. Not even Ashan. Only me, and my human-born conscience.

It should have been easier to silence.

The next few days passed in silence, a kind of tense standoff of waiting. Part of me felt at ease now; the stubbornly Djinn part was aware of how much risk there was, and what a subtle web it had woven around me. No more children visited the barn. In fact, I only saw them at a distance, always close to the school and their teachers. I never caught any sight of Zedala.

Merle continued on as he had, without any incident, until the third morning. It took me a short while to realize that although the other workers in the field beyond the barn were familiar, there was no sign of Merle.

I took it upon myself to visit the food hall and return with a heavy pitcher of cool water and a cup, and made the rounds of the sweating workers to deliver the refreshment with a smile. When I got to Will, he wiped his damp face, gave me a blindly sweet smile, and drank two deep cups before sighing in gratitude.

"Where's Merle?" I asked, looking around. "He's usually here, isn't he?"

Will had been stretching his long arms, but now he lowered them to his sides and looked sidelong at me, brows raised. "Usually," he said. "Why?"

"No reason. I just wondered if he was all right. He seems quiet lately."

"I don't think he worked out," Will said.

That sounded offhand . . . and ominous. I drank some water myself, trying to decide how to approach the subject, and finally abandoned subtlety. "Did he leave?"

"Yes," Will said. "He left." After an awkward second of silence, he nodded. "Thanks for the water. I need to get back to work. These rows won't tend themselves."

I walked back to the food hall to return the pitcher, thinking hard. Merle *might* have been able to leave without incident; they *might* have allowed that.

But I couldn't believe it, not really. He'd seen the incident with Zedala. He knew the children were at risk, and that made him a dangerous witness indeed. They would never let him simply walk free, even if they hadn't suspected him of being some sort of spy.

As I put out food for the pigs, greeting them with friendly pats, I ascended into the aetheric to get a glimpse around me. Merle had been solidly visible before, an easily recognizable target to locate ... but now I could see no sign of him. My attention was drawn instead to a spot of darkness on the aetheric, like a wide, violent splash of blood. It was in the field, and it was far beneath the surface.

It was the shape of a corpse. No ... not just one corpse. I counted four, at least, all buried deeply in the earth.

All fresh enough to retain their basic human shape, and the aetheric stain of their death struggles.

One of them had to be Merle.

The emotion of it hit me a moment after the factual information: Merle, as competent and careful as he was, had been killed. I was alone here. No friends, no allies, no chance of leaving with my life. Like Merle, I'd seen too much, asked too many questions. I was trapped.

But I wanted to be trapped. Didn't I? Hadn't that been my purpose in coming here all along?

Still, in that moment, seeing the blunt reality of what had happened to a man who had seemed, in many ways, indestructible, I felt fear, real and visceral. If I died here, I'd leave Luis and Ibby without ever really reconciling with them. They would believe that I hadn't really loved them, really wanted to stay.

You're not here to love them. You're here to save them. And that, too, was true. I had been sent to this world as an avatar of Ashan's wishes, and I knew that; he'd manipulated me into believing that it was my own will, but I knew the hand of the master at work. Ashan couldn't lose this game, not with the position in which he'd placed me; if I couldn't find a way to destroy Pearl, I would be driven to the last extreme, and destroy the human race that anchored and fed her. I was his cat's paw, and if I was destroyed in the process, then that was a price both he and I knew to be acceptable, given the stakes.

I hadn't intended to feel so much, or so deeply. Not for myself, and this fragile shell of flesh that sustained me, in any case. It should have been a temporary, uncomfortable prison, but instead—instead I felt as human, as afraid, as any of the people around me.

I spent the rest of the day feeling disconnected and alone, lost with my hideous secret beneath our feet. Will didn't know, nor did the others. I thought the boy Warden, the one who'd buried me briefly, had been the one to carry out the executions. It was a neat, mess-free way of disposing of those they no longer needed; it would have been a horrible way to die, suffocating on your own grave dirt, but I didn't suppose the boy cared.

He was a true believer, after all.

I was on my way to the food hall, exhausted and more than a little angry at my own indecision, when I saw a small shadowy figure lurking near the corner of my lodge building.

Zedala. She had managed to create a veil for herself, and done it well; I drifted her way slowly, almost by accident, and put my back against the side of the lodge wall beside her. The night was chilly, and she was shivering in her thin clothes. I was wearing a quilted jacket, which I stripped off and dropped beside her. She quickly picked it up and put it on with a quiet, trembling sigh of gratitude.

"What are you doing here?" I asked her. I kept watch for any sign of observers, but although there were people about, they didn't pay any obvious attention to me.

Zedala continued to huddle in her veil, but finally replied, "I was looking for you. You tried to help me."

"And?"

"I need to get out of here." She looked up, and the

faint, fading light shone on tear tracks on her face. "They say I failed. They say I'm not powerful enough; I'm not the one they need. So they say I'm going to go home. But I'm not going home, am I?"

I thought of the bodies under the tilled field. "No," I said. "I don't think they'll let you go home."

"Can you help me?" she asked in a very faint voice. "Because there's nobody else. Nobody."

I closed my eyes. The pain in her voice pierced me, but I knew what Ashan would want me to do. What the old Cassiel, the Djinn Cassiel, would have done. I knew I should have walked away, left her there in her tears and desperation, and preserved my chance to win the day.

But she had no chance without my help. None. By dawn, I'd be finding her corpse buried next to Merle's. I'd be imagining a child's last, frantic, desperate moments. A child whom these people professed to honor and protect.

I might be a good Djinn if I allowed that to happen, but I would be a monster of a human being.

I opened my eyes and said, "All right. Can you veil yourself until I come and get you?"

"I think so." Zedala wiped her face with her sleeve and looked up at me with hope dawning warm in her eyes. "You're going to help? Really?"

"Yes," I said. "I'm going to help. But you have to promise me one thing."

"Okay."

"You have to promise me you won't stop running until you reach the Wardens. Tell them I sent you for help."

She nodded solemnly, and I pushed away from the wall and went into the lodge. My shower seemed to take an eternity, as did the dinner that followed. Will tried to distract me with amusing stories, but my smiles were all halfhearted.

Oriana was gone, too, I realized, as I looked around. Merle and Oriana, both missing, both likely dead.

I would be next, or the child would. I couldn't let her suffer for my mistakes.

After dinner, I willed myself to return to the lodge. Oriana's bunk above mine was neatly made, but any personal effects were gone. Instead, it was ready for a new occupant, complete with the same welcome gifts she and I had received upon our arrival. I undressed and got into bed, and waited for the hours to pass.

In the full dark, I rose and dressed as silently as I could, went to the restroom, and pried open one of the small windows at the back. I would never have made it in my original Cassiel form, but Laura Rose was smaller and lighter-boned, and I squirmed through the narrow opening and dropped to the ground outside. The moon was dark, so I had only starlight to navigate by. Apart from the rustle of the wind in the trees, there seemed to be no one about at all tonight. I spotted the subtle glimmer of Zedala's veil; she was where I had left her, close against the wall of the lodge building. I hesitated for a moment more, breathing in the sharp evening air, all senses alert, but I heard and saw nothing else.

I moved toward her under cover of shadows and crouched down next to her. She was wrapped in my quilted jacket, but still shivering. Nevertheless, she gave me a wan smile when she saw me. "You came," she whispered. "You came."

"Of course," I said. "I wouldn't leave you."

I helped her up, took her hand, and after another careful survey of the area, led her across the dangerously open area toward the fence. It was a significant barrier, but not for an Earth Warden; I had no more fear of disguising my power, because I knew that in order to allow Zedala's escape, I'd have to betray myself.

It felt like a positive step, until I remembered the

friends I'd made, the peace I'd felt here. Until I imagined the look in Will's eyes when he learned of my
betrayal.

"Are you okay?" Zedala whispered. We were at the
fence, and I was at the moment of truth now. No more
delays, no more doubts. I had to do this, or the child
wouldn't survive her next encounter with her *teachers*.

It would cost me my chance at Pearl if I did this, but
if I stood by and allowed a child's death as the cost . . .

No. I was willing to pay a high price, but not that. Not
that.

I extended my hand, exerted a delicate flow of power,
and the metal mesh of the fence began to split and peel
back like the edges of a sharp, dangerous flower.

Something hit me in the back of the neck with a stunning blow, and then again, even harder. A wave of dis-
orientation, darkness, pain, and then I was falling to my
knees, struggling to turn my power on the one who'd
attacked me . . .

. . . until I saw Zedala's face, alight with triumph and
malice. She still held a bloody rock in her hand. She
raised it over her head and screamed in triumph—a
warrior's cry, chilling from such a small, fragile girl.

"Why?" I asked. I was clinging to consciousness only
with the greatest of effort, and there was something terribly wrong with my head. The world tilted, sliding me
toward the black edge.

For answer, Zedala hit me again. I heard answering
cries, hot with approval, and this time, I couldn't hold on
to the world at all.

Cass. Cass! Wake up!

Luis's voice, whispering urgently in my ear. I didn't
want to wake up. The darkness was kind; it cloaked the
pain and dulled the betrayal, but the whispers reached
me even there, dragging me into a dull twilight full of

agony. The pain drove me upward, into a harsh light that made me groan and twist aside from the glare.

"She's waking up," someone said. Not Luis. I ached to feel his presence, his comforting, healing touch, but instead there was only pain, and isolation. I couldn't move far. I was tied, or otherwise restrained. When I opened my eyes, the blaze of sun made me want to retch in anguish. There were dark shapes around me, distorted and sinister. "Block her! Don't let her get at her power!"

A child-sized hand flattened against my forehead, and I felt a cold, iron-hard wall come down, severing me from the reservoir of warm golden power that had accumulated within me. Luis had been feeding it to me, I realized; he'd been trying to heal me from afar, but now I was adrift and alone, and without that constant pulse of power, I was beginning to die. Oh, it was a slow process. It would take days of agony and terror, but my flesh would rot, and then the core of me would starve and flicker out like a blown flame.

I blinked away the glare, and the shadows wavered into the shapes of faces and bodies. Zedala's face came first. She was kneeling next to me with her hand on my forehead, and it was she who was cutting me off from my source. From Luis.

Zedala looked up, and I saw a boy of about her own age standing there staring down at us with a cold, remote expression. The Earth Warden boy, the one who'd staged that elaborate charade in the field to draw me out. There were two more children as well—a small, delicate girl who almost vibrated with the energy of Fire and a golden-skinned boy with silky black hair who radiated . . . nothing. Absolutely nothing.

There was something terrifying about him, and the look in his eyes. He couldn't have been more than nine years old, but that was an ancient, awful thing inside of him.

There was an adult woman with them as well, one of the teachers in a red bandanna. She was standing back, head bowed, hands clasped together. I thought for an instant that her obedience was directed toward the children, but then I realized that there was another presence in the room, standing farther away and somewhere past my aching head.

I pulled in a shaking breath as I felt the tidal force of her presence wash through the room.

I'd sought Pearl here.

I'd found her.

"No words, sister?" Pearl walked slowly into my field of vision. She was tall, graceful, beautiful as a blinding star; the dream vision I'd had of her had been an accurate representation of her human avatar, except that she wore her thick, silky black hair piled in intricate knots on top of her head to emphasize the long sweep of her neck. Unlike her followers, she was dressed in lush patterned silks that swept the floor as she walked. Her feet were bare and perfect. "No threats? No apologies? I'm disappointed. I wouldn't expect you to give up so easily."

I held my silence, since it bothered her. My head felt wrong and tender, and I was almost sure that my skull was fractured. The pillow beneath me felt sticky with blood, and I could smell the iron reek of it. Nausea twisted inside me like smoke, but I contained it. I couldn't heal myself, and cut off from Luis, I had no chance of surviving such an injury. Pearl knew that.

She was enjoying it.

Zedala and the other children looked at Pearl with expressions of utter devotion. In turn, Pearl trailed her long, lovely fingers over the hair of the smallest girl and favored her with a slow, cool smile. "Do you know what I've done, Cassiel?" she asked. "Do you understand the astonishing thing that's been accomplished here?"

"You've perverted and destroyed children," I said.

My voice sounded weak and dry, no match for her elegance. "It's not so astonishing. Humans have been doing that to their own for millennia." A pulse of hot, stabbing pain bolted through me, and I tensed and cried out.

Zedala gave me a wolfish grin. "Don't be rude to the Lady," she said. "You're not good enough to look at her. I should put your eyes out."

For an awful second, I thought that Pearl would allow that; she considered it, as she wandered over to the Earth Warden boy and caressed his face with idle affection. "No," she finally said. "Show me her base human form first."

Zedala cocked her head, staring at me, and then power burst out of her like a flood from an exploding dam, such astonishing power that it overwhelmed and drowned me, ripped me apart in its turbulence, then subsided in a slow, sticky tide. I felt myself changing. Bones shattered and re-formed. Skin melted and healed. I screamed; I couldn't stop the flood of agony, or my body's primal, visceral response of horror.

The only part of me that didn't suffer was my left arm, from the forearm down. Instead, the fleshy disguise I'd adopted melted away, leaving a cold, gleaming bronze appendage in all its minutely crafted detail, down to the whorls of artificial fingerprints on metal fingers. I'd sliced away my arm to save myself, and replaced it with a Djinn-crafted duplicate; it seemed the only respite now from the pain Pearl and her children seemed intent on causing me.

I could move it, just a little.

By the time Zedala burned her way down my body, I had gained a foot in height, and my skin had been restored to its ivory color. My hair as well—it had grown out, and been bleached to its normal ice-white.

"There you are," Pearl said, and shrugged. "Or the human vessel of you, at least. Tell me, sister, how long since we've been together, even in our Djinn forms? Human time has no measure, does it? So long ago that you killed me."

I had killed her, or at least I'd believed it was so. And it had been the only possible response to her crimes, which had driven Mother Earth mad with pain. I'd destroyed her, and I'd thought I eradicated all traces of her . . . but some part of her survived, tenacious as the roots of a weed. It had taken her aeons to gather her strength, but finally she was here, present, physical again.

And deadly. So very, very deadly.

"These," she said, and placed a kiss on Zedala's braided hair, "are part of me now. They believe implicitly in my cause. They understand how dangerous the Djinn and the Wardens are. They are my warriors. My avatars. My *children*. And when the end comes—and it will come for you, Cassiel, for all of you—these will survive with me. Out of the ashes, a new Mother will rise."

My mouth went dry. "You."

"Yes. Of course. Who is more deserving?"

Pearl's ambition was greater, and more insane, than I'd ever dreamed. Not annihilation, as grandiose as that might be; she still planned to destroy the Wardens, the humans, the Djinn, and indeed all life, but she planned *more*. She planned to kill her own Mother, the life spirit of our planet, and she planned to *become* that life spirit.

A corrupted, damaged, evil spirit. I couldn't imagine what would spring forth from her, as she breathed her power over the dead land—whatever it would be, it would be nightmarish, twisted, and a perverse mockery of all the beauty and diversity of this world.

The Djinn didn't know this. Couldn't imagine it. If they had, if they'd been able to comprehend the danger, they would have bonded together to destroy her regardless of costs.

Even Ashan would have set aside his personal ambitions for that.

Now I had a new mission—not killing Pearl, although that was still my greatest goal. No, I had to get this knowledge out, to the Djinn, to the Wardens, to anyone who could take up arms and defend against her. I had no choice now but to survive, and run.

If I could.

"I won't insult you, or myself, by asking you to join me," Pearl continued. "I know you won't. There is a core of stubbornness in you, Cassiel, that does you no particular credit. I suppose some would see it as heroism; I see it as arrogance. You have no cause for that, dear sister. You're not nearly what you once were."

"Who is?"

She laughed, a golden bell of sound that sounded so lovely it was easy to forget the rotten darkness in her core. Pearl was seductive; that was why this camp existed, why these children had been so badly and fatally bent to her will. That was why, even now, the Djinn hesitated to move against her—that, and their own self-interested instincts.

Even I felt her attraction, and had ever since I'd stepped into this camp. Here, she put forth her charm, her glamour . . . and everyone responded. Even, I suspected, the human FBI had succumbed, outside the gates. Perhaps she'd merely made them decide to abandon their posts. I wouldn't have put it past her abilities, not anymore.

Merle had resisted. Look what that had earned him.

I had to get free. Somehow, insane as it was, I had to find a way out of this.

"She's plotting," the boy Earth Warden said—Pearl's personal executioner, as Zedala had become her personal torturer. "She's going to try something."

"Not yet," Pearl said serenely. "She's injured, and

she's alone. She'll bide her time. Cassiel is good at that. But I, my sister, am far, far better practiced." She bent over me, and brushed her smooth, damp, cool lips against mine. I resisted the urge to bite, only because it wouldn't help—or even hurt her. The touch gave me the truth of her human form—it was still artificial, not genuinely human. She didn't yet have the real power to create a body down to the cellular level. This was a shell only, lovely as it was. "If you're counting on your Warden lover, I wouldn't," she continued, still bent close to me. Her eyes were black, lid to lid, and shimmering like oil. "He won't leave the child's side, not to rescue you. And if he does, I'll have you all, won't I? Foster father . . . foster mother . . . and child."

"You'll never have Isabel," I said. "She's free now."

"You think so?" Pearl's smile was nauseating, seen at close range—not in the least human. She straightened, and glanced at Zedala.

"You'd better kill me," I said, and meant it. "If you don't, I promise you, I'll destroy you. At whatever cost."

"You can't do anything without power," Pearl said, "but I was planning to kill you, sister. No reason to waste you, though. My children need practice."

She nodded to the small black-haired boy, the one from whom I sensed no identifiable kind of Warden power at all . . . and he reached out a single finger, and touched me just as Zedala yanked her hand away from my forehead.

Void.

His power was its absence. He lived and breathed, but what filled him was cut off from the roots of life. He existed without connection, and as his touch bridged the gulf between us, I felt the organic parts of me being shredded into rags, lost in a vortex of hungry emptiness. I couldn't even scream. There were no human sounds for the agony of cells imploding into absolute nothingness.

It would be slow, and I would feel every second.

I was going to die, in a way more painful than I'd ever imagined, and more thorough than any other kind of death. It would devour the very Djinn nature of me. It would erase me.

And there was nothing at all I could do to stop it.

Chapter 12

THE DJINN PART OF ME, the Cassiel part, was no more than a whisper, but it did not want to die. I felt it flow through me in a silvery thread, coiling in the power that I could now reach, since Zedala had withdrawn her block—but the power couldn't survive against the black-hole pull of the Void.

The organics of my body were coming apart. Instead, the power flowed into my inert metal hand.

I was no longer consciously directing the power; it was driven by Djinn instinct, by the primal need to survive. My metal hand malformed, changed, and re-formed into a sharp-edged metal blade, which sliced through the bonds holding my left hand and foot to the bed where I lay.

And then my Djinn self, my cold and true self, slashed the blade through the air toward Pearl's lovely shell. It sliced through her neck, and her body collapsed in a nauseatingly empty sack of meat—lacking organs, bones, muscles. Just a shell of flesh, and the power inside escaped.

The mocking echo of her laughter remained.

I had no choice of what to do next. I slashed across my body, and cut off the finger of the Void conduit where it pressed against my skull.

The boy screamed and fell backward. He sounded

like a wounded child, not a vicious empty *thing*, and for a fatal second, I hesitated with my blade ready for a killing stroke.

That gave Zedala time to lunge forward and grab my arm. A burst of star-hot power blew through the metal, heating it into dripping slag. I threw her off, but it was too late; the moment was gone. The Void child still cowered in shock, but the others were on me.

The Earth Warden boy slapped his hands flat on my chest, and drove me down, down through the metal frame of the bed, down into the wooden floor of the room, down into the hard-packed dirt beneath.

Down into the rock.

I was blind here, but I had power again, and softened the rock and earth to loose, slippery sand, taking away his momentum. We struggled together, lost in the earth. He tried to use his control to shatter my bones, but here, in my element, he couldn't find an easily exploited vulnerability.

I was weak from the Void attack, and still suffering from the beating I'd taken from Zedala. He finally focused on that point of weakness, and I felt his power pushing at it, trying to shatter the cracked skull like an eggshell. If he drove bone into my fragile human brain, I'd be lost. I had to fight, but my strength wasn't unlimited, and in the heat of battle I couldn't draw on Luis, not at this distance.

I was losing.

Something flowed past me, like a shark through water, and slammed bodily into the boy. On the aetheric I saw it as a hard human-shaped light in cool gray, overlaid with the elusive watery spectrum of a Djinn. The boy was fighting it, whatever it was, but for the moment, at least, I was free.

I used the last of my strength to claw myself up at an angle, away from the building where I'd been held, and found the soft, turned earth of the field. I broke the surface and crawled toward the fence. My skull was on fire, and I felt cold and sluggish. I'd bled too much, both in plasma and in power. I had very little left. My mutilated left hand, now just a misshapen, melted blog of metal, made it difficult to claw forward.

Someone tried to grab me and pull me backward. Zedala, who'd chased me. I used the blunt, twisted club that had once been my metallic hand and slammed it into her, and she went down with a scream.

I touched the cold metal of the fence, but I didn't have enough power left to do more than bend the links.

Trapped.

I felt that human/Djinn presence cutting through the soil beneath me, and it erupted in a spray of dirt like a geyser.

Will. It was *Will.*

He grabbed my shoulders even as the fence blew outward in a spray of melted metal behind me, and dragged me through to the other side. Zedala had rolled to her feet, feral and furious; the blood on her face only added to the savagery of her expression. As she lunged at Will, he drew back his hand, gathered power, and threw it in a tight, silver ball at her chest. It hit her and slammed her backward to the soft earth. She slapped at it, trying to throw it off, but it ate its relentless, merciless way through her body until she lay still and silent in the dirt.

Will's face was smeared with dirt and mud, and now I recognized his eyes, those gray, emotionless eyes. I recognized the implacable rage with which he'd just killed the girl.

He turned it on the boy Earth Warden, who lunged up from the dirt and took a tearing grip on my hair. I didn't see what happened to the boy, but I felt it. I saw the blood explosion on the aetheric, and saw his violent streaming colors go pale, then black.

"Stop," I whispered. "Ashan, *stop.*"

"No," he said, and kept dragging me. "They have to be destroyed. All of these abominations must be *ended!*"

"No!"

He dropped the human disguise of Will, abandoning the warmth, the sweetness, the lovely and seductive illusion. What was left was the prince of the Old Djinn, a cold silver flame of fury barely contained by a human-shaped shell. My brother. My king.

He was also a cruel, conscienceless murderer, and now he turned that focus to the boy containing the Void, who was coming after the two of us with a fanatic's disregard for personal safety.

The boy could kill a Djinn. Easily.

"Don't touch him!" I screamed to Ashan. "He'll destroy you!"

Ashan, who'd been reaching out to rip the boy in half, spun away at the last moment. The boy's grasping hand brushed Ashan's side, and I saw a black gouge appear in his body. He twisted away, and the shout of pain vibrated on the aetheric, and snapped branches from trees in the physical world. Ashan stumbled back and, with a fluid motion, caught one of the large, heavy falling branches. He let its momentum spin him, threw physical force into it, and slammed the branch home into the boy's body.

I heard the wet snap of breaking bones, and tried to roll to my knees. I managed that much, but my balance failed as I tried to climb to my feet. I grabbed the trunk of a tree and watched as the boy—crippled now—clawed his way on, still determined to destroy Ashan no matter the cost.

"Stop!" I screamed again, as Ashan lifted the branch for a killing blow. "Ashan, *no*, not this way—"

He didn't listen. I turned my head at the last moment, but that didn't block out the sound of the impact of the branch, or the boy's choked last gasp. "No," I whispered, but there was no strength in it, or in me.

Ashan grabbed me and lifted me in his arms, and I saw the last of Pearl's chosen children, the tiny Weather girl, summoning power in both hands with a dexterity that was chillingly beyond her years. Beyond her, the camp was massing—people I had known, and liked, armed with whatever they could find. They would rush us, kill us if they could. The fury was like fire in the wind.

Ashan looked down at me, and for a second I saw Will, the man I had felt such kinship to—and then Will was gone and only Ashan remained.

"Hold on," he said, and stepped into the aetheric just as lightning exploded where we had been, burning a crater twenty feet deep in the smoking earth.

Make no mistake: I do not like Ashan. Even among the Djinn, Ashan inspired fear, not love; his arrogance— and his power—were legendary. He had, however unwillingly, bowed his head to one Djinn only, and when Jonathan had been destroyed, he owed loyalty to no one. He'd claimed by right to rule, after, and I had never contested that, though I could have. So could Venna, the oldest of my siblings, but we were both content to be what we were, and allow him his power.

That didn't mean we liked him. It meant we respected him.

In this moment, though, weak and fragile as I felt, overwhelmed as I was, I loved him and hated him with an intensity that made me want to weep bitter human tears. I clung to him as we passed in a mist through the aetheric, speeding away from the camp. Most Djinn couldn't bring humans through the aetheric, not intact, but Ashan could, when he wished.

Which was seldom, if ever.

We stepped out into night ... a thick, full, velvety

darkness, somewhere far enough from human civilization that no hint of lights glimmered, save the stars. The wind hissed through the pines, and Ashan bent to lay me down on a bed of fallen leaves. Starlight painted him in stark contrasts—his eyes had turned full silver now, his skin almost the pale color of mine. We looked like kindred now, except that his beauty was Djinn to the core, remote and hard, and mine was soft and frail and broken.

"You pretended to be human. To be Will," I said. "Why?"

"Like you, I wanted to see," he said. "I wanted to know what she was doing, and why. I couldn't depend on you, Cassiel. I had thought I could, but you began to care too much for them. You aren't as you were when I sent you here."

"Neither are you," I said. "You feigned a human far too well not to have liked being in his skin. I thought we both despised them."

"We both did," he said. "But perhaps you're right. We've both changed."

"You knew who I was all along. You recognized me."

"No," he said, and turned away to stare up at the stars. "I didn't know, not at first. I felt . . . something. But you disguised yourself well, just as I had. We both fooled her, for a time—and we fooled each other as well."

"We won't fool her again."

"No, not again. She's beyond playing coy now." He turned back to me. "What did she tell you?"

"What we knew: She plans to destroy us. All living things. Even the Mother." I pulled in a painful breath, and tasted blood in the back of my mouth. "She plans to take her place."

That froze him. I had rarely seen Ashan surprised; I'd *never* seen him afraid, but this time, I saw a flash of real alarm blaze around him in the aetheric. He controlled it almost as swiftly and said, "Do you think she could?"

"I don't know," I confessed, and rolled on my side to cough. Something in my side hurt, and I spat up blood. "I need to rest."

"Rest won't help you," Ashan said. "You're broken." He said it with a remote kind of recognition, nothing more, but when he knelt down and touched me, his hand felt warm and almost gentle. "Stay still."

"I don't need your help."

He smiled, sharp as a knife. "Then I should have left you there to their mercies. My apologies, Cassiel. I didn't realize you had the situation so well in hand."

I stubbornly reached out to Luis through the frail connection between us, and felt it snap apart with a painful jolt. Terror bolted through me, and I sat up, heedless of my injuries. "No!" I rose up into the aetheric, flailing to regain that thread between us, but it was gone, melted away.

He was gone.

"You don't need him anymore," Ashan was saying, down in the human world. "No need to humble yourself further, my sister. You understand now the gravity of the situation, and what has to be done. I won't have you tethered to a human, not with what you must do. I can be merciful."

I stared at him with deadened eyes. "You cut the link." He didn't answer. "Give it back, Ashan. Now."

"No."

"Give it back."

"You've played human long enough, Cassiel. Enough of that. Take back your place, and do what you have to do."

"Do it yourself!" I snarled. The anger in me had a sickening quality to it, a nightmare intensity. More than that, my human body was starting to fail, and he knew it. "Kill them *yourself* if you think it's so vital!"

"I can't," Ashan said. "It will destroy me, and I'm the True Djinn's connection to the Mother. It'll poison all of them. You know that."

I hadn't thought of it in such terms, but he was right. Ashan risked bringing down the Djinn if he struck at the humans, and that was why he needed me to do it.

Because I was, at the last, expendable.

I felt the pressure that had held me in human flesh suddenly ease, like a door coming open in an airless room. The relief of that was intense and shattering. Flesh was a cage, a prison, and now I could abandon it, rise up to the aetheric and stay there, where I belonged. If I wished to visit this plane, I could descend like an angel at will. Or abandon it completely.

He was offering me my eternal life back, something that I had longed for, something I *needed*.

It was like being dropped in water after an eternity of thirst. I'd forgotten how it felt, to be so free, so pure, so utterly complete.

It was more seductive than anything I had ever known.

I kept staring at him, reading ages and distances in his silver eyes. He was old, Ashan. Very old. Very powerful. We had that in common, still. We had so much history that we had witnessed.

He thought he knew me.

But in this, this one simple thing, we were completely different, because I had breathed, wept, bled, *lived*. And he never had, not fully. Not even at the camp, when he pretended to be Will. I could see it in him now, that lack of empathy and understanding; it was possible he *could* learn, but he had *not* learned. Not yet.

I wanted to let go, to succumb to that soft, welcoming

embrace of the eternal. I wanted to be what I had been, vast and powerful and perfect.

But part of me was always going to be here, in the dirt, in the blood, in the sweat and heaviness of a body. There was a strength and a power in that, too. One Ashan couldn't really understand.

And it allowed me to close the door between us.

"No," I said again, softly but very firmly. "I won't abandon them. I can't."

Ashan stared. I had, again, surprised him. "Not even to save us. Not even to save the *Mother*."

I was silent on that point. I pressed a shaking hand to my injured side. The pain turned glassy and sharp. Broken ribs, I imagined. The head injury had taken on a remote, unreal aspect; I still felt blood trickling down my neck and matting in my hair, but the pain had subsided to a dull, throbbing ache. I didn't know if that was better or worse.

Ashan was considering what I'd said. He finally shook his head. "You're not in your right mind," he said. "You're injured."

It was kind of him to notice. "It doesn't matter if I'm injured or healthy. I won't kill them. If you want them dead, do it yourself."

"One of us must lead," he said. "We've always agreed that it would be me, Cassiel. Always. And a leader must order others into battle."

I felt a cold wave of anger push back the simple human anguish of my injuries, and I looked up sharply at him. "Maybe it's time for a change," I said.

He laughed. "You won't fight me. Look at you. You can't stand on your own, and you refused my gift. You can hardly exist at all."

I climbed slowly to my feet, moving with great deliberation. I didn't wince, even when the pain bit deep;

I didn't allow so much as a flicker of hesitation. I never looked away from him as I stood, unaided, and faced him.

The wind bent the trees around us, and pitiless starlight rained down. The silence seemed to stretch for an eternity.

"All right, enough," Ashan said, finally. "I never doubted your stubbornness. Only your ability."

"I have ability," I replied. "And will. And I don't need more than that."

"I'm not battling you. It isn't the time, or the place." Ashan's pale lips twitched into a brief, very cool smile. "If you would be polite enough to wait, it's more than likely I will be destroyed soon enough. We live in a dangerous world, Cassiel. And all of us will pay a price for survival, if we survive at all."

"I've never heard you say such things." Ashan was, after all, self-interested and a coward first, before all things except his protection of the Mother herself. That made him less of a pessimist than most.

"There has never been such a time," he said. His tone was calm and dispassionate, and all the more powerful for it. "The disease the Wardens have brought to this world may destroy us yet; even Pearl has taken advantage of it, in her use of the Void. With Pearl seeking our destruction at the same time as the Wardens' mortal enemies, do you really believe we can win without great loss?"

"I'm only surprised you even consider that *you* may be one of those losses."

He bared his teeth in an almost genuine smile. "David has no reason to protect me."

"Nor you him, though it hasn't seemed to have worried him a great deal."

David, the leader of the New Djinn, probably bothered far less about Ashan than Ashan did about David;

I suspected that David's intense and legendary love for the human Warden Joanne Baldwin had wakened both contempt and confusion within my brother, which manifested in—predictably, for Ashan—real hatred. David, from the few encounters I'd had with him, held little or none.

My attempt to show strength was spoiled as my knees weakened. My body gave me no real warning—a thick wave of dizziness, and then I felt myself falling. I put out my hands to brace myself—or my one human hand, and the misshapen lump of bronze that weighed down my left arm—but I never hit the ground. Instead, Ashan stepped forward, caught me, and eased me down to a kneeling position. I was having difficulty breathing—my lungs felt thick and wet—but I still managed to wheeze, "This is how you like me, on my knees to you," before I began to cough, explosive mouthfuls of hot blood.

Ashan made a sound of frustration, and I felt a cold silvery power glide through me, from the crown of my head downward. I tried to resist it, but his touch was seductive and powerful, and the comfort it left behind it was so extreme that I felt an urge to weep. I didn't. My eyes were dry by the time Ashan stepped back, and I looked at myself disorientingly from the aetheric.

My head still ached, but the broken skull was fused together, and the ragged tear in my scalp had closed. The broken ribs had likewise reset, and the blood in my lungs was gone. He hadn't bothered with my collections of bruises, but overall, I was in sound condition, considering my recent injuries.

"I could have destroyed your physical body," he said. "But I wasn't sure that even at the last, you'd choose to regain your rightful place. This has to stop. I need you with me, Cassiel. We can't allow Pearl to pursue this course, and there's still only one way to stop her."

"Genocide," I said.

"Extinction," he corrected me. "As it has been before, as it will be again. It's the reason we were created, to protect the Mother. And we will, with or without you."

I got off my knees. "Then you'll do it without me," I said, brushing the dirt from my filthy, shapeless gray uniform with both hands . . . and only then did I realize that he'd repaired my metallic left hand. I left it to the faint starlight, examining the finely detailed flexible metal skin, the precise movements of the metal fingers. He'd done a better job of it than I had, originally. I rubbed my fingertips together, and the sensation that came to me was absolutely realistic. Except for the warm matte color of my forearm and hand, it might have been the original appendage.

"That's a gift," he said, nodding toward it. "And I think you'll find that in the end you'll know I was right about the humans. They were a mistake, and they need correcting."

I sensed he was about step into the aetheric and leave me behind. "Wait! My connection to Luis. Restore it."

He met my eyes, and in his silver ones I read a trace of the man I'd liked, back in the camp. A trace of regret, and kindness. Then Ashan blinked, and it vanished. "Very well," he said. "But you won't like what you find. I was trying to spare you the pain."

I felt a hot snap inside—not something breaking, this time, but something reforging. It burned, then cooled, and I felt . . . nothing for a few seconds.

Then, distantly, I felt pain, echoing through the connection like a scream from a long distance away. Pain, anguish, fury, fear.

I opened my eyes and stared at Ashan. "What have you *done*?"

"Nothing," he said. "You destroyed Pearl's brightest acolytes. Did you think she would simply let that go? She's like you. Emotional."

The shock of it wore off, and now the dread set in, heavy and black in the pit of my stomach.

I'd done this. *We'd* done this. Luis was under attack, injured, maybe dying. I had a flash of Manny Rocha, my first Warden partner, dying in a hail of bullets while I'd stood at a distance, unable to save him—only this was more intense, worse, because what I felt for Luis—no, the *love* I felt for him—left me horrified, frantic, and desperate.

I *had* to save him.

Ashan was already beginning to fade away. "No!" I screamed, and lunged for him. His form was solid, then softened into mist. For an instant he stood in his True Djinn form, something human eyes weren't meant to comprehend. I had to look away.

"Please," I said. "Please take me there. *Please*, Ashan. I will beg, if that's what you want."

"It isn't," he said, and I felt him slip away, into the aetheric. Only his voice remained, a whisper on the wind. "I want you to remember what it means to be one of us, not one of them. If you'd chosen to join me, you could have saved him. You could have saved them all."

And then he was gone, and I was alone, cold and alone, in an unknown forest.

And far away from me, my love was fighting for his life.

I let out a scream that shook leaves from the trees, and began to run.

I had only gone perhaps a mile before I ran into Ashan again, standing in my path, shining like the moon. He looked at me strangely, as if he'd never seen me before.

"You run," he said. "You have no idea where you are, and yet you run."

I could feel Luis's presence, like a compass tugging me onward. I didn't slow down, only ran around Ashan's still form and kept going. I didn't know how far it was; I only knew that I couldn't risk *not* trying.

If Luis died, I would die with him, one way or another. And I would wish it to be so.

Ashan, again, standing near the trunk of a massive, shadowed tree. I was remotely thankful for his presence, as he illuminated a hidden branch that stretched across the trail and might have tripped me. I vaulted it and kept running. "You won't make it!" he called after me. "Cassiel!"

He was lying to me. I had to believe he was lying.

And so I ran. I ran until I was breathless, shaking, covered in sweat. I ran until my muscles trembled with exhaustion. Ashan continued to appear like a ghost in the darkness, silently watching me.

I didn't stop, until with Djinn suddenness he formed right in my path, close enough that I had to slide to a flailing halt to avoid hitting him. He caught me silently when I faltered, and held me there, staring down at me. He was dressed in an immaculate gray suit now, human but with an inhuman perfection to him. His eyes, and his tie, were teal blue, with glints of silver. I had never felt so grubbily human as that moment, face-to-face with the eerie beauty of what I'd left behind.

"Enough," he said. "If you must destroy yourself, do it in battle, not . . . like this. Not uselessly."

And he whirled me away into a nauseating swirl of color, sound, taste, the rancid scent of death . . . and out again, into a blast of cold air, smoke, and the roar of fire.

I tripped over a corpse and fell face forward into bloody, churned ground.

Chapter 13

THE CORPSE I'D TRIPPED over was someone I didn't recognize—a man, dressed in dark clothing. He had a rifle with him, and a handgun holstered on his belt. I tugged it free, picked up the rifle, and slung it across my shoulder as I rose to my knees.

Ashan had brought me back to the school, but the school was unrecognizable. It was a burning inferno, only vaguely defined by the shapes of walls; the fire was incredibly hot and violent, with the flames in places leaping fifty feet into the night sky. Trees burned from their leafy crowns downward all around me. At first I thought that the school had been in the path of a forest fire, but that made no sense; there were powerful Fire Wardens present who should have been able to turn the flames away, even if they hadn't been able to extinguish them completely.

No, this was an attack.

And a successful one.

I didn't hear the sound of the shot fired at me, but I felt the bullet slice across the meat of my upper arm, drawing a bloody slash; it felt like a hot poker applied to my skin, and for a second I didn't register what had occurred. My instincts saved me; I threw myself flat and crawled to take the only shelter available—behind the corpse that I'd fallen over earlier. I rolled him on his side and curled up, unshipped the rifle, and carefully looked around for my assailant. It was impossible to hear the shots, but I saw a spark of misplaced flame from the trees—a muzzle flash in the darkness—and aimed and fired, using the power of the Earth to guide my shot to its target.

I sensed the shock of the bullet's impact through bone, brain, and out the other side as my shot found its home, and then I took another moment to study the scene more carefully. He seemed to have been the only remaining gunman, or the one assigned to prevent reinforcements from arriving; no one else fired on me.

But I felt a harsh ripple on the aetheric, and turned toward it just as I saw the trees bending, whipping, and cracking. Something was coming for me, coming fast, and it was big. Very big.

I glimpsed something dark, but it wasn't an animal; the power driving it felt alien at its core, cold and lifeless. *Void.* Someone was driving a moving sphere of void through the forest, devouring all it touched, and it was heading straight for me.

I couldn't fight that, and it was too late to run. I got up to my feet, took three long steps, and prepared myself. There was a dead tree trunk lying at an angle nearby, and I ran for it, up its incline, and on the last step channeled power into my legs and jumped.

The black sphere charged through the space where I'd been while I hung at the apogee of my jump, fifty feet overhead, and then landed crouched on the branch of a tree above. It hesitated, circling, and then zipped off in a different direction. It had found another target, and I heard someone scream.

It was quickly cut off.

From this vantage, with the treetop aflame above me, I could see the devastation wrought on the Wardens' stronghold. The attack had shredded the metal fencing around the building, but it was the building itself that had sustained the most damage—concrete walls shattered, wood burned away, and now almost every part of the interior seemed to be burning with a white-hot intensity that was at odds with a normal blaze. It was being fed by a Fire Warden of abnormal power and concentration . . . one of Pearl's, I imagined. I could feel the dark shimmer of her power in the air, though I couldn't locate her presence.

Evidently her adept that was managing the Void was less well equipped, because after several moments the black sphere faltered, smashed through a few more unlucky trees, then abruptly shrank to a pinpoint and vanished with an implosive *pop* louder even than the roar of the fire. I jumped down from the tree and began hunting for the rest of Pearl's attacking force.

Instead, I saw a Warden—one I recognized, though I didn't know her name—waving at me frantically as she rose from behind the cover of some bushes and dropped what must have been a very, very good veil. I raced to her, keeping low, and as I ducked behind the brush I saw that she wasn't alone—she had dozens with her, including most of the other Wardens. Almost all of them were injured or exhausted from the fight. "Thank God," she said. She was holding a bloody bandage to her side, and offered me a real, though tense, smile of welcome. "I'm Gayle."

I nodded, scanning the weary faces. "Where are the rest?" There were too few children, and no sign of Luis and Ibby. Gayle's smile faded, and she looked back at the burning inferno of the school.

"I'm sorry," she said. "We couldn't reach them. Marion, Janice, Luis, Shasa, Ben—at least five of the kids. We tried, but we were under attack. We had to save those we could reach. I'm so sorry."

I shouldn't have blamed them for that, but in that

moment I felt a surge of pure hatred nevertheless. *You left them to die.* Gayle must have known that, must have seen it burning in my eyes, but to her credit, she didn't back away. Maybe she was simply too tired, and too badly wounded.

I turned away and stared at the burning ruins. Adrenaline and fear made it difficult to sort out my emotions, but I calmed myself and listened, listened for that tiny whisper that always existed—that fragile yet steely-strong connection with Luis.

I felt a discordant jangle of emotions not my own.

Alive. He was alive, somewhere in there.

I opened my eyes, turned to Gayle, and said, "They're inside. We must get them out."

She looked at her exhausted, wounded band, and the huddled, frightened children they protected. "I can't. I'm sorry, but we have to concentrate on protecting these kids. We can't go back in there. I have only one living Fire Warden, and she's badly injured."

I couldn't fault her logic, or her judgment, but I wasn't willing to accept defeat that easily. Not when it meant the lives of those I loved. "Then watch my back," I said. I handed her the rifle, and she checked the clip with a competence that gave me confidence.

"Good luck." She nodded. "If you can get them out, head for the fire road to the east. If everything works right, we should have rescue transportation coming in the next twenty minutes, but we can't wait for you for long if it means risking the lives of those we already have."

I rolled to my feet and ran, keeping low, around the side of the school. The flames weren't as intense here—in fact, part of the wall seemed intact, though heavy iron gray smoke poured through shattered windows. The door was open, and two small bodies lay huddled together on the bare ground outside.

I ran for the fence, still largely intact on this side, ripped it apart with Earth power, and left it dangling open behind me as I scooped up the two children and dragged them away from danger. Both were almost unrecognizable under the thick layers of soot on their faces, but I knew the bright red blaze of her hair—the girl was Gillian. It took me longer to work out the boy's identity, but of course it was Mike, her constant companion and protector.

Mike was dead. I checked him to be sure, and tried all the techniques I knew to revive the boy, but his spirit was gone, and his body unresponsive. He'd been badly burned, his lungs scorched beyond any survival. Mike, the Fire Warden, had been overwhelmed by the blaze he'd tried to manage.

But he'd saved Gillian—no doubt at his own expense. She was unconscious, and suffering from smoke inhalation, but alive. I poured power into her to stabilize her condition, and then plunged back through the fence and handed her off to Gayle, who put her with the other injured children.

The door into the building was firmly closed and blazing hot, but so far there were no flames at the window where the two children must have escaped—only a thick black river of smoke pouring out.

I climbed in.

The smoke closed around me like hot, smothering cloth, and I immediately dropped to the floor to try to find anything like breathable air. It was there, but very thin and tasting of toxins. I couldn't see well—between the billows of gray and the dazzling leap of fire on the far wall, it took me a moment to realize that I'd dropped into some kind of library. Books were aflame at the far end of the room. A plastic chair and table were in place, but melting into surrealistic shapes as the flames approached. I crawled, feeling the synthetic carpet clinging and sticky beneath me. It, too, was melting from the heat. Breathing turned more difficult as I approached the far doorway; there were flames pouring through it, but moving along the ceiling, and only gradually descending toward the walls.

Still possible, if not safe.

In the hallway, I came across another body—a Warden. It was young Ben. He'd been shot in the back three times—center chest twice and once in the head. Dead. I left him and crawled on, not knowing if it was even possible to find the others. All I knew was that Luis, at least, was still alive, somewhere in this inferno.

And I had to find him. I couldn't leave him to face this alone.

At the end of the hallway, a curtain of intensely hot flames burned—intensely hot, and oddly *directed*. Focused. Pearl's attackers were focusing their efforts here, which meant that there was some reason for it.

Someone was conducting a spirited and lasting defense.

It was counterintuitive to head *for* the worst of the blaze—not to mention insane—but I sensed the roil of power that overlaid the conflagration. That wasn't merely fire ahead of me; it was a weapon, wielded by a master.

And there was an equally expert defense, mounted from the other side.

I had no protection I could summon up for the risk of burning, but there was no question in my mind of turning back. Luis was beyond that thick wall of destruction. *Isabel* would be there with him.

And I would not abandon them.

I should have taken Ashan's offer. As a Djinn, I could have entered this fight with significant advantages ... but at the risk of losing what made me *want* to fight so hard. It was the losses I'd suffered that made me part of this world; Djinn had no such connection. Not the Djinn I had known, or been.

I couldn't give up my hard-won humanity for power. I had to find a way. I rose to a crouch, readied myself, and closed my eyes.

And then I raced forward, into the fire.

Humans have an atavistic terror of burning, and I hadn't counted on it being so strongly encoded in the cells of my body, but the instant I felt the flames hiss through my hair and clothes, my body went into terrified overdrive, releasing massive amounts of adrenaline, blocking out pain. The world shrank to a single, unalterable imperative: *run*.

And I ran, straight and fast, through a roaring fury of heat. Even with the deadening influence of the adrenaline, I distantly felt the lash of pain as my clothing caught fire and burned around me. Every step forward seemed to take a nightmare hour, though it couldn't have been more than a few seconds before I hit the barrier at the end of the fire.

It was an impenetrable barrier of stone, flung up out of the Earth's bones.

I couldn't stop. I reached out to Luis and pulled an enormous, crippling flood of power that melted the stone in front of me in a rippling wave. It was extraordinarily dangerous, and I felt the pressure being exerted from the other side to block me out. The stone hardened, and I faced a nightmare possibility of being trapped, sealed in the rock, crushed . . . but then the pressure fell away, and I tumbled through into hot, smoky air that felt as cold as ice against my scorched body. I hit the smoldering wooden floor and rolled. Someone threw thick cloth over me, and I felt hands slapping at me, trying to douse the flames. At the same time, someone sent an enormous burst of power toward the stone wall through which I'd come, to seal it shut again.

The first face I saw as the blanket was withdrawn was Luis's. His eyes widened, and his lips parted in either horror or astonishment—it could have been either, given my current state—but then he pulled me up to a sitting position and hugged me fiercely. The adrenaline was fading as quickly as it had dumped into my bloodstream, and the pain that flashed through me was agonizing . . . and then muted, as his healing power began to do its work.

No, not just his power . . . Isabel's, as well. She was beside me, too, and her hand was resting on my shoulder. The two complex signatures of power, as distinctive as types of wine, mixed inside me and exploded in a powerful new way, driving my cells to heal at a dizzying rate.

I hugged them both close, shuddering in shock and gratitude, and felt Isabel's arms wind around my neck. *Oh, child. Beautiful child.* I kissed Luis quickly, put my hand on his unshaven cheek, and said, "Ben's dead. So is the boy, Mike. Gillian is alive—I got her outside the fence. Gayle has most of the others hidden outside, waiting for transportation."

"We've got almost everyone else," Luis said. "It happened fast. I don't know how; Ben must have been taken out first just as the fireworks got started. They meant to burn us all."

I didn't think so. I looked up at the others, who were sitting or lying in the small defensive space left to them. Marion still had her wheelchair, and she took time to spare me a quick look from her maintenance of the barrier that held back the ravening fire. "Thanks for joining us," she said. "But it might not have been a good idea. We're not doing so well."

She was right about that; the situation looked bad. Earth could defend against Fire, but not for long. Ben's Weather skills had been their best possible option; he could have kept the air fresh and clear, and starved the fire, given enough time and power.

The elderly Earth Warden, Janice, was in charge of the children, who were huddled close against her for comfort. She'd put two of them under, and they seemed to be sleeping with unnatural peacefulness. When I met Janice's eyes, she said, "We can't have them panicking." And she was right about that; having these extraordinary children losing control of their talents here, now, would be deadly to us all.

Isabel tugged on my sleeve. I looked down at her in distracted affection and kissed her forehead, but she only tugged harder. She leaned in and whispered in my ear, "We're in trouble."

"I know that, Ibby."

"No, we're in *trouble*. Really."

"Can you get through the fire and get out?"

"Sure," she said, and shrugged. "But I can't get anybody else out. They'll let me go; they already told me so. And Sanjay and Elijah, too. But nobody else. And I can't leave Uncle Luis."

"You may have to," I told her. "You may have to take the other two and leave, if they'll let you."

She gave me a long, sober look. "That's what they want us to do. They want us to go back to the Lady."

My arms tightened around her. I thought of Zedala, of those other fanatical children; Ibby, Sanjay, and Elijah would make perfect assassins, if she continued their indoctrination. I couldn't allow that to happen to them.

But at least they'd be alive. My alternative might be to watch them die in a particularly horrible way.

I turned to Luis, but he was moving toward Marion, who was beckoning for his help. He was limping, and there was a broad, bloody stain on the leg of his pants. A bullet wound, but one he was managing well.

Ben had also been shot, from behind, by someone he must have trusted. He'd been heading to join Marion, or to warn her. "Ibby," I said. "You said we were in trouble. You didn't mean the fire, did you?"

"I saw her shoot him," Ibby said, still in that tense, quiet whisper. "I didn't know how to stop it. You should have showed me how to stop the bullets from exploding, and I could have stopped her from killing Ben. But it was too late then. I couldn't bring him back. Nobody else saw it, and I don't think she knows that I know."

My gaze moved around the room, and fell on Shasa, who was deep in concentration, hands held palms out. She was sending waves of control against the fire, but whatever or whoever directed it against us was stronger. She was shaking, and damp with sweat as much from effort as heat.

"Not her," Ibby whispered. *"Her."*

I turned and met Janice Worthing's calm, kind eyes— only in that instant they weren't calm, or kind. Only blank with calculation. And I felt something go still and very quiet inside me.

I had known. On some level, I'd been uneasy with the woman, though everything and everyone around me had given the lie to that instinct. I should have listened to my Djinn side, I realized, the cynical and mistrustful side that had refused to be swayed and charmed by her subtle use of power.

Janice Worthing had been the traitor in the heart of the school, and no one, not even Marion, had suspected her. I wondered how long she'd been waiting to strike— months, maybe years. Maybe she'd been an early convert of Pearl's, or maybe she'd simply been for hire. She didn't, even now, strike me as a true believer—more of a mercenary.

She was holding little Elijah, the youngest of the children, in her arms. He'd been sent into a deep artificial sleep; to all appearances, her cradling of his body was gentle and protective, but suddenly I saw it differently.

Suddenly, Elijah was a shield.

"Let go," I said to Ibby. She shook her head. "Ibby, let go and go to your uncle. I don't want you to get hurt." This was, in many ways, more dangerous than anything else that might have happened . . . that the traitor was locked in here with us, in this desperate last stand, ready to strike at will. I wondered why she hadn't done it already, but I thought I knew. She didn't dare strike until she could ensure that she would take out *all* of the remaining Wardens in one blow—Marion, Luis, Shasa, and now me, to complicate her problem. Janice's mission must have been to gather the most powerful children and bring them out alive to Pearl.

She'd gathered them. Now she simply had to kill the rest of us to ensure her victory.

I peeled Isabel's arms away from my neck and pointed her at Luis. "Stay with him," I said, and she backed toward him, never taking her wide dark eyes from Janice.

Janice cocked her head slightly to one side, and I saw the recognition in her eyes. She knew that I knew, and that Ibby did as well. Her charade was ending.

"Well," she said, "it was nice while it lasted." She extended one hand toward Luis, and the bullet wound in his thigh suddenly broke open, pumping bright red blood in a fountain. Ibby stopped, shocked, and backed away from the spatter in instinctive horror. Luis let out a choked cry and grabbed for his thigh, squeezing with both hands; Marion spun her chair toward him and slapped her hand atop his. She was splitting her concentration dangerously, and as I'd noted when I'd left the school, she'd already been tired. She had to pull away as a fresh attack pounded against the stone walls she'd

thrown up, and the bleeding increased again as Luis
sank down to a sitting position on the floor. Ibby ran to
him and put her hand on his shoulder.

"No, no, Isabel, you're in no shape to do that kind
of work," Janice said, and I felt a subtle, wrong shift in
the energy coming from her. The edges of it brushed me,
and I felt sick, wrong, *twisted* . . . but it wasn't directed
at me.

It was directed at Isabel, who screamed and dropped
to the floor beside her uncle, writhing in the grip of one
of those seizures I'd witnessed before.

Janice had induced it. Deliberately.

I snarled and turned on her, every instinct—Djinn and
human—screaming inside me to destroy the woman . . .
but I couldn't. She had Elijah's neck in her hands, and
the boy was asleep. He couldn't fight back.

"I'll flay you," I said, with an eerie control that I
didn't feel. "I'll flay you and feed your skin to the pigs
while you watch. *Stop hurting them.*"

"Back off, and I will," Janice snapped. "Ah, ah, Marion, stay where you are. Don't make me start thinning
the herd."

Marion's face was frightening to behold, but she
stopped her slow advance toward Janice. I could feel her
gathering up her power, getting ready to strike, but like
me, she was at a severe disadvantage.

As long as Janice had the children gathered around
her, we were limited in what we could do.

Shasa's concentration broke as the situation in the
room finally dawned on her. She opened her eyes, startled, and glanced at Janice with a frown. "What the hell
is going on?" It was only at that moment that I realized
how much Shasa's power had kept the ravening inferno
at bay around us; smoke poured through tiny cracks in
the stone, and the rock itself snapped and hissed under
the pressure of the heat. Marion's barrier couldn't ex-

ist for long without Fire Warden assistance. "Janice? What's she talking about?"

"Nothing," Janice said in that warm, soothing voice that had lulled so many into trust. "She's a traitor, Shas. She's one of them. She left us to give them intel, and now she's back to finish the job. She brought this on us, and we let her inside."

That held just enough truth to distract Shasa for another critical moment . . . and then Janice extended her hand and tapped the Fire Warden on the shoulder. Just a light tap, but I felt the cold breath of power settle around the girl.

Shasa collapsed as her eyes rolled back in her skull. She looked fragile, suddenly, like a broken doll. Without her power supporting it, the defenses around us began to snap and shift under the pressure of the forces outside.

Pearl's forces.

My lips peeled back from my teeth. I glanced over at Luis, who looked pale and shaking, but he'd stripped off his belt and was twisting it around his thigh, attempting to slow the loss of blood. Isabel had collapsed against his side, trembling and writhing in the grip of the seizures, and the sight of that fueled my rage to dangerous levels.

I turned to Janice. "Put Elijah down," I said. "Now. Or I destroy you. You're no match for me."

"Oh, you're right about that," she replied, and gave me her sweet little grandmotherly smile. I almost preferred Zedala's fanaticism, in that moment; Janice's violence and cruelty were coldly calculated, and in a sense that made it all the more horrible. "But then again, I've got some advantages, don't I? If you want the bleeding to stop, and Ibby to survive this latest attack . . . you'll stand aside. I can call off the attack. We can arrange a peaceful exchange—these children for your lives."

"And yours."

"Well"—she shrugged—"naturally someone has to

go with them to take care of them. And I'm one of the best." The smile turned hard around the edges. "Even Marion said so."

Marion remained silent, but her expression could have shattered stone. I'd never seen a human look so implacably angry. That was the kind of rage that Wardens tried to avoid—the kind that drove them to extremes even a Djinn couldn't comprehend. This offended her in every way possible, from her compassion for the children to the massive and unthinkable betrayal of trust Janice had perpetrated.

"I think Cassiel is wrong," she finally said, very softly. "Flaying is too good for you, Janice. I'll have to think of something . . . better."

Janice lost her smile altogether. "The New Mother is going to kill you all, in ways worse than you'd ever think of trying on me," she said. I realized, with a grim, bleak amusement, that Pearl had given herself a title. How very like her. "Don't be stupid. Let me have the kids. Let me walk away. I can guarantee you'll live to lick your wounds."

"She's lying," Marion said. "She doesn't intend to let any of us out of here alive."

"And I don't intend to allow her to live, either," I said. "Stalemate."

Janice laughed. "Is it getting hotter in here, or is that just me?"

It was. The stone around us was cracking, friable under the unrelenting pressure of the fire. Smoke poured thinly through the cracks, adding to the oppressive heaviness of the air. I realized I was breathing more and more deeply. The fire outside was turning the air toxic, and without a Weather Warden to cleanse it, we had very little time left, even if the fire didn't reach us first.

Janice was no match for me, not in strength; that was why she had Elijah, and the other children. Human

shields. Any of us would hesitate to use full power with
them in the way; it would be hideously easy for her, as
an Earth Warden, to kill them before we could act.

"If I'd been able to keep Gillian, I could have solved
this little problem," Janice said. "You can blame that one
on Ben. He lost his backbone."

Ben. Weather Warden. I suddenly understood who it
was who'd ambushed me with the mudslide on my way
back to the school, before . . . It was Ben; it had to be.
Janice had recruited him, or he'd been placed, like her,
in the heart of the school . . . but he'd had a change of
heart. Probably, I thought, because of the children. I'd
seen him with them, and he'd seemed genuinely moved
by their plight. I'd been an easy, justifiable enemy for
him.

Not the children.

He'd been shot ensuring that Mike and Gillian were
able to escape . . . or Gillian, at least. In that end, there
had been honor.

"You can't want this," I said. "I've seen you working
with the children. You're not cruel, Janice. You care for
them. You can't want them to be used, twisted, made
into killers."

"You think these children aren't already killers?"
Janice touched Elijah's forehead, then Sanjay's. Both
boys stirred, looking dazed. She altered her tone again
and projected a subtle variation of her normal warm
reassurance—this one had an edge of fear, and pleading. "I need you, boys. You have to protect each other,
and protect me, too."

Sanjay looked up at her with absolute trust and devotion. "Miss? From what?"

"From them," she said, and nodded at Luis, Marion,
and me. "From our enemies."

And like the good soldiers that Janice must have
made them behind Marion's back, Sanjay and Elijah

climbed to their feet and faced us with identical expressions of determination.

Ready to fight, and die, for the cause.

"No," Marion breathed. She sounded aghast, and deeply betrayed. I could understand that. . . . She'd been just as seduced by Janice's powers as anyone else. Janice had a rare gift of influence, one that had served Pearl far better than stronger, more overt talents. She'd manipulated absolutely everyone, to one extent or another. I was willing to bet that gathering the children at the school, logical though it might have seemed at the time, was also an idea that sprang from Janice's suggestions.

While Marion had been focused on healing the children's physical damage, Janice had been conducting a different kind of campaign . . . one of steady, damning indoctrination, taking place right under the noses of the Wardens set to guard the children. Even Luis, warned that there was a traitor, had been blind to her.

As cynical and suspicious as I was, I would have chosen her last. There was something about her that simply defied reasonable doubts.

"Sanjay, Elijah," Marion said, "don't *do* this. We're not your enemies. Your enemies are out there. They're the ones trying to hurt us all."

"No," Janice responded. "She's lying to you. Those people out there, they're trying to get to us. To save us. We need to help them."

"She's right. They're trying to save us," Sanjay said. He sounded utterly certain of it. "*You* want to hurt us."

"No, sweetheart, I don't." Marion's anguish was palpable, but it was not reassuring; the boys drew a step closer to Janice, seeking the numbing, gentle warmth that she radiated. Only Ibby had broken with it, and only, I thought, because she'd seen Janice without that mask while she killed Ben. "Please don't do this. You know we're trying to help you. We've always tried to help."

Her argument wasn't going to win; I could see that. Sanjay and Elijah had both endured pain in the healing process, and they were too young and fragile to understand that the pain was necessary. Janice had chosen her willing avatars well, because even I, pragmatic as I was, wouldn't strike against them unless forced to do so. They were a deadly combination—too small, and far too powerful.

Marion cast out a sudden strike of power, meant to send the boys to sleep, but Elijah batted it away with contemptuous ease. It was the wrong move, although if it had succeeded, we might have had a chance. As it was, whatever doubts the boys might have held were wiped away in the face of what they saw as an attack against them.

Elijah pushed power outward in a bone-crushing wave, directly at us. That, Marion and I blocked easily enough; it was our own specialty.

But he wasn't our only problem.

"Down!" I yelled, and toppled Marion's wheelchair to one side as Sanjay raised a hand. Flames exploded from the padding of her chair, but I pulled her safely out before she could be more than singed.

"I have to hold the wall!" she shouted at me, and I saw the torment and fury in her face. "I can't split my attention; I'm too tired. You have to take them down, Cassiel. Do it fast."

Elijah must have heard, because he sent another attack flying at us—no, not at us. At Luis and Ibby, wounded and defenseless now. I lunged in front of it and turned the power back at him in a hot golden flare. It knocked him backward in surprise—but not down.

I rolled out of the way of another bolt of power from Sanjay, which splashed against the stone . . . directly into

another send by Elijah, which closed crushingly around
my bones, trying to shatter them like glass. He could
squeeze me to a pulp in an instant before I could get my
defenses in order . . . but something interfered with him.

Isabel. She was lying on her side, eyes wide, face pale
and ghostly under a coating of sweat. She was weak and
terribly vulnerable, but she threw out just enough power
to disrupt Elijah's hold on me. Just enough to allow me
to break it and throw him back, again.

He and Sanjay had an excellent strategy working . . .
I had no effective counter to Sanjay, but avoiding the
strikes left me off balance and vulnerable to Elijah,
whom I *could* counter, if given an instant to prepare.

They didn't intend to give me that instant. Sooner
or later, I would make an error, fall short, and they'd
have me. Both of them. I needed Luis, but he was even
weaker than Isabel; the bleeding from his leg continued,
slowed but not stopped by the tourniquet he'd applied.
Neither Marion nor I had the time or space to apply
any kind of healing, and he was too weak to try it on
himself. Earth Wardens were notoriously bad at self-
administering their power, in any case.

Hold on, I begged him silently through our link.
Please hold on.

We have an ace, he whispered back. *Time to use it.*

I didn't understand for an instant, and then I did, as
Luis fumbled in his pocket and pulled out a small, thick
bottle topped with a black rubber stopper.

He put his thumb on the stopper, preparing to pop
it open. Preparing to release Rashid, and order him to
save us.

"No!" I screamed. "Luis, *don't*!"

He seemed startled to hear me say it, and shook his
head. He was starting to lose focus from the bleeding; I
could see the vagueness in his eyes. "Only way," he said.
"Need his help."

"He'll *kill* you! You're in no condition to manage a Djinn!"

He wasn't listening. I lunged. He pulled back, but I didn't have time to wrestle with him for the bottle; I balled up my fist, put a burst of Earth power through the muscles of my arm, and punched him in the jaw, a neat right uppercut that snapped his head back and sent him reeling.

He let go of the bottle, still stoppered. I caught it, fought off his dazed attempt to get it back, and retreated to the middle of the room. Across from me, one of the stone walls that Marion had erected shattered under the force of the flames beyond, and a rippling wall of fire burst through, seeking the cooler air of our little shelter. Marion flinched, but she couldn't seem to repair the damage. She crawled to Shasa's side, fending off an attack from Elijah as she did, and shook her awake just as a huge white-hot fireball shot through the opening. I lunged for Luis and Ibby, covering them as it bloomed overhead, filling the room with unbearable heat and glare.

Shasa came upright, screamed out raw defiance, and crushed the fireball into a marble-sized ball of plasma, which she grabbed and threw back out to the other side of the gap. I felt her shield go back up, and for the next few seconds, at least, she held off the attack.

Sanjay closed in on Marion, who was struggling to put the stone barrier back up.

Isabel squirmed out from beneath me, staggered to her feet, and got in his way.

"No!" Marion shouted, but it was too late; Isabel channeled a raw amount of force that shocked even my Djinn senses and sent Sanjay flying against Janice before he could pull enough power to strike. "No, Cassiel, stop her! She's not ready—this will kill her!" She choked and coughed, retching as the almost unbreathable air finally became too much.

We were all in danger of death, I thought, but didn't have the breath left to speak. The air was thick and fetid, and it was an effort to even try to draw it in, as shimmering and hot as it was. Around us, the school was crumbling under the attack, and our circle of safety felt now like a slower, crueler way to die.

I looked down at the bottle in my hand and scrambled up to my knees. Luis struggled to get up, wiping blood from his mouth, but he was done. There was little strength left in him now. Certainly not enough to manage a Djinn imprisoned against his will, like Rashid.

Rashid would help us. Perhaps. But like all Djinn, he hated being compelled to do anything. Even his regard for me, even his distant appreciation for the humans around me, might not be enough.

He might find a way to allow us to die, simply out of a basic, inhuman need for revenge. It would be easy for him, so easy.

I couldn't give him a reason.

I dropped the bottle to the floor, unopened, and grabbed a fallen slab of rock. Luis, guessing what I was about to do, flailed a weakened hand toward me, but he was too late.

I smashed the bottle with the stone, and felt a gust of something that was not quite wind, not quite power blow through us like a shock wave. It felt like a sigh.

"No," Luis whispered. There were tears in his eyes as he collapsed with his cheek against the stone. "No, Cass, *why*? Why did you—"

"No other choice," I choked, and fell beside him. Even Janice had collapsed to her knees, though Elijah and Sanjay were still moving, still a threat. "Can't compel him."

He was our last hope, but Rashid didn't appear. Seconds ticked by, brutal and hopeless. Isabel went down, and Shasa; I dropped the stone and crawled to her, pull-

ing her into my weak arms. The power inside me boiled
impotently. There was nothing it could do. I tried to
soften the stone beneath us, provide an escape route, but
our enemies had thought of that, too.

No way out.

Elijah began to claw at the walls with his power, fighting Marion for control. He had more power, and he was
winning.

"Give up," Janice said between coughs. Her eyes were
bloodshot and strained from gasping for what little air
was left. She no longer radiated warmth and comfort,
only desperation and fury. "Why won't you *just give up*?
Do you really think you can *win*?"

I didn't give up because I couldn't. That, I thought
was something Janice, a mercenary at heart, could never
really understand . . . that there were some battles too
important to retreat from, at any cost.

I'd gambled on Rashid, but that might have been my
own blindness. I trusted a Djinn because I'd once been a
Djinn, and yet I knew all too well that he had no obligation, no reason to help us. Luis had been ruthless, but he
might have been right to keep Rashid captive.

No. I had done right.

I would die doing right.

I would die beside Luis, holding Isabel, and at least
we would be together. At least that.

A blast of fresh air swept through the room, sweet
and cold, and I gasped it in with helpless hunger. Luis's
lungs heaved, too, and Isabel's. It braced all of us, and
gave us a precious few more moments.

Unfortunately, it also gave Sanjay the fuel he needed
to ignite an intense, tightly compacted fireball in the
palm of his small hand, and fling it directly at me.

I had no chance of avoiding it, or of turning it aside. I
reached for Earth power to try to form a shield of stone,
but he'd acted so quickly I was drastically unprepared.

Luis lunged across me and intercepted the strike.

The incandescent ball of boiling plasma hit him in the chest, and threw him like a rag doll into the cracked, smoking wall. He screamed, and convulsed, and I tried to get to him. I tried, but Sanjay threw another bolt, and this time I was able to raise the stone in time to block it, but *Luis* . . .

He was lying motionless, limp as an animal broken at the side of the road.

The scream that came from my throat left it bloody and raw, and instead of relying on power I rushed the boy, shocking him, and grabbed him in my arms in a tackle. He felt scalding-hot, as if in the grip of a killing fever. I put my hand flat on his forehead and managed to moderate the power that I poured into him, although my instincts were to kill, to punish. . . . But it wasn't the boy I needed to kill.

It was the old woman, with her fixed and mocking smile, who watched from behind Elijah, with her other sleeping hostages around her. I lunged for her.

Elijah simply batted me aside, as if I were an insect, and sliced his hand down at my neck. I sensed the force he was wielding, blunt and brutal; he'd have crushed my flesh and bones, destroyed me without a single moment of mercy.

Something caught his hand on the way down.

Rashid.

The Djinn's perfect suit and tie were at odds with the feral twist of his lips and the fire in his eyes—silver and as hot as the blaze bursting the stones around us. He held Elijah by the arm and looked down at where I lay dazed on the floor. "Get up," he said. "And don't think this makes us even, Cassiel. Your human owes me debts that will take generations to repay."

"I know," I said, and rolled to my feet. "Is the air your gift?"

"I couldn't have you dying before I reaped my rewards." Rashid looked down at the boy, who was struggling to break free. "This one's stronger than I'd expect." And Rashid was controlling him without much apparent effort. Impressive.

"Don't harm him," I said.

"Really, do you think I am so cruel?" Rashid did a good job of seeming offended, but I knew he wasn't; I knew him too well to think he would blink at any action, no matter how morally offensive to a human. "Hush, child. Enough." He touched a fingertip to Elijah's forehead, and the boy went limp. Rashid dropped him to the floor and extended his hand to me. I wasn't too proud to accept the help.

"Luis," I said, with dawning horror. "Luis was hit—"

"Yes." Rashid didn't move; he didn't so much as glance at where Luis lay. I rushed past Rashid, but he caught me and dragged me to a sliding stop. "Wait." He held up a sharp finger to silence me, more of a threat than a gesture. Then he tilted it toward Luis.

Who was sitting up, staring down at the charred hole in his shirt. It was a black-edged gap of more than ten inches across. Beneath it, his skin looked normal and undamaged.

I wasn't imagining it this time. His flame tattoos *moved*, shifting like shadows in nervous flickers, and then went still again.

Luis touched the burned edges of the fabric and looked up at me, lips parted in wonder.

"What happened?" he asked. He still looked pale and ill, but he should have been *dead*. That plasma ball from Sanjay had hit him with full force, and as an Earth Warden he had no real defense against it.

As an *Earth* Warden.

Luis, whether he recognized it or not, was manifesting a critical second power. I'd seen it, from time to time;

I'd felt it in those inked tattoos, but I hadn't understood what it was. But I did know that this time it had saved his life, and mine as well.

"As you see," Rashid said, "he's in no immediate need of my help. Not that I would give it."

"He's still bleeding," I said.

"Survivable. And also not my problem."

I had half expected that. "Then can you help us out of here?"

Rashid's handsome, inhumanly sharp face relaxed into an unexpectedly charming smile. "For a price, of course."

There were too many lives at stake to play this game. "I freed you," I said, and held his gaze. It wasn't easy, with those hot silver eyes boring into mine. "I freed you, and that is price enough, Rashid. Don't push your luck."

"Don't push yours, friend Cassiel. One day you'll need me more than you need me today."

I looked around at the collapsing shell of our safety. At Shasa, somehow holding back the fire, at the last edge of her strength. At Marion, doing the same with the crumbling stone barrier. At Luis, Isabel, the fallen children. "If I need you more than this," I said, "then I don't think even you will be enough."

Rashid cocked his head, as if surprised by that, and nodded. "Await me," he said, and walked out, through the barrier of flames. Fire didn't bother Djinn. In fact, it strengthened them. Djinn were born of inferno, long ago; that was why we'd been named devils, from time to time. But we were simpler than that.

And much, much more.

The attack against us fell into confusion, and then died away. The fires, left undirected by someone with that affinity, snuffed themselves out; they'd long ago exhausted their natural fuel. A few guttered in the ashes, but most of it was smoke, and even that quickly thinned.

Rashid came back, dragging two bodies. I didn't know either one, but he hadn't left much to recognize, either. He dropped them at my feet, like a cat leaving kills for its owner, and turned toward Janice.

I'd almost forgotten her. She was moving quietly toward the back of the room, where the stones had broken. No doubt she'd planned to slip out while we were distracted.

She was carrying the two boys in her arms, one on each hip.

Rashid looked at me. "Yours?" he asked.

"Mine," I said. "Thank you."

"Oh, there will be a charge. We'll discuss that later. Privately." He grinned again, and then turned his attention to Luis. "And later for you, too, *Warden*."

Luis didn't try to speak. He just shook his head. I glanced at him, tormented; he needed healing, and quickly. Rashid wasn't about to do it; in fact, as I turned toward him, the Djinn evaporated into flickers of darkness and was gone.

Marion waved me on. "I'll take care of him," she said. "Go. Get her."

I rolled the tension out of my shoulders and walked toward Janice. She tried to move toward the exit, but I easily outmaneuvered her. Anger made me quick, and feral.

"I can still kill them," she warned me. "Doesn't take much. You know that."

"It wouldn't take much to kill you, either," I said. "And I'd do it before I let you go. I don't want the boys harmed, but if you do it, it's your choice. Mine is to stop you."

"At any cost," she said. "Really."

"Yes." I felt more like a Djinn in that moment than at any point I could remember since falling into flesh. "I promise you, you won't leave here alive unless you put those boys down, safely."

Janice flinched. What she saw in me woke fear, and obedience. She bent and carefully laid Sanjay down, then Elijah. As she straightened, she held up her hands in surrender. "All right," she said. "They're down. Deal?"

"Deal," I agreed. And on the aetheric level, I wrapped power around her rapidly beating heart. She tried to stop me, but in the end, without her glamour, she was far weaker than I'd expected. "I didn't tell you I *would* let you leave alive. Only that you wouldn't if you failed to do what I said. You bargain badly."

And then I killed her.

It was a great deal more merciful than she deserved.

Marion was dangerously weak, but her power and mine sufficed to heal the ragged tear in Luis's artery, at least well enough that he could move safely. The volume of blood he'd lost was another matter. We accelerated the production of it, but it would be days before he was himself again. Still, he was conscious, steady, and able to walk, if stiffly; that was a great deal better than either of us had expected.

There was a bruise forming on his chin. He rubbed it as I helped him to his feet. "Damn, girl, you didn't have to make your point quite that hard."

"There wasn't time for polite argument," I said. "And you deserved it."

He sighed. "Yeah, I kinda did. But you're not going to hear it again. I'm blaming it on the blood loss."

His sense of humor was back, for which I was heartily grateful. I braced him until he could stand on his own, and tried to step away.

He didn't let me. His hands went around my upper

arms, and held me in place, close to him. "You bet our lives," he said. "On a Djinn's goodwill."

"It was better than betting it on his obedience," I said. "You tricked him into the bottle. It wasn't his choice. This was. You have to trust Djinn, Luis. You can't force them to be what you want them to be."

I was speaking of Rashid, most certainly, but I was also speaking of myself. And he knew that.

"You still hate me?" he asked. "Don't go saying you didn't. I felt it. I know how much it hurt you, what I did. What I said, sure, but mostly what I did. I never wanted that, Cass. Never."

"And I never wanted to leave you," I said. "Please believe that."

He nodded, eyes gone dark. "Did you find her?"

"Yes."

"Did you hurt her?"

"Some," I said, and shook my head. "Not enough. Not nearly enough."

"You will."

"*We* will."

"Yes." He kissed my forehead, with so much tenderness it melted the last of the icy pain within me. "We will."

We left the ruins behind.

The other Wardens had met us on the way to the fire road, to the east . . . a ragtag, injured bunch, but they hadn't lost anyone else. A few asked about Janice. None of us commented on her loss with more than a brief acknowledgment of it. I wondered what Marion would say, in the end. She, more than anyone else, had made a catastrophic mistake in allowing Janice such unfettered, trusted access to her most vulnerable charges. The pain of that weighed heavily on her—visibly, in fact, in the slump of her shoulders and the new lines on her face. I'd managed to retrieve her wheelchair from the ruins, but the electrical power had been destroyed, and no one had the energy left to repair it. She pushed herself along the rocky path, face welded into an emotionless mask. Alone with her thoughts, and her failures.

Miraculously, only one of the children had died: Mike, whom I'd found outside of the building. Gillian seemed inconsolable; she'd sought out Isabel, and the two girls walked together, hands clasped. I wondered how that friendship had developed. They didn't seem at all similar, really.

Humans often confused me, though.

The Wardens traveled in unexpected silence, communicating in careful whispers and gestures as we moved down the twisting path. At regular intervals, we paused to take a head count.

Just before we reached the fire road, we stopped for the last one. Luis and I stood together, not touching but closer than we'd felt since the decision to bring Isabel here. I still didn't know if that had been a mistake, or a necessary evil; she seemed better, despite the desperate last stand in the school. Maybe Marion's treatments had helped, though the seizures she'd suffered still frightened me, as did the pessimistic estimate of her chance of long-term survival.

I looked around for her, but there were two other Warden children behind us. "Ibby?"

Someone shushed me. Gayle passed me, rapidly conducting her head count. Then she came back, frowning, counting again.

Dread gathered in my stomach. I stopped her. "What is it?"

"Two short," she said. "I didn't see anyone leave."

Neither had I, and it alarmed me. I'd been vigilant. Whoever had left the party had done so under cover of a veil, and a very good one.

Luis and I exchanged a look of perfect understanding, and spun away in separate directions, checking faces. When I reached the end of the line, I turned and ran back to meet him halfway. We instinctively grabbed hold of each other.

"She's not here," Luis panted. "Ibby's gone. The other girl, too. Gillian."

Gillian, who had been so distraught. But had they gone on their own, or had they been taken?

"We have to look for them," Luis said. "They've only been gone fifteen minutes, since the last check. Can't have gone far."

Gayle grabbed him and pulled him to a halt. "Hey!" she hissed. "We've got refugees and wounded, and we don't know that they're safe yet! We can't go tearing through the woods shouting!"

He shoved her back, but he must have known, as I did, that she was right. "Then what?" he spat back, but quietly enough. "Someone *took her*! I'm not just giving up on her!"

"We may be able to track her on the aetheric," I said quietly. "And we don't know that she was taken, Luis. We don't know that at all."

I was trying to prepare him, because I didn't believe, not for a moment, that Ibby had been spirited away against her will. The child was, if nothing else, a fighter; she'd been taken once, and she would never go quietly again. Added to that, she was in the midst of a group, and no one had noticed her, or Gillian's, disappearance.

She'd gone willingly, wherever she had gone. And she'd taken Gillian with her.

"Well?" Gayle whispered. "We can't wait. I have to keep them moving. We're vulnerable out here."

"Go," Luis said. "We're staying." I nodded. We stepped out of the group, and Gayle, after a troubled frown, led the others on into the dark. It took surprisingly little time before we were lost in the dark again, just the two of us.

Luis limped over to me as I stood surveying the dark, cold woods. The school's fires had gone out, or at least sunk to sullen ashes; it was once again full, true night, and a moonless one. "Let's go," he said, and limped on, back toward the trail. "We might be able to pick up their tracks where they left the group." I didn't move. After several steps, he stopped and looked back. "Cass?"

"Stay where you are," I said softly. "Don't move."

I heard a soft, whispering laugh through the trees. "You're good; I'll give you that," said a woman's voice. I recognized it all too easily. "*Mira*, he's a tasty one. Yours?"

Luis started to turn, but Esmeralda—Snake Girl—whipped out of the shadows with blinding, reptilian speed, wrapping coils around him with crushing force. Her human half rose up, beautiful and terrifying as she hissed and bared her venomous fangs. Luis struggled, but Esmeralda was too physically strong to budge ... and when I tried to break her hold, my Earth-based powers bounced off of her without effect. In a very real sense, Esmeralda *was* part of that power. It had taken a Djinn's death to seal her in the form she was in and take away much of her strength; that only served notice of how incredibly powerful and dangerous she'd once been.

I thought I could defeat her, but not with Luis held hostage in those muscular, tensing coils. She could crush him before I could save him.

"*Very* tasty," Esmeralda said, and lowered herself to look into Luis's eyes. "You have good instincts, Djinn. This one's no rabbit. He's more of a tiger."

Luis tried something—I couldn't tell what, but it didn't matter; at the first sign of his drawing power,

Esmeralda tightened her coils, and I heard bones and muscles creaking under the stress. He gasped, and then couldn't pull in another breath to replace the one he'd lost. The panic in his face made her smile. "Definitely a tiger," she said. "But tigers die just like rabbits, *hombre*. So play nice."

"Let him breathe," I said. "Please."

She glanced at me, raised her eyebrows, and tossed her dark hair back over her shoulders. "Since you ask so nice, sure." Her smile was real, and vicious. "You want to ask me why I'm here?"

"I know why you're here," I said. "You're here because Ibby told you to come here. When?"

That startled Snake Girl, and once again I saw that flash that betrayed her genuine youth. She might exude self-confidence, but beneath it she was still a girl, one who'd made tremendous mistakes. "Who says I come running when some little brat calls?"

"Because you liked her. Because you saw in her what you once were. And because she asked your name."

"You think I'm that simple?"

"No," I said. "I think you're that lonely, Esmeralda. How did she send for you?"

Es slowly unwound herself from around Luis's body, and he staggered and backed away toward me. The two of us against the monster . . . but I wasn't seeing a monster anymore.

Es settled her coils comfortably, a glistening mound of sinuous flesh, and propped her chin on one hand. Her elbow rested on the top of a coil. "She called the shop and left a message to tell me where she was. She said she liked it here, but she figured things would go wrong. She thought I could help. She said it was the least I could do."

"Can you help?"

"Yeah, probably." Es shrugged. She studied her fingernails, and frowned at the dirt she found beneath them. She'd been traveling a long way, I realized; her shirt—the only clothing she wore—was dirty and torn, and her previously shiny, perfect hair was rough and tangled. No doubt she could manage to hide herself effectively with what remained of her Earth powers, because otherwise her travels would have been brief, and full of general panic. But even then, she hadn't had an easy time of it.

I was willing to bet it was the first time she'd risked the outside world in quite some while.

"The girls," I said. "Do you know where they are?"

"Ibby and the redhead? Yeah. I know where they were going."

"And you just let them go?" Luis said. His fists balled up, and I saw the black tattoos on his arms glitter in the starlight and start to smolder. His use of fire was purely instinctual now, not directed with anything like precision. I laid a hand on his shoulder, and felt him deliberately reach for calm. "Where are they?"

"Doing something brave," Esmeralda said. "They knew somebody would be coming for the convoy you have on the road. They split off. They're going to intercept them."

Luis spat out a curse. "We *already* had perimeter security," he said. "The last thing we need is two of these kids out there handling power they shouldn't be touching!"

"Listen, man-cake, I already slithered past your so-called perimeter security, like, fifteen times." Es sighed. "You Wardens. *Es stupido.* You'd do better with third-rate rent-a-cops; at least they'd have guns. Ibby was right. If you want to keep your convoy from getting trashed, you'd better get your best on it. And the kids, they're good. Better than you."

"Es," I said, "the more those girls use their powers, the more broken they become. They started too young. You understand that better than anyone."

The Snake Girl looked away, and didn't comment. Her coils shifted restlessly, and there was a slight, instinctive buzz from her tail rattle. "They'll be okay," she said. "Look, you can't protect them. They're going to do what they're going to do."

"It's killing them," Luis said.

Esmeralda's dark gaze flashed up to lock with his. "And?" she asked. "What do you think making them *not* use it is going to do? Kill them slower? Some of them won't make it. Some will adapt. That's the way things go in this world. You can't stop it, and you'd better not get in the way."

"I'm not letting her do this," he said. "Cass. Let's go."

"You won't find them," Es said. "One thing that kid knows how to do is hide. You won't find them unless you trip over them by accident in the dark."

"Can you find them?" I asked.

Es considered the question, and then tilted her head a little. "Maybe," she said. "Maybe I don't want to, though."

I had let this go on too long, I decided. I was a little fascinated with Esmeralda, the way a mongoose is fascinated with a snake, but enough was enough. Luis was right. We couldn't allow a six-year-old child to fight a battle for us.

I had been sending tendrils of power out through the roots of trees around us, and now, with a snap of will, I triggered the trap. Branches slammed down, forming a thick, springy cage around her. Roots squirmed from the dirt and wrapped around the branches, weaving it together.

Esmeralda let out a hiss of surprise, and I heard the dry rattle of her alarm. She battered the cage with the coils of her body, but it was tightly woven, and impossible for her to get real force into her struggles. "Let me go, you cold bitch!" she screamed, and ripped at the wood with her hands—but those were merely human hands, without the strength necessary to shred the tough fibers. "Let me *go*!"

"Once you tell me where they are," I said. "You know this is too dangerous for them. Don't let them down, Esmeralda. They meant for you to tell us. They hoped you would."

"That's not what she said." The snake's coils pulsed against the cage, trying to push it apart, but the trees were firmly rooted deep in the earth. Esmeralda subsided, panting, glaring through the mesh at us. Her knuckles were white where she gripped the branches. "She said not to let *anyone* find her."

"She's a child," Luis said. "And she's too brave for her own good. She needs us. Tell us where she is or I swear to God I'll rip off your rattle and feed it to you!"

Esmeralda was silent for so long I wondered if she *would* tell us, and then she finally said, "I'm not afraid of you. I'm telling you because I think the *gringa* bitch is right; the kids shouldn't be doing this alone. I was going to go help them anyway."

"Where. Is. She?" Luis almost snarled it, and I felt the burning aura of fire around him again, a kindling that raised the temperature by several degrees.

Esmeralda sensed it, too, and went very still. The dry buzz of her rattle grew louder as she reacted to his threat, but she had nowhere to run, and she couldn't strike to defend herself. Luis wouldn't burn her alive—at least I didn't *think* he would—but his rage was clear.

"If you stand between me and Isabel, I'll wipe you off the face of the earth," he told her. "You take us to her. Do it *now.*"

He nodded to me, and I released the cage of branches, which sprang back into their normal positions with a creak and rustle of dry needles. The roots shriveled back into the ground.

Esmeralda was free, but she still didn't move. The steady, unnerving buzzing continued, like bones in a bottle.

"You keep it in mind," she said. "I'm not your bitch. I'll crush you and eat you if you mess with me."

Luis brushed it aside with an angry swipe of his hand. "We can kill each other later. *Ibby*. Now!"

She relaxed a little, and the rattling slowed, then stopped. "All right," she said. "Try to keep up, asshole."

She could move with astonishing speed, and with a quick, sinuous flash, she was already disappearing through the trees. The pale white of her rattle was the only visible sign of her.

"Run," I said, and took off in pursuit.

Chapter 14

IT WASN'T THAT I had forgotten Luis's leg injury, but I'd known he wouldn't allow it to slow him down too much. Even so, he labored very hard to keep the pace, gasping for air, and when he faltered I grabbed him and pulled him along. He dug deep for the strength to deny the pain, and I blocked it as much as I could. The patch to his torn artery was holding, and that was all I could hope for now. This pursuit might do irreparable harm to him, but he wouldn't give it up. There was no point in asking.

Esmeralda's snakelike form whipped around trees, threaded between boulders, slipped over shadow-protected drifts of snow that hadn't yet melted. I expected her to slow, but if anything, she increased speed, and the starlight wasn't enough to keep her in sight. I tracked her on the aetheric; her aura was eerie and weirdly wrong for the shape she held in the human world. It was more as she imagined herself ... but she wasn't human at all. A feathered serpent, magnificently colored, gliding silently through the world above. The deadly sense of menace from her was even stronger in that realm of force and will, and I realized once again what a power had been leashed inside those snake's coils.

Whoever the Djinn who'd defeated her was, he must have been astonishing. And remarkably selfless.

It took a quarter of an hour, but Esmeralda's progress abruptly ceased, and I dragged Luis to a panting, trembling stop a few feet behind her. Her rattlesnake-patterned coils pulled themselves together in a tense pattern, bracing her for a strike, but the rattle remained silent.

Luis collapsed to one knee, and I heard a soft moan out of him, something he tried to muffle but couldn't. The pain was intense; I felt it burning between us, and touched his damp shoulder to try to numb the screaming nerves. He shook me off. His long, dark hair was soaked with sweat and clung to his face in sharp, sticky points. "Is she here?" he whispered. I shook my head. I didn't sense her, but there was something gathering on the aetheric around us, dark as a coming storm.

There was a flash of blue-white light to the east, and in its glow I saw Isabel standing back-to-back with Gillian. They were surrounded by what looked like half a dozen wolves—big, rangy ones, circling and charging in to nip at them. It wasn't natural hunting behavior, although wolves could certainly hunt humans if they chose. I felt the pressure on the animals in the aetheric, heavy enough to make my head ache even at this distance. The wolves were letting out soft yips—not excitement, but pain.

They wanted to run, but couldn't. Instead, one darted forward, lunging for Gillian, but the young Weather Warden was ready; a blast of air met it and slammed it backward, tumbling through the air to land splay-legged ten feet away. It trembled with the urge to flee, but inched forward again, dragged against its will.

"Es," I said. Her human face turned toward me. "You handle the wolves. We'll handle the real enemies."

Her eyes narrowed, but she nodded, and in a flash she was heading for where we'd seen Isabel and Gillian fighting for their lives. There was another flash of light—Isabel, throwing fire—and in its glow I saw that one of the wolves had grabbed Ibby by the front of her shirt and was dragging her like a cub across the ground as she fought. The fire sent it yelping away, and Ibby scrambled back to where Gillian was batting another wolf away. There was a tornado forming above them, and I felt the whipping, ferocious winds from where I stood. Gillian planned to bring it down around them, leaving them in the protected eye, but it required control and great precision. It was a good plan, if she could make it work.

But out in the dark, someone sliced into her careful construction, and the tornado wobbled, lost cohesion, and became an uncontrolled downburst that snapped off trees and slammed Gillian and Ibby to the ground.

The wolves closed in, but before they could sink their teeth into the girls, Esmeralda was there. She hit the wolf pack like a wrecking ball, slapping her coils into them, crushing some and throwing others at bone-breaking speed into trees. I turned away as she hissed and struck at the one closest to Isabel. I didn't need to witness it to know that she would keep the girls safe . . . at least from the wolves. Whether they would be safe from *Esmeralda* was a larger puzzle, but it had to be risked.

Luis nodded to me, and we moved toward the place from which the Weather Warden had struck to disrupt the tornado. On the aetheric, there was a black tangle, impossible to sort out—it could have been one, or twenty.

It proved to be three, and they were once again children. One Weather, one Fire, and one Earth. There was no sign of the Void represented here, which relieved me greatly. It was possible that Pearl had not been able to train enough of those kinds of soldiers yet, or that they were rare. I was glad enough not to face one.

The children were focused on Esmeralda, as I'd hoped, and Luis and I got within striking distance without being noticed. He took down the Earth child first, clapping a hand to the boy's forehead from behind and dragging him off his feet; at the same moment I took the Fire Warden child, another boy. Mine went down more easily into an enforced, deep sleep; Luis's fought, and I had to jump to his side and add my strength to his to overcome the boy, even taken by surprise as he was.

That left the Weather Warden, an older girl of about fourteen. She was legitimately old enough to come into her powers, but her fine control and raw strength were far from natural; she'd used the seconds of warning well, and as Luis and I tried to grab her, she pulled a massive amount of power from the air around her, drenching us with moisture and then ripping away energy to create ice. It wasn't thick, but it was shocking, and it slowed us down long enough for her to scramble backward and launch her next attack, directly from the clouds overhead: lightning. I felt the buzzing whisper of power beneath my feet, of electrons turning and seeking alignment with those above. Even a full Djinn hesitated to take the force of a lightning bolt. I was not at all sure that I could survive a direct hit.

Flesh is an imperfect conductor. The delicate mechanisms of life are not suited to channeling that much raw energy, and I didn't have the natural advantages of a Weather Warden to allow me to absorb the shock.

What I did have was a connection to the Earth, and the ability to alter my own body chemistry. It was risky, but the only possible defense I could muster in the second of warning I had. I increased my electrolytes, coating my skin in them in the form of sweat, and focused the energy downward, through my feet.

No one had prepared me for the pain. I'd been Tasered recently, and that had been painful, but this was like having every nerve in my body stripped raw and screaming, and then shaved with razors. It seemed to go on forever, and I felt my heart struggling not to seize up, fibrillating in the current ...

... And then it was gone, and I dropped to the forest floor, unable to move. Alive, but trembling with agony. What I could see of my hand seemed intact, though the sleeve of my jacket breathed wisps of smoke.

Luis hadn't stopped. He had launched himself in a purely physical attack, barreling into the girl and slamming her down into the leaf litter on the ground. She screamed out raw defiance and rolled him over, pushing her palms down on his chest.

I saw his eyes go wide, and he struggled to breathe.

No! She had taken away any kind of breathable air in his body. She could suffocate him this way—it was difficult for an Earth Warden to escape this particular sort of attack ... hard to hold on to focus and power while drowning in clear air.

She thought I was down, out of the fight.

I wasn't.

I lunged forward, grabbed the girl's long, braided hair in my metallic left hand, and yanked her backward. She shrieked and reached instinctively for her head, and I wrapped my arms around her to still her struggles. Luis rolled over, climbed to his feet, and put his hand on her forehead. She fought, but couldn't ride the tide of darkness. It took her under.

I let her fall, and collapsed next to her, gasping. My nerves still didn't seem free of the random, coursing energy; I felt oddly displaced, light-headed, numb. *I shouldn't have been able to survive that*, I thought, but that, too, seemed distant, almost unimportant.

Esmeralda's coils writhed into view, and she wrapped her body around the base of a tree. Isabel and Gillian were with her. I saw no sign of the wolves, living or dead; I hoped most of them had escaped with their lives, but Snake Girl looked suspiciously well fed.

"You've got them," she said. She sounded surprised. "Not bad."

"Glad you like it," Luis grunted, and sat down—more of a controlled fall, really. "Damn, Ibby, what were you thinking?"

She came to him and gave him a hug, a long one. "I'm sorry," she said. She didn't really sound sorry. "Es told us they were out here. I was afraid they'd hurt somebody else. I didn't want them to get Sanjay and Elijah."

"What if they'd gotten you two?" Luis asked, and hugged her again. "You've got to be more careful, *mi hija*. You can't put yourself at risk."

Ibby looked at him with sad, sober eyes, and said, "It's too late for that. You know it is. The Lady wants us, and she's going to come for us. We're going to be trouble for you until she gets us."

"Ibby," I said. "Your plan wasn't just to come out here to fight them, was it?"

She shook her head, looking so much older than her years. Older, perhaps, than Esmeralda. She looked at Gillian, who nodded.

"We were going to let them take us," Ibby said. "If we do that, we can help. We can make the Lady trust us. We can stop her—I know we can."

"Sweetheart," Luis whispered, and put his hands on her small, sweet face. "Sweetheart, that's very brave, but it's also very stupid. We can't let you do that. It's very dangerous."

It was also too much of a risk in another way, one he wouldn't acknowledge . . . because Ibby had been convinced by Pearl once, and although I knew she was a strong, independent child, she could be subverted again, perhaps without even realizing it.

"It's dangerous to stay here, too," Gillian said. Like Ibby, she no longer sounded much like a child. She'd seen and experienced too much. "They'll keep coming for us. People will get hurt trying to protect us. Innocent people." I saw the grief in her face, and the glitter of tears in her eyes, and knew she was thinking of the boy, Mike, who'd given his own life to save hers. "It's better this way."

Perhaps Esmeralda knew what they were going to do; I felt her shifting restlessly, heard the soft, tentative hiss of her rattle.

But neither Luis nor I was prepared, really.

Ibby had her arms around her uncle, and she kissed him on the cheek. "Sleep," she said, and I sensed the sudden black wave that crushed down on him.

He fell as if she'd killed him, but I knew she hadn't; I felt the continued, quiet beat of his heart, the steady pulse of his lungs and his life.

He slept, like the three children we'd taken down.

"Cassie," Ibby said. She was still looking at her uncle, not at me. "Are you going to let us go?"

I was too weak to fight her, and Gillian, and I didn't know which way Esmeralda would fall, or if she'd take a side at all. "Take me with you," I said. "I can help you. I can make sure you're safe."

"Nobody's safe," Ibby said, and her tears fell on Luis's burned, torn shirt. "Not me, not you, not him. Not the world. Can't you feel it?"

Esmeralda looked up, and I heard the buzzing of her rattle burst into frantic, loud life.

The night sky was silent, full of stars, but what I felt, what I heard, wasn't coming from the sky.

It was a scream, and it was growing louder and louder,

and it was coming from the aetheric, and the ground beneath us, and the trees, and the *world*.

It was the scream of awakening, of pain, of the sudden and irrevocable changing of our lives.

Isabel stood up. So did I. Esmeralda slithered closer, her rattle shaking out a steady, adrenaline-fueled alarm, Gillian pressed closer against my side, and I put my arm around her for comfort.

The screaming grew so loud it burned in my head and drove me to my knees. The aetheric was burning red, burning like the end of the world.

And I heard Her voice. The Mother. Only the vast, rolling sound of it, the voice of thunder and hurricane, rock and boiling volcano. The scream of life in all its violent, striving agony. There was no meaning to it, no way to interpret it, but I knew what it meant.

It meant that my time was up, and so was Pearl's. Whatever her plan, she had no time left to prepare. The Mother was *awake*, and the fury of her pain would drive the Djinn to her defense, like white blood cells racing to contain infection . . . and that infection most certainly was *humanity*.

Ashan hadn't triggered this. I didn't know what wound had been made in the world that had brought it on, but it no longer mattered. The Mother was awake, and the Djinn would be under *her* command now, no longer individuals choosing their paths. Even Ashan would be one of that army, mindless and effectively quite insane.

If I'd taken his offer, if I'd returned to my Djinn strength, I would be just as helpless as the others now.

In a perverse sense, this worked *for* Ashan, not against him. He wanted humanity gone, and the defenses of the Earth would begin to do that bloody work for him. Millions would die. Chaos would descend.

Pearl would have no one to oppose her now; all their

energies would be devoted to survival. She could amass her forces and wait for the end, and no one would oppose her.

No one but us.

"We have to go," Ibby said. "You have to make Uncle Luis understand, Cassie. We need him, too."

"I know," I whispered. I swallowed and tasted blood, and ash, and the oncoming deaths that this would bring. "I'll make him understand."

There was no place for protecting Ibby now, or Gillian, or any of them.

There was only total war.

TRACK LIST

I found these songs were the perfect inspiration to get through the writing of *Outcast Season: Unseen*. Here's hoping you enjoy them, too! (As always: Artists exist because you support them *economically*. Please buy music—don't steal it.)

"To Hell with the Devil"	Jim Bianco
"Tomorrow Is Another Day"	The Stone Coyotes
"Nostalgia"	Emily Barker and the Red Clay Halo
"Steal Your Heart Away"	Joe Bonamassa
"Quarryman's Lament"	Joe Bonamassa
"Telephone"	Lady Gaga and Beyoncé
"Back Against the Wall"	Cage the Elephant
"ROTUB"	The New Hotness
"I Know Who You Could Be"	Butcher Boy
"Lost Art"	Mere Mortals
"Boys and Girls"	Mon Roe
"Resistance"	Muse
"The Pigeons Couldn't Sleep"	Peter Himmelman
"It Dawned on Me"	Calla
"Teardrop"	Jose Gonzalez
"Saint Veronika"	Billy Talent
"So Long, Good-bye"	10 Years
"A Place Called Home"	PJ Harvey
"Any Other Way"	Colin Blunstone
"Not As We"	Alanis Morissette
"Gives You Hell"	The All-American Rejects

"Piano Fantasy"	William Joseph
"Alice"	Avril Lavigne
"Whataya Want from Me"	Adam Lambert
"Complicated Shadows"	Elvis Costello
"I Should Be Born"	Jets Overhead
"Hold On"	KT Tunstall
"Mykonos"	Fleet Foxes
"Robots"	Dan Mangan
"Why Try to Change Me Now"	Fiona Apple
"To Ohio"	The Low Anthem
"Be OK"	Ingrid Michaelson
"Now"	Dave Carroll
"21 Guns"	Green Day (featuring the cast of *American Idiot*)
"Light On"	David Cook
"Symphonies"	Dan Black
"Kandi"	One eskimO
"Walter Reed"	Michael Penn
"Wars"	Hurt
"We Are Young"	3OH!3
"Make Me Wanna Die"	The Pretty Reckless

The brand-new series from

RACHEL CAINE

THE OUTCAST SEASON NOVELS

Undone

Once she was Cassiel, a Djinn of limitless power. Now,
she has been reshaped in human flesh as punishment
for defying her master—and must live among the
Weather Wardens, whose power she must tap into
regularly or she will die. And as she copes with the
emotions and frailties of her human condition, a
malevolent entity threatens her new existence...

Unknown

Living among mortals, the djinn Cassiel has developed a
reluctant affection for them—especially for Warden Luis
Rocha. As the mystery deepens around the kidnapping of
innocent Warden children, Cassiel and Luis are the only
ones who can investigate both the human and djinn
realms. But the trail will lead them to a traitor who may
be more powerful than they can handle.

**Available wherever books are sold or at
penguin.com**

Available Now

from

Rachel Caine

THE WEATHER WARDEN NOVELS

ILL WIND
HEAT STROKE
CHILL FACTOR
WINDFALL
FIRESTORM
THIN AIR
GALE FORCE
CAPE STORM
TOTAL ECLIPSE

**"You'll never look at the Weather Channel
the same way again."**

—#1 *New York Times* bestselling author Jim Butcher

**Available wherever books are sold or at
penguin.com**

Welcome to Morganville, Texas.
Just don't stay out after dark.

The *New York Times* bestselling Morganville Vampires series

by Rachel Caine

College freshman Claire Danvers has her share of challenges—like being a genius in a school that favors beauty over brains, battling homicidal girls in her dorm, and finding out that her college town is overrun with the living dead.

Glass Houses
The Dead Girls' Dance
Midnight Alley
Feast of Fools
Lord of Misrule
Carpe Corpus
Fade Out
Kiss of Death
Ghost Town

rachelcaine.com

R0036